Predator One

Jonathan Maberry

Predator One

A JOE LEDGER NOVEL

St. Martin's Griffin
New York

This is a work of fiction. All of the characters, organizations, and events portrayed in this novel are either products of the author's imagination or are used fictitiously.

PREDATOR ONE. Copyright © 2015 by Jonathan Maberry. All rights reserved. Printed in the United States of America. For information, address St. Martin's Press, 175 Fifth Avenue, New York, N.Y. 10010.

www.stmartins.com

The Library of Congress Cataloging-in-Publication Data is available upon request.

ISBN 978-1-250-03345-1 (trade paperback)
ISBN 978-1-250-03344-4 (e-book)

St. Martin's Griffin books may be purchased for educational, business, or promotional use. For information on bulk purchases, please contact the Macmillan Corporate and Premium Sales Department at 1-800-221-7945, extension 5442, or write to specialmarkets@macmillan.com.

First Edition: April 2015

10 9 8 7 6 5 4 3 2 1

This is for dear friends Keith Strunk and Laura Jo Swanson.
And, as always, for Sara Jo.

Acknowledgments

As always, I owe a debt to a number of wonderful people. Thanks to Doctor John Cmar, of the Infectious Diseases Department of Johns Hopkins Hospital; Doctor Todd Humphreys, the University of Texas at Austin; Doctor Steve A. Yetiv, professor of political science, Old Dominion University; the International Thriller Writers; my literary agents, Sara Crowe and Harvey Klinger; all the good folks at St. Martin's Griffin: Michael Homler, Joe Goldschein, Aleksandra Mencel, Rob Grom; and my film agent, Jon Cassir of Creative Artists Agency. Thanks to Clint Blackwood, Michael Bailey, and Vinessa J. Olp for the computer info.

Thanks to everyone who participated in the food-bank fund-raiser: Lani Jones, Michelle Woodstead, Lynne Dempsey, Shannon Sauter, Geoff Brown, Kya Aliana, Joanne Durann, Brad Tappin, Thomas Stoops, Tabitha Floyd, Patrick Freivald, Eric Besel, Nick Pulsipher, Jason Manning, Jason Stout, James Shields, Justin Estes, Sandra Gurin Krieg, Bob Murphy, Tafmara Brown, Mindy Rimel McGee, David Alspector, Eugene Johnson, Stephanie Daugherty, Brian Anderson, Michael Chrusciel, Kirk von der Heydt, Richard Pione, Bryan Thomas Schmidt, Jonathan Lambert, Elektra Hammond, Cheryl Rimel, Larry Martinez, Angie Courville Green, Dennis Marcello, Mike Jackson, Stacy Kingsley, Garrett Ison, Rob Montgomery, Kee Lee, Traci Loya, Linda A. Colandrea, Brandon Pruchnik, Roger Cox, Jennifer Dee, William Tilly, Kevin Bosemer, Brandon Botley, Patrick Seiler, Irene and Chris McCann. Thanks for being Joe's "friends in the industry."

Thanks and congrats to the winners of the various Joe Ledger contests: Jay Faulkner, Tom Erb, Joseph Capozzi, Sinh Taylor, Mike Jacobus, Michael Daugherty, Daniel Johnston, Michael Keenan, Brandy Buchanan, Rob Meyer, Jonathan Clark, Gavin Cooksley, Jason Stout, Lindsey Ann Brewer-Muñoz, Mary Gavin Kurec, and Craig Curnew.

Part One
Ghost in the Machine

History is a set of lies agreed upon.

—NAPOLEON BONAPARTE

Chapter One

When the technology of war becomes so easy anyone—and I mean anyone—can use it, then we are in deep shit.

And we are in deep shit.

Chapter Two

The Resort
208 Nautical Miles West of Chile
October 12, 9:41 P.M.

We dropped like dead birds from the clouds.

Four of us.

Me.

Top and Bunny. My right and left hands. The guys who have been with me since I started this game. Brothers who have walked through the valley of the shadow with me so often we'd carved our initials in the landmarks.

And Sam Imura. Our sniper. Cool, quiet, lethal at any distance. Handgun, long gun. If he wants to punch your ticket, then don't double-park your car.

Four of us.

Falling.

Falling.

"HALO" is a nice word. Calls to mind angels and the glow around the heads of saints in old paintings.

In military parlance it's an acronym for a specific kind of parachute jump. High altitude, low open.

Those are two concepts that are antithetical to a quiet life. I am not, as

I believe I've told you before, a fan of jumping out of perfectly good airplanes. Neither God nor evolution saw fit to give me wings. I'm not made of rubber, so I don't bounce worth a shit. Skydiving is a sport for madmen. Anyone who says different should switch to decaf. Diving from so far up that you can't even breathe, so far up that you need to wear an oxygen tank? That's just nuts on too many levels to contemplate.

The "low open" part of this was just as bad. The whole science of landing safely after you throw yourself out of that nice, safe airplane is to open your chute in plenty of time for physics to waft you down like a goose feather. That is the only reasonable way it should be done, right? Oh, not so. Some genius in the military long ago reasoned that if you fly the plane so damn high that radar can't see it and then you fling yourself out and wait until you're close enough to the ground so you can count the cigarette butts in the gutter, then no one will detect you. Personally, I think they'd hear the big splat when you hit the ground. It took some convincing at jump school to prove to me that low-open jumps can be done safely. Or, as they added with tight little smiles, with a measure of safety.

We needed to get onto this piece of real estate without being spotted. There were radars looking for us. There were guards and watchtowers and all that shit. The people at the facility did not want visitors and were willing to be real damn nasty if any showed up.

We were on our way to showing up.

I hate my job.

Before a jump like this, you do forty minutes of breathing pure oxygen to chase the nitrogen from the bloodstream. You also have to dress for it. It's about minus forty-five up there. Frostbite is a real risk, even though we were dropping down toward Chile. I had a set of polypropylene undies under my battle-dress uniform and other gear.

We dropped from thirty thousand feet.

Six miles.

They call the rate of fall "terminal velocity." Unless the word "bus" or "train" is in the mix, no phrase using the word "terminal" offers any comfort. Not to me. In regular jumps there's a margin for error, time to open the backup chute if there's a failure with the main chute. In HALO drops? Not so much.

Despite all of that, we rolled out and fell into the midnight blackness at 122 miles per hour.

We deployed our chutes, and there was that moment when the differential between your mass falling at uncontrollable speeds meets a degree of resistance. Slam your necktie in the side door of a race car and see what happens when it goes from zero to sixty. Feels about the same.

The ground still seemed to be coming up way too fast.

Too fast.

Too fucking fast.

It never feels like the chute is doing enough of its job on a HALO drop.

I shifted my position and tried to land the way Top and Bunny landed. Like a professional who isn't afraid of heights and isn't a hiccup away from crying for his mommy.

You're a big, tough, professional soldier, Ledger, I told myself. Stop acting like a pussy.

I told myself to shut the fuck up.

And then I was down.

I went limp and fell sideways, doing everything right. But I was convinced I'd ruptured everything, including the tonsils I no longer had.

But I was down.

Sam Imura touched down twenty feet away. He landed at a walk, turned, gathered his chute, detached, bunched it up. All with complete calm. I wanted to shoot him.

I didn't think kissing the ground beneath me would do anything to inspire confidence in my subordinates, so I scrambled to my feet and stowed my chute and began a rapid postlanding equipment check. Top and Bunny appeared out of the gloom, and the four of us knelt, each facing outward in a different direction, flipping on our night-vision goggles. We were using a new prototype developed for the Department of Defense by, of all people, Google—an advanced variation on their Google Glass. The goggles had interchangeable lenses for different kinds of light and could be controlled by light touches to the temple, a trackball on our belts, or—in a pinch—voice control. A nonmilitary version is scheduled for the public market under the name Google Scout. However, we had them exclusively for eighteen months.

Developed by one of Mr. Church's friends in the industry. He seems to have friends in every industry.

We each scanned 120 percent of the area around us, which meant there was a significant overlap with what the guys on either side of us were seeing. The Scout glasses recorded everything and fed it via secured uplink to a satellite that in turn bounced it in real time to the TOC—the tactical operations center at the Hangar, the main DMS headquarters located at Floyd Bennett Field in Brooklyn. Church was there, along with Aunt Sallie, Bug, and all the senior staff. This was a very important mission.

It was also highly illegal.

It was unauthorized and prohibited, and, if we were captured or identified, would result in the shutdown of the DMS and lengthy jail terms for all of us. Unless the mission was successful, in which case we'd all be heroes with the thanks of a grateful nation. The middle ground between those two possibilities was about an inch wide.

So, no pressure.

The Scout glasses threw data streams onto the edges of the goggles, giving us a mission clock, temperature, info from thermal scans, specs and intelligence details sent to us from Bug, and other spiffy stuff. Remember the screen display from the Terminator movies that showed what the cyborgs were seeing? Like that. Only we weren't robot assassins from the future who had, for inexplicable reasons, Austrian accents. Instead, we were government agents going way, way off the reservation.

Breaking the law.

About to break a lot of them.

Chapter Three

Brentwood Bay Resort and Spa
849 Verdier Avenue
Victoria, British Columbia
October 12, 10:12 P.M.

His name was Doctor Michael Pharos and he was a monster.

A very select kind of monster.

He knew it. He was aware of the shape and dimensions of the thing that he'd become. He knew exactly how ruthless he was, and how ruthless he was willing to be. He understood the ways in which old splinters of regret and conscience still jabbed at him. He was fully cognizant of the steps he'd descended from the Hippocratic Oath and the rule of "First do no harm" to his present state of "Do whatever harm is necessary to get the job done."

For the last twenty years, his job had been enabling even worse monsters to do great harm to a vast number of people. Although he was a medical doctor by training, he had discovered that his genius was in organization. Management.

He seldom devised a moneymaking plan—he knew that he was not particularly inventive—but he was the man everyone counted on to make sure the plan was carried through. Dot all the *I*s, cross all the *T*s, bury all the important bodies.

That's what Doctor Pharos did.

He managed the machineries of corruption, terrorism for profit, extortion of key figures, the transfer of stolen monies, and all the other cogs and wheels. Pharos specialized in that, and he did it, he was sure, better than anyone alive.

And he did it on a grand scale.

Global.

Historical.

Not an exaggeration, though he was aware that at no point was his name ever the one to appear on a Most Wanted list, or the evening news, or a CIA kill order. He was a ghost. The password for his laptop was even *zeitgeist*.

The ghost in the machine.

For most of his adult life he had been managing an engine of great cultural destruction and enormous financial expansion. The people for whom he worked—the ones who designed and built the machine—asked that he ensure that the machine would continue to run despite any foreseeable disaster. Even in the event that the creators themselves were removed by death, flight, or imprisonment. Pharos did that, though he never expected such a catastrophe to occur.

When it did, the machine he'd managed kept running.

Running.

Running.

Bills were paid, paychecks cut, employee benefits seen to. Equipment and supplies were regularly purchased and shipped. Tier upon tier of lower-level management kept everything greased and tuned. The great destructive machine functioned as it always had, even though there was no one at the controls anymore. The designers, the creators, the planners were gone. The worst-case contingency had, in fact, come to pass. None of them were in prison, none were in flight.

They were dead.

All but one.

And there was barely enough of the last one to even call "human." Just a burned and crippled lump of diseased flesh hooked to devices that breathed and excreted and pumped for him.

The organizational machine did not falter. It never so much as hiccupped.

Pharos had managed it too well to allow mistakes.

It ran and ran.

And ran.

Primed and ready.

Ticking like a bomb.

Ticking.

Ticking.

Ticking down to boom.

Chapter Four

The Resort

208 Nautical Miles West of Chile

October 12, 10:13 P.M.

"Clear," said Top, and the others echoed it.

"Clear," I agreed.

We were in a field of tall grass near the rocky coast of an island off the coast of Chile. Just far enough off the coast so that it rested in international waters. Way, way outside any claim of American sovereignty. Technically you could do almost anything out here and get away with it.

There were exceptions, of course. You couldn't build a nuke. You couldn't set up a lab to create doomsday pathogens. NATO would frown on it. UN peacekeepers might crash your party.

But that left a bunch of things you could do. Start a space program. Develop drugs of all kinds that could be sold to countries that don't regulate that stuff. Set up the world's biggest meth lab. Engage in illegal cloning. Build a sweatshop and use slave labor to make brand-name sneakers. Participate in the global sex trade. Establish a totalitarian dictatorship and oppress your own people. Stuff like that. Stuff that doesn't generate enough political backlash to make the superpowers feel they have to act. After all, as they see it, defending oil wells and keeping their fellow nations from becoming nuclear powers have always been far more important than freeing the twenty-plus million people who currently live as slaves here in the twenty-first century.

The whole world is bug-fuck nuts. Don't try to make sense of it or you'll hurt yourself.

Sadly, none of those things were the reason the four of us fell out of that airplane. We were not hunting mad scientists with the next superweapon. We weren't here to liberate the oppressed or overthrow a murderous dictator. That would have been much more fun. We might have even been able to get a grudging go-ahead nod from Washington. It would have made good press, and there are always elections coming up.

No.

This island was owned, through dozens and dozens of arcane removes, by a private corporation that was actually a front for Uncle Sam.

Or, at least, a seedy, jackass nephew of Uncle Sam.

This place was a prison.

Think Gitmo and Abu Ghraib, and then lower your expectations. Go farther down the crapper. Remove all traces of sanity, compassion, common decency, and humanity. Then double that, and you have this place.

They called it the Resort.

Not sure if that was done as a joke or as cover. Either way, it made me want to hurt whoever came up with the name.

The Resort.

The island was three miles long, two wide, and most of it was nearly impassable volcanic hills, dense rain-forest growth, noisy parrots, and every son-of-a-bitching biting insect known to the fossil record.

We were seventy yards inland on the east side, having come in on the angle our computer models picked as the one with the worst visibility for security. The terrain to the west would have frightened a mountain goat, and foot patrols were infrequent. There were tower posts with motion sensors, but Bug made short work of those. He used MindReader to hack the feeds, created a forty-minute loop, and, as soon as we were within a thousand yards of touchdown, fed the loop into the system. Their security guys were essentially watching a DVR'd version of a quiet night. Bug did the same with the motion sensors and thermal scans. Bug loves this stuff. He's better at it than anyone, and it's a very, very good thing that he's on our side.

Even so, we moved with great caution.

"Cowboy to Deacon," I said, using the combat call signs for me and Mr. Church. "Down and safe."

"Proceed," said Church's voice. We were on a team channel, each of us with an earbud tuned to the mission channel. "Good hunting."

"Hooah," murmured Top and Bunny. Top's full handle was First Sergeant Bradley Sims, former Army Rangers. His call sign was Sergeant Rock. Bunny was an ex-marine by the name of Master Sergeant Harvey Rabbit. Real name. His father is a bit of a prankish asshole. We all called him Bunny except on a mission, and then he was Green Giant.

Sam Imura was Ronin.

Bug was Bug. He was monitoring the security room, so he'd give us a heads-up if they tumbled to our presence.

"Everything's copacetic," he said in our ears. "Two guards on duty. They're talking football."

"Foot patrols?" I asked.

"Sending you their locations, Cowboy," he said, and immediately one lens of my goggles showed a soldier walking a perimeter line. This faded back to a white dot on a satellite map of the compound. We had markers on every warm body on this island.

Nice.

Top, Bunny, and Sam are all experienced operators. Each of them could lead any team of first-chair shooters anywhere in the world. The fact that they were my team, key players of Echo Team, always gave me confidence. They didn't need to be told what to do. We had rehearsed this mission fifty times, with the other members of Echo throwing all kinds of variables at us. We had it down, we knew our jobs, and we went about it like professionals.

And, yes, that still means we knew that things could, and often did, go wrong. If you do this kind of thing for a living, you accept that as part of the mission planning. You're never locked into one way of doing things. Reaction and response is every bit as important as intelligence and planning.

Like four ghosts, we left the grassy field and moved into the foothills of broken volcanic rock, following a path picked for us by a geodetic-survey software program. The easiest safe path. The path that wouldn't burn us out. Safety takes time, so we moved only as quickly as common sense allowed.

I saw an armadillo waddle into a hole, and I stepped around it, not wanting to disturb the animal. A few minutes later a chinchilla shot out from in front of Top, and he very nearly put a hot round into it.

"Fucking thing wants to be dead," he muttered.

Farther up the mountain slope a vicuña raised its ugly head and watched us go past, munching on a midnight snack of green leaves. Bunny stopped for a moment and stared eye to eye with it. The animal didn't move except to continue its slow mastication of tamarugo leaves.

Bunny blew it a kiss, and we moved on.

It took an hour to go one mile inland. Serious rocks. A lot of caution.

We fanned out to preselected spots and considered the compound.

There was a fence, which was no problem. There were guards on patrol. That was problematic. We weren't here to kill anyone.

Absolutely no one.

Let me tell you why.

We were here to break one of the world's worst terrorists out of a secret prison.

But it was a prison run by the Central Intelligence Agency.

Chapter Five

Sam Imura faded off to the north and vanished. He had two rifles slung over his back. Aside from his usual sniper rifle, he had one retrofitted to fire tranquilizer darts at ultrahigh rates of speed. The tranqs would drop anyone in their tracks. The darts could do some damage, but nothing that wouldn't heal. They were filled with an amped-up version of the veterinary drug ketamine mixed with a mild psychotropic. No one who wakes up from it is a reliable witness for anything within a couple of hours before or after being juiced. It has a long technical name. We call it "horsey." So, whoever got darted with horsey would waft off to la-la land and probably dream of sexy rainbow-striped unicorns. Something like that. Haven't tried it myself, but I've heard stories.

I nodded to Top and Bunny, and they peeled off to the south, then split up to go over the fence at two different points. I went more or less straight in.

As I ran low and fast toward the fence, I removed a device approximately the size of a deck of playing cards. One of the wonderful little gadgets developed by Doctor Hu's science supernerds. Just as Bug inserted a video loop into the cameras, this more or less did the same thing for the juice in the electrified fence. Bunny and Top each had one, and on my word we simultaneously held them toward the metal chain links. Strong magnets jumped them from our rubber-tipped gloves and attached them to the metal. There was a microsecond of static and then a meter display on our glasses told us that we had a controlled gap in the electricity. The delay lasted thirty seconds. We were up and over in ten. Then the units overheated and fell off. Dead. The electricity on the fence resumed its normal flow.

Nice.

Inside the compound, in the security room, all that would show would be a single, momentary blip. The kind that happens if a small bird gets fried. Happens all the time.

The three big birds were already inside.

That was phase 1.

Sam was high up a tree with his rifle ready, cold eyes searching for targets through a nightscope.

"Talk to me, Bug," I said very quietly. When you don't want to be heard, you speak quietly. If you whisper, the sibilant *S* sounds carry.

"Cowboy," he responded, "there's a two-man patrol sixty-two feet to your . . . no, wait—they're down."

And almost as an after-echo, I heard Sam quietly say, "Got 'em."

"Another one on your two o'clock," Bug advised. "He's walking the inside of the fence."

"Mine," said Bunny.

On the small display inside the glasses, I saw one white dot moving at a slow walk and then a yellow dot coming at him from behind. After a moment, the yellow dot moved off and the white dot did not. I hoped Bunny hadn't dented the guy too badly. Bunny is six and a half feet tall and can bench-press one or both of the Dakotas depending on whether he's really trying.

"Got movement by the first building," said Top.

I moved quickly across the trimmed lawn toward a vantage point beside a parked jeep. From there I could see the buildings. I switched from night vision to my own eyes because there was a row of lights mounted just below the roof level. I kept the glasses on, though, because they still fed the intel and data to me. The compound had three structures on it. The first building was a combination barracks, mess hall, and rec room for the sixteen soldiers and nine technical staff members here on the island. To the right and slightly behind that was the main building, which was a two-story blockhouse that we figured for labs and administration. Then to the right of that, set apart and surrounded by a second electrified fence, was a ten-cell miniprison. Because the wall of an extinct volcano backed up against the compound, there was only a need for two guard towers, and we'd chosen angles of approach that kept us off their menu.

I couldn't see the target Top was closing in on, but then I saw a white dot detach itself from the tracery that gave us the floor plan of the buildings. Must have been someone leaning against a wall. He moved out into the lawn, and I saw that his pace went from slow hesitation to a quick walk.

"Careful, Sergeant Rock," I warned, "he may have spotted you."

There was a moment of silence before Top answered. "Yeah, he did," he said. "But I noticed him first."

On my screen his yellow dot moved smoothly away from another unmoving white one.

Four down.

That still left twelve soldiers and the nine techs.

"Ronin," I said, "what about those towers."

"Gimme a sec," he murmured. There was no sound, no crack of a rifle. His weapon was a highly specialized, max-pressure air gun. "One down." Two seconds later he said, "Two down."

"You are one spooky fuck," said Bunny.

"They don't pay the man to be nice, Farm Boy," said Top. "Cut the chatter."

I said, "Go to phase two."

Top and Bunny headed toward the barracks making maximum use of cover. I peeled off toward the lab building. Even though this was a covert and illegal base, it was run with military efficiency. Vehicles were parked in their appropriate slots, the grass had been mown, the trees were pruned back from the fence, and all the doors, as I found out, were locked.

No problem.

There were lights on in the lab building despite the hour. That would mean the main door alarms wouldn't be active. Only the break-in security would be armed. The keycard reader beside the front door was state-of-the-art, and all the little lights burned red. Not that it mattered, because I had my full junior James Bond kit with me. In the DMS we have a whole different take on what "state-of-the-art" actually means.

I produced another gizmo from a thigh pocket of my BDUs. This one was small and had an adhesive strip on the back. I peeled it off and stuck it to the underside of the card reader. It went to work immediately, hacking into the reader using the full intrusive oomph of MindReader. Our computer system is unique and very dangerous. It has two primary functions. First, it's a superintrusion system that can enter and interpret any other system and then rewrite the target software so that there is absolutely no record of the hack. The second thing it does is look for patterns. Codes are a kind of pattern, and key codes are merely mathematical patterns stored on magnetic strips. Joe Ordinary gets stymied by them. A computer that can hack NASA or the Chinese Ghost Net? Not so much.

In my ear, Bug said, "Go."

I took a blank keycard from my pocket and ran it through the slot. The little red lights turned green, and I heard a faint click.

Easy as pie. I pulled the door open very carefully and eased inside smoother than a greased weasel.

"Inside," I said. "Wait for my word."

"Hooah," said Top and Bunny quietly.

The entrance foyer was short, and there was a second keycard reader inside. I didn't trust that it would use the same keycode, so I repeated the process and used a second blank card. Green says go.

Beyond that door was a hallway with half of the lights turned off. Four doors on the right, three on the left, all closed. None of them had card readers. I drew my sidearm, a Snellig gas pistol. It was a weapon originally designed by some very bad people, the Jakobys, but since they're dead and we swiped all of their technology, we've started using these guns. Like Sam's rifle, it uses compressed gas to fire a dart with a thin shell of a material that structurally acted like glass but that was really a kind of cellulose. Nontoxic and biodegradable. We are nothing if not environmentally conscious here at the DM of S.

The only downside of the guns is range. Handguns as a rule are short-range weapons, but the gas pistols have an effective range of thirty feet. Beyond that it's better to throw the actual gun at your target. Inside that range, though, even a flesh wound will drop your bad guy. Each shell was loaded with horsey.

I ghosted along the hall, stopping at each door, opening it slowly, peering in, finding no one, moving on.

Until door number 5.

Two people sitting at a table, coffee cups nearby, their faces lit from the glow of a pair of computer monitors. I stepped into the room.

"Hi," I said, and shot them both.

A man and a woman. He was in a lab coat; she was in a uniform with lieutenants' bars. The gas darts whispered through the air, and in nine one-thousandths of a second after impact they were out.

Horsey does not horse around.

Bad joke, real assessment.

The woman fell sideways out of her chair. The man did a face plant on his keyboard. As I hurried over, I pulled two uplink drives from my pocket. I pushed the lab guy off his chair and quickly plugged the uplink drives into USB ports on each computer. MindReader stepped right in and began copying everything. Every file, every e-mail, every instant message, every URL. The uplinks had microcharges of thermite buried inside. As soon as the uploads were complete, they'd pop, killing the computers and melting their own innards. No one could trace slag, and no one could duplicate our tech.

We're stingy like that.

I took wallets and ID cases from both sleeping beauties and shoved the stuff into an empty canvas bag clipped to my belt. For later. For after-mission follow-up. Maybe for federal prosecution, if we found what we were looking for. And maybe for quietly disposing of if we didn't.

Then I moved through the rest of the building. In various rooms, I encountered one more soldier and the other eight technicians.

Horsey, horsey, horsey.

Everything was rinse and repeat. Hacking computers, slagging them, taking IDs.

Until I got to the security room.

The room was locked, and I had just begun the process of placing another scanner on the card reader when the door opened and a burly guy with sergeant stripes stepped out. He looked almost exactly like Mr. T, except for the Mohawk. Same face, same muscles. Same attitude.

Sergeant T looked at me in my black BDUs, camouflage greasepaint, and weapons. He did two things at once. He went for his sidearm and he started to yell.

Balls.

Chapter Six

My pistol was still in its holster, so all I had in my hands was a tiny scanning device.

So, I hit him with that.

Hard.

On the nose.

Small or not, the scanner was metal. Sergeant T's nose was cartilage. No competition.

He reeled back, blood exploding from both nostrils. I followed him, hitting him with a palm shot under the chin and a big front kick to the belly. His gut was rock-hard, which was fine because it gave me more to kick against. Sergeant T flew backward into the room and slammed into a second noncom who was rising from his chair, hand already closing on the butt of the Sig Sauer at his hip.

I planted one hand on Sergeant T's chest, used it to launch myself into the air, and delivered a flying punch to the second sergeant's face that broke a whole lot of important stuff. He crashed, bleeding and dazed, into his security console as I landed hard atop the man who was atop him. I hit the sergeant with palm shots to the temple. Again and again. Hard as I could.

He had a head like a bucket and a neck like an oak tree.

It took four palm shots to knock the lights out of his eyes. He began to slump down, dragging the groaning Sergeant T with him.

I staggered back, drew my Snellig, and darted them both.

I was breathing hard. Even a short fight can take the wind out of you. My pulse was jumping all over the place, and I could feel that old familiar adrenaline rush. The room became brighter. Sounds became sharper.

The two security guys were out, but they were hurt. I wasted three seconds repositioning them so they wouldn't choke to death on blood. They were here, and that made them part of something very naughty, but killing them was not on my day planner. There was no way to tell if they were bad guys or merely following orders from bad guys. That was for people above my pay grade to sort out.

Mr. Church would be part of that process, so this was going to get all the attention it deserved. Nobody's going to be putting this on their résumé.

I stopped to listen and assess.

No alarms sounding, no one coming that I could see. There were twelve security cameras in operation around the compound, and each had a dedicated screen there in the security office. I studied them. Most showed nothing except stillness.

One showed the mess hall filled with people.

I tapped my earbud. "Cowboy to Sergeant Rock. All quiet on the western front," I said. "Go."

Something small and metallic suddenly flew in a slow arc over the main table of the mess hall. Several of the soldiers looked up in surprise. Their faces were just registering shock and fear when the gas grenade exploded.

Horsey, horsey.

All fall down.

"Clear," said Top. "Nap time here."

"Shutting down the power to the fence," I said, hitting some switches. "All security systems are now down. Meet me outside the detention building."

I ran down the hall and out through the front door just in time to see Top and Bunny come pelting across the lawn. In a small pack we jogged over to the detention building.

"What have we got, Bug?" I asked.

"Thermals indicate nine people. Two guards in the outer room, one person in each of four cells, and then three signatures in cell six."

"Is that the one with our boy?"

"No way to tell."

Mr. Church's quiet voice said, "Echo Team, proceed with caution."

Bunny knelt by the front door and used the same kind of scanner I'd used earlier to create a keycard.

"Ready, Boss," he said.

I finger-counted down and emphasized the go order with a clenched fist. Bunny swiped the card, and Top pulled open the door.

I stepped inside. "Hey, guys," I said, and shot the closest soldier in the chest. Bunny was right behind me and took the other one.

Everything was going like clockwork. No alarms sounded, no fatalities. Not a single shot fired in response.

We approached the door to the cellblock, once more bypassed the keycard reader, and walked inside, moving on quick, silent feet, guns up and out. There were several prisoners sleeping on cots. The first two were too young. The third was a woman. The fourth was a very fat man.

We found who we were looking for in the last cell. The one where Bug had said there were two other thermal signatures.

And that's when the whole thing went to shit.

The man we were looking for was secured to a sturdy wooden chair with zip ties. He was naked except for a soiled pair of boxers. His body was lean and long-limbed, with graying hair and a whole lot of bruises and cuts. Some of them old, some of them so recent they glistened with blood. The chair was tilted so that the back of the man's head hung over the lip of a big industrial metal sink. There was a towel bunched over his face. There were pails of water on the floor, and a lot of puddles. There were two men, sweaty and angry, standing on either side of him.

It was clear what had been going on.

The spin doctors like to call it enhanced interrogation.

The press calls it what it is. Torture. In this case, waterboarding. Where they pour water over the towel that covers nose and mouth. You can't breath, but you don't drown right away, either. You drown by inches, slow. With great pain and terror.

I know. I've had it done to me. Twice during training, three times by guys who were as ruthless and dedicated to my discomfort as these guys were. I survived it, but I can tell you, when you're bound and brutalized and gargling like that, you take serious stock of what you'd do or say in order to make it all stop. If it goes on long enough, you think about selling out your family, your honor, your values, and your country.

Everyone thinks that.

Not everyone cracks, though.

I didn't.

A lot of guys don't. Waterboarding doesn't work as well as the torturers want. But they keep trying it, because it doesn't leave a mark. And it's a reusable torture. Tearing out fingernails isn't.

These guys looked like they'd been at it for a while. They were stripped to the waist and bathed in sweat. The room was awash.

They heard the door open and turned to us. One in irritation at the intrusion, the other in surprise.

But there was fear in the eyes of both men.

The guy in the chair, though . . .

Yeah. Well, that was the problem.

He wasn't breathing.

"Take 'em," I said, "but keep 'em awake."

Top took the guy on the left, kicking him in the nuts and then clubbing him to the ground with the stock of his M4. Bunny grabbed the guy on the right and literally picked him up and slammed him against the wall. It shook the whole place.

I rushed to the guy on the chair.

I checked his pulse. Nothing.

I turned him and cleared his airway, then I slashed the flex-cuffs and lowered him to the floor. And began CPR.

Breathing. Doing the chest compression. Doing it right.

Doing it for a long time.

Wasting my goddamn time.

The guy Bunny slammed into the wall groaned and shook his head. "We didn't mean to," he whined. "He just . . . stopped breathing. We didn't mean to."

They hadn't meant to.

But they had.

I sagged back, gasping, sweating. Defeated.

The man was dead.

I looked down at him. Late fifties. Six four. Wasted down to a skeleton. Head and beard forcibly shaved. Beaky nose. Dark eyes that looked up at me, and through me, and into the big black.

Dead.

There was a little bit of irony to it. Just about everyone else in the world already thought he was dead. I'd have been A-OK with that being the truth, too. I'd believed the fiction along with everyone else. I'd celebrated it. Bought a round of Kentucky bourbon for everyone at a military bar. Cheered with the news reports.

Right now, though, I didn't want him dead.

He had information I wanted. Needed.

He had been a link to something so big that a lot of people might now die because this source was dry, this door was closed.

Because this man was dead.

We stood there, Bunny, Top, and I. Looking down at him. At that face.

Helpless and defeated.

Staring at the slack, dead features of Osama bin Laden.

Interlude One

The *Astrid*

Gulf of Saint Lawrence

32 Nautical Miles from Gaspé

New Brunswick, Canada

Six Years Ago

Jean-Luc Belmont was a mediocre sailor and he knew it. He'd taken the courses, passed the tests, obtained his license, but in anything except a calm sea on a mild day, he was hopeless. Luckily for him, he had clients who loved to fish, and many of them seemed eager to take the helm and pilot the *Astrid*, a lush Cabo 44HTX.

The boat had a hardtop enclosure—no pesky canvas—that provided climate-controlled comfort, nice ventilation, and a lovely hull profile. The *Astrid* could pave a smooth road through five-foot waves and do so in excess of thirty knots. All of which made for an impressive outing with clients who brought their checkbooks along with their Abu rods and Gander reels.

What Jean-Luc lacked in understanding of boats he more than made up for in his understanding of clients. He worked for Belasco Arms, an up-and-coming weapons manufacturer that was making a dedicated run at becoming a real threat to Colt Canada. The Belasco B9C assault rifle was outselling Colt's C8A1 carbine and their C8FTHB special forces weapon in several key markets. Jean-Luc found that a day on the water hauling in northern pike and other sport fish, combined with lots of very good alcohol, was a great way to do business. Once they were back and showered, there would be steaks and more drinks, as well as some female entertainment for those guys who wanted to leave their wedding rings in their hotel safes.

The four men aboard the *Astrid* with Jean-Luc were all experienced fishermen and boat handlers, and they seemed to accept as a gift his willingness to turn the boat over to them. They worked the mouth of the Saint Lawrence, and one of the men pulled in an astounding forty-one-inch pike that weighed twenty-six pounds. It wasn't one for the record books, but it was the biggest of the species any of them had pulled in. They were all jazzed about it, and that amped up the general air of holiday.

Jean-Luc was delighted. All three of the potential buyers worked for companies that provided security specialists and private contractors. Jere Flanders, COO of Blue Diamond Security, was the man who caught the fish. The others were Bill Allen, of Blackwater, and Huck Sandoval, of The Martinvale Group. Technically competitors, but not really. There was a heavy demand for private contractors these days, especially since the Americans pulled most of their people out of Iraq and Afghanistan. The regular soldiers had gone home, but there was a great need for competent field operators who could—and would—pull a trigger.

The fishing party had set out from Gaspé before first light and was well past Forillon National Park on the end of the peninsula. When they saw the humped silhouette of Brion Island, they dropped a sea anchor and broke out their rods. The island was a bird sanctuary and mostly uninhabited except for some government parks people. The day was quiet, the air crystal-clear. The men spent hours fishing, telling lies about past catches, hauling in pike, taking photos with the big ones and then throwing them back, drinking, talking some business.

They were all pretty well hammered when they saw the flash.

"Hey," said Flanders, tapping Sandoval on the arm. "You see that?"

"Yeah," agreed Sandoval. "Big flash."

The sun was in a different part of the sky, and there was no chance this was lightning. They all agreed on that.

They listened and heard a faint throb of noise. Almost felt more than heard.

"Was . . . that an explosion?" asked Jean-Luc.

Allen nodded. "It damn well was. On the water, too, I think."

The others nodded, too. They all knew what a blast signature sounded like, and that's what they'd heard.

"I think that was Semtex," said Sandoval, but then he shook his head. "No. Too heavy."

"C4," said Allen, and again the others nodded.

"Lot of it, too," said Flanders.

They stared across the water, but there was nothing to see except a small and fading glow.

"Boat?" asked Jean-Luc.

Instead of answering, Sandoval climbed up to the bridge and started the engines. The others pulled up the anchor and stowed their rods. Within two minutes they were smashing through the small waves, racing toward the horizon line. Jean-Luc used the shipboard radio to call it in to the Canadian Coast Guard.

They did not find a boat, and, given the heft of that explosion, none of them expected to. That had been a lot of bang.

What they found were pieces of a boat. Splinters. A lot of pieces spread out over a half mile of water. The closer they got and the longer they looked, the more they were convinced that they weren't going to find anything. Or anyone.

They were wrong.

It was Jean-Luc who spotted the body.

If it was a body.

It bobbed in the choppy water like a lump of greasy red chum.

Sandoval slowed the boat and swung around broadside to the corpse.

"Jesus Christ," he murmured.

The body had ragged stumps for legs, one ending midthigh, the other gone below the knee. The left arm was a mangled slab of nothing. The right hung down into the water. What face there was had been burned hairless; the heat had melted its features so that they no longer resembled anything human. It was impossible to tell much about it, except that it had once been male and that it had died badly.

"Poor bastard," said Allen. "At least it was quick."

He was wrong about that. They all were.

The bobbing chunk of meat turned over in the water. At first Jean-Luc thought that a predator fish was hitting it from below. A shark maybe. There were more than two dozen species of shark known to visit or live in these waters, though shark attacks were rare. Jean-Luc had seen a brute of a Greenland shark, as well as an eight-meter-long basking shark and a four-meter-long great white. Mostly farther out on the salt, but sometimes here in the more brackish waters.

But that wasn't it. The body didn't pitch and jerk the way it would if a shark was hitting it. Instead, it . . . *rolled over.*

The remaining arm broke the surface tension of the water and flopped toward the *Astrid.*

The hand, blackened and raw, opened and closed.

Reaching for the boat.

Reaching for life.

Using the last of his strength to find anything that would let him cling to the world.

The men in the boat cried out. Shocked and stunned. And repelled.

And then Jean-Luc kicked off his shoes, threw his watch and wallet onto the deck, pushed between Sandoval and Allen, and dove into the water. He was no good at piloting a boat, but he could swim. He reached the dying man in eight quick strokes and wrapped his arm around the burned torso.

The man screamed.

It was a high, shrill, and inhuman shriek of agony.

Then his grasping fingers closed around Jean-Luc's shoulder and clung on as the salesman kicked out toward his boat and the reaching arms of his customers.

The *Astrid* was already punching its way toward the mainland when the Coast Guard arrived.

Chapter Seven

The Resort
208 Nautical Miles West of Chile
October 13, 1:01 A.M.

My guys stood and watched me make the call. I'd rather have knee-walked across broken glass.

"Cowboy to Deacon," I said.

"Go for Deacon."

"The tires are flat. Repeat: the tires are flat."

There was a long pause. Heavy. Pregnant. I could imagine the faces of everyone at the TOC staring at Mr. Church. Via the lenses of the Google Scouts, they'd have already seen it anyway, but this needed a verbal confirmation. Someone had to own it, and that someone was Mama Ledger's firstborn son.

If I expected Church to fry me, though, I was wrong. Maybe he was bigger than that, or maybe he was saving it for a face-to-face. Or maybe he was simply enough of a realist to accept that this happened. The man was dead before we entered the building. If there hadn't been the very real risk of a no-win firefight, we could have tried for this building first and maybe gotten here before the interrogators accidentally killed him. We'd X'd that out during the planning, though, because finding him had been half the job. Getting him off the island alive was the other half, and that could not have been accomplished with all those troops awake and trigger-happy. No, it had to play out the way it had. This ending was unfortunate.

Damn unfortunate.

Church even said that. "This is unfortunate."

"Copy that," I muttered. "Call the play."

"Secondary objectives are now in effect, Cowboy," he said. "A helo is inbound. LZ is the front lawn. Thirty minutes."

That was that.

I tapped my earbud to leave the mission channel and nodded to Top and Bunny to do the same. Sam would remain in position until the chopper got here.

We squatted down and made a huddle.

"This is messed up, Boss," said Bunny.

"Yes it is."

Top pinched bin Laden's chin with a thumb and forefinger and moved his head side to side.

"Wouldn't a minded killing this fucker my own self," observed Top dryly.

"Word," agreed Bunny.

"Yesterday's box score," I said.

Bunny shook his head. "Still can't believe this is him. I mean . . . holy shit. You know?"

We all knew. Everyone at the DMS knew. And we were freaked out and furious.

When SEAL Team Six entered Pakistani airspace and breeched the compound in Abbottabad, they thought they were hunting the real deal. The guy who'd orchestrated 9/11. Those heroes went in to do a job, and they did it and earned their places in the history books. Unless this all became public knowledge, they would go on believing it.

Hell, even the president of the United States thought he'd dropped the hammer on bin Laden. We all did, except the conspiracy crowd, who kept ranting that we'd faked bin Laden's death. They supported this claim by openly wondering why there were no pictures of bin Laden's corpse.

I could answer that. The semiofficial story was that bin Laden didn't die from the head shot and was thrashing and twitching on the floor, so they capped off a bunch of rounds to finish him. Those rounds tore up the body to the point that photos would be very nasty. That was only partly true.

Except that there is a different chapter to that story because a bunch of ass-hats from the CIA have been running a long game on everyone.

On the whole world.

Short version is this: The real Osama bin Laden was more than the point man for al-Qaeda. He was also a member of a group of what could, for lack of a better word, be called "financial terrorists." Or maybe "global criminals" is a better phrase. Not sure. They both seem to apply. The group had set themselves up as a secret society. Called themselves the Seven Kings. And they deliberately and carefully hijacked much of the mythology of other real or imagined societies like the Illuminati, Order of the Temples of the East, the Fraternitas Saturni, the Arioi, the Carbonari, the Ethniki Etaireia, the Palladists, the Order of Heptasophs, and others, including some outright fictional groups like the Priory of Sion, the Millennium Group, and—according to Bug—the Order of the Phoenix from the Harry Potter books. They used the Internet and a disturbing level of computer-hacking savvy to seed their pseudo histories into the pop-culture conspiracy-theory ocean. With all that, a woman who called herself the Goddess began making predictions of disasters. Each of her predictions came to pass. Why? Because the Seven Kings were making them happen. But because the predictions were couched in religious ambiguity, they had the odor of prophecy rather than guilty knowledge. At least as far as the conspiracy-theory crowd went.

The Kings' go-to model for making a lot of money was to covertly fund radical political and religious groups, nudge them toward committing large-scale terrorist acts, and then make billions from the resulting swings in the world stock markets. There are always a lot of people who run for cover as soon as anything happens. "Flight to safety" it's called. If you knew in advance when something as big as the attack on the Towers was going to happen and were already in position with buy orders and calls, then as soon as the shock waves hit, you start shoveling Franklins into a wheelbarrow.

The attack on 9/11 was theirs.

How'd they orchestrate that so smoothly?

Real simple.

One of the Seven Kings, specifically the King of Lies, was Osama bin Laden.

Yeah. Take a moment with that.

Thing is, that ole Uncle Osama wasn't doing it for Allah. And he wasn't doing it in order to further a religious movement. This wasn't fatwa or jihad for him. And he did not give a naked mole rat's wrinkly ass about the followers of Islam. For him, it was all about the money. Lots and lots of money. All those deaths, the resulting wars, the ongoing "war on terror"? Shit. Every new death, every new headline, every instance of political divisiveness put more money in his pockets.

His pockets, and those of the other Kings.

Bin Laden, and the other Kings, were essentially apolitical. For them it was all a running con, albeit the most dangerous one in history. Fighting the Kings was a bitch. They were a massive organization, built over decades, with thousands of operatives seeded carefully into world governments, multinational corporations, and law enforcement agencies. They constructed a kind of bureaucracy so sophisticated that any single one of the Kings could run it all. Hell, it could probably run without any of them. As long as the money trickled down from the top—from well-established bank accounts—then the agents buried into society would continue to do their jobs. Which meant that they were always ready to strike, to disrupt, to do damage. All it took was a phone call, a coded e-mail, a text message.

And they have continued to stay busy. Kings operations have been on-going, and we see their fingerprints in terrorist attacks, suspicious oil spills, domestic insurrection in countries that produce key commodities, and so on.

The DMS has been working very hard to tear the whole damn thing down. The King of Plagues, Sebastian Gault, was presumed dead along with the Goddess. The founder of the whole organization, Hugo Vox, the King of Fear, was definitely dead at Mr. Church's own hand. Two reliable informants—the former assassin Rafael Santoro and a former aide to the King of Plagues, Alexander Chismer—provided us with enough action-able intel to go after the others. I'd spent a lot of time over the last few years making some pretty serious house calls.

The King of War had been a high-level member of the Israeli military. We sent a team to extract him, but he didn't want to come quietly. He was killed during a mother of a gunfight. Pretty much the same thing happened with a Russian manufacturer who served as the King of Famine. Right around the time we breached his defenses in a remote site in Siberia, he ate his gun. The Italian banker who called himself the King of Gold swallowed eighty Vicodin when his sources told him we were closing in.

We were able to arrest the King of Thieves, a French commodities bro-ker, but he managed to get himself killed while in custody. Exactly how that happened is a matter of some concern, and there's a hunt for a spook within the marshal's office.

Bin Laden was the last.

We didn't want him dead, though. If our theory was right and the Kings organization was essentially running itself, then we needed insight into the infrastructure. We wanted to stop the runaway machine. We placed a lot of stock in swiping bin Laden from the Resort and encouraging him to help us with that.

Now, though.

Damn.

When SEAL Team Six went to Pakistan, much of the intel upon which they acted came from MindReader searches, from clues provided reluctantly by Santoro and willingly by Chismer, familiarly known as Toys. We shared that intel with the CIA, and the mission was set.

What we didn't know then and found out the hard way later was that there is a splinter cell buried like a tick within the skin of the CIA, and it wanted bin Laden alive. They knew that bin Laden had at least five surgically altered and very well trained stand-ins. Much like the ones used by Stalin and Hitler. And, if the rumors were true, by William Taft. The stand-ins were either true believers who were happy to surrender to the knife in order to further Osama's cause. Or they were on the payroll. Some of bin Laden's family knew about the switch. Some of those were believers. Others were agents of the Seven Kings. It's a complicated mess of duplicity and intrigue. The guy living in the cave in Afghanistan was only one of the fakes. So was the guy on dialysis. Funny thing is, the real Osama had been healthy and fit and hadn't been inside either Iraq or Afghanistan since May of 2001. He hadn't been in Pakistan since 2008.

The CIA splinter cell knew this. They knew it because eighteen months ago they located and apprehended the real Osama bin Laden. It was done very quietly, with their captive taken from a sprawling banana plantation in Guatemala and brought to this island for interrogation. Osama had been living under the false identity of a retired textbook publisher from Tel Aviv. Funny, huh? He had a Guatemalan wife, and he had four children who believed themselves to be half-Israeli. The CIA team raided his plantation in the middle of the night and whisked him away. To cover their tracks, they even sent a series of ransom demands as if they were local thugs. No one suspected a thing.

If I didn't hate those pricks so much, I'd applaud them for their investigative brilliance.

Since then, the CIA has scored a surprising number of big-ticket arrests of actual al-Qaeda terrorists, thanks to information coerced from bin Laden by the splinter cell. This resulted in a new veneer for an agency that has taken a lot of drubbing over the last—oh, I don't know . . . forever. Congress was so happy with them that when it came time to review the annual budget, they pretty much handed the Agency a blank check.

When Mr. Church and our crew found out about this through some creatively targeted computer hacking, we decided that Osama should come live with us. We weren't here to "rescue" him per se. Hardly. Nor were we unduly concerned about the violations to his civil and human rights. Normally, that kind of thing torques my shorts. Less so in this case.

All we wanted was to turn him into an information source for us. There have been rumors in the intelligence pipeline for a couple of years now that something big was coming. Something massive. Something tied to the Seven Kings. The CIA splinter cell caught wind of it, too, but they dismissed it. The Kings were not on their to-do list. The Kings case belonged to the DMS.

So close.

So damn close.

What was the big project they had in development? Was there, in fact, a project at all? Bin Laden would have those answers. The King of Lies would know the truth.

If he was alive to tell us.

Now he was cooling meat.

Balls.

Interlude Two

The Imperial Condominiums

Unit 6A, Edgewater Drive

Corpus Christi, Texas

Four Years Ago

The girl's name was Boy.

It was the only thing anyone ever called her. If she had a real name, it was buried in the dirt of the past. She wouldn't answer to anything else.

Boy.

She was closing in on her twenty-fifth birthday. The last ten years of her life were the only years she cared to remember. The decade before that belonged to a different person. The decade before that belonged to a different story. A horror story.

No one sane mentioned her early years. No one smart asked her about them.

Doctor Pharos was the only one who could have that conversation with her, but he never did. He'd been the one to take her away from it, so he didn't need to comment on it.

Because he'd taken her away from that life, and because of the things he had done while taking her away, they were connected. Bonded.

Family.

Doctor Pharos and Boy.

Not the Boy. Just Boy.

They shared no other obvious connections. Not gender, not race, not cultural background. Certainly not any religious ties, except that neither of them prayed to a god or believed one existed.

The reality of their connection was something about which they never really conversed. Not a philosophical dissection of it. Not a deconstruction of motive or sources of gratifications. It existed, and they knew it. It worked, and they worked with it. It grew, and they cultivated it.

Their connection was terror.

It was something Doctor Pharos required of her.

It was something she existed to provide for him.

And it was the source of her joy.

Doctor Pharos loaded her like a bullet in the weapon of his intention and fired her over and over again at the targets of his need. He did this in the past in the service of the people they had both served. That time had passed, and now he did it to serve his own needs.

Today he had fired her in the direction of a scientist and college professor who probably thought his life was good, his job satisfying, and his future assured.

In this he was mistaken because he did not know that he was the target of the bullet fired by Doctor Pharos.

Boy waited in the dark.

She liked the dark.

It was like a glove that fit all of her curves and extrusions. It kept her safe and reminded her of her power.

She sat cross-legged on the dining room table in a nest of steel. Each of the eight steak knives and eleven assorted cooking knives had been driven into the tabletop. She had taken great pains to make sure they stood perfectly straight, a precise half circle. She didn't use forks. Forks were stupid. Who would use a fork?

Knives, though.

She got wet thinking about knives.

Her flesh trembled as she sat in her nest.

Waiting.

Waiting.

The man was late tonight. That was okay, though. It was a variable in a predictable pattern. He was sometimes late. A drive through for takeout. Dry cleaning. Sometimes a trip to the bookstore for magazines. She thought it strange that he only read magazines. There wasn't a single book in the house.

People were strange.

She waited.

The music coming through her earbuds was *pinpeat*. Elegant Cambodian ceremonial music that once played in the courts and temples. Ten instruments collaborating to form a sensual cloud of beauty that was unlike anything Boy had ever heard except the *pihat* ensembles of Thailand. So lovely. So serene.

She liked playing it very loud at times. It was more appealing than the sound of screams.

Now it played softly. A whisper.

Her heart fluttered with the tinkling notes of the *renard-ek*, the high-pitched bamboo xylophone. Her breathed flowed in and out with the extended notes of the *srelai thom*, the large quadruple-reed flute.

So lovely.

Her eyes wanted to drift shut, but she knew that if that happened she would fall asleep. This music could do that to her too easily.

Instead, Boy kept her eyes open and slowly, methodically counted the lines of wood grain in the tabletop.

When the key turned in the lock, she was awake, alert, and calm.

The table was not in line of sight with the front door, else she would not have chosen it as her place to wait. The man entered the house. Boy heard him toss the keys into the ceramic dish he used for that purpose. She heard him turn the lock. The whap of mail landing on the coffee table. One thump, two thumps as he kicked off his loafers. A click, and the TV was on. CNN. Wolf Blitzer was talking about something nobody cared about. He sounded desperate to be relevant.

The man—Professor Harry Seymour, chairman of the experimental aeronautics department at Texas A&M, Corpus Christi—came around the corner and into the dining room. Looking over his shoulder at the TV. Looking the wrong way.

Boy smiled.

She waited until he turned around. Waited until he saw her.

Waited until he stiffened with shock and fear and outrage.

Waited until Professor Seymour began to yell.

Attempted to yell.

She did not actually permit him to get a shout as far as his mouth.

As Seymour opened his mouth, she pivoted sideways, supple as a dancer, and kicked him in the throat.

The professor crashed sideways into a breakfront, fell heavily and badly, and hit his head on the way down. He slid all the way to the carpet, choking and gagging, trying to speak, trying to yell, trying to groan, trying to cry out.

In all of those things he failed.

Boy slid off the table and landed on cat feet. She bent over him and punched him in the face three times using a single-knuckle punch that was delivered with a whip of the wrist. No thrust. A thrust would injure her hand. A whip injured only him.

One blow to his left sinus. One blow to his right sinus. A third to the bridge of his nose. His head snapped back from the foot pounds of force lurking within the speed of her punch. The back of his head hit the breakfront.

She knelt quickly and struck Seymour again. A loose slap with the pads of her fingers upward beneath his testicles. A harder blow would galvanize him, coax a scream from him. A loose slap has an entirely different effect. Immediate and comprehensive nausea.

He rolled over onto hands and knees and vomited.

She stepped back and let him.

Vomiting was good. It reduced a man of this kind to shame and the helplessness that came with shame.

She walked behind Seymour and used the tip of her sneaker to kick him in the perineum, exactly between scrotum and anus. The blow was delivered at a slight angle so that the correct nerve clusters would be stunned.

They were, and immediately his bowels let loose. The rich stink of feces filled the room. The man groaned. Another wave of pain and shame.

Those were two of Boy's favorite tools.

Combined, they were far more effective than agony and fear. Pain—controlled, specific, and moderate—was one key, one dial she turned on people. If the pain was too big, then system-wide shock set in. The body released the wrong chemicals; it sparked a different psychological reaction. It was why classic torturers put bamboo shoots under the fingernails rather than cut the fingers off.

The professor began to cry.

Boy nodded, satisfied.

The man on the floor was big. Two hundred and fifteen soft pounds. She weighed ninety-eight. She was as slender and hard as the knives she loved so dearly.

Boy knelt beside the man and bent close. She kissed his cheek. She ran a tongue around the curve of his ear. He cringed and tried to close into himself. Boy leaned so close that her breath was hot in his ear.

"It doesn't have to get worse than this," she said.

Professor Seymour almost stopped breathing. He lay there, rigid, hanging on whatever she would say next.

"You want to talk to me," she continued. "You want to whisper to me. I know you do. I can feel it. You want to share things with me."

She reached a hand and gently stroked his crotch, letting each separate fingertip find and caress his flaccid length. His penis twitched.

And what a wonderfully mixed signal that would send to this man's brain. Boy knew that. Even laying there, beaten, his underwear filled with his own shit, he had just reacted to a woman's touch.

Exactly as other men had done before this one.

Exactly as Doctor Pharos had said they would when he taught her his methods.

As she continued to touch him, the shame of defeat, the worse shame of having soiled himself, the pain in his nose and sinuses all triggered the first flow of tears. Injuries to the nose always made the eyes water. To the overwhelmed it is impossible to tell the difference between the body's automatic reaction to facial injuries and tears that are shed as a response to personal weakness. It is because of this unavoidable reaction that so many brave people doubt their courage and believe in a previously unknown cowardice. It's a way in which the mind breaks itself.

Seymour began to cry.

To sob.

And it was then that Boy knew he would tell her anything.

She stroked him. And she felt him, against will and circumstance, grow hard. If she had started with sexual touch first and proceeded to pain, he would not be able to get hard. One had to know the patterns of things.

Boy knew those patterns so well.

"Please," begged the professor. And in that moment he probably did not know what he was begging her for.

She smiled.

Yes, this one would tell her anything.

Everything.

Chapter Eight

The Resort

208 Nautical Miles West of Chile

October 13, 1:11 A.M.

"Let's do this and go home," I told my team. "Gather all intel. Anything on paper goes with us. Maybe they have some Kings stuff. Maybe we'll get lucky."

"Maybe blue pigs will fly out of my ass," muttered Bunny. I ignored him.

"Double-check that we have IDs on everyone. Disable all weapons. Collect all cell phones, trash any hard lines or radios. Basically, vandalize the crap out of this place."

"Hooah," said Top. He stepped out of the cell for a moment, then hurried back. "The other prisoners are in moderately poor shape. Lot of obvious wounds. Untreated cuts. Dislocated fingers."

"Some 'resort,'" said Bunny, and then he shook his head. "I am having some weirdly conflicted feelings here, guys. I mean, our intel says that most of the prisoners here are actual scum suckers. Really-bad bad guys. And if I thought there was a bomb about to go off and any of these pricks knew where it was or how to de-arm it, then, well . . . shit. I guess I'd put my conscience on a back shelf and go all Jack Bauer on them. But that's, you know, heat-of-the-moment stuff. Needs of the many and all that stuff."

"You walking in the direction of a point?" asked Top.

Bunny looked at the door to the hallway. "Not sure what I'm saying."

We all got it, though. We were all warriors. We were all killers. But we were all, each in our own way, idealists. Working for the DMS will do that. It's nudged us away from either the right or the left side of politics. I had my left-wing, bleeding-heart-liberal moments, and I had my hard-line conservative moments. Pretty much in equal measure these days. It didn't exactly make me a centrist, and it certainly didn't make me a libertarian—besides, soldiers shouldn't play politics. I occasionally did appalling things because the situation was fragile and innocent lives would be lost if I didn't act. All three of us had. Sam, too.

And yet . . .

The line between immediate need and breaking the law is blurry at the best of times. And I'm not talking about the laws of states or nations. I'm talking about the laws of basic humanity.

It's so hard to decide how to think about it. When I first joined the DMS, I was appalled when Mr. Church used deception and carefully worded threats to psychologically coerce crucial information out of a suspect. Church broke the man. As a result, we gained information that ultimately saved millions, perhaps billions, of lives.

Not too many months later, I needed to get a certain code from a man who was about to launch a series of designer pathogens that would have wiped out everyone who didn't conform to a certain standard of acceptable "whiteness." Again, billions would have died. He was an old man, and he was injured. However, the clock was ticking down to boom time, and so I did what I had to do. The information he ultimately gave to me stopped that genocide.

So, how was this different?

I don't really know if I can answer that question. A lot of what was being done to these prisoners was part of a fishing expedition. The prisoners were believed to have knowledge of imminent or long-range threats against America. Due process was denied to them by the Patriot Act because the legal method can be used against itself. That's something I understand, but on the whole I wouldn't wipe my dog's ass with the Patriot Act. It was quickly written and is poorly thought out, bad policy. People on both sides of the aisle should be working together a little more diligently to replace it with something smarter and saner.

This prison, the Resort, was illegal. No doubt. Any useful intelligence obtained was, in fact, saving lives. However, it was funneled through certain Agency channels for the career benefit of a select few.

Does that matter if the effect is still the saving of lives? Sure, but how much is something that still needs to be looked at.

Is the systematic and continual torture of prisoners justified if they do, indeed, have guilty knowledge and if that information is crucial to saving lives?

That's what had Bunny's gut clenched. Mine, too. And Top's. Standing there in that cell, with no one around but varying degrees of criminals, it was hard to pin your sympathies to the right wall.

I sighed and called it in. Church said that a medical team was on board the chopper.

"What about the staff?" asked Bunny once I was off the call. He looked at the two men who had been interrogating bin Laden. They cowered against the wall in horrified silence.

"P-please!" said one of them, holding up his hands. Throughout our conversation, he'd been pretending to be a hole in the air. Like maybe he thought we'd forget about him. "Please . . . we were following orders to—"

"Really?" I said. "You're going with the 'only following orders' thing?"

They began protesting. Then begging.

Top drew his Snellig and darted them both.

"Thank you," said Bunny.

Top shook his head slowly as he shoved his pistol into its holster. "I could have worked on my uncle's farm. Getting fat and rich growing peaches."

"Right now," said Bunny, "that sounds like heaven."

I nodded to the unconscious men. "Secure them. They've got cells waiting for them back home."

"Be mighty uncomfortable," said Top. "Them tied up and all. No food or water. No bathroom runs."

"You have a problem with that?" I asked.

He said, "Nope. Just noting it."

We nodded to each other. Each of us aware of the conundrum's souring our collective moods.

"Feeling the need to vent a little here, Boss," said Bunny. "Might slash some tires and break some windows."

"Hooah," Top said again.

"None of that goes outside of the mission protocols as far as I'm concerned," I said. "Indulge yourself."

We tapped back into the mission channel. "Tell the helo pilot to brew a fresh pot of high-test, and I don't want to hear the word 'decaf,'" I said. "Going to be a long night."

Chapter Nine

The Capitol Building

Washington, D.C.

October 13, 1:15 A.M.

"Home, James."

It was a running joke every time the president climbed into the back of the Beast, the presidential state car.

The driver, a sergeant in the White House Military Office, was actually named James. The driver grinned, as he always did, even though the joke was as stale as Christmas fruitcake. But the basic rule was that the president's jokes were always funny, even when they weren't. The rule applied to any joke told by any president. As a result, a lot of former commanders in chief left office convinced that they were hilarious.

Being seen to visibly appreciate the joke was even more important tonight, because the man sharing the backseat with the president was Linden Brierly, director of the Secret Service. Brierly, though not James's boss, had unquestioned influence over all matters of security personnel.

So, the driver, Leonard Allyn James, chuckled at the joke and waited until the senior motorcade NCO gave the go signal. The long line of vehicles switched on their red and blue flashers and the procession pulled away from the Capitol for the six-minute drive to the White House.

The Beast was a heavily armored Chevrolet Kodiak–based, Cadillac-badged limousine. It was referred to in most official documents as Cadillac One or Limousine One but called the Beast by everyone in the presidential motorcade.

Another running joke was that the motorcade was longer than the route between the two buildings. Most often there were forty-five cars in the procession, with one or two dummy versions of the presidential state car. All for a drive of one-point-seven miles. For what would otherwise be a nice stretch of the legs.

In the back, the president rubbed his eyes and sank wearily into the cushions.

"Long night," said Brierly.

"Long damn night," agreed the president.

The third person in their conversational cluster nodded, but added, "Good night's work, though."

Alice Houston, the White House chief of staff, somehow managed to look fresh and alert despite this being the middle of the night. Everyone else who had spent the last fourteen hours hammering away at the budget bill looked wasted. The elderly congressman from West Virginia had drifted off to sleep five times and had to be shaken vigorously to give his opinion on alterations in a bill that would keep the lights on in government facilities across America. Later today, the House would receive the bill and vote on it, hopefully in time to beat the midnight shutdown.

"I think we have something we can all live with," said the president. It was not the first time he'd said that. Not the tenth. They all repeated it like a mantra. In truth, the bill was a pale shadow of the one they'd tried to pass. The original bill, drafted by a close supporter of the administration, took several hard stances that were fiscally sound. They were also politically indefensible. They required the kind of bipartisan cooperation that only ever happened in heartwarming and naive political comedies. That bill assumed that the phrase "in the best interest of the American people" meant just that.

"I wish we could have taken Donald's suggestion," muttered the president.

Donald Crisp was a junior senator whose idealism was dying a quick death in Washington. His suggestion, intended only as sarcasm, was that all further discussion of the merits of the bill be conducted only after every person in the room had been hooked up to lie detectors. That was a riff on a Jimmy Fallon bit about how cool it would be if the participants in political debates were hooked up to polygraphs. A nice idea, but it would cause armed insurrection on Capitol Hill.

Everyone in the room tonight had laughed. A lot.

Even Donald Crisp.

Now, in the car, the chuckles were less jovial. There was more evident regret that the world did not, and never would, spin in that direction.

"Can't wait to see what the press does with the bill," continued the president.

"I don't think it will be too bad," said Brierly. "Nobody wants to see the government shut down. Again."

"Sure they do, Linden," said Houston. "News is news is news. And it's pretty quiet out there." She gestured to indicate the world as a whole. With the war in Afghanistan more or less over and things in the Middle East simmering on a moderately low boil, the big story had become the impending shutdown. With a bill that was all compromise, the pundits would have to feed on something, which meant that they would milk the bill—and the participation of the key players—for as much sustenance as they could. "Once the 'shutdown averted' headlines have their fifteen minutes, then they're going to go snipe hunting in D.C."

"That might be an imperfect metaphor," murmured the president.

Houston opened her mouth to reply, but the car suddenly jerked to a halt with such abrupt force that they were pitched forward against their seat belts.

Brierly punched the intercom. "James—what's wrong? What's happening?"

"No threat, sir," said James. "The brakes locked up."

The whole motorcade screeched to a stop. Doors opened and sergeants swarmed the Beast. Most of them had guns drawn.

Brierly turned in his seat. "Mr. President, are you okay?"

"Yes, yes, sure. No problem," said the president, waving him off. He unbuckled his seat belt and reached a hand toward Houston. "Alice—?"

Houston was flustered, but she nodded. "I'm fine, I'm fine."

"James," growled Brierly, "talk to me."

"Must be a malfunction. Hold on, I think I—."

Then the car suddenly lurched forward, snapping them back against the cushions. The president had been half turned toward Houston, and Brierly had been leaning in toward him, but the jolt bounced them together. Brierly's forehead struck the president's cheek with a meaty crack.

The car stopped and oscillated on its springs. The siren blared on and off. The headlights cycled from running lights to driving lights to high beams to off, and then through the same pattern. Door locks popped up, then down, then up.

"Jesus Christ!" cried the president, reeling back, a hand clamped to his cheek.

"What's happening?" shrieked Houston, terrified.

"Goddamn it, James!" snarled Brierly. Then he yelled into his cuff mike, calling for a medic.

The car jerked forward again, and once more Brierly and the president collided. The president snapped a hand out to fend off a second collision and accidentally struck Brierly's mouth. Blood erupted from the director's mashed lips.

"The onboard computer's going crazy," bellowed James. "I can't turn it off."

The doors of the Beast were whipped open and hands reached in, closed around the president, and pulled him out. He was immediately surrounded and, in a run-walk, taken to a second car. Two WHMA sergeants piled into the Beast. One released Houston from her belt and began guiding her to the doorway; another slid in beside Brierly, whose lower face was painted with blood. James was pulled out of the driver's seat.

The car jerked forward again. And again, throwing Brierly and the sergeant to the floor. The edge of the door clipped Houston's ankle and tripped her, and as she fell, she dragged her escort down.

Then the lights switched off, the horn stopped blaring, and the Beast's engine growled down to silence.

WHMO sergeants and Secret Service agents assigned to the motorcade pointed guns in a dozen useless directions, including at the car itself. One agent took a risk and leaned quickly in to throw the car into park. But it already was. When he turned, confused, he saw James hold out the keys.

Four heavily armored cars peeled off into a smaller motorcade and whisked the president away. The rest of the vehicles and all of the remaining agents stared at the car, uncertain about what had just happened. The driver had put the car in park, turned off the engine, and removed the key. However, the car had still jerked forward, and its engine had run for several seconds after that.

Linden Brierly, holding a compress to his torn lips, expressed the thought that was on everyone's mind.

"What the hell——?"

Chapter Ten

The Resort
208 Nautical Miles West of Chile
October 13, 1:23 A.M.

"I uploaded a lot of data to MindReader already," I told my guys. "Do the same with any computer you see. If bin Laden told them anything about what the Kings have running, maybe it'll be on the drives."

"You think that's likely?" asked Bunny. "It's my impression that the assholes in the splinter cell were still more or less on our side, just going about it the wrong way. If they caught wind of anything, there's a dozen ways to slip that info to us."

Top shook his head. "You more trusting than I remember, Farm Boy. I think you been hit in the head too many times."

We left it at that. Everyone went about their jobs.

The lab building was mine. I placed Bug's uplink doodads into the USB ports of every computer I could find. MindReader gobbled up all of their data.

"Geez," said Bug, "there's a lot of stuff here. A lot of eyes-only and above-top-secret files. Encrypted, but that won't be a problem."

"Let me know if you get anything on the Kings."

"There might be, but you know the Agency. They have code names for everything. They might have reams of stuff hidden under some name we won't recognize. I'm seeing files labeled Dora the Explorer, Getaway Weekend, Cinco de Mayo, Mr. Smith Goes to Washington. These guys are hilarious."

"Yeah, I'm laughing my balls off. Pull it apart."

"Sure, just know it'll take time. Nikki's doing a simultaneous pattern-and-keyword search as this stuff comes in."

While that process ran its course, I scouted around for anything else of use. Except for the computers and some personnel records, there wasn't anything lying around with the word "Evidence" stenciled on it. These guys were careful. Had to keep looking, though. Found a porn stash in one guy's desk. DVDs with cover images of Asian girls who looked way too young to be in the kind of horror show they were in. Some of those kids couldn't have been older than ten or twelve. Disks were from some illegal pirating group in Malaysia. I found the name of the person who sat at that desk and matched it to the sleeping prisoners. The guy with the kiddie porn was a big slice of white bread with lots of tough-guy tattoos. I kicked him in the balls. Real damn hard.

Will I kick a man when he's down?

Nah.

But I'll kick a pedophile from any angle at any time.

I went back to my search without a flicker of guilt.

Interlude Three

The Imperial Condominiums

Unit 6A, Edgewater Drive

Corpus Christi, Texas

Four Years Ago

The car idled outside the Imperial Condominiums, engine quiet, driver silent. No radio, no conversation, even though there was a second man in the front passenger seat. They sat and waited.

They were slim men. Midtwenties. Average height. Average weight. Average in every useful way. Forgettable.

The car was a medium blue Ford Focus.

The men were dressed like grad students. The driver wore a print dress shirt and moderately tasteful Dockers. The passenger wore a Texas A&M, Corpus Christi, basketball sweatshirt over pressed jeans and New Balance running shoes. They looked like what they wanted people to see. They did not look like who and what they were.

The man in the Dockers was currently using the name Jacob. It was listed as the most popular name for boys based on statistics from the Social Security Administration. The man in the jeans was using the second most popular name, Mason.

Before coming here they had been at a Starbucks on Ocean Drive. Jacob pretended to read the paper. Mason pretended to surf the net on his iPad. They sat near each other, but not together. When they left, Jacob went out first, walked around the corner, and got into his car. He circled the block and picked up his companion one street away. The driver made sure he was not being followed.

They were both very careful men.

Then they drove over to Edgewater and parked outside the condos. Engine on, both of them waiting.

Jacob had a Ruger SR22 pistol snugged into an ankle holster. Mason had an identical gun in his zippered tablet case. They always carried the same make and model of handgun. It made it easier for sharing ammunition. These were efficient men.

However, both of these guns were their backup pieces. Neither of them preferred to kill with them.

They used something else for that.

The cell phone that rested on the dash vibrated.

The driver picked it up, thumbed the green button, and said, " 'Āllō."

He listened and then disconnected without a comment, switched the engine off, and got out of the car. The other man removed a small hemp-handled paper bag. The bag was from Starbucks. Two plump one-pound bags of Pike Place blend peeked out of the top.

Together, Jacob and Mason approached the building.

They pressed the call button for unit 6A. A moment later, it buzzed and the door lock clicked.

They entered and took the stairs. They did not go to unit 6A. Instead, the driver led his companion to unit 12B. It was at the end of a short hallway. The hall was completely empty and very quiet. They knocked on the door and waited until a woman answered it. She smiled expectantly at them. They were unobtrusive and well-groomed young men. Everyone in this building worked at the university. Nearly every tenant was a professor. It was not at all unusual for a couple of grad students to visit.

"Yes?" said the woman.

"Mrs. Harrison?" asked Jacob.

"Yes."

"We work with your husband. Doc Harrison asked us to bring this over." He held up the Starbucks bag.

She was still smiling, but there was as much frown as smile on her mouth. "He's in the shower, but I can—"

Mason punched her.

Once, very hard, in the throat. He used the folded secondary knuckles of his left hand. A leopard's-paw punch.

The blow crushed her hyoid bone and larynx. It silenced her voice. She collapsed immediately, and he stepped forward to catch her. He smiled at her as she turned purple. Trying to breathe, trying to find even a whisper of breath in a throat filled with shattered debris.

Mason caught Mrs. Harrison and laid her very gently on the floor, holding her down to keep her heels from hammering on the hardwood as she died.

Jacob closed the door. He took the coffee out of the bag and removed a pistol. It was not another .22. It did not fire bullets at all. The weapon looked vaguely like a silvery space pistol from a bad science fiction movie. It didn't look entirely real.

It was.

The weapon was a Jarvis USSS-2A pneumatic mushroom-head non-penetrating stunner. Very effective for the quick and humane slaughter of cattle. Unlike the captive-bolt stunners, this one did not even break the skin. No risk of contaminants. No need to meticulously clean the fittings to remove DNA.

"Doris—?" called a man's voice from down the hall. "Who was at the door?"

They could hear the shower water running.

Jacob nodded to Mason, who rose from the corpse, and together they walked down the hall toward the bathroom.

Sixteen minutes later, they were in the Focus driving away.

The two men were in the front, Boy was in the back. She had been waiting for them in the lobby.

There were three corpses in the condominium.

Professor Milo Harrison, deputy department chair of applied robotics at Texas A&M, Corpus Christi, and his wife, Doris. And Professor Harry Seymour, chairman of the school's experimental aeronautics department.

The car moved at a comfortable pace along Edgewater.

Away from the three dead bodies.

Away from the Imperial Condominiums.

Away from the column of dense smoke that rose from that building.

Several fire engines screamed past them. Five separate police cars roared by. No one took note of the nondescript car with its nondescript passengers.

They drove to a motel outside the city limits and checked into their rooms. They left all of their equipment in the car. A minute later, a silver-gray Toyota Camry and a beige Honda Civic pulled into the lot and parked in front of the rear exit. The drivers of those cars got into the Focus and drove it away. They took it to a scrapyard on Holly Road, got into a black SUV, and left. The Focus was crushed within minutes. Later, it was added to a load of scrap metal that would be taken by heavy truck to the docks and included in a shipment bound for Japan.

At the motel, Boy went into one room and the two graduate students went into another.

Boy stripped off her clothes and stuffed them into a plastic container. All other personal effects went into the same container. Naked, she went into the bathroom, took a shower, dried herself thoroughly, removed an aerosol can from a bag on the sink, and doused herself with a dark spray-on tan. She put contact lenses in her eyes, injected collagen into her lips, slipped on a blond wig and padded clothing. The last thing she did was put on padded shoes that added two inches to her height.

After she left, a cleaning woman came in, took a hazmat suit from her cart, put it on, and proceeded to clean every inch of the room with industrial cleaner and bleach. She poured acid down the drains to dissolve any traces of hair or other DNA. Another cleaner did the same in the room used by the two young men.

The plastic containers of clothing and personal effects were taken to a waste site and dumped into a tub of hydrofluoric acid. The residue was mixed with plastic and ball bearings and allowed to harden. The hardened blocks were dumped from fishing boats out at sea.

All of this took place within a few hours of the three murders at Imperial Condominiums. It is possible, even likely, that more than half of these procedures were unnecessary, even wildly so. They were done anyway. Nothing was left to chance.

No trace was left.

Boy drove her new car to New Orleans. The trip took nine hours.

Mason and Jacob drove a more leisurely route along I-10 west to Alamogordo, where they checked in to the Holiday Inn Express. And waited.

They had no idea how long they would have to wait. Nor did it matter.

Instructions would come.

Instructions always came.

They spent the time swimming in the hotel pool, watching pay-per-view movies, playing video games, and making love to each other.

In New Orleans, Boy checked in to the Hotel Monteleone, ate room service food, and read three novels. When she wasn't actively working, Boy read all day and into the evening. She was currently working her way through the entire works of Elmore Leonard, having just finished all the Travis McGee novels by John D. MacDonald. Reading calmed her. It allowed her energies to idle in neutral.

She did not make any calls. She did not feel the urge to check e-mails. She had no Facebook or Twitter pages. She was patient and in her patience was content to wait. Doctor Pharos would call her.

He always called.

There was still so much left to do.

The world was still on its hinges.

For now.

Chapter Eleven

The Resort

208 Nautical Miles West of Chile

October 13, 1:38 A.M.

"Cowboy," came Bug's urgent call, "be advised we have incoming."

"Incoming what?"

"Looks like a UAV coming in low and fast." UAV was shorthand for unmanned aerial vehicle. A drone.

He read off the coordinates and vector, indicating that it was coming from the west. From the seaward side of the island. I hurried outside. Top and Bunny were already there, each of them fitting on their night vision.

"What's this shit?" asked Top.

"This some Agency thing?" growled Bunny. "They have a second location out here? Another island we don't know about?"

"Nothing on the satellite maps," I said. "Bug, give me something. Who's toy is this?"

"Unknown, Cowboy," said Bug. "Definitely not one of ours. The only drones we have are running surveillance between here and the mainland. This one just appeared on the radar. Probably launched from a boat."

"Boat," echoed Bunny nervously. "Chilean navy? They could have launched one from a submarine out of Talcahuano. They got a couple of those Type 209 German-made boats."

"Got Exocets on 'em, too," said Top. "Don't want to overstay our welcome and get a missile shoved up our asses, Cap'n. We ain't supposed to be here."

"I don't think so," said Bug. "This is a small signature. Don't think it's military. Not big enough to carry heavy weapons. Coming right at you, though. Seven miles and closing. We have two helos heading to intercept, but the UAV will get to you first."

"Frigging drones are a pain in my ass," said Top.

I had to agree. These days they were everywhere. The military had a lot of them, but they were also being used not only to map streets and, by law enforcement, to conduct aerial surveillance and patrol the border but also to film sports events, take real-estate photos, and even deliver goods. Amazon, Barnes & Noble, Domino's, Taco Bell, and hundreds of other companies had applied for licenses. The FAA kept trying to fight it, and for very good reasons. UAVs could be used to deliver a lot more than chalupas or the latest Janet Evanovich novel, but the agency was losing most of their cases.

"Still not seeing it, Bug," said Bunny. He held a muscular AA-12 shotgun with a drum magazine. It was a monster. Fully automatic and drum-fed, it fired five 12-gauge shotgun shells per second. Very reliable, very little recoil. I've seen Bunny fire it one-handed. And for times when a hail of hot buckshot isn't enough of a crowd-pleaser, he could swap in another drum loaded with Frag-12 high-explosive or fragmentation grenades. He calls it Honey Boom-Boom. Bunny has issues.

We listened.

Drones are very quiet. Maybe if there weren't a million crickets and cicadas filling the night air with their steady whistling pulse, maybe—just maybe—we'd have heard it. Maybe not.

"Infrared," I said, and we cycled through the Scout's lenses until the world was painted scarlet.

"There it is," said Top as he raised his M4. "Two o'clock. Fifty feet above the trees."

"C'mon, Bug," I said, raising my own rifle. This wasn't the time for horse tranquilizers. "Tell me something useful or we're going to blow this thing out of the air. Not in the mood for surprises."

"I got nothing on it, Cowboy. Satellites are not picking up an active weapons system."

"Doesn't mean it ain't a bomb," observed Top.

We all saw it then. A pale blotch of heat painted against the fifty thousand shades of red and gray that made up the forest. It was a four-rotor quadcopter and it was bigger than I thought. Maybe six feet across. It wobbled slightly as it flew, pushed out of true by a freshening easterly breeze. It flew just above the tree line until it hit the clearing between trees and fence.

"I don't see a payload," said Bunny.

"No rocket pods," agreed Top.

"I got it," said Sam Imura's voice over the radio. "Call it, Cowboy, and I'll switch off the lights."

"Everyone hold fire," I said. We kept our guns on it as it flew closer.

"It's slowing," Bunny said.

It was. The machine crossed the fence line very slowly indeed and drifted over twenty feet of lawn, coming straight for us. Then it stopped; hovering there as if painted on the night sky.

"Cowboy," said Bug urgently, "be advised, we're picking up a strong, active video feed. It's going up to half a dozen satellites."

"Who's satellites?"

"It's crazy—it's hacking into every communication satellite in range and bouncing them all over. This thing is broadcasting this live. It's showing up on TV and the net."

And there, lying on the ground at our feet, was the corpse of Osama bin Laden.

Dead and in color.

"Jam the signal!" I shouted.

"Can't do it, Cowboy—it's already out there."

The drone hovered there. Mocking us with what it could do. Mocking us with what it was already doing.

"Take it out," ordered Church. "Right now."

Sam fired first, but I think we all hit it. We blasted the drone out of the sky and into a thousand fragments of metal and plastic. The motor core exploded and shot firework sparks into the dewy grass as the parts rained down.

I could hear the beat of helicopter rotors far off to the north, as our evac bird came hustling through the shadows to take us home. We stood and waited, watching the last of burning sparks drift down to the lawn. None of us said a word. What was there to say?

The video feed was out.

"Well, fuck me," breathed Top.

It was damage done. We pulled off the Scout goggles, but I didn't want to meet anyone's eyes.

Very quietly Bunny said, "Without the beard and hair . . . maybe no one will know who it was."

Top gave him a withering look. "You're out of your damn mind, Farm Boy. Hope you had all your shots 'cause we are about to be well and truly fucked."

Our Black Hawk swept over the trees accompanied by a big Chinook transport helicopter. They descended like monstrous birds from the night sky. But even their combined and powerful rotor wash couldn't sweep away the weeds of doubt that were trying to take root in the soil of my soul.

Interlude Four

The sign outside said it was a hardware store. The store was open, fully stocked and staffed, and did good business.

The three floors above the store were not used for stock, offices, or employee break rooms. They were nicely furnished apartments. The doors were of the best quality, the security systems state-of-the-art, the staff fully trained. Two of the agents on each shift were Israelis on the payroll of the CIA. The other two were MOSSAD agents. Three men, one woman. They spent a lot of time together. They talked shop, they played cards, they surfed the net, they watched a lot of TV. Mostly, though, they read reports. This station was one of several joint operations that formed small but valuable links in the intelligence chain that was looped through every town and country in the Middle East.

The lead agent was named Dor Ben-Shahar. His mother was a Tel Aviv Israeli; his father was from Brooklyn. Both of them were experienced agents, both second generation Agency operatives, which made Dor a third-generation spy. He treasured his agency legacy as much as his ethnic and religious heritage. His grandfather had fought in the Six Day War. One of his uncles was at Entebbe. His great-aunt had been part of Operation Wrath of God following the Munich Massacre. There was no one in his family, on either the American or Israeli side, who hadn't seen active combat. Not one.

Dor Ben-Shahar was different only in that he never wore a uniform, but he'd seen his full share of dirty little actions. He had blood on his hands, and most of it was guilty blood. Bad guys who needed to die. A few drops of blood were from civilians caught in the cross fire. Collateral damage. Unfortunate but unavoidable.

Lately, though, Dor hadn't had to use his gun or any of the skills he'd learned from the Agency trainers or from his friends here in Israel. He hadn't touched his gun at all except to clean and oil it. Lately he'd put on three pounds from eating too much falafel and doing too few crunches.

Lately, he had become a babysitter.

Part, in fact, of a team of babysitters.

All for one man.

A little pip-squeak of a guy from New Jersey. An egghead. A scientist.

Doctor Aaron Davidovich.

Dor thought the guy looked like a tailor. Or maybe a bookie in a 1960s New York gangster movie. Beard, big nose, thick glasses, delicate hands, bad breath. Not the kind of guy you'd want your sister to marry, unless you didn't care much for your sister. Dor's sister, Esther, was in Army Intelligence. He did like her, and her taste in men tended toward Navy SEALs or Delta gunslingers.

Not creepy little guys like Davidovich.

Dor's job was to protect the scientist and guarantee that he would be fit, healthy, and whole so he could make his presentation to a joint panel of military strategists from the United States and Israel. All very hush-hush. All tied to a new phase of the drone project. All part of a new level of warfare that would—if Davidovich was as good as his promises—significantly increase the tactical effectiveness of UAVs used in surgical strikes while decreasing collateral damage among civilians. Bystanders were martyrs waiting to happen, children doubly so. Nobody wanted them killed. Not even the kind of people who didn't give a cold, wet shit about Muslim children as long as the target was secured. Those ultrahawks weren't motivated by compassion. Not even a little. Any concessions they made to reducing civilian casualties were measured against negative political pressure because political pressure was often tied to defense-budget purse strings.

Dor, though a warrior and son of warriors, was a family man. He considered himself to be a good man. Not really as devout as he might be—his wife had to all but threaten him at gunpoint to get him to synagogue except on the High Holy Days—but he believed that warriors were defined by their skill, not their body count. If it took a little more work and time to reduce unwanted nonmilitary casualties, then so be it. Otherwise, a warrior became a barbarian. A Philistine. Dor took pride in what he did.

If Davidovich could accomplish both goals—increasing the likelihood of killing high-level targets while decreasing unwanted casualties—then Dor was more than happy to do his part to keep him safe.

Shame the guy was such a drip.

"You want to play cards?" asked Dor.

Davidovich didn't look up from his laptop. "I'm busy."

He wasn't working. Dor could see that easy enough, even without the laptop beeping and booping as the guy battled his way through some old retro arcade game. Ms. Pacman for god's sake. Guy writes artificial intelligence software for drones and he can't play anything more challenging than Ms.-fucking-Pacman? Seriously?

"You want coffee?"

Davidovich ignored the question. He paused his game play, put earbuds into his ears, turned up the volume on his iPod and resumed chasing energy dots and fleeing from ghosts.

Dor sighed. He shared a look with the other agent working this shift, an Israeli national named Tovah. She made a face and shook her head. She understood.

Dor went to the kitchen to make coffee for himself. Tovah was drinking Coke.

The coffeemaker began beeping, and at the same moment there was a knock on the door. Dor and Tovah exchanged another look, and this was of an entirely different frequency. Without saying a word they both stopped what they were doing, drew their guns, and took their positions. Tovah hooked Davidovich under the arm and pulled him gently but firmly up from the couch and away from his game, then guided him quickly down a short hall to the bedroom that had the reinforced door.

Meanwhile, Dor went to the door, standing to its left side, which was the wall with the steel sheeting hidden beneath the drywall and wallpaper. Without opening the door, he said, "Who is it?"

"Delivery for Yev," said a voice.

Dor relaxed. That was the correct day code.

He replied, "Mr. Yev is not here."

"This is for his mother."

All correct, and the voice sounded familiar.

Even so, he kept his gun down at his side as he disengaged the lock and, with the chain still on, opened the door one inch so he could peer outside. As he did so, he asked the final verification question.

"Is it still cloudy?"

"No, the sun is shining. It's a nice day."

Dor exhaled and grinned. "Simon," he said, "you're early."

Simon Meir was his relief man.

"Let me in," said Simon. "I have to use the john."

Dor closed the door, slipped off the chain, opened it, and died.

Just like that.

Simon's gun was fitted with a sound suppressor. The bullet entered under Dor's chin and punched a hole at an angle that blew off the crown of his head. Dor stood straight and still for a moment, his head raised as if listening, though he was already past hearing. His body was caught in a moment when it was balanced only by skeletal alignment, the muscles not yet responding to a lack of signal.

Then Dor's knees buckled and he puddled down.

By then Simon Meir and his companion were already inside the apartment. Simon closed the door while the second killer—smaller, slimmer, female—hurried down the hallway toward the secure room.

From the mouth of the hallway, Simon called, "Tovah. I brought some falafel. You hungry?"

From inside the room, Tovah laughed. "I'm always hungry," she said as she opened the door. "Hope you brought enough for—"

And she died.

Boy put three rounds into her: one in the heart, two in the head. Boy used a .22 with a Trinity sound suppressor. The shots made only small, flat noises. There were no exit wounds. Almost no mess. Tovah staggered, tried to catch the wall, failed, and fell.

Then Boy and Simon entered the secure room, guns up and out. Doctor Davidovich began backing away from them, his eyes wide and filled with the sure and certain knowledge that his world—everything in his world—was going to change. That everything had already changed.

He held up his hands. Tears sprang into his eyes. He sank to his knees.

He said, "No . . . please, no . . . "

Boy smiled as she holstered her pistol and removed a syringe.

"Please . . . ," whimpered the scientist.

Boy liked it when they begged.

Chapter Twelve

The president sat slumped on a sofa in his apartment in the White House. The room was filled with people. Secret Service agents, senior staff, his body man, a military doctor and nurse, and Linden Brierly, who had four stitches in his lower lip. The first lady was in Detroit on a speaking tour.

Brierly, despite the pain and discomfort of his injury, was doing most of the talking.

"We're tearing the car apart," he explained. "So far, we've eliminated simple mechanical problems. The senior mechanic thinks that the onboard computer system is the culprit."

"The car was turned off," said the president. "Isn't that what you told me? James had the key in his hand."

"He did, and I'm not trying to protect one of my own when I say that I don't think he is in any way to blame for—"

The president flapped a hand. "Oh hell, of course not. And I don't want to hear about James being transferred to the dark side of the moon. I can't see how this is his fault. He's a good kid."

"We think the problem is in the autonomous vehicle software."

"The what?"

"Autonomous—"

"I heard you. I mean . . . since when do we have that installed in the Beast?"

Alice Houston answered that. "Eighteen months ago, Mr. President. You, um, were briefed on it when you took office."

"Oh," said the president. "Right."

Brierly said, "The systems were installed to allow the car to operate in a defensive and protective manner, sir. Even if the driver were incapacitated, the car would use its GPS and other software to get you out of there. It's tied to all of the internal security systems and countermeasures and is in constant contact with the White House Communications Agency. The idea is to make sure you're never sitting in a dead or driverless car."

The president gave a sullen nod. He was a year and a half into his presidency, and the glamour of the gizmos and geegaws had long since eroded, revealing a set of security protocols that were ponderous and annoying. Necessary, sure. But annoying. The Beast was a perfect example of what he considered overpreparedness. It was sealed against biochemical attacks and had a full medical kit in the trunk, including pints of blood in the president's type—which he found deeply unnerving. It even had its own oxygen supply. And it was so heavily armored that it barely got eight miles to the gallon.

Now this. An autonomous driving system.

"I would have assumed," he said acidly, "that someone was supposed to vet this system before we paid whatever we paid—probably fifty times what we should have—to have it installed?"

"Yes, Mr. President," said Brierly. "The operating software package has been thoroughly tested by DARPA and some independent labs."

"Then explain to me why and how this happened, Linden."

Brierly had no answer to that.

No one did.

The president got wearily to his feet. Everyone else got to their feet as well. "I can't do this anymore. I need some sleep. Alice, you kick whoever you need to kick, but by the time I wake up, I want to know why my car turned into a Transformer. Are we clear? No excuses, no buck passing. I want a clear and cogent answer. Capisce?"

"Yes, Mr. President," she said.

The crowd began edging toward the door, with the president walking behind them, arms wide, like a shepherd driving his flock into a pen. When they were outside, he closed the door and turned and leaned back against it, blowing out his cheeks.

"Damn," he said, sighing out the word so that it was stretched as thin as he was. After a moment, he pushed himself upright and had just hooked his fingers into the knot of his tie when someone knocked on the door.

Very hard, with great insistence.

"Jesus H. . . ."

He bellowed, "Come in, damn it."

The door opened and two heads leaned in. Alice Houston and Linden Brierly.

"It's too soon for good news," grumped the president. "So, if it's bad news, I don't want to hear it."

"Mr. President," said Houston, pushing past Brierly to come in. She crossed to the TV, snatched up the remote, and clicked it on. "You have to see this."

The screen filled immediately with a video already in progress.

Three hulking armed figures in dark clothes stood in a tight cluster around the nearly naked corpse of a man.

One of the men barked out a command in American English.

"Jam the signal!"

The president said, "What the hell is this?"

Chapter Thirteen

Brentwood Bay Resort and Spa

849 Verdier Avenue

Victoria, British Columbia

October 13, 8:16 A.M.

The oncologist had the kind of face that always seemed to be in pain. His expressions shifted from one version of a wince to another. Even his smiles looked pained, though he rarely smiled. It seemed to be a trick of a perverse god or one of life's little ironies that the doctor's name was Merriman.

Emerging from the big private suite's master bedroom, he closed the door quietly and was ushered onto a balcony by the patient's personal physician, Doctor Michael Pharos. It was an unseasonably warm morning, and the balcony faced the sun. A silent maid poured tea for Merriman and coffee for Pharos, then retreated inside and pulled the balcony doors shut. Birds sang in the trees, and the sunlight glittered on the countless wavelets on the waters of the Saanich Inlet. Down at the dock, a cluster of expensive boats rocked gently against their fenders.

"You can speak frankly, doctor," said Pharos, getting right to it. He was a very direct man most of the time. Less so in the presence of his last remaining employer, the sick man in the master bedroom. "I suspect you'll have few surprises for us."

Merriman sipped his tea and nodded as he set the cup down. "The results from the needle biopsy bear out what we expected to find, I'm afraid. We found a malignant neoplastic growth and—"

"So, it's bone cancer."

Merriman nodded. "Yes."

"Has it metastasized?"

The oncologist sighed. "Yes."

"Ah," said Pharos. He placed two cubes of raw sugar into his cup and stirred thoughtfully with a tiny silver spoon. "He has been in a great deal of pain. This explains it."

"Sadly, yes. The invasion of bone by cancer is the most common source of cancer pain. Tumors in the marrow instigate a kind of vigorous immune response that enhances pain sensitivity. As the cancer continues to spread, the tumors compress, consume, infiltrate, or cut off blood supply to body tissues, which is what causes the pain."

"Yes," said Pharos. "I am aware of the process."

They sat for a moment, letting it all sink in. Merriman finally sighed and shook his head.

"May I speak frankly, doctor to doctor?"

"Please do."

"Patients and those who care about them so often rail against the unfairness of it all. They react as if humans were meant to last, forgetting that we are already outliving what evolution intended. Medical science is extending life beyond what is natural. As a result, we have new kinds of protracted illnesses and new degrees of suffering. Even as little as a hundred years ago, most people over seventy-five would have passed. Most of us simply do not have the tenacity, the constitution, or the will to live in the face of catastrophic injury or debilitating illness."

Pharos nodded.

"And then we have cases like this one," said Merriman, nodding toward the house, where the dying man slept. "Here is a man who received injuries that should have killed him. An explosion like that, with the accompanying forced amputations and comprehensive burns. The pain. The constant infections. The damage to organs, the progressive deterioration. And now the cancer?" He shook his head again. "Any of these things would have killed most people, and yet he not only holds on, he fights back with more . . . "

He fished for a word.

"Determination?" suggested Pharos.

But Merriman shook his head. "Many people are determined to live. I'm not even sure he wants to. He knows that he has no real future, no chance of recovery. And no quality of life if he somehow were to go into remission."

"Then what, doctor?"

Merriman turned and gazed toward the closed door. "I believe that the driving force, the *sustaining* force, in our patient is not determination or pride, not a lust for life or anything like that. No . . . If I were to put a label on it, I would say that he is driven by rage."

"Rage." Pharos echoed the word, not quite making it a question.

"Or something very like it. At the risk of sounding melodramatic," said Merriman, "from the things he says, from the passion in his voice at times, it seems as if he has given himself over to a very specific kind of rage."

"And what kind is that?"

Merriman's eyes shifted away from the closed door and locked on Pharos's.

"Malice, doctor," he said.

Pharos smiled very thinly. And he nodded.

Merriman cleared his throat and sipped from his cup, avoiding his colleague's eyes, embarrassed by his own observations.

Pharos waved it away. "What is his prognosis? How long does he have, and how long will he be lucid?"

"Ah," said Merriman, setting down his cup. "First, please understand that this diagnosis is severe. He has G4 bone cancer. It's fully metastasized. He's far beyond the point where we could explore surgical options such as additional amputations. Nor do I think he's a candidate for radiation and chemotherapy. The cancer is so widespread that all the trauma of chemo could accomplish is to hasten the end. It is extremely unlikely that even the most radical measures could do more than cause him additional discomfort."

"Give me a timetable."

"A few months? Four, possibly six. Or it could be weeks."

"I see. What about the issue of lucidity?" asked Pharos. "This is something very important to him. He has many business holdings as well as private monies, and he wants very much to be able to make important decisions before he is too far gone. To protect his family and employees, you understand."

"I certainly understand, and that kind of thinking is commendable. However, lucidity varies. The patient is a very strong-willed man. Remarkably so. And highly intelligent. But, tell me . . . has he been tested for dementia? Or Alzheimer's?"

"He has."

"And——?"

"He has been diagnosed with Creutzfeldt-Jakob disease. Early stages, of course."

Merriman looked aghast. "How on earth did he contract *that*?"

Pharos gave him another thin smile. "A dangerous career side-effect."

"I don't understand. Was he in the medical field? Did he work with the brains of other infected——?"

"He was in pharmaceutical research. Prion diseases were part of that research, and apparently there was an accident or protocol error that he was unaware of. In any case, we can add that to the list of things he has had to deal with."

"Does he know?"

"About the prion disease?" Pharos pursed his lips. "We thought it prudent not to burden him with too many things. He is already quite . . . distraught."

"No doubt, no doubt," said Merriman hastily. "But Creutzfeldt-Jakob disease. God. I can understand your need to resolve the financial and business matters. That disease is very aggressive. It progresses so rapidly."

"It does. So, between the effects of that," said Pharos, "and the loss of physical and mental acuity from the bone cancer, we need to decide how long he has before his decision-making capabilities are no longer reliable."

"But . . . they are probably being affected now. During my examination this morning, he referred to me by several different names. And he asked if President Bush had invaded Baghdad yet. He's clearly disconnected with current events."

Pharos sipped his coffee and studied Merriman over the rim of his delicate porcelain cup. Michael Pharos was a Greek national who had lived all over the world. And although he was very cultured and highly educated, he was also very large and had a face that looked like it had been cut from rough stone. Big hands with callused knuckles. Not a surgeon's hands. A precisely trimmed beard, through which the pale shadows of old scars meandered like small rivers in a black forest.

"Which other names, exactly?" he said, showing a lot of very white teeth.

"Pardon?"

"You said he called you by other names. I'm curious as to which names he pulled out of his memory."

Merriman shrugged. "Does it matter? They were just names. They probably don't even connect with his current life. They could be names he heard on television. Or names of old friends from school."

"Which," said Pharos slowly, "names?"

Merriman sat back in his chair, clearly unnerved. He fumbled for a moment, waffling his way through some pointless nonsense. Stalling while he tried to make sense of Pharos's question, and while trying to remember the names.

"I don't see how it's important, but . . . if you really think it's relevant."

"Indulge me."

"He called me by your name once or twice."

"He calls the nurse and the pool boy by my name. It's currently the one he's most familiar with and therefore irrelevant. What were the other names?"

"Um . . . well, one was an Arab name of some kind. I only caught part of it. Mohammed bin Awad. Something like that."

"I see. And the others?"

"Hugo and—what was the other? It wasn't really a name. Oh, yes— he called me Toys. Is that strange?"

Doctor Pharos turned away to pour himself more coffee. He watched the boats for a long moment. He mouthed those two names.

Hugo.

Toys.

Merriman cleared his throat. "The, um, patient is very likely hallucinating. He is also probably in great fear. Is he a religious man?"

"Why do you ask?"

"Toward the end, as I was finishing up, he kept staring past me into a corner of the room and smiling. When I asked him what he was smiling about, he said that he was happy that his friend had come to visit. I turned to look, but the only thing in that corner of the room was an overstuffed chair. But the patient kept smiling and nodding as if in conversation with someone, even though there clearly was no one there. Every once in a while, he'd say a name. You know, a clerical one."

"What name?" said Pharos, putting a bit of edge into his voice. "What exactly did he say?"

Merriman took a breath. "Every once in a while, after a few seconds of appearing to listen and nod, he would say, 'Thank you, Father Nicodemus.'"

Pharos jerked upright and spilled hot coffee onto his thigh.

"God, Doctor Pharos," said Merriman, half rising in alarm, "are you all right? Your leg . . . "

Pharos came to his senses and hastily brushed at his thigh. The dark coffee steamed as it spread in a big brown stain on Pharos's white duck trousers.

"How clumsy of me. I'll need to clean this up." Pharos stood. "Please excuse me, doctor. I believe you can show yourself the way out."

With that, he whirled and pushed through the balcony doors.

Doctor Merriman set his teacup down, stood, looked around as if the empty balcony could somehow explain what just happened, then picked up his case and left the suite.

His car was brought by the valet, and then he drove toward his office in Black Creek.

Doctor Merriman did not arrive at his office.

His car was later found in the parking lot of the Old Farm Bed and Breakfast on Cowichan Bay Road, near the Theik Indian Reserve. The vehicle was locked, and the interior had been wiped clean with bleach. Doctor Merriman's body was found many months later in a shallow grave farther south at Dougan Lake. He had been shot twice in the back of the head with a .22 pistol. No evidence was ever found, no suspects named.

The strangest part of the case, however, were the footprints found all around the shallow grave and again in the soft dirt near the abandoned car. At first they were dismissed as dog tracks, and there are a lot of dogs in

Canada. One of the camping guides from the Est-patrolas Indian Reserve near Dougan said that they were not dog prints, nor were they coyote. It wasn't until casts of the prints were shown to an exotic-animals expert at the Greater Vancouver Zoo that the identity of the animal was determined. The prints belonged to *Canis aureus*. The golden jackal.

The case remains open and unsolved.

Chapter Fourteen

Over the Caribbean Sea

October 13, 11:48 A.M. Eastern Standard Time

We were on a Lockheed Martin C-130J Super Hercules, cruising at twenty-eight thousand feet. In Chile, we'd switched from the Black Hawk to the plane and had left the resort far behind us. Now the Panama Canal was fading behind us as we headed northeast for the long haul to the Hangar in Brooklyn, where Aunt Sallie's team would be waiting for our payload.

Waiting for a corpse.

While we flew, Top, Bunny, Sam, and I sat in a pressurized conference cabin in the rear of the plane and watched the fallout on TV.

The video footage had gotten out and gone viral.

The clip was forty-seven seconds long. It showed three big men in unmarked black military uniforms, face masks and goggles, all of them armed, standing over the nearly naked corpse. The marks of beating and torture were clear, even in the low-light video footage. The clip included me yelling "Jam the signal!"

However, the drone's camera either stopped taping before it obtained a close-up of bin Laden's face, or whoever controlled the drone deliberately ended the broadcast at that point.

"I don't get it," said Bunny. "They had it. No way they didn't get his face."

"They got it," agreed Top, "but they don't want to show it."

"How's that make sense?" asked Sam. "This is the biggest news story since . . . shit, since they killed bin Laden the first time. Maybe bigger. This is political currency. This could bring down the presidency and maybe put the last two presidents on the hot seat. There's so much damage they could do with this."

"So why aren't they doing it?" said Bunny, nodding. "Why are they holding back?"

I shook my head. "Been trying to work that one out since it happened."

I tried getting Mr. Church on the line, but he was having what I imagined was a very unpleasant phone call with the president.

So, instead, I got Bug on the line for an update on the public reaction. When his face popped up in a window on our conference room TV screen, he looked like he'd just had a lime-juice enema.

"That bad?" asked Top.

"Worse," said Bug. "We hit a wall trying to trace the drone. Was there really no way you could have not blown it to tiny little pieces?"

"Seemed like a good thing to do at the time," I suggested.

"Yeah, okay, but from the pieces you recovered, we got exactly nothing. No serial numbers, no recoverable software, nothing. Maybe when the CPU is delivered here I'll be able to do something with it . . . " He trailed off to suggest that short of performing actual magic on it, the odds of his getting anything of use were somewhere between slim and none.

Sam Imura gestured at the screen with his coffee cup. "What about the video itself? Can we get anywhere with that? Does it tell us anything?"

"Not much," Bug admitted. "The postings were sent from the drone to the net via hacked links to communications satellites. There was no other address or identifying server attached to the feed. Like I said, by destroying the machine, we actually slammed the door in our own faces. The drone uploaded a Trojan horse to each satellite, and that allowed the drone's owner to force the video into the broadcast stream. That made it pop up on everything from YouTube to the morning farm report in East Workboots, Idaho. Everyone's talking about this."

"Okay, but so what?" asked Bunny. "They don't show his face."

"No, but the video feed was encoded with a GPS tracker. It shows a covert military op on an island a couple hundred miles off the coast of Chile. They have time, place, and someone speaking with an American accent."

"In international waters," said Sam.

"The way this is being positioned," said Bug, "it's saying that our special ops guys are out there doing illegal hits. They don't need to prove that. The video footage sells it. Remember, social media's all about the instant buzz. This already has hashtags that are trending pretty heavily."

"The fuck's a hashtag?" demanded Top.

Bunny gave him a pitying look. "Damn you're old."

"Old people kill young idiots while they sleep. Why don't you go take a nap?"

Bug grinned. "A hashtag is what they use on Twitter so people can follow a specific conversation or topic. Right now there's #SpecOpsKillers and #AmericanKillList and #USKillersWhoDiedNow. Like that. People are posting all kinds of theories about who the dead guy is."

"Anyone calling it right?" I asked.

"Not even close, thank God. Pretty much everyone still thinks bin Laden is dead."

"He *is* dead."

"You know what I mean. No one would look at what's on the net and think it's Uncle Osama."

Top shook his head. "Don't make sense. Why not just show his damn face?"

"Because that's a different trick," said Bug. "First you have to build the need to know something so that it grows as big and as demanding as possible. Then you start dropping clues. I bet you that's what we're going to see next. Whoever took that footage is building toward something, and they're going to ride a social media wave until they're ready for their reveal."

The images on the screen were abruptly replaced with the unsmiling face of Mr. Church. He's a big guy with an even bigger presence. North of sixty, but not in any way that sanded off his edge. Blocky body, cold eyes, dark hair with some gray.

He said, "There's been a development."

"I don't want to hear it," I said.

He ignored that. "Someone has stepped forward to take credit for the video."

I nearly came out of my chair. "Who?"

"They call themselves the Friends of the Truth."

"Catchy," said Bunny. "Look real nice on a travel mug."

Sam asked, "We ever heard of them?"

"Not until now," said Church.

"I'll run a search," Bug said, then turned aside to speak to someone off camera, firing off a string of orders in computerese.

"I doubt you'll find much," warned Church. "We got this from a call to the White House switchboard. It seems that they are being very careful not to leave an Internet footprint. I'll play the message for you." He tapped a button on his laptop, and a voice began speaking. It was a distorted machine voice.

"We are the Friends of the Truth. We are the servants of justice. We have taken actions that will force you into the light so that everyone will know who you are and what you have done. You have lied to your own people. You have lied to the world. You have lied to God. How much will He punish you? How much should the whole world punish you? You think you have seen fatwa? You think you have seen jihad? You have not. But you will."

The call ended.

We sat in silence for a moment. Only Top spoke, and it was a quiet, "Well fuck me blind and move the furniture."

Chapter Fifteen

Brentwood Bay Resort and Spa
849 Verdier Avenue
Victoria, British Columbia
October 13, 11:51 A.M.

Doctor Michael Pharos sat beside the hospital bed until the burned man woke up. He then adjusted the bed to approximate a sitting position, offered the man some water, and then settled himself back into the leather visitors' chair.

"Where is Doctor Merriman?" asked the burned man.

"Gone."

"When will he be back?"

"He's not coming back," said Pharos. "He's gone."

"Ah." A long pause. "Why?"

Pharos considered how best to answer the question and ultimately decided on the truth. A species of it, at least. "You were half asleep during part of the examination. You spoke in your sleep. You mentioned some names that Doctor Merriman did not need to hear."

The burned man was not able to blush. The artificial skin that had been grown over his scars did not permit that. But he looked away for a moment.

"I see," he said. Without turning, he added, "What names?"

"A few of note," said Pharos. "Hugo Vox and—"

"Gault is dead."

"Toys—"

"He should be dead, the little shit."

Pharos inclined his head. "And you mentioned Father Nicodemus."

The burned man hissed as if scalded. "I did not!"

"It's unlikely Doctor Merriman could have invented that name."

Finally the burned man turned back to him. "He's a monster, you know."

"Oh, yes," said Pharos. "I know. Don't forget, I knew him long before you did. I've seen what he's capable of."

"Some," corrected the burned man.

"What?"

"You've seen some of what he's capable of."

"I saw and heard enough."

The burned man stared at him, and something seemed to shift behind his one remaining eye. "Not me."

"Pardon?"

"I haven't seen enough of what he's capable of. If we're going to complete our project before I'm effing worm meat, then maybe we need someone like him to help move things along."

"Surely you can't be serious."

"Why not? We've used him before."

"And look where it's gotten us. The Kings have fallen. You're all that's left. One king. Hugo Vox practically worshipped Nicodemus, and now he's dead and his fall nearly crashed the entire system."

"The system, Pharos, cannot be crashed. Isn't that what you've bloody well told me a thousand times? It's on autopilot. It's a perpetual motion machine. Those are your words."

"I know, but—"

"But what? Don't give me another speech about how this will all work without further influence or action from the executive level. I'm not denying that. But look at me. I'm more dead than alive. Those tests Merriman did? They were cancer screens. He's been testing me for bone cancer, and the very fact that you haven't leapt to give me good news lets me know that the news is all bad. I'm dying even faster than we thought. And you know as well as I do that there's something happening inside my head. Dementia, early-onset Alzheimer's. Something. My cognitive functions are dicey at best. My memory is for shit. I can't remember your name half the time, and the other half of the time I don't remember what happened to me or how I got like this. No, no, Pharos, your perpetual-motion machine might succeed in bringing down the American government—and it probably will—but I won't live to see it."

"You don't know that."

"Fuck if I don't," snapped the burned man. "If I live until May or June, it'll be a sodding miracle. Don't treat me like an idiot, Pharos. Don't you dare do that."

The words disintegrated into a spasm of wet coughs that shook the ruined body and made bloody tears leak from the corners of both eyes— the sighted one, and the dead one. Pharos began reaching out to help, but the burned man snarled at him between the coughs, damning him and ordering him back.

Pharos sat rigid and still and waited for the burned man to be able to speak again.

"Bloody hell . . ." gasped the dying man. Then he stabbed a finger toward Pharos. "Don't ever try to tell me a lie about what's happening to me. So help me God if I find out you're hiding things from me, I'll have you skinned alive. You know I'll do it, too."

Pharos said nothing. He waited through another coughing fit.

When it was done, the burned man's lips were flecked with new blood, and he looked a thousand years old.

"I . . . I . . . want him," he gasped. "I want him right fucking now."

Pharos did not ask who. He closed his eyes and sighed. Instead, he got heavily to his feet. "Very well," he said. "I'll make some calls."

"Don't fail me on this, Pharos."

"I won't."

With that, he turned and shambled from the room, heading toward his office. Going to make the call that would bring Father Nicodemus there.

Chapter Sixteen

The White House
Washington, D.C.
October 13, 3:23 P.M.

Linden Brierly met with the head of the White House Military Office, the chief of staff, two representatives from DARPA's autonomous-vehicle-design program, and the senior mechanic from the White House motor pool. They spent a grueling two hours going over the data from the complete inspection of the presidential state car.

No obvious problems were found.

"We've pulled the vehicle's CPU," explained one of the designers.

"And?" asked Brierly. It had been a long night since the incident with the Beast and the far worse revelation that a CIA splinter cell had been committing a very bizarre form of treason. Even though the media sensation of the short video clip had calmed down, no one in the White House was getting much sleep.

"Well," said the designer diffidently, "there's not really much that we can find wrong with it. A little code error, sure, but we don't really see how that could have resulted in the vehicle doing what it did."

"No," agreed the second designer. "Nothing in the actual programming should have been able to do that."

"I was there," said Brierly. "So was Ms. Houston."

"Oh, we believe you," said the first designer quickly. "It's just that we can't really understand how this happened."

"You're telling us," said Houston slowly and with no warmth, "that you don't understand the quirks of a system you yourselves installed in the president's car?"

Neither designer wanted to tackle that. They looked everywhere but at her.

Finally, the second one said, "We've, um, replaced the whole computer and installed a brand-new software package."

Alice Houston narrowed her eyes. "When you say 'new,' do you mean a different version of the same software?"

"No. A totally different system," said the first designer. "The one that we'd originally installed was the SafeZone version of BattleZone, which is a part of our Regis program. This isn't the combat-software package, though. It's essentially the same autonomous-control program we developed as a smart-system backup for manned aircraft. Like for when the pilot is incapacitated or the plane's been hijacked. It's a backup system."

"But," said the second designer, "the version in Cadillac One only has about a hundredth of that code. It was redesigned for that car. We did five thousand hours of test drives and simulations with it. It's a good system. It's pretty much foolproof."

"Tell that to my lip," said Brierly.

The designers avoided his eyes this time.

Houston said, "So, what did you replace it with?"

"Ah," said the first designer. "Something really cool."

"Cool?"

"Um, what I mean is, something better. It's a brand-new AI program that is about four jumps past SafeZone. Really sophisticated, but also simple. The driver has a kill switch, too. And there's a voice command that we're synching with the senior NCOs on the motorcade detail. If anything ever happened—"

"And it won't," assured the other designer.

"—one command phrase will initiate an immediate code reset. Bang, the whole system becomes passive and the AI goes off-line."

"You're sure?" asked Brierly. "We don't want another fuckup."

"Absolutely sure," they said in unison. "This new system is the best of the best of the best."

"What's it called?" asked Houston.

They grinned.

"It's the absolute king of autonomous, self-guiding software. The king."

The first designer said, "We call it Solomon."

Chapter Seventeen

Church called back to give us an update. Mostly to say that the news media was trying to build something out of the video, but there wasn't enough of it for them to use.

"Does the president know about this?" I asked.

"He does."

"And—?"

"He is not a happy person," said Church. "POTUS had wanted to stay out of the loop on the Resort operation until it was done and we had a clean case to take to the attorney general and Congress."

"Plausible deniability," I said in exactly the same way you'd say "jock itch."

Church didn't comment. "He is very much in the loop now. I shared the mission specifics with him. We cycled the AG and the judge advocate general into the conversation. It was not the most pleasant half hour I have spent."

"I can imagine. Will the DMS take the hit for this?"

"No. However, this will be very bad for the Agency. Probably bad enough to damage their effectiveness."

I nodded glumly. While we all despised the splinter cell within the CIA responsible for the bin Laden con game, the Agency as a whole did a lot of good. This could—and probably would—crush it. Maybe to the point of having it replaced by another department. That would be a logistical nightmare, and it would very likely open up a lot of vulnerable holes in our intelligence-gathering process. If that came to pass, people would die. No question about it. From the grim look on Church's face, he knew it, too. Our operation had been intended as a bit of surgery—cutting off necrotic tissue in the hopes of saving the healthy flesh. Now . . . this might become one of those instances where the surgery was a complete success but the patient dies.

"Mind playing that one more time?" asked Top. Church did, and we all listened to the mechanical voice make its threats.

When it was done, Bunny asked, "So . . . this is who? Al-Qaeda? Hezbollah? The frigging Taliban?"

"If it's any of them," I said.

They all looked at me. Church said, "Go ahead, Captain. What are you seeing?"

"Well, I'm sure as hell not seeing this for what they intend," I said. "I mean, come on, they get the most damning footage imaginable, but they release it in bits? Bug was explaining to us about building a viral message with social media. They're doing that."

"Clearly," agreed Church. He reached out of frame, took a vanilla wafer from an unseen plate, and bit off a piece. "Go on."

"We've dealt with every kind of religious nut in the world. Extremists of all faiths, every splinter group, sect, and cult that thinks their version of god needs to kick everyone else's god's ass. And one thing that marks genuine religious extremists is the clarity of their message. When they make a statement, they make it big, and they shove it up the ass of everyone else. Doing that not only scares the crap out of their enemies, it also serves as a clear rallying call to their followers. We've seen that with al-Qaeda. We saw it with the Soldiers of Jesus. We saw it with that Buddhist kill squad. Religious nuts are not particularly subtle. They can't afford to be, because if they do anything that makes it look like their agenda is anything other than a mandate from God, then they know how much public support— active or tacit—they'll lose."

Church ate more of his cookie and waited.

"So, we have this message. It appears to be another call to arms for a militant group within Islam. They drop the right words. 'Fatwa' and 'jihad.' Everyone knows that those words are scary as hell. Not just to non-Muslims, but to the bigger part of Islam, to the Muslims who don't want to burn down the rest of the world."

Bunny frowned. "How's that not this?"

"'Cause," said Top, stepping in, "they didn't hit us with the full punch. They put part of the video on the net, and they made their statement to a switchboard. No, I'm with the cap'n on this. It's too calculated and restrained for outrage. You know what would be going on right this damn minute if they tagged that message onto the full video and put that on the net?"

"Sure," said Sam with a shudder, "there'd be blood in the streets. Cities would be on fire. All over the world. But none of that is happening."

Church nodded. "Yes," he said slowly, "and isn't that interesting?"

Chapter Eighteen

Brentwood Bay Resort and Spa

849 Verdier Avenue

Victoria, British Columbia

October 13, 3:49 P.M.

After he had made the call and finalized arrangements, Doctor Pharos returned to the burned man's chambers. He opened the door very quietly and looked in on the twisted lump of a thing on the bed. A nurse came out with a clipboard.

"The Gentleman is sleeping," she said.

"Good," said Pharos. "Send someone in to clean him up. He's likely to have a visitor."

She nodded and left.

When he was alone, Pharos walked over and studied the sleeping man. Despite the frequent hostility between them, it saddened Pharos to see the once-powerful man so badly wasted. The Gentleman was a lump. His face and torso were a red landscape of melted flesh. He had one eye with minimal vision; the other was gone, as was one ear and most of his nose. His legs were gone, victims of the boat explosion that had nearly killed him. His left arm was a stub, amputated at the elbow. There were bags attached to his penis and rectum and wires of every kind snaking in and out of his sickly gray flesh.

It was science, and not the grace of any god, that kept the man alive. Science and the will of so many devoted people. Many thousands of them, hidden in plain sight inside the government, in the military, in banking systems and universities. Hidden everywhere. Some of them knew about this man, but most of the cogs in the great machine had no idea they were involved in something illegal. A culture of secrecy and lies, of misinformation and disinformation, of corruption and coercion.

And this dying madman was the heart of it all.

The last beating heart, at least.

Most of the employees in the upper tiers thought that there were several people running things from the top. If not Seven Kings, then at least a majority of them. Doctor Pharos made sure they kept believing that. It was a useful fiction; just as it was useful not to let them know that their hopes and dreams, their plans of financial security and benefits, rested on the thready pulse of a rotting piece of meat tethered to life by eight hundred thousand dollars' worth of medical equipment.

And by Doctor Pharos, of course.

The loyal servant. The faithful and attentive doctor. The doting friend.

He had to fight to keep a sneer from his mouth.

The Gentleman was losing it; that was clear.

But he had not lost it all quite yet. Pharos knew for certain that the charred bastard still had certain secrets locked away. Not in vaults or encrypted onto computers. No, the bastard had them memorized. Long strings of numbers. Banking access codes and routing numbers. Beyond the millions on the organization's operational accounts, there were billions—tens of billions—in offshore numbered accounts. And as the Regis project unfolded, many more billions would flow in as the global stock markets tore themselves to pieces. All of that money would flow into the accounts controlled by the burned man. After all, he was the last man—Pharos paused here in his musings. The burned man was hardly the last man *standing*. Merely the last man. His value as a human being, his total value to Pharos, and his sole protection *from* Pharos were in that set of numbers. Those banking codes.

Once Pharos had those—or even some of them—the burned man would be far less important. Pharos had a splinter of sentimentality left for him. So, maybe he wouldn't actually abandon him to rot and starve. A bullet or an injection would be the merciful, compassionate, and companionable thing.

Once he had the fucking codes.

For now, though, they were all in that dying, demented brain. In the lump of gray that was being turned into Swiss cheese by the relentless march of Creutzfeldt-Jakob disease. Spongiform encephalopathy. A degenerative neurological disorder, a human variation of mad cow. Prions. Misfolded proteins that led to rapid neurodegeneration, causing the brain tissue to develop holes and take on a spongelike texture. Incurable, untreatable, and fatal.

The fact that *this* man, in particular, should be dying from a prion disease was all the proof Pharos ever needed that there was not only a God but also one with a wicked fucking sense of humor.

Despite how amusing it was, it was also dangerous. If the Gentleman descended too far into madness, then those codes would go with him. Much would be lost.

Many billions.

And the world . . . ?

The great plan, the *project*, would still unfold, even without this last King. It was a time bomb of procedure and process. When it detonated, this ugly world would continue spinning; however, the American government would cease to exist in any recognizable form. The dollar would be relegated to a footnote in history. There would be global war. There would be chaos, and therefore a delicious opportunity to plunder more wealth than had ever been taken in the history of larceny.

"The codes, the codes, the goddamn codes," he muttered to himself.

Two nurses—one male and burly and the other small and delicate— came padding up, and he waved them inside. Then Pharos crossed his arms and watched as they managed the padded straps and pulleys as they moved the Gentleman from his bed to a special bathtub. They washed him with chemicals that soothed his burns and disinfected his entire body. Then they hoisted him out again. Water dripped from the man's slack flesh, and steam coiled up from his chest like the heads of pale snakes. Pharos removed a package of cookies from an inner pocket of his sports coat. A small six-pack of Nilla Wafers.

It made him smile to eat them.

It reminded him of the people who were going to suffer—so much, and for so long.

It also calmed him, and he needed to be calm because of the impending arrival of Father Nicodemus.

"Good God and all His angels," murmured Pharos as he chewed. He did not speak loud enough to be heard by the nurses or the bastard they were now arranging in the bed.

Father Nicodemus.

If there was ever a real boogeyman, then the little Italian priest was it. Pharos remembered the first time he had met the man. The priest had been staying at the house of Hugo Vox. Pharos had been introduced by Vox and had made the mistake of letting manners get in the way of his instincts. He'd offered his hand, and the priest had taken it.

It was the single most disturbing memory that Pharos possessed. The priest had clasped the proffered hand in both of his, and his hands were small and delicate and damp. And they were different. One hand, his right, was as hot as if he'd been holding a steaming cup of coffee; the left was cold, the skin icy.

Pharos had instinctively jerked back, but the priest, a man half his size and twice his age, had tightened his grip and would not release his hand. Instead, he pulled Pharos's hand forward and pressed it to his own chest. Pharos could remember how that bony, meatless chest felt through the thin fabric of the cleric's black shirt.

"Feel that?" asked Nicodemus, smiling at him the way the snake probably smiled at Eve on that distant misty dawn morning. The way the Roman soldier had before he unlimbered his whip as he approached a kneeling Jew in the governor's court. As the German technicians had as they closed the iron doors to the gas chamber. Even at his most corrupt, Pharos had never before seen such a smile look back at him from the mirror. "Do you feel that, boy?"

Boy? Pharos had been thirty-five at the time. Tall and powerful.

"Stop messing with him," said Vox from the wet bar, where he'd been building himself a Scotch. "He doesn't understand your jokes."

"Oh, he understands," said Nicodemus, using his grip to pull Pharos closer. He dropped his voice to a whisper. His voice had been cultured and accented, but in the next sentence it changed to a backwoods drawl. "There's a darkness in this one, Hugo. It's a twisty-turny kind of darkness. You better watch this one, or he'll be sitting on your throne one day."

That's when Hugo turned away from the wet bar and crossed to stand next to the priest. The big American and the strange little priest had studied him for a long, terrible time. Pharos felt as if his hand was simultaneously burning and freezing. Sweat ran down his face, and he almost cried out, almost begged for the priest to let him go.

Almost.

But he had not.

Instead, he ground his teeth and took the pain, endured the stares. Survived the moments.

Then Hugo Vox reached down with his free hand and touched Nicodemus's thin wrist. The priest looked disappointed, but then he smiled, shrugged, and released the grip. He turned away and began placing kindling into a cold and darkened hearth.

Pharos winced as he cradled his hand to his chest. Vox sipped his Scotch and regarded him.

"More things in heaven and hell," he said. Then he winked and turned away.

That was the only time Pharos had spoken with Father Nicodemus. It was enough. He knew that he had been scarred by the encounter. Exactly as the old priest had intended.

Pharos ate the six cookies very slowly. Then he wiped the crumbs from his tie. The Gentleman was in his bed now. The burly nurse had switched on the iPod, and soon the subtle violin stylings of Gehad al-Khaldi flowed from the speakers. Violin Concerto no. 2 in E Minor, by Felix Mendelssohn-Bartholdy. The Gentleman had no particular passion for Mendelssohn, but this piece had been playing at the bank in the Seychelles when Pharos had accompanied the man there. Perhaps it would help him remember the routing numbers.

It was worth a try.

If it was a good day for the Gentleman, maybe today Pharos would coax him into giving one of the bank-account routing numbers.

Wouldn't that be delicious?

Interlude Five

Ha-Nagar Street
Above the Stein Family Falafel Shop
Ashdod, Israel
Three Years Ago

"Scream if you want to," said Boy. "Scream as loud as you want to. It's okay. You probably should."

Doctor Aaron Davidovich did.

He screamed.

He yelled.

He thrashed against the zip ties that bound him to the heavy wooden chair.

Boy sat crossed-legged atop the kitchen table. Jacob and Mason sat together on the couch. They were holding hands, fingers entwined. The CD player was working its way through a mix. Mostly electronic dance music, with a bias toward Deadmau5 and Daft Punk.

There was an open bottle of water on the floor in front of Davidovich.

He had not been given water or food for thirty-two hours. He had not been allowed to use the toilet. His legs, hips, and the chair on which he sat were streaked with urine and feces. The stink rose around him and filled the room. Boy, Mason, and Jacob occasionally rubbed mint ChapStick on their upper lips to kill their sense of smell.

The three of them waited with calm patience as Davidovich fought to get free and cried out for someone—anyone—to help him.

No one did.

Not that time, and not the five other times he'd been brought to consciousness.

The apartment was soundproofed. None of the people who came and went to the falafel shop downstairs heard a thing.

When Davidovich could scream no longer, when his throat was so raw he spit droplets of blood onto his naked thighs, when he slumped forward, weeping and spent, Boy nodded to the two men.

They rose as one, graceful and silent. Jacob picked up another of the heavy wooden chairs and carried it into the living room. He set it down in front of Davidovich. Mason went into the smaller of the apartment's three bedrooms and returned carrying a body over his shoulder. A man who was secured by the wrists and ankles.

Jacob went and helped lower the man into the chair. They tied him in the same way as Davidovich, using the plastic ties to secure him firmly to the arms and legs of the chair. The man wore only striped boxers and a ribbed tank top. Both undergarments were stained with blood and spit, though the man did not look to be seriously injured. Merely unconscious.

"Wake him up," said Boy, and Jacob nodded. He went to a closet and removed two items. One was a leather gladstone bag of the kind doctors once carried when making house calls. The other was a slim zippered vinyl case. Jacob handed the doctors' case to Mason and unzipped the smaller case himself. From it he produced a prefilled disposable syringe. Jacob squirted some of the liquid into the air, tapped the barrel of the syringe with a fingernail, and then jabbed the needle into the unconscious man's arm.

The effect was nearly instantaneous. The man jerked as if shocked, then began blinking and sputtering. He raised his head and looked wildly around.

"Oh God," he said in a voice that was already cracking with fear. "No. No more. Please, for the love of God, no more."

Boy unfolded her legs and walked over to the man, who cringed back from her. The man was in his early forties, with an intelligent face and bright blue eyes that were wet with unshed tears. Boy cupped his chin and raised his face to hers. Then she quickly bent and kissed him. It was a long kiss. She pushed her tongue against his teeth until the man opened his jaws, and then she stabbed her tongue deep into his mouth. She straddled him and ground her pelvis against his crotch. Despite everything—despite his terror and the bizarre circumstances—the man grew hard. His penis poked out through the opening in his boxers. Boy broke the kiss and slid off of the man's thighs, sinking to her knees in front of him. She kissed the swollen shaft and then took it in her mouth, working up and down to make him harder still. Her head bobbed faster and faster, and the bound man moaned in equal parts fear and passion and horror and shame.

Then Boy raised her head, letting the engorged glans pop from between her lips, though she continued to stroke the man's hard length. She turned and smiled at Davidovich, her lips wet with spit, her eyes smoky and glazed.

Her smile was a devil's smile. Filled with the promise of so many wicked things. Her hand moved up and down, up and down.

"Now," she said softly.

Behind the bound man, Jacob and Mason opened the gladstone and began removing their instruments. Skinning knives. Scalpels. Bone saws. The bound man saw none of this. Only Davidovich did. He began to scream a warning, but Boy put a finger to her lips.

"Shhhh," she said.

Her other hand continued to move up and down, and the bound man's back was beginning to arch as he neared an impossible, improbable, and entirely unwanted orgasm.

"Now," she said again.

Jacob and Mason approached the man. Both of them wore identical expressions of complete indifference. The knives gleamed in their hands, reflecting the twisting figure.

Boy's hand was a blur as it moved up and down, and the bound man cried out as he came.

He threw his head back.

And he saw the knives.

His scream changed in frequency and volume and emotional content.

Davidovich screamed, too.

He screamed so loud.

He kept screaming and screaming and screaming as the knives did their work.

The bound man screamed, too. He was able to, because he did not die.

Not for a long time.

Not for a terrible, long time.

Chapter Nineteen

Brentwood Bay Resort and Spa

849 Verdier Avenue

Victoria, British Columbia

October 13, 9:22 P.M.

"Is he here?" asked the burned man.

"Yes," said Pharos. Fear sweat ran in lines down the sides of his face and gathered in pools inside his clothes. His hands were clasped with knuckle-hurting tightness behind his back. His buttocks and stomach muscles were clenched. His single word of reply came out almost as a squeak.

The burned man smiled. "Good. Then send him in."

Pharos did not risk saying anything else. He was afraid a scream might bubble out. He bowed and scurried toward the door.

It opened before he got to it.

And *he* was there.

Smaller than Pharos remembered. Older. His skin as dry and withered as oak bark. Eyes whose color seemed to flow and change. A smile like some hungry thing from the pit. Pharos stood aside, and, as the old priest entered, he bowed again. It was more appeasement than respect, and in this one case Pharos did not castigate himself for acting like an obsequious toady. He kept his eyes averted until the priest had passed into the room. Then Pharos exited quickly and pulled the door shut behind him. The click of the lock was like a splash of cool water on his hot face. He leaned against the door, chest heaving, heart pounding, sweat running.

Then he licked his pasty lips, pushed away from the door, took two staggering steps, and stopped, fighting to pull the pieces of his armor back into place.

No one ever affected him like this.

He doubted anyone could, even if he was brought in chains to a private meeting with Mr. Church.

No . . . this man was different.

This little priest.

This monster they called Nicodemus.

Whatever he was.

Pharos, feeling faint, hurried away.

Interlude Six

Ha-Nagar Street
Above the Stein Family Falafel Shop
Ashdod, Israel
Three Years Ago

Boy sat on the floor.

The floor was awash in blood, and she sat in that. In a lake of red.

Davidovich sat on his chair six feet away. Blood spatters painted him from hairline to toes. Mixing with his tears and with the muck that ran down his chair legs. He panted like a man who had run up fifty flights of stairs.

Behind Boy, the lumps of things that had been the bound man sprawled on, and over, and around the chair.

Jacob and Mason were in the shower, cleaning each other off. Their laughter and snatches of song drifted through the noise of the spray. They were always happy. After.

Davidovich was no longer screaming. That time had passed. All he could do now was stare. Not at the ruin of the stranger. At Boy.

"You understand now?" she asked.

The scientist was so terrified that he did not dare answer.

"Do you understand?" she repeated.

He nodded. Shook his head. Nodded. His expression told her that he was trying to tell her what she wanted, to agree to anything. A stalling tactic, but understandable.

She pulled her crossed ankles under her and rose. Blood dripped from her shorts and ran in crooked lines down her slim legs. She did not have any on her hands. She padded across the room to the entrance to the kitchenette, took her laptop from the table, and brought it over. She turned it toward him so that he could see the pictures on the screen.

Three people in small video-feed windows. An old woman seated at her kitchen table doing the newspaper crossword with a blue ballpoint. A woman soaking in a tub, a wet rag across her eyes, a glass of wine on the flat rim. A fifteen-year-old boy walking beside a school soccer field while he read text messages on his cell phone. It was obvious that they were being filmed, just as it was obvious they did not know it.

Davidovich goggled at them.

He found that he could scream again after all.

The three people in those three little video squares were his mother, his wife, and his son, Matthew.

The only three blood relatives Aaron Davidovich had in this world.

Boy stood next to the destroyed red debris that had been a man and showed the images to Davidovich.

"Do you understand?"

"Please . . . " His voice was barely a croak.

"They have not yet been harmed, but if you do not do exactly what we want, you will sit there and watch what happens to each of them. This," she said, nudging a piece of meat, "is not the worst thing that can happen. Do you understand that?"

He stared at her, his horror so great that it detached him from any possible intelligent reply. Boy understood this. The man needed some help.

She shifted the laptop to one hand and dug her cell phone out of her shorts pocket, punched a number in, and waited for an answer. She put it on speaker.

"Yes?" said a male voice.

"Take Matthew Davidovich. Send me his balls and his eyes but leave him alive."

Davidovich launched himself at her with such fury that he stood up, the heavy chair still attached to him.

"You fucking bitch!" he screamed. "You motherfucking bitch!"

Boy kicked him in the chest. Very fast, very hard. A ball-of-the-foot thrust to his sternum. It knocked him backward so that the four chair legs crashed down and pulled him with them, back into almost the exact spot where he'd been.

"Not my son," moaned Davidovich. "Please don't! Please, please . . . "

"Wait," Boy said into the phone.

"Please don't hurt my son. He's only a kid. You can't."

Boy yawned and held out the phone toward him. "Would you prefer we take your mother? She's old. She probably wouldn't last more than three days. Or do you want to kill your wife? I can have a dozen men over there in half an hour. They can make her scream for days. For weeks. And then they will begin cutting parts off of her. They'll mail them to me here. By the time they arrive, I bet you'd be so starved that you'd eat them."

Her voice was soft, quiet, almost without inflection.

Which made it all so much worse.

"No," begged the scientist. "No, no, no, please God, don't hurt them!"

She squatted down and looked up at him. "You have the power to kill them," she said. "Or to save them. You have that power. You say the word, and I will tell my people to do whatever their imaginations can conjure. Can you imagine what we could do to a little boy? Picture it, doctor. Put those thoughts in your mind."

"No, no, no, no, no . . . "

"Or," she said, and watched how that one little word made Davidovich freeze and listen with every atom of his being. "Or . . . you help us. You do some work for us. Freely, without hesitation or reservation. You do exactly what we want. You come to work for us. You become part of us. You do that, and your mother, your wife, and your son, Matthew, will never be harmed. They will prosper. They will be protected from any harm. That tenth grader who has been tormenting your son? We will make him go away. We will keep them all so safe. Safe." She leaned closer. "But it's all up to you. What orders will you let me give? How will you use your power, Doctor Davidovich?"

Davidovich began weeping.

And nodding.

And begging.

Boy smiled and smiled and smiled.

Into the phone, she said, "We've reached an understanding. Remain on station. Wait for my next call."

Chapter Twenty

Brentwood Bay Resort and Spa
849 Verdier Avenue
Victoria, British Columbia
October 13, 9:25 P.M.

The little priest came and sat in a visitors' chair beside the hospital bed. For a few moments he said nothing, did nothing except look at the machines, following each pendulous plastic tube, each trailing wire.

The burned man watched him with his one good eye.

"You came," he said.

"Of course."

"Thank you. I—didn't know if you would. After all, we never actually met. You were in prison when I—"

"I was never in prison."

"What?"

"Someone was in prison who wore my name," said Nicodemus, "but that wasn't really me, was it?"

They studied each other for several burning moments.

"No," said the Gentleman. "No, I suppose not."

Nicodemus glanced at the closed door. "Your keeper is out there."

"Pharos? He's my doctor."

"Don't be an ass. He's a vulture sitting on your tombstone."

The Gentleman flapped his hand weakly. "Maybe. He's harmless, though. He takes care of me because he wants something I have."

"Routing and account numbers?" asked Nicodemus, arching his eyebrows as if surprised at what he was saying.

"How do you know—?" began the burned man, but let it hang. "Yes."

"Will you give them to him?"

"If I do, he'll pull the plug on me."

"Maybe he won't."

"Why on earth would you say that?"

Nicodemus smiled. His lips writhed and twitched when he smiled. "He still has some conscience left. Not a lot. But some. I think he actually cares for you."

"Bullshit."

"No," said the priest. "He cares, but he isn't really aware of it. It makes him feel conflicted." He spoke that word as if it tasted delicious.

The burned man shook his head. "He'll leave me to rot if I give him the numbers."

Nicodemus shrugged. "Or giving him one or two would be a gesture."

"Of what? Of kindness?"

"To him, probably. For you, it would be control." He chuckled. "Think about it. People can surprise you."

"People disappoint me."

"That's why you're miserable," said Nicodemus, licking his lips. "I find people so . . . mmmmmm . . . satisfying. And entertaining."

"Yes . . ." said the burned man distantly. "Hugo said that you had certain appetites."

The priest nodded approval. "Do you know who I am?"

The word "who" hung twisting in the air between them—as if it was the wrong word, deliberately chosen. The real word remained unsaid, but it screamed in the burned man's mind.

Not who.

What.

"I think I do."

"Do you?"

Instead of directly answering, the burned man said, "Do you know that I was in infernos twice? How many men can say that? The first time was in Afghanistan. The sands were melted to glass, and they stabbed me through the flesh, into my bones."

The priest nodded.

"Then there was the explosion on the boat. I was on fire, burning like a torch, as the force of the blast sent me flying through the air. My skin kept burning even after I fell into the salt water."

"Yes."

"That was six years ago. Do you think that I have stopped burning yet?"

"No."

The man in the bed fixed the priest with his one fierce eye. "Everyone who burns knows your name."

"Everyone?"

"I dare say the effing saints knew your kiss in those last moments when the flames reminded them that they were not angels yet."

The priest stood, bent, and kissed the burned man on both cheeks and then on the forehead.

The kisses were scalding.

The burned man hissed in fresh pain.

As he sat, the priest was smiling.

"You asked me to visit you, my son," said the priest. "What is it you want from me?"

"You know what I want."

"You have to tell me."

The burned man ran a tongue over his melted lips. "Church. Ledger. The DMS. All of them."

"You want them dead? Don't disappoint me now that we are getting so close. You have an army of thugs to do scut work."

"If I'd just wanted them dead, they would be dead," snapped the burned man. "You know that's not what I want."

"Then tell me."

The Gentleman's one remaining hand snapped out with reptilian speed and clamped on the priest's wrist. He pulled himself half upright, and through clenched gray teeth hissed out his reply.

"I want them to *suffer*. That's what I want. Can you do that for me?"

The priest placed a hand over the burned man's. For a moment, for just a fleeting moment, the shrieking nerve endings all over the dying man's body fell silent. For just a moment there was no pain. For just a moment his mind was clear again, sharp again. He could even, in that fleeting moment, feel his missing legs and lost arm; and his dead eye could see.

For a moment he was himself again. Whole. Powerful.

Alive.

He screamed. Not in pain but in sudden, overwhelming joy.

And then the priest pushed the burned man's hand away and released him.

The moment passed.

Everything came crashing back. All the pain, the weakness. The darkness at the edge of his perceptions.

Everything.

It was a terrible, terrible thing.

It crushed the burned man against his mattress like a bug.

It left him gasping and whimpering.

The priest sat like a gargoyle on his chair, watching, watching.

"Can I make them suffer?" he asked. "Why don't *you* tell *me*?"

The burned man said nothing.

With a satisfied grin on his ugly mouth, the priest leaned back and crossed his skinny legs. "Besides . . . I've already got a dog in this hunt."

"What does that mean?"

The priest shrugged. "Let's just say that I'm already invested in this particular matter. The games, as they say, have already begun."

Interlude Seven

Ha-Nagar Street
Above the Stein Family Falafel Shop
Ashdod, Israel
Three Years Ago

Doctor Aaron Davidovich stood naked in the shower. He'd been in there for almost thirty minutes. Lathering furiously, scrubbing at his skin, rinsing, repeating. Nothing he did, no amount of soap and hot water he used, seemed able to wash him clean. First his own shit and piss. Then the blood of that man.

Then the images that still burned in his mind.

His mother.

Clara, his wife.

Matthew, his son.

Each of them in little windows on a laptop. Innocent. Unaware. Untouched.

Unsafe.

Vulnerable on a level that Davidovich never imagined.

He snatched up the bar of soap and began once more working up a lather on his skin, on his chest, over his heart.

He was so hungry, though he could not imagine eating. Not after what he'd seen. Not after what he'd imagined.

Not after what he'd agreed to.

I am in hell.

Those four words burned in his mind.

He scrubbed and scrubbed and scrubbed.

When he staggered from the shower, gasping and weak, he saw that they had laid out clothes for him. His own clothes, taken from the safe house. Davidovich dressed in clean underwear, khakis, a checked shirt. No belt, no socks, no shoes.

"You won't be going anywhere," said Boy. "It's warm enough in here without shoes. If you get cold, we can get you slippers. Would you like that? Some fuzzy slippers?"

He said nothing.

Boy smiled as if had. She stood and watched him get dressed. The woman was about five feet tall and couldn't weigh a hundred pounds. Davidovich thought he could take her in a fight. He'd taken some aikido classes in college. He had a yellow belt, though he hadn't been inside a dojo in fourteen years.

The woman clearly knew some martial arts. Could he take her?

These were stupid questions, and he knew it.

He turned away to finish buttoning his shirt. It took a while. His fingers kept losing the buttons. He wished his hands wouldn't shake so much.

The bedroom in which he dressed was the smallest of the three in the apartment. Just a twin bed, a cheap dresser, and a window that was sealed with heavy wooden panels bolted to the walls.

When he had wrestled the last button through the hole, Boy led him out of the room and across the living room to the second bedroom. Davidovich did not look at what Jacob and Mason were doing. They had black plastic trash bags, mops, and a bucket of hot water and bleach. A fan blew vapors out a window.

In the other small bedroom, there was a mission table and two comfortable leather office chairs with wheels. On the table were three computers. Two laptops and one heavy-duty, high-end unit of the exact kind he used in his own office back in D.C. Along the wall were other machines, including a sophisticated portable supercomputer. Davidovich knew the model. It had a 12-core, 24-thread 2.7GHz Intel Xeon processor that turbos to 3.5GHz and up to 32GB of DDR3 1600MHz memory. A row of expensive, networked, thirty-petabyte external drives lined a shelf.

"This is where you will work," said Boy. "E-mail and Internet access is restricted. All of your work will be monitored. There are many people working on this around the clock. You will always be monitored, Doctor Davidovich. Please remember that. At random times throughout each day and night, I will need to make a call to tell our field teams not to do the things to your family that you know we will do. Do you understand this?"

He did not dare speak. Instead, he nodded.

"It will make everything so much easier if you bear it in mind and act accordingly. There is no way to bypass our security. We are too good at it, and we have been doing this for a long time. You cannot break our pattern without killing your family. Please grasp that concept, doctor. Your cooperation and enthusiastic dedication to your job will keep your family alive and safe. Only you, through some act of stupidity, can guarantee that your family will suffer and die. If you accept this, then your life will not be filled with horrors. When you are done doing what we ask, you will be released unharmed. Your family will never know the danger they were in. You will be given your life back."

"How . . . how can I trust you?"

Her smile was radiant. "Why would we need to lie to you? We own you now, doctor. We own your family. You have already agreed to work with us. It would be petty to lie to you at this juncture. We are many things, doctor, but we are not petty."

"Who are you?"

Boy cocked her head to one side. "I could answer that question. I will answer it, if that's what you want. But, tell me, which of your loved ones will I kill in exchange for that information?"

Davidovich nearly fell down. "No! No, I take it back. Don't tell me. I don't want to know."

"I know you don't." She reached up and stroked his cheek. A gentle touch that was perhaps the most perverse thing he'd so far experienced. He shivered with revulsion.

Boy stepped away from him and gestured toward one of the chairs.

"There is a folder with your name on it stored on the laptop. In it are PDF files with instructions and a list of tasks. You will read those instructions very carefully and thoroughly, and then you will get to work. If you have any technical questions, we have a coded e-mail address for you to use. That e-mail will only go to one destination. If you attempt to use it in any other way . . . well, we don't want to explore that, do we?"

She spoke with perfect phrasing and word choices despite her Cambodian accent. Davidovich found himself hanging on her every word.

"Let me know if there is anything you need," she said, then made a kissy mouth at him and, laughing, left the room.

Aaron Davidovich sagged back against the wall, feeling the knives of despair and defeat stab him through the heart. He stayed there for a long time. As long as he dared.

Maybe a full minute.

Then he sat down at the laptop, booted it up, found the folder with the PDFs, and began reading. The longest of the files was marked REGIS. As Davidovich read it, he discovered the full extent of what they wanted. The last page of the Regis file had a long list of tasks. Each one was something that he knew he was uniquely qualified to accomplish. So much of this was built on a scaffold of his own work for DARPA.

He printed the task list and held it in his hands for nearly five full minutes. Tears rolled down his cheeks and fell onto the page.

Then Aaron Davidovich placed the list on the table near the keyboard, flexed his hands, took a breath, said a prayer to a god he feared had abandoned him, and began typing.

Writing code.

Taking the first steps down into the valley of the shadows.

Part Two
Clockwork Devils

Humanity is acquiring all the right technology for all the wrong reasons.

—R. BUCKMINSTER FULLER

Chapter Twenty-one

National League Baseball Opening Day

Citizens Bank Park, Philadelphia

March 29, 12:52 P.M.

Nobody is allowed to die on the opening day of Major League baseball.

If it's not an actual rule, it should be.

We can all agree on that.

The sky over Philadelphia was so blue it hurt the eyes to look at it. There were a few clouds up there. I figured that God and all his angels were sitting on them, harps tossed aside, schooners filled with ice-cold lager. That's the way the universe is supposed to work.

Since joining the DMS I haven't made one opening day. Not one.

This year, I had tickets. Rudy was with me in a box that Mr. Church finagled from one of his friends "in the industry." I was on my second big red cup of Yuengling. Ghost was in his service-dog disguise, drinking covertly from some beer I accidentally spilled on the ground right in front of him. Twice. The dog's a lush, but he loves baseball.

My buddy, Patrick Seiler, was with us. He is a former San Diego cop who is now a financial advisor. My advisor, actually, which is weird. I never had much beyond checking and a lot of bills. But Church pays his people well, and my lady, Junie Flynn, has some money. Patrick's helping us grow it in case I live long enough to retire.

Patrick had on a Phillies home-game jersey. Rudy and I were both wearing Baltimore Orioles away-game shirts to show our solidarity with the city that would be our home for six more days. This was our way of saying good-bye.

Patrick, Rudy, and I were making professional-grade headway into the stadium's supply of cold beer. We were telling jokes and telling lies, and the cares of the world were a million miles away. We could have been anyone. We could have been three old high school friends meeting for a day of balls and bats. We could have been business friends taking a day off.

We could have been happy, and we were.

Beer and baseball, sunny skies and laughing crowds. There are a lot of good reasons to be in great seats at a baseball field on opening day. If I have to list them all, you'd need help or some kind of cultural intervention. But on that particular day there was an added bonus. Colonel Roger Douglas was going to throw out the first ball.

Douglas is The Man—capital *T*, capital *M*.

He's the guy who saved all those soldiers during Operation Anaconda back in March 2002. It was the second large-scale battle of the Afghan war. The biggest one to use mostly regular ground troops instead of special ops teams. A collaborative op of the U.S. military and CIA paramilitary teams, along with allied Afghan military forces and both NATO and non-NATO forces. The drama played out in the Shah-i-Kot Valley and the Arma Mountains southeast of Zurmat. Seventeen hundred U.S. troops led the way to take control of the valley. It became an instant shitstorm. The Taliban and al-Qaeda, dug in like ticks, were firing mortars, antitank weapons, and heavy machine guns.

Colonel Douglas—then a captain—was flying an A10 Thunderbolt, and he'd been in the thick of it. He was returning to refuel when a call came in about a platoon that got trapped deep in the badlands when a Taliban push cut them off. The soldiers were surrounded, low on ammunition, and taking heavy fire. No other resources were available to rescue them. Douglas's bird was low on fuel, but he requested permission to make a run to lay down some cover fire for the platoon. Permission was denied, and he went anyway. There's been a lot of debate in the press about just how badly damaged Douglas's radio was, or if it was damaged at all. He claimed that he heard only static and never received the recall order.

Instead, he peeled off and flew back, emptying everything he had: his last missiles, his last rocket, and a whole bunch of machine-gun rounds. He all but popped his canopy to throw his watch and shoes at the Taliban. His assault opened a very small, very narrow window, and in the last few seconds before he reached the point of no return in terms of fuel, the platoon sergeant radioed that his men were clear.

The Thunderbolt limped home on fumes and set down on a secure strip in the staging area.

There were some who wanted to hang Douglas for insubordination and a list of violations a mile long. There were others, wiser and saner people, who decided that heroism should be rewarded, not discouraged.

Colonel Douglas flew thirty-one subsequent missions. No one has a better record for doing damage to the enemy while protecting civilian and military lives.

I think the guy's a frigging saint. If I had a daughter, I'd let her marry his son. Patrick thought so, too. He had friends who'd been part of Operation Anaconda.

So, having Colonel Roger Douglas step out onto the pitcher's mound to throw out the first ball? Oh hell yes. We toasted him with fresh cups of beer.

When they announced Douglas, the whole damn stadium went totally batshit crazy. He's that kind of a guy. Tall and good-looking. Denzel Washington is going to play him in the movie. Huge white smile, and darn if he didn't look good in his uniform with all those medals and ribbons. The air force color guard was with him, and Beyoncé was there to sing the national anthem.

On a day like that, no-damn-body needs to die.

The Goodyear blimp was overhead, and its whale of a shadow moved across the field. Douglas shook hands with the umpire, with the presidents of both ball clubs, with the mayor of Philadelphia, and with James Wolcott Ledger, who was the two-term mayor of Baltimore and its former police commissioner.

My dad.

For me, watching dad shake hands with Douglas was like watching Superman high-five Captain America.

I knew my brother, Sean, and his son would be watching the game on the big-screen TV I'd given them for Christmas. Top and Bunny would be watching, too. Probably most of my guys would be.

As the press swarmed around to take the photos that would lead the news stories around the country, I saw something out of the corner of my eye.

At first I thought someone had jumped from one of the upper tiers of the stadium on the far side from where I sat. But that wasn't it. The shape did not plummet but rather soared outward, and for an insane moment my fear of a man falling changed into a delusion that I actually was seeing Superman. It wasn't that, either.

It was a plane.

As the plane soared over the tops of the cheering crowd, I could see the long body and fixed wings, the bulbous cockpit, and the two barrels of the engines mounted high on either side of the tail.

It was far too small, though.

A toy plane.

A toy jet.

"Hey," said Patrick, "look at that."

The plane swooped down toward the field and then began a high, climbing turn around the mound. As it passed third base, I could see that it was even smaller than I thought. Maybe forty inches across at the wings, thirty-five in length. Gray. Sleek. You see them in fields or over beaches where crowds of enthusiasts fly them. Perfect replicas of full-sized planes.

I heard people laughing. I heard Rudy laugh. Patrick, too.

Even Colonel Douglas looked up and smiled as a remote-controlled model version of his own A10 Thunderbolt circled above him.

After a moment of surprise, Douglas began to applaud.

The crowd erupted into thundering applause.

The plane waggled its wings, and the audience laughed.

The plane buzzed the commentators' skybox. It buzzed both dugouts. It circled completely around Beyoncé, who curtsied to it.

Everyone was clapping and laughing.

Except me.

I grabbed Rudy's arm, and the face he turned to me was one of the happiest and least stressful I'd seen on him since he was hurt a couple of years ago. It was uncomplicated and a million miles away from the hurt and harm that is our daily lot.

Except I didn't think we were as far away as we needed to be.

When Rudy saw the look on my face, the joy on his crumbled into dust.

"Cowboy—what's wrong?"

I pointed at the plane. "That shouldn't be here. Not here."

"What do you mean?" asked Patrick, setting down his beer and getting to his feet.

"Stay here," I said. "Keep your eyes open. I'll be right back."

"Why?" demanded Rudy. "What's wrong?"

I didn't answer. Instead, Ghost and I began fighting our way through the crowd. I dug my cell phone out of my pocket, punched in a three-digit speed dial, and immediately got the duty officer at the Warehouse. Ghost barked at people, and those who didn't move out of my way got immediately out of his.

"DeeDee, this is Joe," I yelled and told her to check with the FAA and the baseball commission to see who authorized the use of a UAV at Citizens Bank Park.

Unmanned aerial vehicles were everywhere these days. More and more companies were winning their legal battles with the FAA to use them to deliver food and products. But they were damn well not licensed to fly inside a packed arena like this.

Maybe I was being paranoid, but my tolerance level for drones had bottomed out back in October.

"DeeDee, get me whoever's in charge of this field and patch in the head of security here. His name is Tom Rollins. He knows me. I want everyone on the line right now."

I'd struggled through the press all the way to the entrance to the inner corridors of the park. The noise was like thunder. The park seats nearly forty-four thousand people, not to mention staff, teams, and the press. Everyone was yelling. Everyone was clapping and whistling.

As I waited for the connection, I could feel my heart pounding. My dad was down on that field. My dad. Sweat popped out all over my face, and I had to paw it out of my eyes.

Maybe this was a prank. A couple of guys snuck in the pieces of an F10, assembled it on the sly up in the nosebleed seats, and decided to launch it as a tribute to a great man. Maybe that was it. Maybe they were soldiers, or family members of soldiers who had been saved that day. It could have been that. I wanted to sell that to myself.

I tried real hard.

Tom Rollins came on the phone. Head of security and an ex-cop. A good guy I'd known for years.

"Tom, are you seeing this?" I bellowed.

"Yes, I am," he growled back. "We've got people working their way up to where we think it was launched."

"You need to clear the field."

"We can't do that, Joe. It would cause a panic."

Ghost stood at the entrance, barking at the buzzing plane, the white hair on his back standing straight.

"C'mon, Tom, you know this isn't right." Through the open mouth of the third base tunnel, I could see the F10 take another spin and then head upward, coming toward home plate, rising toward the control box high overhead.

"Joe—it's a prank. We'll find out who did this and let them spend a couple of nights in jail. Then we'll sue their asses and—"

That was as far as Rollins got.

It was the last thing he said. The last thing he ever would say.

He was in the control center. I was in a corridor, so I didn't see the actual blast.

I heard it, though.

I felt it.

And then I heard the screams.

Chapter Twenty-two

Seahawk Place
Del Mar, California
March 29, 12:54 P.M.

Junie Flynn stood on the balcony and looked out at the ocean. It was a deep blue, and it went on and on forever. The sky was flawless. Far out to sea, a flock of seagulls was settling down onto a kelp bed to hunt for the small fish that swam among the flowing plants.

"It's perfect," she murmured.

"Yes, it is."

She turned to see two women come out onto the balcony. One was tall and pretty, with dark hair and pale eyes. Donna Strauss, a longtime friend of Junie's and her travel companion for this house-hunting trip. Donna was a healer from Pennsylvania.

The other was a newer friend—Doctor Circe O'Tree-Sanchez. She was a lovely woman with a heart-shaped face and curly black hair pulled back into a loose ponytail. A pair of glasses was perched on the end of her nose. She was shorter than Junie and of a different physical type. Circe was rounder, with more voluptuous curves and olive skin. Junie was tall and lithe, graceful in the way dancers are, with long, wavy blond hair that fell down her back and danced whenever she moved. Both women were beautiful but in such different ways that there was no tendency to compare them.

One difference, though, seemed to fill the air all around them. Circe was pregnant and close to her time. Donna had joined them on this round of visits to prospective apartments in case someone with medical knowledge was needed. And because she had a good eye for beauty and value.

This was going to be Circe's first child.

It was an experience Junie ached to share but never would, thanks to an assassin's bullet that had done wicked damage to her uterus. The wound had healed; the ache had not.

Even so, Junie wanted to be happy for her friend in the most supportive and uncomplicated way. But it was hard.

It was so hard.

The bullet she'd taken last year had done terrible damage inside her. And though all the surgeries and physical-therapy sessions were done, there was an ache in her heart that no amount of physical healing could ever remove.

Circe must have caught a flicker of something on Junie's face because she frowned and touched her arm. "What is it, honey?"

"Nothing," said Junie, dialing up the wattage of her smile. She knew full well that she had a great smile. She'd used it as both a shield and a distraction her whole life. She could stall almost any man to a mumbling confusion with it. She could charm her way out of a traffic ticket or make a barking dog begin wagging its tail. Knowing one's gifts and using them was a quality of controlled self-awareness, and Junie was very aware of who she was and how people were reacting to her. Even smart, perceptive people like Circe could be deflected by that smile. "I guess I'm dealing with sticker shock," she lied. "This place is not cheap."

"Too pricy?" asked Circe, falling in line with the deception.

"Oh, I don't know," said Donna. "This view is beyond price."

Junie shrugged. In truth, she could afford the place pretty easily. She had quite a lot of money squirreled away in bonds and stocks, and there was still a big chunk left untouched from her father's estate. She never mentioned any of that to Circe. Like most people, Junie didn't talk about money. Joe didn't even know how much she had, and he'd never asked.

"No," said Junie after a moment, "I think this is just right. Joe will love it. I can already see him and Rudy sitting out here with beers, watching the dolphins and talking baseball."

"Rudy's been making a slow change from beer to martinis," said Circe. "I think he's trying to convert Joe."

"Good luck with that. The only thing Joe likes more than beer is coffee. I sometimes think I should wear eau du lager perfume. He'd go wild."

They laughed about it, and if Junie's laugh was forced, Donna and Circe didn't seem to notice. Or, if they noticed, they were too polite to call her on it.

"Quite a view, isn't it?" asked a fourth woman as she came out to join them. Slim and wearing stylish business clothes, she had a long fall of dark hair brushed back from her face. Irene McCann was a real-estate agent from the Coldwell Banker office in La Jolla and a longtime friend of Junie's. This condo was the eighth property she'd shown Junie, and it was clear from her smile that she knew she'd saved the best for last.

Junie leaned on the rail and looked down. There was a pool and hot tub below, nearly hidden among the green succulents and palm leaves of the sculpted garden.

"It's really spectacular," said Donna, and that was no lie. The place was perfect.

Irene smiled, and for a few minutes the four of them stood on the balcony watching the ocean and said nothing.

"Really spectacular," Junie echoed after a moment. Almost to herself she said, "I think we can make a life here."

There was movement down on the bluffs as something broke from the bushes and darted along the footpath.

Half smiling, Circe said, "Is that a coyote?"

The other women looked. The animal was silhouetted against the glare coming off the waves.

"It's too small," said Donna. "Might be a fox."

"Del Mar is a very dog-friendly town," said Irene. "A lot of mixed-breed rescue dogs. Could be anything. If you meet the owner, they'll probably give you the whole story. A lot of them even do DNA tests on their dogs."

The animal vanished into another patch of brush and did not reappear.

Junie nodded. "Joe's dog, Ghost, is a big goof. He's a white shepherd. He'll be our ambassador of goodwill. He'll help us make a lot of friends out here."

Circe took her hand and squeezed it, and for a moment Junie thought it was a girlfriend thing, a congratulations thing, an encouragement thing on the brink of a new and bold decision.

Then Circe's grip tightened to crushing force.

She cried out so sharp and loud that it sounded like a seagull.

Junie and Irene turned and lunged forward as Circe O'Tree-Sanchez's eyes rolled back in her head, and then her knees buckled and she pitched forward. Her swollen belly hit the metal rail, but Donna caught her before she could fall over and down.

Chapter Twenty-three

The Bluffs
Del Mar, California
March 29, 12:55 P.M.

The animal stood in the shadows beneath a twisted eucalyptus tree.

Watching the figures a hundred yards away. Listening to the cries of fear and panic.

Eating the pain in their voices.

Savoring the separate flavors.

It stood unmoving for many minutes and only turned away when the air was split by the wail of an ambulance siren.

Another delicious sound.

The animal's eyes swirled with colors. Browns and greens and grays that had no correlation to things that grew and prospered in sunlight.

Then with a small bark that might have sounded like a grunt of satisfaction had anyone heard it, the jackal turned and trotted along the bluffs.

Chapter Twenty-four

If a giant had reared back and then punched the stadium with all of his strength, it would feel like this.

A single massive *WHUMP!*

The concrete floor beneath my feet shuddered, and I felt myself falling sideways. Ghost began barking hysterically. People everywhere were screaming the kinds of screams that were torn from deep places in the chest. Raw, ragged, absolutely terrified.

I staggered out of the tunnel as the whole building continued to tremble from the rebounding shock waves. As I emerged, I turned and looked up to see a cloud of fire expanding outward from where the control box had been. Then I turned and covered my head with my arms as debris showered down.

The crowd went insane.

There's no other word to describe it.

Insane.

They panicked, recoiling from the blast. Pieces of masonry, pieces of melted chairs, pieces of burning plaster fell onto the seats below. Pieces of people, some of them still screaming, flew as far as home plate. The crowd slammed into the entrance ways, and I could actually hear bones break as thousands crushed dozens. People fell, and the crowd surged over them, everyone becoming savage in their terror. I saw a mother punched in the face so that she fell away from her screaming six-year-old. I waded into the crowd to try and help and was immediately shoved and clubbed and kicked from every possible direction. Ghost leaped and barked, but then I heard him yelp as someone kicked him in the ribs. An instant later, I heard a very human shriek buried beneath a canine snarl of reciprocal fury.

Something hit me on the temple, and I pitched sideways, and before I could regain my balance the human tide carried me halfway into the tunnel. I tried everything I could to fight against the current, but, tough as I am, there's no amount of martial arts or military or police training that offers an adequate response to thousands of people moving in blind panic.

I lost all track of Ghost.

The crowd spun me and turned me and pummeled me. Then I was falling backward through an open door into a small service corridor. I landed badly but scrambled instantly to my feet, calling for Ghost. There was no sign of him as a torrent of screaming people rushed past the open doorway.

There was another bang. Smaller, hollow, and in my disorientation I could not at first understand what it was. Then I saw one of the panicking people in the hallway go down, the side of her face blooming with bright red blood.

Then I understood.

I whirled and saw that the hallway behind me wasn't empty.

There were two men there.

One of them had a big wooden crate on a hand truck.

The other was pointing a gun.

At me.

His first shot had missed me and hit a woman trying to run to safety.

The hall was sixty feet long and ended at a T junction. A service corridor for event staff. These guys were in the kind of nondescript coveralls you'd expect of maintenance staff or equipment handlers.

Except that they both had ski masks pulled down over their faces.

Oh shit.

The guy with the gun fired again. And again.

He emptied a whole clip at me.

I dove through the doorway of a broom closet, but the rounds passed me and punched into the people in the main corridor. I couldn't see the hits, but I heard the screams.

Rage ignited inside my chest.

I spun as I drew my off-duty piece, knelt, reached around the doorjamb, and fired blind. Most rounds fired in any firefight do not hit a useful target. Ask any soldier. Especially when firing from cover. You can slant the odds in your favor by aiming center mass at average height.

I heard the scream as at least one of my rounds found something meaty.

The gunfire paused.

Then I was up and out, swapping magazines, bringing my gun up into a two-hand grip as I broke from the broom closet and ran toward the guys in ski masks. I saw one guy down on his knees, both hands pressed to his lower abdomen in a vain attempt to stop blood from pouring onto the floor. His gun lay in a spreading pool.

The other guy had abandoned the hand truck and was unzipping his coveralls to get at his pistol.

I ran at them full speed. Powered by rage and fear.

I shot him in the chest. Twice.

I shot the other guy in the face.

Fuck it.

As he pitched back, I jumped over him, skidded to a stop at the T juncture, and looked up and down the hall.

There were more of them.

Five more, pushing two more big crates on hand trucks. All of them in coveralls and ski masks.

Technically, I should have used the edge of the juncture as cover, identified myself as a federal agent, pointed my gun at them, and told them all to give up.

I didn't.

I opened up on them.

Why? Because fuck it, that's why.

People were still screaming, running, hurting, dying. The echo of that explosion was burned into my eyes. My father was here. So was my best friend. And so were a lot of innocent people, some of whom were now dead or wounded.

So, yeah. Fuck it.

They were thirty-five feet away. We were in a concrete corridor. Missing the target was harder than hitting it.

I hit what I aimed at.

Body shots. I wanted them hurt. I wanted them to scream. But later I would want them to talk. I would want them to give me some goddamn answers.

Two of them returned fire, but I had the advantage.

They all went down.

And, yeah, they screamed, too.

Suddenly, bullets whipped down the hall and chipped the wall a foot above my head. I threw myself backward, but my mind was replaying the flash image of two more men coming out of another door. Same kind of guys.

I dropped my magazine and fished for a replacement.

Which I did not have.

This was my day off. One loaded magazine in the gun, one spare. Both spent.

I heard the men running.

I took a risk and bent low to sneak a peek. They'd stopped beside the tangle of their bleeding comrades, but they weren't offering first aid. Instead, they were tearing at the fastenings on the crates.

One of them saw me looking, and he whipped his gun up and fired. I ducked back with no time to spare as bullets tore the corner of the wall to gravel. Stone chips chased me backward. Then I got to fingers and toes and launched myself the way I'd come. The gun from the first guy I shot was useless. It was soaked with blood. I pulled the other guy's coveralls open and stole the gun he'd failed to pull. A Glock 26. Two spare magazines. Nice.

As I turned back to the T junction, I saw something that made no sense at all.

A pigeon flew around the corner.

Then another.

And another.

Gray pigeons. Like you see everywhere in Baltimore and Philly and New York.

They flapped at full speed right past me, and I ducked backward out of the way. Three of them.

And then nine more.

I said, "What the fuck——?"

Four more flew past, rounding the corner from where the last two guys had been.

Raising the new pistol, I raced back and dropped to a crouch, leaned out, and pointed the barrel.

At nothing.

The two men were gone.

The two crates lay open and empty.

The men I'd wounded lay there, but none of them moved. Or ever would.

Each of them had been silenced with shots to the head. Cold, efficient, brutal.

It made no sense.

I tapped the earbud I always wore and tried to get Bug, but all I heard was static. Damn it. Probably damaged in the struggle outside. So, I pulled my cell and tried to call my office, the Warehouse.

I got no signal at all.

Nothing.

There was no way a professional stadium would have cell-phone dead spots, so this had to be something else. It had to be deliberate. Someone jamming the cell signals. Ditto for my DMS transmitter.

Shit.

Far behind me, nearly lost in the roar of the frenzied crowd, I heard a dog barking in wild panic.

Ghost.

I whirled and ran.

Chapter Twenty-five

Tanglewood Island
Pierce County, Washington
March 29, 1:01 P.M.

The Gentleman hung like a spider in a web.

Sickly but venomous. Consumed by hate, but fed by it as well.

Diseased. Burned. Wasted. Repulsive even to his own eye.

The Gentleman. A joke that he had come to appreciate as much as Pharos and the rest of the staff did.

Gentleman. A shared absurdity.

He was neither gentle nor still a man. Not anymore.

He knew that he was a dead man. A pernicious ghost that would not fade until the blackest desires of his heart were fulfilled. It was melodrama, certainly, but it was a glorious melodrama. Operatic. The only thing he had left. The one thing he had to live for.

His bedroom was silent except for the screams that came from the television speakers. The wall in front of him was lined with HD screens, each turned to a video feed from a separate tiny camera. The images jumped and shook as the drones in which they were mounted flew, wheeled, turned. Exploded.

Some of the screens had already gone dark, their feeds terminated in just the right way.

Others kept running with real-time images.

People running.

People screaming.

People flying apart into crimson nothingness.

And there, running along a corridor, gun clutched in a bloody fist, was a man.

Big and blond. Healthy and whole. Cold eyes and a brutal mouth.

Running toward the sound of screams.

The burned man raised a withered arm and extended one skeletal finger. "You *see*? That's *him*."

Beside him, his only companion leaned forward, elbows on knees.

"Oh, yes," said Doctor Michael Pharos. "I see him."

Chapter Twenty-six

National League Baseball Opening Day
Citizens Bank Park, Philadelphia
March 29, 1:03 P.M.

The crowd hadn't thinned much when I reached the doorway to the main corridor. The stadium had been packed, and there were thousands of people fighting their way from the stands through the halls that led to the parking lot.

As I pushed my way out of the corridor, I saw that many people were bleeding and bruised. How much of that was because of the blast and how much was because of panic was anyone's guess.

Then I spotted Ghost. He was on the far side of the hallway, crouched down beside a pretzel cart that had been toppled onto its side. Ghost was barking at everyone and everything. There were some smears of red on his shoulders and muzzle. He saw me and became hysterical, snapping at people as he tried several times to enter the flow. Each time he shied back.

Several people took swings at him. Nobody got near to his teeth. Ghost had lost several teeth during a mission in Iran. They'd been replaced by gleaming titanium fangs, and his broken jawbone had been surgically reinforced and strengthened. People couldn't know that, but a hundred-plus pounds of shepherd with metal teeth wasn't something to mess with. Not even when running for your life.

Getting to him would be like trying to cross a raging river.

I tried to yell at him to stay there, to hide in the shelter formed by the fallen cart and the wall, but he was too deep inside his own wildness. He lunged into the crowd in a mad attempt to get to me. Immediately, people collided with him and accidentally kicked him and fell over him. Ghost instantly turned and bit, more out of reflex and fear than anything. I saw blood.

I saw Ghost go down under the feet of the crowd.

I very nearly fired into the crowd.

No joke. I'm not proud of it, but I almost shot the people who were trampling my dog. He means that much to me. Brother in arms. Pet. A member of my family.

So, instead of committing wholesale murder, I flung myself into the throng and began fighting my way to him.

Within seconds, I was beaten down to the ground.

Kicked. Stepped on. Stomped. But I reached Ghost and wrapped myself around him to keep him from being stomped. And to keep him from killing anyone, because he was as far out on the ragged edge of panic as I was. We folded down, and the crowd crammed us into a cleft of wall and floor.

It was like being caught in a riptide and dragged through a rocky reef.

I screamed.

And I could not do a fucking thing about it.

The tide roared as it surged past.

All I could do was ride it out and wait for it to be over.

But it was not over.

Not even close.

Interlude Eight

Aaron Davidovich sipped coffee and studied the code he'd just written, tapping a key to scroll the page. The coffee was excellent, better than any of the piss water his Agency watchdogs had provided for him at the safe house. The croissant he'd just finished was top quality, too.

He sipped his coffee and read.

One small part of his mind was detached from the meticulous process of reading computer code. That part stood to one side and observed. He was aware of it. Davidovich had always been aware of that part of his mind. The part that watched and evaluated everything he did. The nature of the observer shifted depending on mood. For a long time he imagined what Sherlock Holmes, with all of his deductive and inductive reasoning, would make of the little things that Davidovich did. Would Holmes properly interpret the smooth patches of dry skin on his wrists as the result of countless hours of resting on the metal deck of his computer? Would Holmes deduce his general fitness was the natural result of the sedentary habits of a member of an office-based nerd hive?

Sometimes the watcher in his mind was a cop. As when he was clearly over the legal limit of appletinis and was walking from bar to car.

Lately, though, since he'd come to live here with Boy, he imagined that they were watching him all the time. They. Whoever they were.

Even now, six months into his captivity, he didn't know if he worked for terrorists, criminals, or a foreign government. Boy was not an American. Nor, he was convinced, were Mason and Jacob. That left a long list of possibles.

Over time, it mattered less who was watching and more that he give a good impression regardless of whether anyone was watching. He was very careful. He constructed his habits to convey acceptance of his new life, resignation to the situation, and diligence to his tasks.

Even now, sipping coffee and proofreading his code, he arranged his body so that he looked relaxed but alert, showing neither tension nor any of the physical tics of fear. By acting that role, he found, over time, that he actually was relaxed.

It was nice.

After that first horrible day, the whole situation had become . . .

He took a long sip of coffee as he fished for the word.

"Comfortable."

He stiffened and set the cup down, staring at the screen but suddenly not seeing it.

"Comfortable"?

Really? Was that the word? Was that actually what he was feeling?

Suddenly conscious of his inner watcher and the real possibility of hidden cameras and actual watchers, he pinched his nose as if trying to prevent a sneeze. He made a presneeze mouth and took in a breath. Held it. Then sighed, long and with obvious satisfaction of having prevented the sneeze.

All good theater.

All to hide his reaction to his own thought.

Davidovich picked up his cup again and took another sip. It was damn fine coffee.

And, yes, damn it, he was comfortable.

He looked inside to try and read the expression on his inner watcher's face. Would there be disappointment? Contempt? Self-loathing?

Shock and horror?

There should have been.

There probably should have been.

This should absolutely be a crisis moment, the precursor to a dark night of the soul.

Yes, sir.

Aaron Davidovich got up, crossed the room, and got a fresh cup of coffee. Added soy milk and sugar. Sipped, sighed, smiled.

And went back to work.

Chapter Twenty-seven

National League Baseball Opening Day

Citizens Bank Park, Philadelphia

March 29, 1:05 P.M.

Ghost screamed.

Actually screamed.

It was a sound I'd never heard from a dog before.

Pain and fear, blind panic, and a total loss of faith in his pack leader to make sense of the world.

Then there was another sound.

Was it another explosion?

The whole crowd seemed to freeze for one moment to hear. It wasn't behind them, not outside in the stands.

It was inside, in here.

Ahead of where the crowd was trying to go.

In that shocked half second, I struggled to my feet, the gun loose in my sweaty hands.

That sound could have been a gunshot.

Except it wasn't.

There was a faint buzzing noise, and then there was a second bang.

Closer. Louder. A bigger and more hollow sound than either a pistol or rifle round. Way too small to be a shotgun.

It was somewhere ahead. Thirty, forty yards.

The crowd screamed again and sagged back.

I couldn't see what it was, though.

The tide of the crowd was caught between those still pushing from outside and the rest inside, who were trying to avoid whatever was ahead of us. So, I decided to make my move.

I raised my stolen gun and yelled, "Federal agent! Move, move, move!"

The people around me shied away. Ghost got to his feet, shaking and scared, but he was drawn by my attempt to take control back.

"Let me through," I bellowed. "Federal agent, let me through."

This time, with no clear direction in which to flee, they did. Now they needed an answer, and I was the only possible authority they could see.

Bleeding, battered, and wearing a baseball shirt from a different city. Didn't matter. I had the gun, and I was using my best cop voice.

"Let me through," I growled again.

Someone—a woman—screamed, "There's another one!"

I couldn't see what she was pointing at, but above the sudden upsurge in shouts I heard another motorized buzz.

And then . . .

Bang!

Forty yards in front of me, something exploded. I could see the flash and hear the bang, and then I saw blood and red pieces fly as high as the ceiling.

The crowd spun and slammed into me.

I went down again. Harder. Much harder. My head hit the concrete wall.

My gun went flying somewhere.

My legs buckled, and I slid down to the cold ground.

I felt feet running across my chest. My thighs. My groin. I curled into a ball and tried not to die.

I prayed that my dad was okay. Rudy and Patrick, too.

There were more buzzes.

There were more explosions.

And there was more death.

Maybe none of us were going to be okay.

Chapter Twenty-eight

National League Baseball Opening Day
Citizens Bank Park, Philadelphia
March 29, 1:09 P.M.

James Wolcott Ledger stood his ground.

The mayor of Philadelphia knelt behind him, his face streaked with blood, his suit torn and covered in soot. Colonel Douglas lay sprawled. Maybe unconscious, maybe dead. All around him, the stadium seemed to blossom with vast red flowers. Pillars of smoke reached toward the blue sky like the arms of demons. The air was torn by screams, by explosions, by shouts.

He was aware of all of it, but at the moment—inside that moment—his entire body, his reflexes, and all of his heart and soul were focused on the thing that hovered in front of him.

Small.

Shaped like a bird.

Not a bird.

Others just like it flew into the stands and exploded.

This one had swooped down from the upper tiers, canting slightly on a damaged wing but still able to fly. A thin streamer of smoke trailed behind it.

James Ledger ground his feet into the dirt on the pitcher's mound and raised the Louisville Slugger that had been signed by both teams as part of the presentation to Douglas. The bat felt good in Ledger's hands. He'd played ball in college and used to knock the hide off fastballs for the Baltimore Police League. Both his sons had the knack, and his grandson, too. All of them could hit sliders and breakers and break the heart of overeager pitchers.

The drone was moving slower than a fastball. As it swept toward him, Ledger stepped into its path and swung for the bleachers.

The drone darted up and left, and the bat slashed empty air with such ferocity that Ledger was spun three-quarters of the way around. He staggered off balance, took a quick step to catch his balance, turned, and swung again.

Again, the drone flitted out of the way.

A third time.

A fourth.

"Come here, you little cocksucker," snarled Ledger, spitting with fury and feeling, his anger rising even above the level of his terror.

He faked a thrust, faked again, and then leaped forward to bunt the drone. The ash hit the machine and knocked it backward, where it wobbled, trying to level out.

Tried a second too long.

"Up yours," growled the mayor of Baltimore as he swung the bat at full force.

Interlude Nine

Aaron Davidovich lived his life in that apartment above the falafel shop. He worked twelve to fourteen hours each day, a schedule broken up by meals and exercise. Boy and her two male companions—known as Jacob and Mason, though Davidovich was positive those were not their real names—brought in some gym equipment. A Bowflex, small free weights, a jump rope, chin-up bar, push-up handles, TheraBands, a physioball, and a yoga mat. Boy began teaching Aaron how to use the equipment, and, as the weeks passed, Davidovich began losing flab and putting on muscle. After weeks of nightmares, he began sleeping soundly and woke refreshed. Boy made sure that his food was a balance of healthy and enjoyable. Almost no alcohol, though. A few beers a month, usually as a reward for finishing a new section of the design on which he was working.

They arranged to have messages sent to his family. Assuring them that he was alive and being well cared for. None of their messages were ever sent to him, though Davidovich was able to watch them at various times on computer monitors. They were well. They were healthy.

But they grieved.

Even though he was now in high school, Matthew sometimes cried at night.

Davidovich's mother did, too.

His wife . . . ? Not so much.

After seven months of solitude, she began to go out and lie to her son about where she was going. Sometimes she was out all night. Boy's video surveillance showed him what she was doing. And whom she was doing it with. Meeting with a divorced man they'd known for years. Meeting in a motel. Hidden cameras recorded everything.

So, instead, it was Davidovich who wept for her. For the loss of her.

He ached to hold his son. To take him out to basketball games. To talk with him.

It was Matthew who kept him going.

His mother, too. But mostly his son.

Sometimes in the night he secretly wished that Boy would do to his wife the things she'd originally threatened.

The first time Davidovich had that thought, he immediately rushed into the bathroom and vomited.

The second time he had that thought, he just lay there in bed and let the thought play out.

It was the same the third time. And every time after that.

It got easier each time he watched the video feed of his wife in bed with Harvey Cohen. Screaming as she came. Like he was fucking a porn star instead of a goddamn dentist. Doing things with him that had fallen out of the repertoire of activities she'd shared with her own damn husband.

It made Davidovich so mad.

On the days following those moments of video voyeurism, Davidovich found himself working harder at his new job. He threw his anger and frustration into the Regis program. He was even aware that he was channeling his anger and hurt in the worst possible way.

But he didn't care.

It was the only kind of payback that was open to him.

If you can't hurt the one you love, then you hurt anyone you can reach.

BOY WATCHED Doctor Davidovich all the time. She even played back video footage of him from when she was away on assignment or sleeping. She knew every movement, every tic.

Boy saw the way the infidelity of the doctor's wife stuck knives in him. She saw how it changed his sleeping and eating patterns. His workout intensity. She noted how it changed the quality of his work. Boy noted it all down.

Doctor Pharos and the Gentleman, she knew, would be very happy. It was unfolding exactly the way they said it would. Exactly according to plan.

Davidovich would, of course, never be allowed to know that his wife's lover belonged to Doctor Pharos and the Gentleman. Body and soul. Paired very well to seduce the doctor's wife.

So, Boy watched him watch them, and she grew excited. It was as if she could actually see, hear, and feel a great switch being turned on in Davidovich's soul.

From light to dark.

Chapter Twenty-nine

National League Baseball Opening Day

Citizens Bank Park, Philadelphia

March 29, 1:13 P.M.

It seemed to last a long, long time.

I crawled into a corner behind a trash can. This time, it was Ghost who found me. He was limping. His face and shoulders were streaked with blood. His tail was curled under his body, and he shoved himself against me, whimpering, lost and scared.

I felt exactly the same way.

My head was spinning. I know I'd been kicked several times. Maybe a couple of cracked ribs. My groin was a ball of fire. My stomach was in knots.

In those few seconds, at the hands and feet of a crowd of ordinary people, I had taken the worst beating of my life. It was comprehensive, and I had no idea how badly hurt I was. There was blood in my mouth.

I fumbled for my cell phone, but it was gone. I didn't remember dropping it.

There were more explosions. Smoke curled along the top of the curving corridor. It looked alive, like a writhing dragon. Sinister and hungry.

More bangs.

I lost count at ten.

I lost consciousness, too.

Not sure how long I was out. I don't think it was that long.

When I opened my eyes, Ghost was licking my face. He had a crazed look in his eyes, and he was panting way too fast. I pulled him against me, stroked his fur, said meaningless words in a soothing tone into his ear as an ocean of people ran past.

Then I saw what was blowing up.

It was small. No bigger than a . . .

"Oh, shit," I said.

It was a pigeon.

Except that it wasn't, and now I understood what the killers had brought to the stadium in their wooden crates. Not boxes of birds.

These were *drones*.

Small, perfectly crafted to blend into the environment and call no attention to themselves. I'd seen this type before. I'd worked with similar unmanned aerial vehicles.

Pigeon drones.

Not sent out for surveillance.

These were packed with explosives. That's what I'd heard. That was the only thing that made sense.

The fake bird flew toward me, its wings beating at a tremendous rate, more like a hummingbird than a pigeon. Glass eyes seemed to stare at me as it buzzed past.

There were four people between me and the drone. I shoved Ghost to one side and scrambled to my knees despite the sickness in my head and gut. The world seemed to tilt sideways.

"Get down!" I yelled, my voice hoarse and thick.

The people closest to me turned, and I immediately began shoving them toward the walls. I tripped a few, foot-swept a couple of others, knocking them back, knocking them down, trying to get them out of the possible debris field of the drone. Taking shrapnel in the back while laying down would do a lot less damage than taking it in the face. In the eyes.

The drone suddenly stopped in midair, its wings flapping with blinding speed. It seemed to be watching what I was doing. Assessing it.

Which meant that the machine had a camera and someone was watching.

That was not good.

I snatched a bottle of Mountain Dew from someone's hand and hurled it at the drone. It instantly shifted out of the way.

That wasn't good, either. That meant whoever was at those controls had some goddamn fast reflexes. There should have been a lag. I should have knocked the thing out of the air before the video signal could go back to base, be observed, and be reacted to and before a response movement could be sent back to the drone. My bottle should have hit it faster than a person at a remote pilot station could react.

But the drone swerved to avoid the bottle.

It's stupid, it's crazy, but I had the horrible and irrational feeling that it was the machine itself that had reacted. Doing it at machine speed. At computer speed.

The drone rose to the ceiling and turned in a quick circle.

Reassessing?

Accumulating data?

Or picking the best target?

I saw my gun on the ground being kicked as a flood of people ran for the exits, colliding with one another, cursing, screaming.

I aimed my shoulder and drove into the crowd, battering people aside, yelling at them to let me through, shouting "Police!" and "Federal agent!"

Someone to my left yelled back, "Fuck you!"

And he punched me in the side of the head.

It was one of those big, lazy, looping haymakers that, on any other day, would have allowed me to have a sandwich and coffee before yawning my way through a block or evasion. This wasn't one of those days. The guy could hit, too. Damn him.

I went right down.

Even as I fell, though, through the fireworks in my eyes I saw my gun. I stretched out for it as I crashed down. My fingers fumbled over it, and my fingernails caught on the fittings. I gathered it into my hand, turned, rolled onto my back, and brought it up to aim at the drone.

Then it blew up.

A big, solid bang that shook the floor on which I lay.

The people above me seemed to fly apart like corn dollies. Clothing and skin, muscle and bone. It all splashed me. Their deaths prevented mine, but I wore their blood. I heard someone screaming and screaming. Whoever it was tottered on the precipice of a never-ending fall into black madness.

I was so afraid it was me.

It was me.

And I fell.

Chapter Thirty

"Are you watching the news, Father?" asked Boy, the phone pressed to her ear. Her tablet lay on her thighs, the screen filled with images of smoke and blood.

"I am," said Doctor Pharos. "It's very entertaining. I'm very proud of you."

"I'm glad you're pleased."

"Very much so."

"Has the Gentleman seen it?"

"He has. And he was also very pleased," said Pharos. "You know that everything you do pleases us. We're both so proud of you."

She felt her face burn, and she mumbled a reply.

"Boy—?"

"Yes, Father?"

"Are you all right?"

"I . . ."

"What is it?" he asked, his tone gentle. "You can tell me."

"I want to come home."

"Ah."

"I haven't see you in so *long*. I can't . . . I can't stand it."

"Boy—is it the work? Is it getting too difficult?"

"No," she said quickly. "Everything is perfect out here."

"Is there a problem with your people?"

"No. Everyone's doing their job, but—"

"Are there any glitches in the operation?"

"No, it's not that. The machine is the machine. It's perfect the way you made it. That's just it . . ."

"What do you mean?" asked Pharos.

"I don't need to *be* out here anymore, do I? Davidovich is with you now. I don't understand why I'm even out here. All I'm doing is watching. And . . . I mean . . . couldn't I do that there? With you?"

There was a pause. Then Pharos said, "Believe me, sweetheart, that there's nothing more important to me in the world than you. You are my family. *We* are family. You and I."

"And the Gentleman?" She asked the question but tensed against the answer. To her the Gentleman was an almost godlike figure, the last of the Seven Kings. On the other hand . . . Boy almost cringed at the truth in her heart. The Gentleman was dying, and he was crippled—and that made him a burden. If, against all logic, odds, and planning, something went wrong and they had to flee, Boy knew that her father would try to take care of the burned man, try to find some way to flee with him. Boy understood fieldwork better than her father. He had his genius; she had hers. There was no way to flee with an anchor, and the burned man was an anchor. It hurt her heart to think of him that way, but it was true. And, as devoted as she was to the family that was the Seven Kings, if it came down to a choice between saving her father or letting him get taken because of that anchor . . .

Boy knew full well she could put a bullet through the seared flesh of the Gentleman's head. Without a moment's hesitation.

There would be regret later, sure—and maybe reproach from Father. But hesitation? Boy did not possess that particular flaw.

Her father was a long time in answering her implied question about the Gentleman. She knew that he must be conflicted and filled with sorrow at the ill health of the great man.

"Our dear friend," began Pharos, "is a realist."

And that was answer enough.

"I understand, Father."

"I know you do, my sweet. Now . . . is everything in place for the rest?"

"Yes."

"Good. As soon as things are concluded there, I'm going to need you in San Diego. I'll send flight details. It will be outside the no-fly zone. You know where."

"Yes, Father."

"One last job to do," said Pharos. "After San Diego, you come home to me."

Tears rolled down her cheeks.

"Thank you!"

"No, my love, thank *you*. No father has ever been more proud of a daughter than I am of you. Once this is done, then we will slip away like birds on the wind."

It was a line from a very old Cambodian song. He used to sing it to her after her therapy sessions in those days after he took her from the brothel.

"Like butterflies on a spring breeze," she said softly, repeating the last line of that old song. One tear curled over her cheek and found the corner of her mouth. She tasted the salt. Her tears were always so cold. They tasted like seawater.

"I'll send you the details," said Pharos. "You'll need to be strong, and you'll need to be brave. This will be dangerous."

Boy sniffed sharply and swallowed those tears. "I'm ready," she said. "You know I'm ready for anything."

"Yes, I do," said Pharos, a smile in his voice. "But first things first. Finish up there. The Gentleman is counting on you. As am I. Remember that I love you, my daughter."

The line went dead.

Boy pressed the silent phone against her cheek, closed her eyes again, and conjured images of her father. Tall and so handsome. Powerful. Brilliant. Not a King, but kingly in his way.

Then she closed the tablet, turned off the car engine, got out, put her earbuds in, and walked back to the stadium while emergency vehicles and crowds of rubberneckers raced toward the pillars of smoke.

Chapter Thirty-one

California

March 29, 1:17 P.M.

The president of the United States was giving a speech at a brunch for a group of celebrity vintners in Napa Valley. The speech was virtually the same one he'd given to the Deep Sea Fishing Association, the Art Alliance of Berkeley, a group of Silicon Valley billionaires, and a charitable foundation created by the wives of professional football players.

The speech was going well, as he and his team expected. This was one of his party-platform speeches that was flexible enough to allow for subtle changes to make it relevant to any specific target audience. The president had the rhythms of it down, and he'd watched enough playbacks to know when to make lingering eye contact, when to give that confident smile, when to glower like a tough commander in chief, when to beam like the proud father of the nation. It was all theater, but so was all of politics. It didn't make it meaningless, though. The president believed in most of what he said and accepted the necessary compromises of the rest. No president who ever served managed to get everything he wanted. Not even close.

He was just warming to one of his own pet themes, a project to work off college loans built on elements of FDR's New Deal, when Alice Houston came from offstage and bent close to speak to him. It sent an immediate ripple through the audience.

"Mr. President," said Houston, "there has been an attack in Philadelphia . . ."

Out in the audience, people were pulling their cell phones to look at the text messages and Twitter screens.

The news was reaching everyone at once.

Interlude Ten

Tanglewood Island
Pierce County, Washington
One Week Ago

It was a three-mile commute across Puget Sound from the mainland to the small island. As the boat approached the island, Doctor Pharos gestured to the pilot to circle it. The boat began a slow circuit. The craft was a Sea Ray 350 Sundancer. Old, but in excellent condition, with quiet engines and a pilot with a subtle hand. Water creamed along the fiberglass hull and foamed out behind in a widened V.

Tanglewood Island was tiny, like a crumb that had fallen from the vast bulk of Fox Island. It was only eighteen hundred feet long and six hundred wide but densely wooded, with lush growth even this early in the year.

"We're coming up on it, sir," said the pilot.

Michael Pharos nodded. "Circle around so we can take a look at it. Take your time. Let the Gentleman see it."

Beside him, the burned man hunched in his wheelchair, wrapped in layers of blankets, warmed by a portable heater, sustained by the machines fixed to the chair's frame. He wore a fur-lined hat with the earflaps pulled down and heavy protective goggles to shield his eye. The lenses were flecked with spray, and he had to squint to see anything.

"What do you think of our new home?" asked Pharos, nodding to the island.

They both knew that it was very likely the last home in which the Gentleman would ever live. They knew he would die there, and that day was not far away. A matter of months now. The treatments, the surgeries, the mind-clarifying cocktails by Pharos's pet mad scientist, a disgraced chemist named Doctor Rizzo. The man had been fired from Merck for using the R & D facilities to concoct street drugs, and Rizzo had avoided jail only because the company didn't want the scandal. Instead, they'd released him and made him sign papers swearing that he would not seek employment in big pharma for at least ten years. No one but a guilty man who'd been caught red-handed would ever sign a paper like that. Doctor Rizzo had, and three weeks later he'd been recruited by one of Pharos's street scouts.

The chemist had been working on a new cocktail that was part psychic stabilizer and part painkiller. It also had small amounts of different so-called psychoactive "truth" drugs developed for interrogators in various countries: narcoanalytics like scopolamine; potent short- or intermediate-acting hypnotic benzodiazepines such as midazolam, flunitrazepam, temazepam, ketamine; and various short- and ultrashort-acting barbiturates, including sodium thiopental and amobarbital. Pharos could barely make sense of the chemistry.

It was a dangerous brew, but Rizzo said it was all about balancing the trace elements and keeping a bunch of rescue drugs primed and ready. Rizzo was probably certifiable, but he knew his chemistry.

Maybe that would do the trick. Even though Doctor Rizzo had very likely extended the Gentleman's life, there was a line between cutting-edge science and wishful thinking. They all saw that line very clearly.

Pharos wondered if the burned man thought the line was drawn along the dock of the island.

The trip here from the resort in British Columbia was almost too much. No, it probably *was* too much. Pharos was deeply concerned about how hollowed out the burned man looked. How vacant he seemed to be. Not all the time, but too much of the time. The Gentleman seemed to quiver like a match in a strong breeze.

Seeing the process filled Pharos with moody thoughts about the finite grains of sand in the human hourglass. It made him consider his own span here on earth. Sure, there would be decades allotted to him so he could play with his billions in whatever version of the world existed by this time next week, but there would be an end to it. It was sad.

Life was so unfair. So fragile.

So easily stolen away.

The Gentleman did not answer the question, so Pharos repeated it. "What do you think? It's lovely, isn't it?"

Instead of answering, the Gentleman asked, "What about the others? Are they all here?"

"The 'others'?" It took him a moment before he realized that the Gentleman was having a *moment*. The burned man thought that they were going to a meeting of the Seven Kings. It wasn't the first time, but it was the first time in a while. It caught him off guard, though he recovered quickly. "Ah . . . yes. They're waiting for you. I'm sure they'll be happy to see you, sir."

The Gentleman suddenly peered at him. "You think I'm already out of my mind, don't you?"

"Absolutely not." Pharos even managed to smile as he said it.

"You're a lying piece of shit, Hugo. You always were."

Pharos did not correct the Gentleman. He waited instead, knowing that the burned man would catch his own mistake if he was at all lucid. The moment of realization came as a twist of self-disgust on the Gentleman's face.

"Pharos," he muttered. "You know that's what I meant."

"Of course. We all make mistakes . . . and besides, sir, it's been a long trip. I'm sure you're exhausted."

The rheumy eye of the Gentleman studied him. "You're a complete bastard, you know that, don't you?"

Pharos shook his head. "I am your friend and physician. And I am the last person on earth to judge you. The great are not to be judged."

"Such a bastard."

They lapsed into a bitter silence.

The boat completed its slow circuit of the island.

"It's nice to be going home," said Pharos.

The Gentleman said nothing at all, and there was a tear in his eye.

"Very well," Pharos said to the pilot, "take us in."

The pilot nodded and stood with his hand lightly touching the wheel, letting the craft find its way into the boathouse and out of sight of the mainland. He killed the engines and used a remote to close the big wooden doors. Even three miles from land, there was always the possibility of a casual eye looking this way. When the door was shut, lights came on automatically. A man in a black combat-dress uniform was waiting on the dock to make the bowline fast to a heavy cleat.

Silence settled over the boathouse except for the soft slap of water against the exterior walls. Four strong men clambered over the side and, at a word from Pharos, lifted the wheelchair and carried it onto the dock. Embarrassed and angry, the Gentleman tried to turn his face away, but they were on all sides of him. So he glared down at his folded, liver-spotted hand. He did not offer a word of thanks. These men would not expect it of him, and he was too humiliated to want to create that kind of conversation.

Pharos leaped nimbly onto the dock. Showing how fit and strong he was. How young he was. Making a statement to the Gentleman in a way that could not be taken as a direct insult, but which clearly was.

Pharos jerked his head back toward the boat.

"Escort our friend inside," he said.

The guards looked past him and down into the hold. A man sat in a corner, hands bound, a black hood pulled down over his head.

Without another backward glance, Pharos began pushing the Gentleman's wheelchair along the dock to the elevator.

Chapter Thirty-two

National League Baseball Opening Day
Citizens Bank Park, Philadelphia
March 29, 1:59 P.M.

It was Rudy who found me.

Rudy.

I felt hands on me, fingers pressing into the side of my throat. Fingers spreading my eyelids open, and vague shapes leaning close.

"Over here!" he yelled. "It's Captain Ledger. He's alive!"

Alive, I thought. Maybe. Not sure I wanted to be. I felt closer to dead, and death offered an escape from the pain that overwhelmed me.

Rudy.

I tried to say his name. Failed, because it required too much of me.

"*Ay Dios mío,*" he muttered, then he rattled off a longer prayer to Mary and Saint Francis, and, I think, Saint Jude. The prayers were not even a little comforting if they meant he thought I was a lost cause. I wanted to smile, to comfort him. He wasn't a soldier, but he'd come into the smoke and ruin of this building to find and rescue a man who was.

I blinked up through dust and blood and tears and saw his face. Caked with dirt, his one good eye filled with dangerous lights. His lips trembling with stress and horror.

"Joe!" he said urgently. "Joe, can you hear me?"

I couldn't answer his question. It was too difficult. I didn't know which words to use.

The explosions had stopped.

No telling when. I wasn't here for that. I'd checked out and didn't re-call anything other than a dream of falling, falling, falling . . .

There was something big and soft pressing against me. I fumbled for it, tried to push it away, afraid of it. Then something wet on my fingers. A kiss? No, a tongue. Licking me. Small, frantic licks.

I knew there was a name that should occur to me.

It came so slowly and from the wrong closet in my broken head.

"G-Ghost . . . ?"

He barked once. Weak, but certain. I heard a scuffling and saw him crawl-ing toward me. His coat was bloody, and drool flecked his muzzle. I reached out to him, and he nibbled my fingers. I touched his face, his head, his ears. Scratched them. There was a thump-thump of his tail hitting something I couldn't see.

"He's okay, Joe. He'll live."

Those two statements weren't as comforting as they were intended. People don't say "he'll live" when "he's okay" means exactly that. It meant that Ghost was hurt, but not fatally. That still left it open to his being seriously hurt. I flapped out a hand and found a furry shoulder. My fingers came away slick and wet. I knew what that wetness had to be.

Blackness came and went in my eyes and, I think, in my mind.

During one moment of clarity, the shape in front of me moved back, and I could see it now. A man's face. Covered with soot, lined with worry. A black eye patch and tousled black hair, thick mustache.

"Rudy?" I gasped.

"*Me lleva la chingada*, Joe," he said in a quick, nervous voice. "You scared the shit out of me. Are you hurt?"

"I—I don't know. How do I look?"

"You've looked better."

"Great."

I tried to sit up and set my teeth against an expectation of terrible pain. Like splintered ribs or internal injuries, both of which I was positive I had. But my body moved without the grating of broken parts. Everything hurt, but nothing seemed fatal.

"I don't think you should move, Joe."

"Yeah, well, I don't think I should lie here." I sat up and then sagged back against the wall, panting. There were little white explosions going off inside my eyeballs.

The fog in my head began to thin. I gasped and caught Rudy's wrist. "My dad—?"

"He's okay, thank God," said Rudy. "Patrick, too. He's helping with . . . " His voice trailed off.

"What is it?"

"Joe . . . there are a lot of casualties. The police and fire department are still searching for bodies."

"How'd they . . . get here . . . so fast?"

He shook his head. "You've been out for almost an hour. We just found you. The police had you tagged as one of the dead."

"Shit. Help me up."

"No way. Not without a stretcher and—"

"Goddamn it, Rudy, help me the fuck up."

He insisted on checking me for broken bones first. His probing fingers found a lot of places that detonated hand grenades of pain, but nothing moved the way it shouldn't. Rudy stood and pulled me to my feet.

It took a long time and a lot of effort. The corridor tilted and spun, and I nearly fell.

Nearly.

Didn't.

Ghost got up slowly, too. Just as carefully, every bit as shakily. He looked up at me and gave me half a wag as if to assure me he was alive. For some reason, that made me want to cry. I squatted down and pulled him to me, running my fingers through his fur to see how badly he was hurt. It looked worse than it was. A bunch of cuts, but he yelped and whined when I touched different places, clear evidence of the kind of bruises I had. I hugged him and kissed his head, and he licked my chin and nose.

Rudy's words were starting to sink in. Without turning to Rudy, I said, "How . . . how many people?" I asked.

When he didn't answer, I straightened and looked at him. He looked stricken.

"Rude—? How many?"

"They're . . . not sure. A hundred. Maybe more."

"Dead?"

"Yes."

"God almighty."

"Yes."

I looked around. Now that I was on my feet, I could see how bad things were here in the corridor. Bodies lay everywhere. Some of them had been covered with white plastic. Others lay where they'd fallen. There were whole bodies and there were parts of bodies. It was a sickening sight. Not just because of the blood and torn meat, but because these were people.

Ordinary folks. Not combatants.

This was the opening day of the baseball season. We'd all come out to have some fun. Maybe get drunk. Have a hot dog or a soft pretzel. Maybe catch a foul ball. This was all supposed to be fun. A day to remember.

And I guess that's what it was. That last part. A day to remember.

An unforgettable day, for all the wrong reasons.

I tapped my earbud to see if it was working yet.

"There's no radio in here," said Rudy. "Cell phones won't work, either."

"Shit," I growled. "I need to get out of its range. Those sonsabitches might still be in the building."

"Who? Did you see something?"

"Yes," I said, moving as quickly as my battered body would allow, "I damn well did."

Chapter Thirty-three

National League Baseball Opening Day

Citizens Bank Park, Philadelphia

March 29, 2:15 P.M.

I had to fight my way over rubble and around too damn many bodies. Ghost was beside me, and despite his being an experienced combat dog, the blood and death was hitting him hard. His tail was tucked under, and he kept twitching and jerking away from things we found. I made reassuring and encouraging noises and hoped that I wasn't wasting my breath. Just like humans, combat dogs have complex psychologies, and they have their breaking points. I didn't want this to be Ghost's. He was a hell of a lot more than a service dog. He was family.

Rudy was somewhere behind me. He said he needed to help the medical teams. He's a doctor, and that was fine. I was a fighter, and I needed to share intel with other soldiers so we could start to hit back.

If it wasn't already too late for that.

When we reached the main field, I stopped as if I'd run into a wall.

It was like stepping across one of the rings of hell.

The crowd was gone, of course. Many of them had fled. The rest, I suppose, had been ushered out by surviving staff and responding police.

Too many of them, though, were still here.

In the shattered stands.

On the field.

Smoke drifted upward from dozens of spots. Whole sections of the bleachers had collapsed down. The green grass of the field was torn up and splashed red. Scores of emergency vehicles were parked at haphazard angles. Hundreds of emergency specialists were down there. EMTs, firefighters, cops. Volunteers.

It was a scene of stunning horror.

I saw a familiar figure on the field, and he was talking on a cell. There must have been coverage down there.

"Come on," I said to Ghost, and we began making our way to an undamaged set of stone stairs.

The man on the phone heard me calling his name, turned, and saw me coming. He lowered the phone and stared in shock. Even from fifty yards away, I saw the sob that hitched his chest.

Then he was running. Calling my name.

And I called his.

"Dad!"

James Wolcott Ledger pushed past his own police escort and grabbed me in a fierce hug. The hug hurt every damaged inch of me, but I didn't care. His face was wet with tears.

"Oh my God," he said as he held me close. He kissed my head. "Oh my God, Joe, they told me . . . they told me . . . "

"Thank God you're all right, Dad."

He pushed me back and held me at arm's length. Dad is about my height, a little over six foot two, and as trim and fit as when he walked a beat in West Baltimore. Blond hair gone gray and piercing blue eyes. At that moment, though, he looked old. "Christ, you're hurt? What's wrong? Are you all right?"

His questions ran together, and before I could answer, he bellowed for a medic.

Ghost wagged his tail and pressed himself against my dad's leg.

"Dad," I said, "your phone? Are you getting a signal?"

"Yes," he said, "but only out here. Can't get anything in—"

I tapped my earbud. "Cowboy to Bug! Come on, goddamn it. Bug, are you—?"

"Cowboy? Jesus, you're alive. Oh, man, I—"

"Bug, listen to me. I'm at the stadium, and I have intel."

"Cycling in the TOC," he said quickly. "Deacon is on the floor."

"What have you got, Cowboy?" said Church's voice.

I told him what happened in the hallway with the masked shooters.

"Copy that, Cowboy. I have two full teams inbound to you. Echo One and Two are twenty minutes out."

Echo One was Top; Two was Bunny. If they were that close, then they were coming via helicopter, which must be burning its way through the sky.

"I'll secure a landing spot," I said.

"Negative, that's already in hand. SWAT is at your facility. I want you to coordinate with them for a full sweep."

"Haven't they done that already, for God's sake?"

"They have," said Church. "You have not. Take them in again. I'll clear it."

"I'll need a weapon."

"They'll provide."

"There's no radio or cell anywhere but in the center of the field. Must be a jammer. Bug, find it for me."

"Targeting it now, Cowboy. Okay, got it. Looks like the source is inside the Hall of Fame meeting room." He gave me a set of directions.

"Wait for backup," warned Church.

I didn't.

"Dad," I said, "you still have your little friend?"

"Joe, I don't think . . . " But he stopped himself when he saw the look in my eyes. He knelt, tugged up his trouser cuff, and removed a small revolver from an ankle holster. He handed it to me, and I felt the familiar weight. A .38 Smith & Wesson Chief's Special. Five shots. I knew better than to ask about extra rounds. He was no longer a cop. He was the mayor of Baltimore. He carried the gun out of habit but didn't need extra rounds.

I hoped I wouldn't need them, either.

Or maybe I hoped I would.

"Tell SWAT to find me," I said as I broke into a lumpy, limping run-walk toward the same corridor I'd just come out of. Ghost ran after me, and I was heartened to see that his tail was no longer tucked.

As I ran, I passed by a row of bodies under white sheets. The arm of the closest body lay partially exposed. I saw a brown hand and a blue sleeve. Military blue. Air force blue. Torn now, exposing skin that was already going pale with lack of circulation.

I almost stopped running.

I almost stopped everything.

I knew whose sleeve that was, and it broke my heart. Absolutely crushed it.

Colonel Roger Douglas.

Hero.

Victim.

Tears burned in my eyes, nearly blinding me as I ran.

Chapter Thirty-four

Tanglewood Island

Pierce County, Washington

March 29, 2:22 P.M.

Doctor Pharos would never admit it, but he was hiding in his office. Nicodemus had come to Tanglewood and was locked in private conversation with the Gentleman. Pharos wanted no part of it.

Spooky old freak, he thought.

He tried to throw himself into his work. Much of it was mundane, even though it dealt with catastrophic events like what was unfolding at the ballpark in Philadelphia. And all of the other things the machine was primed to process. However, even with all the work, there wasn't enough to capture his whole attention. There was something wrong. There was a flaw in the system. In his personal system.

None of it really *mattered* to him.

Since the Kings organization collapsed, Pharos felt like he was the night watchman in an empty factory. All the machines and computers kept running, but without people at the top to give the organization a sense of grandeur, there was no drama. No excitement.

There was only process.

Sure, there were some things that entertained him to one degree or another. Boy was a lot of fun. Her excesses were legendary, and her degree of efficiency pleased Pharos.

Even some of the byplay between him and the Gentleman was amusing. In a twisted way. Managing the man's deteriorating mind, his rages, his bloodlust, and his secrecy were challenges. Nuts to be cracked, problems to be solved.

Pharos wondered if obtaining the bank codes would energize him.

Hard to say.

Pharos spent most of his time inside his own head. He disliked sharing his insights with others, and certainly never bared his soul to any subordinates. Certainly not to the Gentleman, either. He wondered, though, how much his ennui was clouding his usually sharp inward eye.

"The codes," he murmured aloud. "It's all about the fucking codes."

Which were, sadly, locked in the brain of a madman.

The good news was that Doctor Rizzo had given that madman many new versions of his chemical cocktail to try.

As Pharos shuffled through the papers, he found reports from his training teams about the progress of the field teams. The Kings organization had recruited many hundreds of field operatives. Some had been killers before the Kings offered them employment, while others were introduced to murder for pay after they'd come to work for the group. The bottom line was that no one went out on a field op without already having some blood on his or her hands.

It was important to establish this. Even Pharos had gotten his hands very dirty over the years.

Pharos's phone buzzed softly. The caller ID showed a stick figure. He smiled and punched the button. He'd committed several murders during his rise to power. And it had been Hugo Vox who'd suggested that Pharos cross that line.

"Why?" Pharos had asked him several years ago. "We have people for that kind of thing."

"Right, and they look to us for inspiration and motivation. Manage from the ground up, kiddo," Vox told him. "Go get some grease on your hands and shit on your shoes. Show the people who work for you that you're willing to get dirty and, more important, that you understand that *they* get dirty. If they know that you *get* them, then they'll hand over the pink slip on their souls. Besides . . . I've had my eye on you, kiddo. You got heart and you got feelings. You have to watch that shit. You have to learn how to control it, to shut it down, to turn it off. No better way to pull the plug on your morals than to slowly strangle the fuck out of someone while you look right into their eyes. Do it right and you don't go all psycho. You don't want to wind up with a boner 'cause you're doing a murder. That's weak. No, you want to own yourself. You want to be able to turn on the cold-water tap in your heart whenever you want. No emotional surprises. If you don't do it, then you're setting psychological bear traps, which is also weak, and it's poor process. Take the time now, while you're just getting into all this, and own your power, own your soul."

That's what Pharos had done.

First with men who were criminals standing in the way of the organization. It was easier to start by killing people who had blood on their own hands. It hurt less. But it did put a coat of thick paint over his conscience. With each killing, the paint job became more opaque, so that when he killed someone who wasn't a criminal—just someone who was inconvenient to the organization—there was far less trauma than Pharos expected.

Along the way, however, Pharos learned what most criminals learn who pay attention to the movie projector in their heads. He had limits. He had boundaries. He might participate in programs that would kill mass numbers of civilians, including children, but he would not take a child's life himself. No. That was a door he wouldn't allow himself to open. Pharos had been an abused child in a nightmare of a family life. Although his family's psychodynamics caused him to make the life choices he made, they also etched a line in the sand. A line he would not cross.

When he encountered child abusers, he tended to treat them harshly.

Very harshly indeed.

At one point, the organization collided with a sex-trafficking ring. A big one based in Thailand. Removing key players in the ring was useful to a project the organization had running in Asia at the time. However, freeing the girls and women in the brothels was not part of the agenda, and there had been no reason to place assets or attention on doing so. It would have been enough to crush the organization and let the pieces fall where they may.

Except that Pharos was on the ground during that operation. He was there in Thailand. He saw the brothels. He saw the girls.

One girl in particular. A slender eleven-year-old who had been forced into prostitution when she was eight.

Eight.

That was when Pharos opened a different door in his head. That's when he discovered not only that he *could* kill but also that certain kinds of killing were very satisfying. Not in a sexual way, as it was with some of the murderers and mercenaries he employed. No, this touched his soul. It made him feel like his life mattered. He knew that this was a damaged form of rationalization, but it didn't matter.

He took a team of shooters from Blue Diamond Security, one of the companies covertly owned by the organization, and he tore the infrastructure of the sex-trafficking ring apart.

And he, personally, tore the senior members of that ring apart.

Tore them to red rags.

Killed most of them.

Left a few alive as blind, limbless, disfigured wrecks so they could scream to anyone who would listen that there would be a price for turning little girls into whores.

By the time the organization was done, 179 people were dead, and 418 girls and women had been driven in trucks to hospitals or clinics run by the Red Cross, Catholic missions, and the World Health Organization.

And one child had been taken away by Pharos.

That eleven-year-old girl.

Taken, cleaned up, given medical treatment, given a home, given a life and a future.

Boy.

A name she'd chosen for herself and would not change.

Boy.

His daughter.

Pharos was not sure he actually loved her. Not in the way she loved him. She believed herself to be his daughter on a karmic level. To him, she was proof that his soul was not entirely damned. Pharos believed in God, and when he stood at the gates of judgment, he would point to Boy and those other women and ask to be judged according to that rather than what he'd done for the organization.

He thought he had a shot.

Chapter Thirty-five

I found the Hall of Fame meeting room before the SWAT team found me.

It was in a wing of the stadium that had been mostly empty during the game and the catastrophe that followed. Ash and brick dust covered the floor, and I could see a myriad of footprints. All recent. Most were the shape and tread pattern of police shoes. The gait pattern matched that of officers moving in pairs to investigate and clear a room in haste.

But one set of prints overlaid these.

Sneakers. Small. A young teen or small woman. I knelt and studied the tread pattern. From a closer angle, I could see that the person had come in carefully, walking inside the footprints of one of the cops. Only one step was askew, and that's the one I saw first. This person was very careful.

Unfortunately, the print was going away from the room I was heading to.

I tapped my earbud to see if the jammer had been turned off, possibly removed. But it was still operating.

Interesting.

I hand-signaled Ghost to move ahead and check for people. I reinforced that with a signal for no noise. Ghost is superbly trained, and having specific orders to follow seemed to help bring him back to himself. His body language was shifting from nervous victim to hunter.

Like me, his hunter aspect was very close to a deeper and more savage aspect. For him, the wolf lived beneath the dog hide. For me, the killer— one of the aspects of my fractured persona—was inside my mind, hunkered down in the tall grass, knife drawn, teeth bared, eyes cold.

I faded to the left side of the hall that led to the closed doors. Ghost went right and ahead, sniffing the ground. Not sure how much the prevalent stink of dust, explosive residue, and death affected his senses, but he was still a dog with a dog nose.

He reached the closed doors, abruptly sat down, and looked at me.

That was his signal.

It was what I wanted to see.

It meant that there was someone inside.

I gestured for him to stand and move back from the door, and he took his position behind and to one side of me. Muscles rippled along his flanks as he crouched, ready to spring. The little revolver felt tiny in my hands. I've been carrying an automatic so long that I'm spoiled by having all those extra bullets. Now I had no extra rounds. My only backup was the rapid-release folding knife I always carried clipped into my right front pants pocket. And Ghost.

So, it's not like I was walking naked into this thing.

I squatted and duck-walked to the door, keeping my head below the level of the frosted glass. SWAT seemed to be taking its own sweet time getting here, but I was still cruising on that edge of combat greed where I wanted to be the one to deal the entire play. I wanted to kick some ass and take some names. Literally, take names. I still had no idea who was behind this.

The rules say I should have waited for backup.

Yeah.

Fuck the rules.

Chapter Thirty-six

The Breakfast Place
Mission Beach, San Diego
March 29, 2:29 P.M.

The man was seated at a small table in the corner of a family restaurant on the boardwalk in Mission Beach. He had a plate of eggs and potatoes going cold in front of him. A smaller plate of whole-wheat toast sat adjacent, with one small bite missing from the top slice. Ice melted in a glass. Only the coffee cup was empty, and the waiter came to fill it for the third time.

"Thanks, mate," said the man without looking up. His focus was on the small electronic tablet on a foldout stand. His eyes flicked back and forth as he read one news report after another about what was happening in Philadelphia. It was not technically his business; however, there were aspects of the tragedy that caught his attention.

No, it was less than that. They tickled the edges of a fragment of a memory. Enough that it bothered him and kept him watching the news feeds.

He occasionally toggled over to a special search engine called Xenomancer. It was proprietary software used only by the board of directors and senior staff of FreeTech, the nonprofit company run by Junie Flynn. The firm was dedicated to taking military technologies and repurposing them in humanitarian ways. Hydration projects in draught-stricken areas. Clean water. Renewable clean energies. Sustainable farming sciences. Medical research to eradicate the diseases of poverty. And dozens of other projects. It was an expensive company to run, but private funding kept it going very nicely. Some of those funds were also used for lobbyists, scholarships, lawyers, media campaigns, advertising, and administration for a network of more than six thousand employees.

Xenomancer had been designed by the computer team that worked for the Department of Military Sciences and was given as a gift to FreeTech by Mr. Church.

Life was so weird.

That thought, in one form or another, flitted through the man's head a dozen times every day. Usually when he stopped and mentally stood back to watch what he was doing at any given moment. Writing reports. Attending meetings with administrators of free health clinics. Sending anonymous donations to charities all over the world. Being a good person.

So weird.

He did a lot of his most philanthropic work from that restaurant. The waiters here knew him. He was a regular who tipped very well and kept to himself. They left him alone even though he often sat at that table—a prime spot with a superb view of the rolling Pacific waves—for hours on end.

None of the staff there—not even the manager—knew that the young man owned the restaurant. They did not know that he owned the whole block and all of its businesses. The fair-trade gift shop, the free animal clinic, the sea-conservation museum and lab, the walk-in clinic that provided a variety of free services for women in crisis.

The young man made sure that his involvement with those businesses was never connected to him. This same policy extended to more than seven hundred businesses, organizations, corporations, and foundations that he owned or privately funded. Including FreeTech. He took particular pains to remain invisible to anyone who might want to show gratitude.

Gratitude was something he feared.

Something he dreaded.

To have to accept the heartfelt thanks of an innocent who received his help would kill him. He was positive of it.

It was probably already killing him. He was certain that there was some kind of cancer eating at him in the darkness of his own tainted blood.

That's how he saw it.

Tainted blood.

When he went to church, he spent a lot of time on his knees, praying. He never took confession. He feared what the priest would say.

He was certain that any priest would kick open the door of the confessional and drag him out, beat him, and throw him into the street. That the priest would damn him.

As he deserved to be damned.

As he *expected* to be damned.

But he went to church often. Nearly every day. Mostly Catholic churches because he had been raised in that faith. Sometimes he went to a synagogue. Or a mosque. Or a fire-and-brimstone country revival.

Any church that was open.

Any church that would let him pray in silence.

In none of those places did he beg forgiveness from God in all His aspects.

That, the young man was sure, was an even faster path to hell.

No. He did not want forgiveness. He believed that it was not his to have. Not even from God.

Because there was no way to actually undo the harm he'd done, he didn't see how forgiveness of those sins was valid. Not to a person who had done as much damage as he had. The blood on his hands could not be washed off with holy water and some token acts of contrition.

He wanted something much different than that.

Much different.

He wanted to be of use. To be used. To be useful.

Until he died.

And then he wanted to be forgotten. It was the greatest thing he could hope for.

Now, he sat at his table, his food abandoned, and watched the drama that was unfolding. He listened to the reporters become increasingly ghoulish in their excitement over the disaster and the body count.

It was a bad day in America.

It was another 9/11, they said.

It was another Mother Night Day, they said. Like last year when anarchists set off bombs and released plagues all over the country.

Except that there was something about the attack at the ballpark that made the young man wonder if it wasn't something else entirely.

Something he'd heard about once. Something very much like this. Drones at a ballpark.

His rational mind told him that the thing he'd heard years ago couldn't be connected to this, because everyone involved in that earlier discussion was dead. As far as he knew, he was the only survivor of that group. The only one who was alive to remember the conversation and its grim contents.

Drones.

And a ballpark.

He kept telling himself that this couldn't be that.

"Has to be something else," he said to himself, his voice barely a whisper. "After all, there are a lot of bloody-minded maniacs in the world."

On the screen, they were bringing out the wounded. Many of them were horribly mangled.

"Bugger this," he said, and reached for his phone. He debated whom to call. Mr. Church?

No. This was terrorism that used advanced technology, which meant Church and his people would be involved. Getting the man on the phone was difficult at the quietest of times.

Who then?

His fingers punched buttons as if on their own. The phone rang four times, and he was about to give it up when the call was answered.

"Hello?" said a soft female voice.

"Junie," he said.

"Oh," said Junie Flynn, "Toys. Look, I can't talk right now. Things are bad here."

"Bad where? Are you in Philadelphia?"

"What? Oh, no. I'm in San Diego. At the hospital."

"Why?" demanded Toys. "What's wrong? Are you—?"

"It's Circe," said Junie. "She collapsed. God, Toys, I think she's in a coma . . . "

Junie quickly explained about Circe's collapsing while they were house hunting. Since being brought to the hospital, the doctors had not been able to revive her.

"They're doing all kinds of tests."

"The baby—?"

"They don't know yet. Oh God, Toys, this is so terrible. Rudy and Joe are in Philadelphia, at the ballpark."

"Oh my God."

"Rudy called. He's okay. Joe's hurt, but Rudy says it isn't bad. But they're so far away."

"Stay right there," Toys said. "I'm on my way."

Chapter Thirty-seven

National League Baseball Opening Day
Citizens Bank Park, Philadelphia
March 29, 2:34 P.M.

I listened at the door.

Heard muffled conversation. Men's voices. Low. Speaking quickly. Like people in a hurry.

Not speaking English.

I'm pretty good with languages. I took the door handle and turned it very slowly, met no resistance, opened the door a fragment of an inch. Listened closer.

At least three people speaking.

Definitely not English.

Farsi.

It was the most common language spoken in Iran and Afghanistan.

Not entirely uncommon in the States. Lot of immigrants here. Melting pot and all that. So it wasn't the language by itself that let me know I'd found my bad guys.

It was what they were saying.

Like I said, I'm pretty good at languages.

One guy said, "Your jacket is buttoned wrong."

Another one said, "Let's go. The timer is running."

Then there was the sound of footsteps.

The killer inside my head was growling.

Or maybe that was Ghost.

I whipped the door open and went in low and fast, bringing the little gun up into a two-handed grip, searching for targets. Finding five men, not three.

None of them looked Middle Eastern. No one was an Arab. No one was Persian. They looked like average Americans.

They were all dressed in uniforms.

Four wore the blue shirts and navy trousers of paramedics.

The fifth was dressed in the uniform of a Philadelphia police officer.

If I'd seen them in the hall, I might have bought the con. If I hadn't heard them speaking in Farsi. If I hadn't heard that comment about the timer. Yeah, I might have bought that they were here to help. That they were good guys.

But . . . that ship sailed.

Ghost bared his teeth at them. I pointed the gun and yelled, "Federal agent, freeze!"

Knowing they wouldn't.

Hoping they wouldn't.

They didn't.

One of the paramedics grabbed the man closest to him and shoved him at me. As the man staggered forward, the first man yelled, "Kill them!"

I fired. The guy staggering toward me took the round above the right eye. His head snapped back, but his body continued forward, crashing into me, knocking me back.

I yelled to Ghost, "Hit! Hit! Hit!"

He moved like a white blur, snarling, rising, slamming into the cop. I heard terrible screams as I pivoted to shake off the dead man. But the body shuddered as if punched, and as an aftereffect I heard the pop of a handgun.

With the corpse still atop me, I reached around and fired at movement. Another scream.

I shucked the body off me in time to see one of the paramedics sag back, his stomach pouring red, the gun falling from his hand. I fired two more shots. And another man went down, his lower jaw shot away.

Ghost had the cop down and they were trying to kill each other. No idea who was winning.

Then the fourth man was the only uninjured guy left. I fired my last bullet at him, but he was in motion and the round missed him by half an inch. He tore open his shirt and clawed for a Glock.

I hurled my empty gun at him, and as he dodged I came up off the floor and drove my shoulder into his gut, driving him backward. But the son of a bitch was spry. He took my momentum and twisted, whipping me around his hip. I flew into the wall, rebounded, and crashed down.

The killer dove for his gun, but I snapped a kick out and knocked him down. Then I was on my knees, my right hand going for the rapid-release folder. It was ultra-lightweight and had a small 3.375 blade that popped out with a flick of the wrist and locked in place.

My opponent had a surprise of his own. He slipped a scalpel out of a barrel sheath and rushed me.

In the movies, a knife fight takes five minutes, and the players dance around each other like they're extras from the Michael Jackson "Beat It" video. In real life, knife fights are short, brutal, and messy. The better fighter usually wins right away, and the other guy goes down in pieces.

This was different. The guy with the scalpel was good.

Real damn good.

He body-feinted left and snapped a short circular cut right that traced a burning line from my wristwatch almost to my elbow. Scalpels are wickedly sharp. You don't need muscle to cut deep. I jerked my arm down in the direction of his cut, letting it push me, but even so blood burst out of the wound. It was so slender a cut that it burned like an acid sting.

I twisted my body and hit his elbow with my open palm, then whip-changed back and slammed my right elbow into his biceps. A big torsion-driven one-two. He tried to turn inside the combination, but I checked him again with my left and rebounded my right up and over his deltoid for a very fast left-to-right lateral slash.

My blade caught him on the back side of the big tendon in the neck. It was a big, deep cut. I checked again and corkscrewed the tip into the socket of his throat, punching through trachea and hyoid bone all the way to the spine.

And that, as they say, was the ball game.

He made a terrible wet coughing sound as I twisted my hand to pull the blade free. Just for fuck's sake, I bent and slashed his right knee tendon, sending him crashing and dying to the floor.

Then I wheeled around.

Ghost stood over the cop.

What was left of the cop.

From chin to breastbone, there was only a red ruin. Blood dripped from Ghost's jaws, and in his eyes I saw only wolf. Primal, feral, victorious.

His eyes snapped toward the other two men.

The guy whose jaw had been blown off was thrashing and screaming in a muted parody of a human voice. He might live, but interrogating him was for shit.

That left the second guy I'd shot.

He lay on the floor, hands clamped to the bullet hole in his gut. There was no exit wound, which meant that the round was still in him. He was in terrible pain. Gut shot. Hurts like a mother. Ask anyone.

My sympathy level for him was a few hundred miles below don't-give-a-shit. He could see that in my eyes. I could tell, because I could see the fear expanding in his eyes as I stalked toward him. Ghost crept forward with me, his muzzle wrinkled, bloody drool falling from between his titanium teeth.

The killer knew he was in trouble that went a lot farther down a dark road than a bullet in his brisket. He could see the killer in my head glaring at him. I could tell, because I could see the awareness of it blossom in his eyes.

"Who are you?" I asked.

Not in English. In Farsi.

"Who do you work for? Who did this?"

He licked his lips and shook his head.

"Is there another bomb?" I yelled.

He told me to go fuck a camel. He said it in a way that suggested the camel was also my mother.

I put the tip of my knife against the ragged edge of the bullet wound. Just laid it there, and looked at him while I did it.

"Do you want me to be creative?" I asked.

That's an inexact translation. What I said is probably closer to "Do you want me to do magic?"

He did not. His line of bullshit and resistance only went so far, and then it was he and I in a small room, and we both knew I could make his last minutes on earth last for a thousand years.

He said five words. One short sentence. One name.

The sentence was eloquent in its simplicity.

"It's too late."

And then he clamped his jaws shut. I heard the crunch and knew it for what it was, what it had to be.

Bloody foam bubbled from between his lips. It smelled like bitter almonds.

Hollow tooth.

Suicide capsule.

Cyanide.

Shit.

He went rigid and then collapsed back.

Dead as dead will ever get.

"It's too late."

As much as those words terrified me, it was the name that made it all so much worse.

The name hung burning in the air. Two words that explained everything and told me nothing.

Two words that scared the living hell out of me.

Two terrible words.

"Seven Kings."

Chapter Thirty-eight

I staggered to my feet and began hunting through the room, looking for something very bad. Something with a timer.

I tore open every cabinet, every closet, every drawer. I upended the table. I slashed the sofa cushions and smashed the doors on the trophy case. I looked everywhere a bomb could be hidden.

And found nothing.

Then I started going through the clothes of each man.

That's when I found the device.

Not a bomb. In the pocket of the dead cop, I found a compact and very powerful jammer. Ultrasophisticated. The kind that would link to many smaller relay stations that were probably placed all around the stadium. In trash cans, stuck to the undersides of seats. Didn't matter where they were. They were here and this device controlled them.

On the front of it was a digital counter. A timer.

Ticking down from 305.

304.

303.

Ticking down to what?

I held the device out so Ghost could sniff it, but he had no reaction. If it was a bomb, he'd make a certain small whuff. So, it wasn't a bomb.

It was a jammer.

Which is another way of saying that it was a transmitter.

Icy sweat began running down my spine. When it reached zero, it could do a couple of things. The only good thing I could imagine would be for it to cancel the jamming signal.

I did not believe for one second that this would do only that.

It could also blast out a signal to explosive devices planted in the building. Secondary bombs.

Or . . .

The SWAT guys came crashing through the door, guns out, screaming at me to drop my weapons, to get down on the ground.

"No!" I yelled. "Federal agent. There's another bomb."

They weren't even listening. Two of them grabbed me and slammed me down onto the floor. Ghost began barking, and I had to scream at the top of my voice to keep him back. To order him to lie down. If he didn't obey at once, they would have killed him. Guaranteed.

Ghost looked like he wanted to take them all on. Maybe it was shock or doggy adrenaline, or maybe he was as batshit crazy as me.

"Down!" I shrieked. "Ghost—down now."

He finally sank down. Two SWAT shooters had guns on him, ready to kill. A bad day could have gotten a whole lot worse if they tried.

"Federal agent," I said, over and over again, raising my hands. "We don't have time for this shit."

"Shut up," snapped one of them and kicked me in the ribs. Hard. Ghost nearly came off the ground at him, but I bellowed him back. Then I craned my head and snarled at the man who'd kicked me. "There's a fucking bomb about to go off, asshole. If it does and anyone dies, I'm holding you responsible for it. I will fucking kill you, do you understand me?"

If he was impressed, it was impossible to tell through the mask, goggles, and helmet.

An officer suddenly pushed his way into the room. He knelt in front of me.

"What's your name?" he barked.

"Captain Joe Ledger," I said. "Your name is Hooper. You were told about me. Listen to me, lieutenant. There is another bomb in this building. See that device? That's a timer. It's counting down. We have to stop dicking around and find it."

He gave me exactly one second of appraisal, and then he grabbed my arm and hauled me to my feet.

"Where is it?"

I snatched up the timer. It said 58.

57.

56.

I said, "I don't know. We have to find it."

The jammer was still working.

Their radios were as dead as mine.

We all left the room at a breakneck run.

But we all knew that we were already too late.

We tried.

We really tried.

I don't actually remember the blast. They call it traumatic amnesia. The effect of traumatic shock on the brain. My only splinter of memory was of something white. Just that. A big, white nothing.

I closed my eyes to avoid the glare.

When I opened my eyes, I was in a hospital.

Chapter Thirty-nine

UC San Diego Medical Center

200 West Arbor Drive

San Diego, California

March 29, 3:19 P.M.

Toys saw Junie Flynn at the end of the hall. She was in an ICU unit, behind a big pane of tempered glass, standing beside a hospital bed. There were two soldiers standing guard outside the room. Toys recognized one of them.

Chief Petty Officer Lydia Ruiz.

Lydia recognized him, too.

She said something to the other soldier and then came hurrying down the hall to intercept Toys. She had a rifle slung on her shoulder and a look of complete contempt on her face. It turned her pretty face into something ugly and ferocious.

"Lydia—" began Toys, but she cut him off with a vicious two-handed shove that slammed him in the chest and knocked him against a wall.

"*Chingate,*" she snarled. "*Yo cago en la leche de tu puta madre.*"

Lydia got right up in his face. Her hot spit dottled his cheeks and mouth.

"Listen to me, I—"

"*Bésame el culo, maricón.*"

"If you're going to call me a faggot," he said, "at least have the courtesy to do it in English so there's no misunderstanding."

Lydia grabbed two fistfuls of his shirt, pulled him off the wall, and slammed him back again. She was very strong and very fast. In another time and place, when Toys was a different person, he might have risen to this challenge. He might have wanted to make her eat her words. To make her earn the power she was trying to show him. Toys was a pacifist now, but he had been a killer for most of his life. Ruthless, efficient, and cold.

Even now, he had to fight to keep his balled fists down, pressed against his thighs, shackled by will so that he did not commit another sin. Even the sin of defending himself.

"Lydia!" called a voice, and they both turned to see Junie Flynn hurrying down the hallway, her face grave with concern. "What are you doing?"

"I don't know," said Lydia with a nasty smile. "I'm thinking of dragging this *pinche puta* in the stairwell to see if I can bounce him all the way down to the first floor."

Junie reached out and caught Lydia's wrist. "Don't."

"You got other business, Junie," said Lydia. "Let me——"

Junie stepped very close, forcing enough of herself between Lydia and Toys so that the DMS soldier had to look at her. "I am ordering you to let him go."

Lydia blinked at her. "Ordering? Excuse me, *Miss* Flynn, I know that you're the captain's lady, but this is a DMS matter."

"No, this is a FreeTech matter. I am the director of that company. Toys works for me and with me, and that is by a special arrangement made by Mr. Church. I know that Joe disapproves, but this is no more his call to make than it is yours. Toys is under *my* protection. Let him go right now, or I will have you removed from this detail."

Lydia stared at her. So did Toys.

In the space of a few seconds, Junie Flynn seemed to grow to fill the hallway. Her voice was no longer the soft, almost passive and conciliatory one she generally used. Now it was filled with authority. It was filled with command. And with an absolute confidence in that command.

Lydia Ruiz held her stare for three full seconds. Then, with a grunt of disgust, she shoved Toys away from her. The young man thumped into the wall and nearly fell, but Junie darted out a hand and caught him under the armpit. She pulled him upright but then shifted her hand to the front of his shoulder, holding him gently but firmly against the wall.

Then Junie turned more fully toward Lydia. "This is a misunderstanding.

A difference of opinion. Tell me, Lydia, are we going to have a problem between us now, or are we done with it?"

It took Lydia a few seconds to orchestrate her response. She sighed and stepped back.

"No, ma'am."

"Don't give me that 'ma'am' crap," said Junie with half a smile. "I don't like being called that any more than Aunt Sallie does. I'm asking you a serious question, and I would like the courtesy of an honest answer. Are we done with this?"

Lydia nodded slowly, then said it aloud. "We're done with it."

"Good. And . . . thank you."

She pulled Toys off the wall and gently pushed him toward Circe's room.

Lydia Ruiz stood her ground and watched them go. Then, after a moment, she followed.

Chapter Forty

Tanglewood Island
Pierce County, Washington
March 30, 11:52 A.M.

"You need to rest," said Pharos as he bent over the bed to check the tubes and wires.

"Leave me alone, damn you," snapped the Gentleman. "I'll rest when I'm dead."

"I dare say," murmured Pharos, "but unless you'd rather that be sooner than later, you'll rest now."

"I can't."

"Of course you can. This is over for now."

"Over? Over?" The burned man tried his best to come out of that bed. To grab his doctor by the throat. To throttle the man. Instead, he twitched and wheezed, and his grasping hands closed around nothing. He sagged back, gasping, sweaty, defeated, but still filled with anger. "It's not fucking over. He's still alive. Christ, what does it take to kill one man? We've killed thousands. Tens of thousands. We brought down the sodding Towers. Why can't we kill him?"

Pharos pulled his chair close to the bed and sat down. "So we had a little bad luck. Let it go. I mean, look at what you've accomplished today. You've struck them above the heart. You've hurt them so deeply. This is the kind of injury that will never really heal. Do you think there will ever be a ball game, a concert, an event in which the echo of this won't be felt? Metal detectors, heightened security, paranoia, a loss of fun, a diminution of innocence and cultural arrogance. You've carved your mark into them. They will be talking about this day for a hundred years."

The Gentleman spat. He tried to spit in Pharos's face, but he lacked the lung capacity for that kind of velocity. The lump of yellow phlegm landed on the Gentleman's chest.

Pharos sighed, took a tissue from the dispenser on the bedside table, and wiped it up.

"You are going to win," he said as he crumpled the tissue and dropped it into a waste can. "Don't you realize that? You're going to win. That's your genius, my friend. That's why we all love you."

"Win?" the burned man stared at him, half smiling. "I sometimes wonder which of us is more insane. I've been through trauma, so at least I have an excuse. What's yours? Is this some congenital thing or have you been taking some of Doctor Rizzo's special cocktails?"

"I—"

"How can you think, after all this time, that I give a tinker's damn about winning? Look at me. What good is winning going to be for me?"

"I—"

"Sure, some of you will win. You'll stroll off with billions. So will any of the senior management who are still alive when it's all over. And how bloody nice for you. If that's what you mean by 'winning,' then please have the sense and courtesy not to include me in it. It's rude, and it's insensitive to brag to a dying man that you're going to spend the rest of your life— the years and years you have in front of you—spending all that lovely money. Buying yachts. Getting laid by models and movie stars. Living big. And note that the operative word is living, you miserable prick." The burned man shook his head. "That's your victory, and it doesn't matter one drop to me. How can you not know that? More importantly, how could you have worked for Hugo Vox and the Seven Kings for so many years and not understand what this is?"

Pharos was silent for several moments. Then he said, "I'm sorry."

But the burned man only sneered. "I don't want your apology, Pharos. And I sure as shit don't want your pity. All I want from you is understanding."

Pharos rubbed his eyes and nodded. "I do understand."

"Do you?"

"Yes."

"Then say it. Tell me what I want from this. Tell me what I need from this. Tell me what I will have from this." Spit flew from the melted lips with each word. "Say it, goddamn you."

Pharos said it.

The word.

The single word that meant so much to the Gentleman. A word that had meant nearly as much to Hugo Vox, and to so many of the Kings.

A single word that was the ugliest and most damaging word in the entire dictionary of global politics. A word that must beat like a drum inside the head of creatures like Father Nicodemus. An insane word that held only horrors for Pharos but that meant everything to this dying lump of burned flesh.

He said, "Chaos."

Chapter Forty-one

UC San Diego Medical Center
200 West Arbor Drive
San Diego, California
March 30, 11:54 A.M.

Toys stood in the corner of Circe's room and looked at the woman's chest rising and falling. Her face was totally slack, and if it wasn't for that subtle movement and the pinging insistence of the machines, he would have thought she was dead. Her olive skin had turned a jaundiced yellow. Pale and papery. Her black curls were disordered into tangles of black wire by sweat and trauma.

Junie Flynn sat holding her hand.

Without turning, she asked, "Earlier, on the phone, you tried to tell me something. What was it?"

"Oh, it's probably nothing," said Toys, keeping his voice down to a whisper. Like talking in church. "I should never have called."

"No, tell me."

He licked his lips, stalling as he thought it through. "Um . . . before, when I was with . . . you know . . . "

"Before when? When you were working for Sebastian Gault or when you were living with Hugo Vox?"

She said it bluntly, and it let him know two things about her. First, that she knew a lot about his past, which didn't surprise him. Church had to have told her his background before asking her to take him on in Free-Tech. Fair enough. The second thing, though, was how matter-of-fact she was. She stated facts but didn't front-load them with judgment. He couldn't build a list of people in his life who were able to speak to him without judgment. Certainly no one in the DMS. Even Violin, who liaised with FreeTech, treated him as if he were a hairy little bug. And that was fair enough, too.

Not Junie, though.

She was different.

Though Toys couldn't tell if it was compassion or simply a mind that ran on pragmatism rather than bias.

"Tell me," she urged.

Toys opened his mouth to tell her all of it, but at that moment the bedside phone rang. Junie picked it up, listened, said, "Thank God!"

"What is it?" asked Toys.

Junie put the handset down. "That was Sam Imura down in the lobby. Rudy just got here. He's on his way up."

Part Three
Deus ex Machina

It has become appallingly obvious that our
technology has exceeded our humanity.

—ALBERT EINSTEIN

Interlude Eleven

Caren Fallowfield was texting and parking, but she wasn't driving.

The car was doing that for her.

She typed furiously to her best friend, Meka, who was already inside Princess Hands having French tips put on. Caren's car was working its way into a slot outside. The senior dance was tonight. Both girls had devastating dresses. Meka had one in electric blue with a hint of sparkles that made it shimmer when she turned. There was a tulle sheathing that turned the blue magic of it into smoky mystery. Caren, who had the better figure and they both knew it, went with a red that was so dark it looked black except where it stretched over bust line and hips. And the neckline plunged so far down that she was going to have to use a lot of tape to keep from giving everyone a show. The dress was show enough, thank you very much.

> **MEKA:** I CAN SEE U! U GOT UR CAR WASHED. SO PRETTY!
>
> **CAREN:** LOVE LOVE LOVE THIS CAR!!
>
> **MEKA:** YOU GOT THE HOTS FOR A TRANSFORMER
>
> **CAREN:** :P

The onboard system did not require anything from her. The sensors judged the distance to the cars in front and back, to the curb, and to the traffic whipping past. It made all the necessary calculations in a microsecond and began shifting gears and turning the silver machine at a sedate rate of speed. It was a tight spot that Caren would never have attempted without Optimus Prime, which is what she called it.

MEKA: HURRY UP. SAVED U A CHAIR.

CAREN: OP IS GOING AS FAST AS HE CAN.

MEKA: SLOW BUT RELIABLE. UNLIKE SOMEONE I COULD NAME.

CAREN: DON'T START. JACEN'S GETTING BETTER.

MEKA: HE'S A HORNDOG.

CAREN: SO?

MEKA: :)

The car stopped.

Suddenly and with a jolt. The cell phone fell from Caren's hand, and for a moment she was torn between looking to see what was wrong and grabbing for her phone. She looked around. The car was stopped halfway into the spot. Caren checked the car in front. Still parked, no one in it. She looked in the rearview to see if Optimus had stopped to let the car behind pull out. But it was empty, too.

She tapped the button for the voice controls.

"Continue parking."

"*I will continue to park,*" replied the silky female machine voice.

The car did not move.

Caren snatched her phone up and waited. Nothing.

Another tap on the button. "Continue parking," she said again. With irritation, spacing each syllable.

"*I will continue to park.*"

Nothing happened.

Caren's phone tinkled, indicating a new text.

MEKA: ???

CAREN: STUPID CAR

The car suddenly moved.

Caren huffed out a breath that was half relief and half lingering annoyance.

The car changed its angle to the curb, picking one that much sharper. Caren frowned but did not interfere. She was, she knew, a terrible parker. She could drive as well as anyone, she believed, but parking was not her thing. And not in spots this tight. Optimus was always good at it, so she trusted him. If he needed a different angle, even one that didn't make sense to her, then that was fine. Everything was fine if she could get out of the damn car and inside to get her nails done. They had a dark red polish that would go perfectly with the vampire-red dress. The polish shade was called Secret Passion.

That was fine, because maybe tonight Jacen was going where no man had gone before. The Victoria's Secret thong she had in a bag in the back-seat might see the light of—well, night—if everything went well. Jacen wasn't the sharpest or most reliable guy in the world, but he looked like Theo James and she'd seen him in his gymnastic tights, so there was that. Those tights left nothing to the imagination. She was pretty sure the reason he was called the Hammer had nothing to do with what he did on the rings or uneven bars.

The rear wheel tapped the curb and the car rocked gently. That deepened Caren's frown. The auto-park system wasn't supposed to hit curbs. Ever. That was one of the selling points. She'd read the brochure before she talked her dad into buying it for her. Safer parking. No tire damage. All that.

CAREN: OP'S GETTING WEIRD ON ME.
MEKA: MEN. WHAT CAN I SAY?

Then something happened that shifted Caren from doubt and annoyance to nervousness.

The engine revved.

Like hitting the curb, it should never do that.

Except that it did. She saw the little needle that indicated RPMs swing way up and then drop down. Up and down. Then up and farther up. The engine roar filled the cabin.

"Stop," she commanded. Nothing happened.

Then she remembered that she had to hit the button. She punched it.

"Stop."

"*Stopping.*"

The engine revved even louder. The whole car was vibrating with the power. Smoke plumed up from the tailpipe. Caren saw people stopping to stare at her. She flushed with embarrassed anger.

Caren punched the button again. "Stop auto-park."

"Auto-park disengaged," said the silky voice. Pleasant. Always pleasant. The engine roar increased.

"Stop!" yelled Caren, banging on the button. "Stop auto-park."

"Auto-park disengaged."

The radio suddenly switched up. It began cycling through the preset channels as the volume rose from her usual setting of sixteen to twenty-five, to forty-five, to a screaming and intolerable maximum that blasted everything from her except a shriek.

The steering wheel turned sharply to the left, pointing the wheels away from the curb.

The engine roared.

The radio was a sonic wail so loud that it was no longer music.

Caren's scream was buried inside that cacophony.

Then the autonomous system released the brakes, and the car shot away from the curb and into a narrow gap between the Toyota Camry that had just passed and the UPS truck that was following at forty miles an hour.

Caren tried to hit the brakes.

The brake functions had been disabled by the onboard computer.

There was no time for the truck to stop.

The right front bumper of the truck hit the driver's door at full speed. All those tons of metal punched the door inward against Caren. The air-bag did not deploy, its circuits having been switched off by the computer. The seat belt held Caren in place, so all the colliding steel, aluminum, fiberglass, and safety glass had nowhere else to go.

In the same instant across America, twenty-three thousand vehicles with autonomous systems malfunctioned. Parked cars started in lots and garages and slammed into walls and other cars. Vehicles on streets and highways accelerated or simply switched to park while traveling at road speed. Scores of them hurtled at other cars as if the machines themselves had suddenly gone into a suicidal frenzy.

Chapter Forty-two

"Hey, Boss," said a voice. "Welcome back to the land of the living."

I heard him before I saw a face. But I knew who it was.

I pried open one eye.

The man seated in the visitors' chair looked like a taller, broader, more muscular version of Thor from the comic-book movies. He wore black BDU pants, boots, and a charcoal-gray T-shirt that was a size too small for his bulk. The slogan on the shirt read STERCUS FIT. Latin for "Shit Happens." He had a pair of wayfarers pushed up on his blond hair. His youthful face was creased with concern and offset by a smile that was one part stress, one part exhaustion, and two parts false good humor. He'd been eating Chinese noodles from a white cardboard takeout container. He lowered his chopsticks and smiled at me.

"Bunny . . ." I croaked. Even to my own ears, my voice sounded like an old man's. "Where—?"

"Jefferson Hospital in Philly," said Bunny. "It's tomorrow."

"Huh?"

"That shitstorm at the ballpark? That was yesterday." He looked at his watch. "It's four eighteen in the afternoon of the thirtieth. You've been out for about a full day."

He jabbed the chopsticks deep into the container and set it on the night table.

"Glad to see you awake, though. Been sweating large-caliber bullets waiting to see if you were going to wake up."

"How bad am I?"

"Probably not as bad as you're gonna feel, Boss. Mild concussion, but your skull isn't cracked. I could make a joke about hard heads."

"But you won't 'cause you don't want to die young."

"Which is my point," he said, nodding. "Let's see what else. You have about a zillion small cuts. Thirty stitches here and there. Mostly those faggy little butterfly stitches except for the ones on your forearm. All the rest is bruising. The doctor said he had never seen someone with a bruised liver, pancreas, and spleen before. Not a living person, he meant. Said he usually only sees that stuff in autopsies of people who were run over by cars."

"Lucky me."

"Yeah," said Bunny, this time with no trace of humor. "Lucky you. Lot of people weren't so lucky."

It took me a few seconds to understand what that meant. I had been going on the assumption that I'd been hurt on a mission, but the jumbled pieces of memory began falling back into place a piece at a time.

The ballpark.

The drones.

The bombs.

"Jesus Christ, Bunny," I said, and tried to sit up, to get out of bed, to find clothes.

He got up and body-blocked me. Not that it took a lot. I was empty. No strength at all. I sagged back.

"The bomb?" I asked.

Bunny raised his eyebrows. "Which one?"

"The last one. The timer."

"Oh," he said tiredly, and there was such deep bitterness in his voice. "Yeah. It wasn't one bomb. It was seven of them. In trash cans in different places. Near the exits that the EMTs and emergency trucks were using."

"God."

"Forty-three dead. The bombs were there to hit the emergency responders. Tack those deaths on to what the drones did . . . shit . . . it's so goddam awful."

"How . . . how many all told?" I asked.

He leaned forward to rest his elbows on his knees. "Two hundred and thirty-four dead. At least thirty-eight of them were people who got trampled to death trying to get away from the drones. They're still sifting through rubble. There are a bunch unaccounted for, but we don't yet know if they're buried or just haven't reported in with anyone if they got out. Eight hundred and sixty hospitalized. Fifty on the critical list. Another thousand or so treated and released. Every hospital in the region is jammed."

If he'd grabbed me by the front of my hospital gown and punched me with all of his strength, it wouldn't have hit as hard or hurt me as much. I closed my eyes and tried to will myself back into unconsciousness.

I asked the question I was afraid to ask. "My dad?"

"He's going to be okay. Caught some flying debris, a few cuts. He's at U of P. He keeps calling. But those fuckers killed Colonel Douglas, too."

It felt like there wasn't enough air in the room. Douglas. My god.

"What about Rudy? And Ghost?"

"Ghost's at the vet's. He's banged up like you, but he'll be okay. Rudy's good, but, um . . . "

"What is it?" I asked sharply.

"Look, Boss, Rudy's on a plane to San Diego. Actually, he's probably there by now, or just about. It's, um, his wife. She's in the hospital."

"Circe? Why? What's wrong? It's too early for the baby—"

"Details are way sketchy, but Bug said that she was house hunting with Junie and she collapsed. She's totally out of it. I don't know if it's a coma or what. With all the shit that happened here, it's hard to get straight intel. The doctors are running a bunch of tests, but they don't know exactly what's wrong."

"The baby?"

"No, it's good. She didn't miscarry or anything like that. It's just that she's unconscious. But . . . here's the kicker, Boss, and this is the part that's messing a lot of people up."

"Do I want to know?"

"I doubt it," he said, "'cause it's some weird-ass shit. But based on the timing of Junie's call to 911, Circe collapsed at the same time as the bomb went off in Philly. And I mean the same exact time. Down to the second."

I stared at him. And then I tried to get the hell out of that damn bed.

Bunny put a hand on the flat of my sternum and pushed me right back down. Under ordinary circumstances, he's twice as strong as me. Right then, he was Godzilla and I was Bambi.

"Take your hand off me, Sergeant, or so help me God I will—"

"Yeah, yeah, yeah, Boss. I'm under orders from Mr. Church to keep your ass in bed, and in bed is where your ass is staying. End of discussion. I can get some help in here and can put restraints on you."

I called him a bastard and a bunch of other things. He took it and he held me down and he waited me out. Finally I sagged back, exhausted and hurt. When Bunny met my eyes, I let out a breath and nodded. He removed his hand and stepped back.

"What the hell's going on?" I demanded.

"Yeah, well, we're all real short on answers. Kind of our thing lately. Our new logo's pretty much, 'The DMS: We Don't Know Shit.'"

"Hey, does Junie know what happened out here?"

"Everyone knows. There's no other story on the news. Don't worry, though, Top called her, and so did the Big Guy. Told her you were okay, just scuffed up a bit. She's still in California with Circe. I think she tried to come out here, but there's a no-fly zone around Philly right now except for military craft. We sent Rudy out on *Shirley* 'cause your bird's got an all-access pass. Besides . . . the Big Man wanted her to stay with Circe. I guess he didn't think you'd mind."

"No . . . no, of course not."

Bunny sat back down. "Boss, do you know anything 'bout what happened? Beyond what you told Bug and Mr. Church before you went looking for that jammer?"

"I keep seeing pieces of it in my head," I admitted, rubbing my eyes. "But that's all it is. Pieces. Debris. It's hard to put it together."

"You got anything?" persisted Bunny. "Even something small just so we can start doing something other than sitting around with our thumbs up our asses."

"I'm trying as hard as I can."

"Try harder," said a voice.

Bunny and I turned to see a tall broad-shouldered man standing in the doorway. Three-thousand-dollar suit, quiet tie, tinted glasses, face devoid of all humor and tolerance.

Mr. Church.

Chapter Forty-three

Citizens Bank Park
Philadelphia
March 30, 4:20 P.M.

There were hundreds of them now.

More came all the time.

They'd begun arriving within an hour of the attack.

The first wave had been gawkers, drawn like flies to the smoke and flame, to the echo of screams, to the possibility of seeing the kinds of things they usually only saw on TV.

That was the first wave, and some of them were still there.

The second wave was different.

They arrived more slowly, moving tentatively toward the stadium. They stopped at the police barricades. Most of them said nothing, even to their own companions.

They brought flowers.

They brought photos in frames.

They brought candles.

A few brought toys. Teddy bears and dolls that would never again be cuddled. A baseball glove. A hooded sweatshirt with a middle school logo. A birthday present that had been wrapped but would remain unopened.

There was no plan, no agreement. The first of the people in this second wave showed up before midnight. She knelt and placed her flowers on the pavement. Out of the way of the emergency vehicles. She arranged the flowers so that the brightly colored petals were toward the building. That seemed to matter to her. She was unaware of the tears that fell like rain. The ache in her chest was too big, the chasm in her soul too deep to pay attention to anything as mundane as tears.

She got to her feet and . . . stood there.

Just stood.

Two people joined her a few minutes later. Grandparents who walked on unsteady feet, bearing the impossible weight of loss. Loss of son and daughter-in-law. Of grandson. Nothing in their lives had prepared them for the magnitude of this burden. They laid their flowers near the first bunch and stood staring with eyes empty of all hope and optimism. Too shocked to cry.

Others came. Alone. In pairs. Sometimes in a group that clung together and wept and sometimes screamed.

By noon of the following day, there were more than a hundred of them.

They stood without speaking.

Hours crawled by. The police and firefighters saw them and tried not to meet their eyes. No one tried to move them. No one wanted to engage them.

Twice, reporters tried to interview them, but a police officer working the barricade growled them back. Her rage was so towering that even the sound-bite-hungry ghouls of the press shrank back. They didn't leave, though. The reporters aimed their cameras from a distance and did their stand-ups and drank the pain.

The people gathered around the mound of flowers did not care. Most of them did not even notice.

They lingered because they had nowhere else to go.

Not anymore.

The paths of their lives seemed to have led here.

And ended here.

Chapter Forty-four

UC San Diego Medical Center
200 West Arbor Drive
San Diego, California
March 30, 4:21 P.M.

The receptionist at the front desk was a bright-eyed Asian woman with lots of colorful cloisonné flowers pinned to her sweater. Her name tag read CAROL. She looked up as the small man approached. She hadn't seen him enter the hospital. The man was bent and old, with a deeply seamed face and a tan topcoat over black clothes.

"Hello," she said brightly, "may I help you?"

"Yes, indeed," said the man in a soft southern accent. He loosened the belt of his coat and let it fall open to reveal the black shirt and white collar of a priest. This was done casually, without drama. "I'm here to see Reverend Sykes. Do I need a visitors' pass for that?"

Beverly Sykes was the interfaith chaplain at the medical center.

"Oh, no, not at all."

The priest looked around. There were two city policemen standing by the elevators. City police, and with them was one of the hospital's security guards.

"Is there something wrong?" asked the old priest. "Something going on?"

"Oh, don't worry about that. It's nothing," Carol said, lying easily.

The priest studied the officers for a moment and then turned to look at her. He had the strangest eyes. She couldn't tell if they were brown or green. And his smile, though friendly, was odd in a way Carol could not explain. Later, when police and federal agents interrogated her about this encounter, she would not be able to explain the feelings she got from that smile. All she knew was that it "wasn't right."

That's how she felt about it.

The smile was simply not right. No sir.

Carol would dream about that smile. For years.

But the feeling that the smile was somehow wrong increased with time after she'd given him directions to the chapel and watched him walk down the hall. It wasn't until he was out of sight that she felt her mouth turn into a frown. It surprised her, because the man had neither said nor done anything unusual.

But that smile.

That smile.

Carol Chang had not had a drink in seventeen months.

But for the rest of the day she thought about the bottle of tequila she was going to buy on the way home. That thought was the only thing that kept her from screaming.

Chapter Forty-five

Thomas Jefferson University Hospital

Philadelphia, Pennsylvania

March 30, 4:30 P.M.

"Sergeant Rabbit," said Church, "give us the room. No visitors."

"Yes, sir." Bunny exited and closed the door behind him.

Church picked up my medical chart and browsed it, nodded to himself, rehung it on the end of my bed, and then sat down. "Are you lucid?" he asked.

"Don't you mean, 'How are you, Joe? I'm delighted to see that you're not crippled or dead'?"

He crossed his legs and gave me a long, flat stare. I was welcome to interpret anything I wanted from it. Assuming it was an outpouring of the warm fuzzies would probably be my weakest guess.

"I'm fine," I said. "I want to get out of here so I can start hunting these—"

"Hunting whom, exactly?"

"Whoever's doing this. Bombs here, and whatever's happening to Circe."

He held up a hand. "First, Circe is receiving the best medical care possible. I have experts flying in from eleven countries. Friends of mine."

I looked at him, searching for some flicker of humanity. Circe was, after all, his daughter, his only blood relative as far as I knew. His other daughter and her mother had both died violent deaths, and I was one of the few who knew that their murders had been perpetrated by people who were trying to get to Church. He had many enemies, and many of them would stop at nothing—truly nothing—to break or weaken him. So far, all that those murderous bastards have accomplished was to strengthen an already-iron resolve. I don't know what happened to those killers, but I do not believe for one moment that they are still alive. I also suspect that they died in very bad ways.

Not that revenge brought back the dead or healed a broken heart. And Church's heart had to have been broken. Over and over again. Rudy has tried for years to decode this man, to unlock the mysteries of his emotional and psychological makeup. Since Rudy is a doctor and a man of great personal honor, he hasn't shared with me his professional insights.

"How is she?" I asked.

"She is undergoing tests and appears to be stable. That's all they can tell me at the moment."

"You going out?"

He took a moment on that. "As soon as I can."

"Bunny told me about the timing. That can't be a coincidence."

There was the slightest curl of his lip at my use of the word "coincidence." He detests coincidences. They offend logic. For him, everything is cause and effect.

"We do not yet know how the two incidents are related. Now, as to that, what can you tell me? What is the last thing you remember? Walk me through it."

I did my best. My last clear memory was standing with my dad out in centerfield. I remember telling Church about the drones and the guys I'd fought in the hallway. And about the jammer. And . . .

Something flickered past the window of my mind. I stopped talking. Church waited, letting me work through it. I raised my right arm and looked at the thick bandage wrapped around it. When Bunny had mentioned the stitches there, I hadn't reacted beyond thinking they'd come from the same source as my other injuries. The drone explosions. Now, though . . .

"I think I was in a fight," I said. "A second one, not the one I called to tell you about. Bunny told me about bombs connected to the jammer. That's all tangled up in my head. I thought he was saying it wrong. But he wasn't, was he?"

"No."

"Bug located the jammer, right? And I . . . went to find it. Me and Ghost."

"And—?"

It was coming back, bit by bit.

"I did. But there were five men. Four paramedics. One cop." I told him about using my father's gun. About fighting one of the men. As I recalled and told him one detail, another would emerge. Until I got to the point where I knelt over a dying man and asked him to tell me . . .

And he did.

I sat bolt upright.

"Jesus Christ," I hissed, gasping in pain and shock.

"What is it, Captain? What did he tell you?"

And it was suddenly all in my head. Every last detail. "I know who's behind this."

"Tell me."

"The Seven Kings," I said.

Chapter Forty-six

UC San Diego Medical Center

200 West Arbor Drive

San Diego, California

March 30, 4:31 P.M.

Toys sat cross-legged on the floor beside Junie's chair. There was another visitors' chair available, but it was the one Rudy had been using. Toys felt awkward taking it, even temporarily. He had a Diet Coke resting in the circle formed by his legs and was chewing on a plastic straw.

Rudy was off trying to get his head straight.

Good luck with that, mate, mused Toys. *This bloody thing makes no sense at all.*

It was true. Toys was not a scientist or doctor, but he'd been Sebastian Gault's right-hand man for years, and Gault had been one of the world's most brilliant pharmacologists. Toys had also spent considerable time—albeit reluctantly—with Amirah, Gault's former lover and the head of his science division. Toys had been there for most of the serious discussions about the development of the *seif al din* pathogen. He had a solid working knowledge of medicine and could generally follow even the more arcane conversations between doctors. However, listening to the medical team here go through the battery of tests they'd performed on Circe, it was clear that there was simply no answer. None of their tests could begin to explain why a healthy young woman like her should collapse and then slide into a coma. So far, the tests supported the one encouraging bit of knowledge—that the baby Circe carried appeared to be unaffected.

But Circe was circling the drain, Toys was sure of it.

Rudy had taken the news very hard. He was already worn thin from having actually been at the ballpark during the drone attack. Now this, plus the strain of a cross-country flight in a military transport jet.

The room was quiet except for the machine noises.

Junie sat with her eyes closed, either sleeping or meditating. Toys couldn't tell.

He wanted to close his own eyes and drift away, but he dared not. Someone had to keep eyes on Circe.

Even as he thought that, he knew it was an irrational thought. Circe was in a hospital, hooked to every kind of monitor in the catalog. There were nurses and doctors coming by every few minutes. There were armed DMS agents standing outside the door.

The place couldn't be safer.

Nothing could possibly happen here.

But as he thought that, an older version of him whispered ugly secrets into his ear. Six years ago, the Seven Kings had launched their Ten Plagues Initiative in a hospital. In a manner of speaking.

They'd blown up the London Hospital.

Killing everyone inside. Darkening the skies over the old city.

Proving to everyone who stood on the street and watched or who followed the news on TV that there was nowhere—no place at all—that was truly safe from the Seven Kings.

Get out, whispered the old Toys. The malicious lackey of Sebastian Gault. The toady of Hugo Vox. The Toys who had been a killer and an enabler of killers. *Leave now. Get out before it happens. Get out before you die with these people.*

Toys raised his head and looked at Junie, her face lovely and serene, and at Circe, who struggled to stay alive, for herself and her baby.

"Leave . . . ?" he murmured, his voice as soft as a whisper.

Leave while you can. Save yourself.

Toys looked away, out the window at the scudding clouds.

"Never," he said. Then, a moment later, he repeated it. "Never."

Chapter Forty-seven

Thomas Jefferson University Hospital

Philadelphia, Pennsylvania

March 30, 4:34 P.M.

"The men you faced," said Church, "were they regular troops or Kingsmen?"

I had to think about that. The Seven Kings had used a lot of different kinds of fighters over the years, including security specialists—aka mercenaries—from Blue Diamond and other companies. But their elite shooters were called the Kingsmen. These were men trained to be as dangerous and capable as U.S. special forces operators. Most of the trainers and some of the soldiers were, in fact, former special ops players. Fighting them was how I imagined going to war against Echo Team might be.

I shook my head slowly. "Not Kingsmen. They were tough, but I took them out too easily."

Church called Aunt Sallie in Brooklyn to tell her about the confirmation that we were dancing with the Kings. She was on her way to her townhouse for fresh clothes because it looked like she'd be pulling back-to-back shifts at the main DMS headquarters, the Hangar. I overheard her say that she'd pass the info along, initiate the proper protocols and ring all the alarms.

Church ended the call. "Captain, I think we can now agree that this event is tied to what Echo Team discovered at the Resort."

"No kidding," I said sourly. "But it doesn't tell us who's running this. I mean, sure, the Seven Kings . . . but at last count all seven of them were dead. Who's filled their slots?"

Church shook his head. "To be determined. What concerns me most is their use of drone technology. We've had too many cases involving them. There have been some disturbing developments in the world of UAVs. Bug can explain it better than anyone, and I think you'll want to hear this."

Chapter Forty-eight

UC San Diego Medical Center
200 West Arbor Drive
San Diego, California
March 30, 4:39 P.M.

"There's really nothing you can do at this point, Doctor Sanchez."

The nurse wore one of those smiles that told Rudy what she really meant was "You're being an obstructive pain in the ass, but I can't say that because you're too important." The message was clear, though.

"I'd like to stay anyway," said Rudy.

The nurse shifted slightly to her left. She did not actually plant herself between him and the door to Circe's room, but the motion was every bit as eloquent as her smile.

"They're doing everything they can, doctor," insisted the nurse, "and they are the very best."

It was framed to leave no reasonable room for objection or argument.

Rudy, defeated, turned and trudged away, leaning heavily on his hawthorn cane. A thin, dour black man he didn't know very well followed him at a discreet distance. His name was Cowpers, and he'd met Rudy at the airport. A watchdog provided by Mr. Church. A new hire for the Pier. Rudy had tried to engage the man in conversation, but it had been a nonstarter. Cowpers was his minder, not his buddy.

So, with the lugubrious bodyguard in tow, he walked the halls of the hospital.

He hated to leave his wife.

Since flying out from the horrors at the Citizens Park disaster in Philadelphia, he had hardly been away from Circe for more than a few minutes. He was jet-lagged, traumatized, and frightened.

So terribly frightened.

He also felt like a coward for leaving Philadelphia. His specialty within psychology was trauma, and he knew that he was needed there. Probably more than he was needed here in California. People had died. People had experienced actual terror during and after the bombs. His best friend had nearly died. Rudy's place was out there, helping to address the wounds cut into the minds and hearts of all those people, including the hundreds of professionals and volunteers who were working around the clock to sift through the debris.

That's where he should be.

But that wasn't where he could be.

Circe was here in California. She was here, and their unborn baby was here.

And so Rudy was here.

For once—just this once—be damned to anyone and everyone else. It was a difficult thing for him to think, but it was his thought nonetheless. His family needed him more.

What, though, did they need him to do?

The doctors would not allow him to participate in the testing or research of her case. The conflict of interest was crystal clear, and although Rudy could mount superbly crafted arguments, he had no conversational foothold. They built a wall, with Circe on one side and him on the other.

So he drifted like a ghost. Wandering the halls with a silent killer for company.

Chapter Forty-nine

Thomas Jefferson University Hospital

Philadelphia, Pennsylvania

March 30, 4:42 P.M.

Church opened his laptop and tapped a key, and suddenly Bug's face filled the screen. Bug was brown, young, bespectacled, übernerdy, and smiling. He was born Jerome Taylor but called Bug by everyone, including his mother. He was a thirtysomething computer sorcerer and one of the most trusted people in the DMS. Church allows him—and only him—total access to the MindReader supercomputer. In the wrong hands, that computer could do untold harm. Catastrophic, and that's not a joke. Bug uses it to help Church and the Department of Military Sciences fight the good fight. It's possible that Bug believes MindReader to be a person, and it's also possible he's in love with it on a level that would be creepy for anyone else. Well, actually, it's kind of creepy even with him, but Bug is a friend, and he manages somehow to hold on to some of his innocence without being naive. That's a tough trick.

Then Church turned to Bug. "Tell Captain Ledger about the Regis program."

"The what?" I asked.

"Regis," said Bug, jumping right in, "is a variable-autonomous-operations-software package with military and nonmilitary applications. Developed by DARPA in conjunction with twelve independent contractors working with the Department of Defense. The first thing you have to know is that computer-network upgrades all across the Defense Department are about thirty years behind schedule, and something like seven or eight billion dollars overbudget. It's a mess. We have some jets with next years' avionics and some with stuff you couldn't run on a Commodore Sixty-four. The why of this is too complicated to go into."

"Budgets and bullshit. That part I do understand."

Church removed a package of vanilla wafers from his briefcase, selected one, and nibbled it.

"The problem," Bug continued, "is that we're so big it's hard to fix our own systems. Smaller countries can do it faster because there simply isn't as much to do. Which is frustrating, because we're seeing the arms race become like a dead heat. Not because we don't have the tech, which we do, but because of the logistics involved. And there are so many different kinds of tech—hardware and software—on any given ship, tank, plane, whatever, that we're also losing operational efficiency because these systems were designed by the lowest bidders and not built to work in peak harmony with other tech. You following, Joe?"

"Running with a limp, but yeah."

"Since it's faster and cheaper to install new software than to replace hardware, the Holy Grail of this whole process has been to develop a new kind of artificial intelligence that can recognize disharmonies between existing tech and write its own code for a workaround so that all software works in harmony."

"Wow. Sounds a little like MindReader."

"Similar design theory. A chameleonic system that creates a harmonic alliance with disparate systems."

"Wait," I said, "I think I actually understood that whole sentence."

Church shook his head and tapped crumbs from his cookie.

"Until a few years ago," continued Bug, "that master AI program was a pipe dream. Then someone figured it out. Aaron Davidovich, remember him?"

"Sure, the guy who was snatched in Ashdod a few years ago. Don't we think he's dead?"

"Probably," said Bug.

"Tell me again why we think that."

"Because," said Church, "if he was in captivity, there is a high likelihood that he would have been compelled to complete his design work for a foreign power or to build something new. In either case, his designs are so unique and advanced that they would have his fingerprints all over them. So far, nothing like that has appeared."

"So, he's probably dead," said Bug. "Point is that Davidovich's research was already being developed for active use by his team at DARPA. He called it Regis, but really it's three integrated combat systems and one alternate-use system. The first one, code-named Enact, was designed as a smart system backup for manned craft, mostly for instances when the pilot is incapacitated. That one will even try to land a plane—or ditch it safely—after a pilot has ejected. Enact will also interface with the avionics and weapons control systems in the event the pilot is doing something else. One scenario would be a pilot who is injured from battle or midair collision damage and needs to do immediate first aid like stopping arterial bleeding or reconnecting ruptured oxygen. Enact continues to fly the plane and will even, to a limited degree, attempt to complete the mission. It can be deliberately initiated by the pilot, remotely initiated by a ground station via satellite, or switched on if the jet's internal diagnostics deem it critical."

"Okay," I said.

"Then there's ComSpinner," continued Bug. "That's a true high-end, self-guidance system. This is the one they're installing in missile systems and automated combat satellites. Mostly the weapons are controlled from live operators, but in the event of a catastrophe like the destruction of the command center, the AI will continue to fight the battle."

"Um . . . that's kind of cool, and kind of sick and twisted."

Church merely smiled.

"The third program," Bug said, "is BattleZone. That's your true combat AI. It's what we're putting into drones that we need to operate outside of the range of human control or that are in the presence of jammers that would interfere with remote controls. For countries that can't afford a drone program, developing long-range, high-tech jammers is a growth industry. BattleZone is also being installed into fighters like the QF-16s, the QF-16X Pterosaur superdrones, and a few other birds. There's even a DoD group in Washington State working on adapting it to a bunch of Apache helicopters so they fly missions without human pilots."

"Oh, swell."

"Tell him the truly disturbing part," said Church.

"Wait—that isn't the disturbing part? Self-guiding warplanes?" I said weakly.

"Ah, well, that's the problem with modern cutting-edge tech," said Bug. "There's always something creepier in development. That's where we come to the alternate-use system. It's called SafeZone."

"I can't wait to hear this."

"Because of 9/11 and other hijackings, the Department of Defense is working with Homeland and the FAA to install SafeZone, which is a version of BattleZone, into every passenger jet. They've been doing it on the sly, supposedly so hijackers won't know it's there, but really it's because they know there'd be public pushback."

"Why install a battle program? I don't get it."

"It's not exactly the same system," Bug said quickly. "Say a plane deviates unexpectedly from its course. The assumption is either mechanical problems or hijacking. If the pilot is still in control, SafeZone requires him to enter a reset code within two minutes. If he doesn't—if, say, he's been hijacked—then SafeZone locks out the controls and flies the plane. It interfaces via coded link with air traffic controllers working for Homeland. The program will land the plane at whatever airfield Homeland dictates."

"That actually doesn't suck," I said.

Bug sighed. "There are countermeasures built into the system. This isn't public knowledge yet, and probably won't be unless it gets leaked. Or unless there's a technical glitch and it fires accidentally. Planes like Air Force One can deploy external countermeasures like flares to attract heat seekers. But SafeZone has internal countermeasures. It can modulate temperature and airflow inside the cabin."

"Jesus."

"It's supposed to limit the actions of hijackers without endangering innocent passengers. They wanted to install some kind of knockout gas, but that didn't fly. There would be lawsuits."

"There's going to be lawsuits anyway," I growled. "This is a bullshit idea."

Church nodded. "It has some obvious advantages, but there are too many holes in the operational philosophy. Typical of something designed by engineers at the behest of Congress but without the input of people experienced in the variables of field application."

"What he said," agreed Bug.

"I'm no technophobe," I said. "I love my gadgets—kind of—but giving over that much control to a bunch of ones and zeros does not seem like a particularly bright idea."

"Not even to me, and this stuff's kind of my religion," said Bug.

Church shook his head. "It's typical of a certain mind-set in both Congress and the military, where an improperly considered response is used because it's either quicker, faster, or cost-effective. Though, in this case, many of the contractors are tied to corporations and persons who have powerful lobbies. They are owned by companies that make sizable and regular campaign donations."

"Leaving working schlubs like us to clean up the mess when it goes wrong," I said.

Church smiled. "That is as workable a description as I've heard for the DMS charter."

I chewed on what Bug had told me. "This is what Davidovich was working on when he went missing? This weapons system?"

"It's not a weapons system in itself," said Bug. "It's only a piece of software that makes everything work more smoothly and efficiently. Something that gets all of the other bits of software that have been designed by, like, a thousand other people over the last forty years to talk to each other. Or, maybe, to put it better, it lets all the software talk in the same language. Once the complete installation is done, it's going to upgrade U.S. military efficiency by something like twenty-six percent."

Church said, "You see now why they moved forward with this?"

"Right," I said reluctantly, "it puts us back in front of the arms race."

"Way out in front," said Bug.

"Tell me, though, how thoroughly have they tested this stuff? I mean, what's the margin for error in field tests and—"

Church sighed.

Bug said, "It's been running at a field-efficiency rating of 99.001299 percent."

I stared at him. "That's . . . "

"Impossible? Pretty much. But we, um, borrowed a copy of Regis and ran it through MindReader. And I mean really ran it. It came up one hundred percent every single time. Joe, this is really amazing software. This is why everyone said that Davidovich was the Da Vinci, the Einstein, the Hawking of computers. No one—and I mean no one anywhere—has ever come up with anything half as good as this."

"Not even you?"

"Hey, I'm good, Joe. Maybe the top twenty in the world—"

"Top three," said Church quietly.

"But Davidovich was way, way out in front of all the rest of us. Guy was a social ground sloth and kind of an asshole to talk to, but he was the best of the best of the best. And Regis is work he started but didn't complete. Imagine what he would have come up with if he hadn't been killed."

"Yeah, I am imagining it, and I don't like it," I said. "I distrust perfection except in baseball pitching, craft beer, and short skirts. Otherwise . . . there's always something bad waiting to happen."

"You ever talk to Rudy about that paranoia?"

"Sadly," said Church, "Captain Ledger is frequently correct in his distrust of perfect models. How many times have we encountered a team who has bypassed unbreakable security? Or hacked untouchable defense computers?"

"Yeah, I guess," said Bug dubiously.

"Could someone have stolen Regis? Or made a copy and then used it to control the drones at the ballpark?"

"That's almost impossible," said Bug. "All copies of Regis are stamped with individual ID codes, and all copies are accounted for. And each individual software install has a built-in self-delete subroutine in case one of the planes or tanks falls into enemy hands. If anyone tries to copy or download it without the right permission codes, the CPU erases everything. Davidovich wouldn't have had either the erase or command codes, and even if he had, they'd have been changed the day he went missing, just as all of his DARPA remote-access and Web passwords were changed."

"Come on, Bug," I said, "Davidovich invented this thing, right? You telling me he couldn't have built in a trapdoor?"

"Back door," corrected Bug. "Sure, that's possible, but DARPA's had years to look for it, and they haven't found anything."

"Maybe," I said, taking a fresh swing at it, "if he's still alive, couldn't someone have forced him to re-create it for them?"

"Hey, Joe," said Bug quickly, "if you're asking if he could sit down and rewrite the entire Regis software package for someone else . . . then, no, that's crazy talk. Davidovich had fifty-some engineers working on different parts of it. We're not talking something you can upload with a CD-ROM. This is a massive program. The installation process alone takes specialized training. I don't think Davidovich could possibly rebuild all of that by himself. Second, even if he did, it wouldn't be exactly the same, and DARPA spent three years on it after Davidovich was gone. It's not the same program."

"Okay, one last thing, and then I'll let this go," I said. "About a year before Davidovich was taken, there were two computer experts killed down in Texas."

"What about them?" he asked.

"What if someone had all their research and a living, breathing Aaron Davidovich—what would that do to our Vegas odds?"

Church was silent, considering it.

Bug said, "Oh. Wow. Yeah, I see where you're going with that. But those guys were killed, not abducted."

"Their research could have been stolen," suggested Church. "There was some indication of it, I believe."

Bug hit some keys to look something up. "Yeah, okay, maybe. Their laptops were found in the ashes, but by that point they were melted slag. Someone could have swapped out their computers for dummies before the place was torched. It's what I would do."

"Give us a worst-case of how their research could be applied by a well-funded terrorist organization," I asked. "Like, say, the Seven Kings."

"Geez, talk about a can of worms. Milo Harrison was the deputy department chair of applied robotics, and the applications he was developing were the next couple of generations of mechanical autonomy. He had two DoD contracts tied, including the Regis project. He was a hardware guy, though. Integrative adaptive systems. That's intended to allow multiple autonomous systems to work at maximum efficiency while conserving stored power. A lot of microminiaturization stuff for switches and relays. That was four years ago, and a lot of what he was developing is already in use on just about everything from the latest Apache helicopters to automated systems on submarines. Everyone uses Harrison's stuff because it smooths out the physical application of software commands. Almost zero lag time between order and execution."

"What about the other guy?"

"Professor Harry Seymour was chairman of the school's experimental aeronautics department. Not as much of his stuff is in application, though there are bits of it in BattleZone and in nonmilitary variations like SafeZone. A lot of his research was folded into all three of the Regis software packages. Like I said, pretty much every automated manned combat, flight, or UAV system we have uses one or all of them. And SafeZone's showing up in CCTV cameras, new versions of OnStar, autonomous parking programs for passenger cars. Self-drive trains. Man, it's everywhere. This is the age of autonomy."

"That's hardly comforting, Bug."

"You asked."

"Okay. Now mix Davidovich into that soup. Could any combination of their knowledge be used to take control of one of any of our drones, or anything with Regis in it and turn it against us?"

"Yes," Bug said with hesitation.

Church said, "I can see where you're going with this, Captain, and it certainly gives one pause, but we have no indication at all that this is what we're seeing. It doesn't tie into the ballpark."

"Maybe not directly," I said, and sighed. "But why would we be talking about this if we weren't all thinking that Regis in the wrong hands could be very damn scary?"

Neither of them commented.

"What happened at the park? That could be the Seven Kings testing out some new toys."

Church sighed. "Fair enough. Bug, tell him the rest."

"What 'rest'?" I asked.

Bug gave me a truly disturbing little smile. "The really scary part."

Chapter Fifty

The two forensics collections technicians who followed Jerry Spencer around the ballpark were both professionals, both top of their game. The woman, Gina Robles, had spent the last sixteen years working with the NYPD and was heading up her own division when she was offered a better job with the DMS. Her partner, Laurence Hong, had been with the FBI for eleven years before getting the call. Neither of them held expectations of being lackeys for someone else.

Both had become just that.

It wasn't the official designation, of course. Both of them had impressive titles, breathtaking salaries, nice offices, killer benefits packages. The works. Each of them even had their own teams, ranging from secretaries to dedicated lab technicians to field techs. Each of them believed—truly believed—that they could run the DMS forensics shop.

Just not as well as Spencer.

It's never a fun thing when an expert meets a genius. Robles and Hong talked about it over cocktails quite often.

"This must be what it feels like to be Inspector Lestrade," said Robles one night as she toyed with the olives in her martini. "You know, the cop who's in all those Sherlock Holmes stories."

"I know who Lestrade is, Gina," complained Hong. "He's a fucking idiot."

"No, he's not. That's the point. He's a good cop. A solid investigator. But . . ."

She left the rest hang that night, but it was a conversation they returned to in one form or another a hundred times.

Now, they trailed the genius and kept looking for something useful. Something that would break them out of the lackey role and remind Spencer that they were every bit as valuable as he was.

It was Robles who spotted it.

Down on the field near the pitcher's mound. Explosions had thrown debris all the way out here from the stands. Broken and partially melted chairs, shattered concrete, torn and bloody clothing, a baseball bat, trash.

Ambulance crews were removing tagged bits of red meat so ragged that they would require lab analysis to identify which parts of what kind of body they came from. Male, female, young, old. As Spencer, Hong, and Robles passed by, heading toward a spot where a piece of what could be a control circuit had been spotted, Gina Robles saw something.

It was broken and covered with brick dust, but it was there.

"Wait," she said, touching Hong's arm. "What's that?"

They both stopped, looked down. Their hearts jumped a gear at the same moment. Robles knelt and leaned forward, studying the shape that was almost completely hidden by dust and bits of rubble. Almost.

But not entirely.

"Jesus Christ," said Hong, who stood behind her. "Holy Jesus fuck."

Robles immediately turned, cupped her hands around her mouth, and yelled at the top of her voice.

"Jerry!"

Chapter Fifty-one

Thomas Jefferson University Hospital

Philadelphia, Pennsylvania

March 30, 4:51 P.M.

"It gets scarier?" I asked. "Are you going to tell me that the drones at the park were using a proprietary military program?"

"Not exactly," said Bug. "If that was the case, we could probably backtrack those drones to where the software was stolen from. No, it's trickier than that. After Regis was developed and sold to the military, DARPA licensed a stripped-down version of it for sale to commercial markets."

"What? Why?"

"Money. Piles of it. I mean, are you kidding me? Drones are so hot right now. Everyone wants them, and hundreds of companies are building them. It's a growth market worth billions, and it's only going to get bigger."

"And the FAA and FTC have been fighting this every step of the way," I said.

"Fighting and losing," said Church. "Though they thought they'd won a major battle when Congress decided that all drones need to have a reset subroutine that can be activated in case of illegal misuse."

"Right," said Bug, nodding emphatically.

"I'm not following," I admitted. "You're saying DARPA gave them Regis?"

"They gave them a version of it," said Bug. "A fragment. Actually, it's a commercial version of BattleZone that's been retooled for nonmilitary use. It would allow civil authorities to take operational command of a commercial drone under certain specific events. Homeland worked out the details."

"That's not necessarily a good sign," I said.

"Hardly," said Church. "Bug and his number two, Yoda, were able to crack the security in under ten minutes. They could take over any drone licensed for business or private use."

"Shit," I said.

"Which means," said Bug, "that if we can do it—"

"Yeah, yeah. The Kings and everyone else can do it."

"Well," Bug said diffidently, "the talented people could do it."

"This is nuts. If those drones have Regis, can we track it to point of sale?"

Bug laughed. "Right now, just about everything has Regis. Every jet, every submarine, every tank has the full military package. All commercial drones have the stripped-down SafeZone. And just about every single drone on the shelves at BestBuy, Target, Walmart, Sears, and Brookstone. Hell, Costco has them. Regis is everywhere."

I said, "Jesus Christ."

Chapter Fifty-two

Thomas Jefferson University Hospital
Philadelphia, Pennsylvania
March 30, 4:56 P.M.

Church said, "Captain, tell Bug about how the drone evaded the bottle."

I did.

"Weird," Bug said, frowning. "That's too fast for pilot handling."

"What does that tell us? Is that the commercial version of Regis?"

"Definitely not," said Bug. "I'm not even sure it's the full military version."

"What do you mean?"

"Well . . . the software used for some drones has a react-respond sub-routine, but it's designed specifically for the bigger UAVs. Raptors, preda-tors, and the retrofitted QF-16's target drones, and the experimental QF-16X Pterosaur combat drones. Haven't seen it on anything as small as a pigeon drone."

"Could it be done? Adapted, I mean? Is that possible?"

"Just about anything's technically possible, just not probable. But . . . to clarify," Bug said, "is there any chance someone on-site was operating it? I mean, right there in the hall with you?"

"No way to know, but I doubt it. There were plenty of Kings goons in the building, but I didn't see anyone in what you'd call line of sight."

"Besides," said Church, "there would have had to be someone operat-ing each of the drones for that scenario to work. We'd have had some eye-witness accounts, and there has been nothing like that. No, I think Captain Ledger's assumption is correct. This was the drone itself reacting."

Bug whistled. "That's awfully fast. That's like animal-kingdom fast. Wasp-reaction speed, at least. Perception, threat assessment, and action in a microsecond? Damn. If we're not talking RPA—remote-piloted aircraft—then we are talking some serious software."

"How serious?" I asked.

He sucked a tooth for a moment. "Not . . . sure. From what you de-scribed, that pigeon would have had to be operating using adaptive-control techniques. We're talking software that would allow the drone to learn on the, um, 'fly' and then strategize based on acquired data and ongoing variables."

"Can it evade attack?"

"Up to a point. AI software in the Predator drone is adaptive, and this seems to be, too, but it's not reacting in the same way. Regis is pretty much the cutting edge as we know it."

"One way or another," I said, "the drones at the park had to be using some version of BattleZone, right?"

"You'd have to know computers and AI to understand why I don't think so, Joe."

"Then give me the short-bus version."

"Well, you have to start with the nature of UAVs and the software that runs them. There's a difference between an unmanned aerial vehicle following a preset computer program and something that actually thinks for itself. Most of what is called self-guiding software isn't really. Mostly it's programming that allows for a lot of obvious choices. It's task-driven. Stuff like fly here, drop this, whatever. That's nothing really new. I have a Rumba in my apartment that follows a set of programs to clean my rugs. And it has sensors that allow it to perform simple react-and-respond functions like not hitting walls and adjusting suction for carpet and hardwood. But that's not what you described, Joe. You said that it evaded an object thrown at high speed and then seemed to scan the crowd to assess the best possible attack vector. We could be talking AI complete here."

"What's that?"

"In the artificial intelligence field there are different classifications for function, for response, for problem solving, and like that. When a computer encounters a problem that it can't solve—something that requires human intervention or cooperation—we call it AI complete. Or, sometimes, AI hard. This is when simple, specific programming algorithms aren't going to get the job done. AI-complete problems crop up a lot when vision is required in order to understand a task. Camera lenses, even those that have thermal scans and that operate in a range of visual spectrums, still don't do what the human eye and its nerves can do. Same goes with what programmers call natural language understanding. You can program a computer to understand anything in the dictionary, but it can't interpret inflection, sarcasm, or other parts of human speech. Not yet. So, what you described is something a computer probably couldn't deal with on its own. Selecting you as a threat, evaluating the potential personal harm of what you threw at it and reacting so smoothly, and then planning a counterattack."

"Even at computer speed? I thought these machines could outthink us. Or close enough."

"Ha! Computers don't actually think as fast as humans. Not even close. Look, computers are calculators. That's what they were designed to do. Every function they perform, from finding a Web site to playing a game is a mathematical process. This plus this equals that. Computers seem smarter because they can do a lot of calculations at high speed. Such high speeds that it looks like it's doing a lot at once. But the human mind is the ultimate thinking machine. It does trillions of things at once. Everything from the release of hormones to regulating heartbeat to solving a Sudoku puzzle. All of the functions of cells and organs and proteins and all that organic stuff is happening simultaneously. Computers have been built to simulate that by performing calculations at such high rates of speed that it gets to the same result as fast or faster. But we're not there yet. No computer, not even MindReader, actually works as efficiently as a human brain."

"Oh," I said, more than a little confused. "Are you saying it was pure AI or that AI-complete thing?"

"That's just it," Bug admitted, "I don't know. It's strange. If this is only the drone, then were not really talking about AI. Maybe what we're talking about is actually AGI. Artificial general intelligence."

"What's the difference?"

"Well, for one thing, AGI doesn't exist yet. It's a hypothetical kind of artificial intelligence that is supposed to one day perform any task that a human being can perform. A true thinking robot or thinking computer. AGI is also known as full AI, and it's a computer mind that crosses the line from ultrahigh simulation of the human mind to something that is a machine parallel. Something that can actually think for itself. Something sapient and sentient. Something that's self-aware."

"Bug," I said, "I know that the drone evaded faster than it should have. So it's either one of these self-aware computer systems or there was someone at the controls who had some spooky-fast reflexes. Not really crazy about either of those scenarios being the case."

"No argument," Bug said quickly. "Tough to know which one, though. Right now, the main focus of drone R and D is intelligence, surveillance, and reconnaissance. However, with the complexity of target acquisition in remote areas like, say, the mountains of Afghanistan or the jungles of Mexico and down in South America, some generals at the Department of Defense have been putting pressure on the guys at DARPA to come up with AI programs that will allow an automated system that can select and eliminate its own targets."

"How?"

"That," said Church, "is the question at the center of the debate. The science is called neurotechnology. The argument for these kinds of machines is that they could be programmed with a specific set of the rules of war, which would include facial recognition and other identifying software that would allow the UAV to identify targets with a high degree of probability and then selectively remove them. It's an attempt to realize true AGI and marry sentient computers to independently operating military machines."

"You don't sound like a fan," I said.

"Hardly."

"The conspiracists out there," said Bug, "say that because the government has not officially sanctioned that kind of program, some black-bag organization went off the reservation and is funding it under the table."

"I want to throw the name Seven Kings out here and see if anyone thinks they're good for it."

"It would take their kind of money," said Bug. "We're talking hundreds of millions of dollars in R and D."

"It's in keeping with their level of sophistication, too," agreed Church.

"Which," I said, "makes me want to circle back around to the idea that someone has Aaron Davidovich's research."

Bug sighed. "That would seriously suck."

"The other possibility we have to brace for," said Church, "is that the Seven Kings have Doctor Davidovich himself."

I nodded. "Which makes me wonder if we shouldn't ask our pet tarantula about that."

"Who?" asked Bug.

"He means Toys," said Church.

"How would he know? Davidovich was taken a couple of years after Toys, um, had his change of heart. Or whatever."

I made a rude sound that Church chose to ignore.

Church gave me a considering look, however. "It seems like a cold lead, but I'll call and ask."

Chapter Fifty-three

The gathered students and faculty members joined the president in a moment of silence. On the big screen that covered the rear wall, there was a live but silent feed of people standing vigil before a growing mound of flowers, children's toys, and photographs.

The president raised his head and said, "Thank you."

The quiet persisted, however. The hall was packed, and this gathering was as somber as the one on the screen. The continual flashes of the press cameras gave the scene a strange strobe quality that seemed to enhance the stillness rather than add an element of movement.

There were synched teleprompters on either side of the podium, but the president didn't look at them. Instead, he gazed out at the sea of faces.

Finally, he nodded and began to speak. Ignoring the script. Speaking for once truly from the heart.

"I'm standing with you here," he said slowly, "and together we stand with the families and friends of the people in Philadelphia who have suffered terrible losses. Just as all America has stopped to look east, to the birthplace of our nation and the cradle of our liberty."

He shook his head.

"America is the most powerful nation on earth. In terms of our economy, our military, our potential. We all know this. The risk of being so strong, however, is that we sometimes fall into a dangerous complacency. We begin to believe our own fiction, our hype that we are not only unbeatable but untouchable."

He paused and looked at the faces who watched him.

"After Pearl Harbor, when America was delivered a crushing blow in a cowardly sneak attack, we got up from where we'd fallen, we brushed off the dust, wiped away the blood, and stood together to rebuild, improve, arm, and react. We became the world's first true superpower. And from then until the end of the twentieth century, we were that powerful. No one struck us. No blow landed on us."

He shook his head again.

"And then on September eleventh, 2001, early in the twenty-first century, we were struck again. Not on an island thousands of miles away from the mainland. But we took an arrow to the heart. New York City. Hijacked planes flew across our skies and struck the World Trade Center. The Towers, symbols of American power, trembled and fell, and that sent a shudder of fear through the veins of this nation. Another plane hit the Pentagon, and a fourth crashed in a field, taking with it heroic citizens who, in the moment of crisis, stood together to fight back. On that terrible, terrible day, the belief that we could not be hurt was proven to be a lie we, in our vanity, told ourselves."

He looked around.

"And what was our reaction? Did we lay down and give up? Did we lose hope in our strength? Did we lose faith in our God?"

He smiled. A small, sad smile.

"Of course not. We stood up again. Now—I will not discuss whether all of the actions we took in the wake of 9/11 were the appropriate ones. Second-guessing and Monday-morning quarterbacking are for historians. When that happened, I was a small-town mayor making a run at the governor's office. I was not called upon to vote for or against the policies of that time. It would be unfair of me to criticize anyone who had to think through their own shock and hurt in order to make a decision. No, I won't throw that kind of punch."

A fresh flurry of camera flashes bathed him in light.

"I am the president now. Today. And yesterday our country was struck again. Bombs were detonated at a baseball stadium in Philadelphia. Citizens—our fellow citizens—died. Many more were injured, some critically. This time, I must react. This crisis is mine. Possibly the defining moment of my presidency. I wish it could be different, that I would be offered a better choice. But one thing that the powers of the presidency does not include is choice. Not that kind of choice. This is mine, and I accept it. Now I must make decisions that will determine how America responds to this crisis. Tomorrow morning I will be in Philadelphia. I am in constant contact with all of the emergency-response teams and investigative agencies that are already on the ground."

He leaned on the podium and stared into the burning lights of the press cameras.

"We don't yet know who is behind this attack. I have placed all of the resources we possess—our military, our intelligence networks, our federal, state, and local law enforcement—to determining who is responsible. For now, those cowards are hiding from us. They will not be able to hide forever. They will not be able to hide for long. We will find them. We will learn who they are and where they are. And we will hunt them down."

He spaced those last three words so that they hit like punches.

"Right now, this moment, I am speaking to the people who did this and to anyone working with them, helping them, or hiding them. Listen to me. Hear me. We are coming for you. Don't think that you are too small to slip between our fingers. You are not. Don't believe that you can hide. You cannot. Don't fool yourself into believing that you can hide inside the borders of a sovereign nation, or that we will not cross those borders to find you. We will. I tell you now, before the people gathered here, before my fellow Americans who are watching, before the world, which has paused to listen, we will find you." He paused and his lip curled for a moment, giving his face a feral cast. "America is coming for you."

There was a moment when nothing happened.

Then thunder shook the hall as everyone leaped to their feet and applauded. The crowd shouted. They yelled. The flashes pulsed.

Every reporter began screaming questions.

The president of the United States stood there and glared, his face as hard and unforgiving as stone.

And then the tone of the audience changed. There was a moment when every reporter froze, most of them touched earbuds or pressed cell phones to their heads as they listened to something. Many of them stared into the glow of their smartphones or tablets. Eyes bugged wide, mouths dropped open.

Silence held the room in its fist for just over seventy-one seconds.

The president leaned toward his chief of staff. "Alice, what's going on?"

She touched her own earbud, and her face went dead pale.

That's when the reporters began raising their heads. They were like a pack of jackals who suddenly smelled blood in the air. Their eyes raised toward him, and the look the president saw on each face was filled with anger, hurt, outrage. And hate.

They all began shouting at once.

They actually rushed forward in a pack, and for a moment the president had the bizarre feeling that the crowd was going to fall on him, to drag him down and tear him to pieces. Everyone was screaming. Alice Houston was yelling at the Secret Service to get the president out of the room. Agents were closing in to body-block the president from the pack of reporters.

Through it all, two words kept slashing through the din. And as the president heard them, he understood.

And he realized that the world was going to catch fire.

Right now.

His world.

The whole world.

The two words were *bin Laden*.

Chapter Fifty-four

Thomas Jefferson University Hospital
Philadelphia, Pennsylvania
March 30, 5:13 P.M.

"If the Kings have Davidovich," said Bug, looking genuinely scared, "then we also have to bear in mind that he's had four years and an unlimited budget to develop his programs. Remember, Joe, he's the Einstein of the computer world. And he knows his hardware, too. If he's actually out there and he's somehow working for the Kings? Jeez . . . Just knowing what I know about what he had on his to-do list scares the crap out of me."

"You mean Regis?" I asked.

"No, I mean what he said he was planning to do after Regis was done."

"I know I don't want you to answer this, but . . . what was he going to do?"

"In his lectures and articles, he said that he was going to try and crack the science of building a quantum computer."

I said, "I know I keep asking this, but . . . what is that?"

"I sent you a report on this three years ago."

"Which, clearly, I didn't read. Just bring me up to speed."

"Okay, okay. Digital computers have memories made up of bits, right? Each bit represents either a one or a zero."

"Yeah, I get that much."

"No, let me finish. A quantum computer has quantum bits. These are made out of quantum particles that can be zero, one, or some kind of state in between. In other words, they can be both values at the same time. A quantum computer maintains a sequence of qubits. A single qubit can represent a one, a zero, or any quantum superposition of these two qubit states. A pair of qubits can be in any desired quantum superposition of—"

"Stop. I'm not following any of that. I have a head injury, son. Have a little mercy."

Bug gave me the kind of pitying look highly intelligent people tend to give to the mentally challenged. Not mean, just exasperated. "Okay. Look, Moore's law states that the number of transistors on a microprocessor continues to double every eighteen months, so within a decade or so circuits will need to be on a microprocessor measured on an atomic scale. So, the logical next step will be to create quantum computers, which would harness the power of atoms and molecules to perform memory and processing tasks. Quantum computers have the potential to perform certain calculations significantly faster than any silicon-based computer. Like insanely fast."

"Sure, but how does that make for a more dangerous computer?"

"Because a normal computer has to go through all the different possibilities of zeros and ones for a particular calculation. But because a quantum computer can be in all the states at the same time, you just do one calculation, and that tests a vast number of possibilities simultaneously. That speed not only gets you a faster answer, it gets one based on better statistical probability of being the right one for your needs. Remember, we're talking AI. You match the need for autonomous decision making in the field with a computer that can perform faster and with more creativity than your opponents and, well . . . you get the picture."

"Okay, now you're scaring me."

"It gets worse. The biggest and most important potential use for a quantum computer would be its ability to factorize a very large number into two prime numbers. The reason that's really important is because that's what almost all encryption for Internet computing is based on. A quantum

196 of Church 196

computer should be able to do the same kind of superintrusion stuff that MindReader does. And it would do it a whole lot faster."

"Could it attack MindReader?" I asked.

Bug didn't answer.

Church said, "Yes."

I said, "Shit."

"It could do worse than attack it," Church explained. "It could hide from MindReader."

The room seemed to be getting colder, and I don't think it had anything to do with the thermostat. "Doesn't that open the door to the possibility that the reason we haven't been able to find anything about this is because a quantum computer is blocking our play?"

"That's always been a potential danger," said Church.

"Yeah," said Bug. "But I don't think we really have to worry about it yet. Some labs have already built basic quantum computers that can perform certain calculations; but the common thinking around the computer geekverse is that a genuinely practical quantum computer is still years away. Decades."

"Even if Davidovich is working on it with unlimited funds and a gun to his head?" I asked.

Bug chose not to answer that question.

"The drones at the ballpark," I said. "How much of one of them would we have to recover in order to determine if it's using a quantum computer?"

"A whole one. Undamaged."

"Oh," I said. "Crap."

"Thanks, Bug," said Church, and ended the conference. Before I could ask him any questions, his phone rang. He held up a finger to me as he took the call. He said very little, listened, and closed with, "Send it to Doctor Hu and let Bug know it's coming. This is very encouraging. Good work and—"

He stopped abruptly, the other party clearly having hung up on him midsentence.

"Let me guess," I said. "Jerry Spencer"

"Yes."

"He hang up on you again?"

"He did."

"He have anything?"

"It seems that he does, and we may have caught our first significant break. I know Bug will be happy."

"What did he find?"

"A complete pigeon drone with its CPU intact. Someone apparently knocked it out of the air with a baseball bat, and that canceled out the detonation codes. Jerry said that the onboard computer looks like nothing he's ever seen."

"Are we talking a quantum computer?"

"Bug will tell us. It's already on its way to him."

"Maybe God doesn't actually hate us," I said.

Chapter Fifty-five

UC San Diego Medical Center

200 West Arbor Drive

San Diego, California

March 30, 5:19 P.M.

Rudy Sanchez haunted the cafeteria for a while, aware that Cowpers was loitering nearby. Never at the same table. Never actually next to him, even on an elevator. Rudy drank six cups of incredibly bad coffee and ate yellow lumpy mounds of hot mush that were supposed to be eggs. Then he went into the bathroom and threw most of it up.

He wasn't sick, but his imagination was conspiring with his medical knowledge to conjure terrifying scenarios to explain what was happening to Circe. When he came out of the toilet stall, Cowpers was there, leaning against the closed bathroom door, blocking anyone else from coming in.

"You need me to do anything?" he asked. It was almost the only thing he'd said since meeting Rudy at the airport.

"N-no," gasped Rudy. He lumbered to the sink and splashed handfuls of water on his face.

"You sure? I can get someone."

"I'm fine."

Cowpers nodded, folded his arms, and said nothing else.

Rudy leaned on the sink and for a full minute did nothing more complicated than breathe. When he raised his head and studied his face in the mirror, he saw a man who looked old and unfamiliar. His hair was tousled, droplets of water glistened in his mustache, and his eye patch was slightly askew.

Ay Dios mío, he thought. *If I saw that face on the street, I'd cross to the other side.*

He tried to smile at the joke, but the effect was ghastly.

Rudy straightened; took a long, deep, steadying breath; then spent a few minutes washing his hands and face, combing his hair, and straightening his clothes. It was odd to do all this with someone watching him, but he pointedly ignored the agent.

Then he stepped back from the image in the mirror as if he was backing out of a suit of clothes that didn't fit. He turned and headed for the door, paused to allow Cowpers to open it for him. He did not look back to see if the man followed. Of course he did.

Rudy asked the first nurse he saw where the chapel was, and was given directions. It was only when he reached the small room that he stopped and faced Cowpers.

"I would prefer to go in there alone."

"Not going to happen."

"Make it happen," said Rudy.

Cowpers studied him for a moment, though his face showed nothing of his thought process. Then he nodded, pushed past Rudy, and walked the length of the chapel, poked into the small confessional, and finally came out.

"It's clear," he said. "I'll be right here. Call if you need anything."

Rudy shook his head and went inside.

At first the chapel appeared to be empty. Then he noticed that a man sat to one side. He was small and dressed in black. As Rudy approached, he saw that the man wore a Roman collar.

A priest.

"Father?" asked Rudy quietly.

The priest looked up. He was a white man with a Mediterranean complexion, dark hair, and green eyes that were older than his face. Worldly eyes.

"Hello," he said, smiling and rising. "May I be of some assistance?"

"I hope so," said Rudy. "I could use someone to talk to."

The priest gestured for him to have a seat. "This seems like a good place for a conversation. Please, make yourself comfortable and tell me what's troubling you."

"It shows?" Rudy said as he sat down.

"It shows."

Rudy looked at the altar. There were items representing Catholicism, Judaism, Islam, and some generic protestant iconography. A generic all-purpose hospital chapel.

"Are you a multifaith chaplain?" asked Rudy.

"I'm a priest. Several of us share this place."

"I see."

"Would you prefer to speak with someone else?"

"No, no, that's fine. I'm Catholic."

"Did you want to make a confession . . . ?"

"No. Just to talk."

The priest nodded encouragingly. "I'm a good listener."

Without naming names or mentioning any connections to the DMS or the bombings in Philadelphia, he talked about the high level of stress in the work he and Circe were engaged in. He referred to her job as a consultant, which was true enough in its way. She consulted on the politics and theology of terrorism, with related observations on symbology and anthropology. Circe was a complex woman. Brilliant, multifaceted, and insightful. Rudy found it challenging to skirt around specifics, though. The priest listened patiently, nodding occasionally. He seemed too savvy to ask probing questions when clearly Rudy did not want to open certain doors. That kind of attitude made it increasingly comfortable to talk with him. Then Rudy circled around to Circe's pregnancy and her collapse.

When he was finished, they sat in silence for a moment, both of them considering what Rudy had said and how he'd phrased it. In his own review, Rudy knew that he was being very careful in his word choices, building Circe's collapse and coma into a temporary thing that would prove to be nothing of note and that had no dire implications for the baby or mother. He knew that if he'd heard a patient say this to him during a session, it would not come off as optimism but rather bald desperation, as a declaration made to try and convince the speaker by trying to convince the audience.

The priest clearly had the same thought. "And how do you really feel about what's happened to your wife?"

Rudy almost blurted out more of the rationalization. Instead, he made himself take a moment. "I—don't know what I feel."

"Is that the truth?"

Rudy sighed and shook his head. "No . . . no, Father, it is not."

The priest reached out and gave Rudy's hand a squeeze. His hand was surprisingly strong, and his skin was oddly hot.

"No," he said, nodding. "You're afraid she's going to die."

Rudy almost jerked his hand away. "No," he said quickly. "No, I don't think that."

"Don't you?"

"No."

"Aren't you afraid that she and the baby are going to die." The priest continued to squeeze his hand. His skin was so hot that it burned. The contact was painful.

"Father . . . please, you're hurting my hand." He tried to take his hand back, but the priest's grip was like hot iron.

The priest smiled at him. He had very white, very wet teeth. "You not only think they'll both die," he said, "you think they deserve to die."

"No. Father, please . . . "

The priest increased the pressure of his grip. "You know they're going to die, don't you?"

"No!"

"Don't lie to me, Doctor Sanchez," said the priest. "Don't you know it is a sin to lie to a priest? It's a sin to lie in church."

Rudy stared at him, suddenly very afraid. "How . . . how do you know my name?"

"You come to the house of God and you commit sins. Tsk, tsk, tsk."

"Father, I did not tell you my name. How do you know my name?"

"You told me, Doctor Sanchez. You told me your name."

"I did not."

"Oh—not today," said the priest, squeezing so hard now that Rudy gasped. "You told me when we met before."

"That's a lie. We've never met before."

"I warned you about being disingenuous."

"No. Let go of my hand."

"You don't remember me, doctor?" The priest's voice seemed to change. It slurred into a kind of southern drawl. But not a real one—a cartoon one. Like someone pretending to be southern. "Don't you remember me at all? We had such a lovely conversation, oh yes we did. We spoke of many things. We spoke of shoes and ships and sealing wax, of cabbages and kings. Surely you remember that."

The light in the chapel seemed to shift and change, and with it the color of the priest's eyes changed. They were no longer a medium green, but instead seemed to swirl with colors. Bad colors. Ugly colors. The green was now the sickly green of toad skin, and eddied with a fecal brown and infectious yellow. A sudden stink permeated the room. An outhouse stench of putrescence and human waste, of methane and sulfur.

Rudy recoiled and pulled furiously to free his hand, but the priest held on to it. Easily. With no visible effort, even though he was much smaller and slighter than Rudy. The heat of his touch increased, and now Rudy could feel his flesh begin to blister. Steam rose from between the priest's fingers. The pain of that burning grip was intense.

"I weep for you," said the priest. "I deeply sympathize. To lose everything that you love. To have them taken from you so cruelly, so completely. How will you ever survive it? How will you live, Doctor Sanchez, when your whore and that insect that curls asleep in her womb have turned to rot and ashes?"

Rudy's cane was hooked over the back of the pew, and he snatched it up with his free hand, raised it, and brought it whistling down on the priest's forearm. The shock of that impact was incredibly, insanely powerful. Pain shot like electricity through Rudy's wrist and up his arm, and his hand spasmed open. The cane rebounded and flew from Rudy's hand, falling with a clatter on the seat of the pew.

The priest looked at the hand-carved cane. He bent and sniffed at the wood, then winced and swatted it away from him as if it was something vile.

"Hawthorn and silver," he said. "You must think I'm a witch. Or a vampire."

He opened his mouth and laughed.

And laughed.

And laughed.

As he laughed, his mouth seemed to open wider and wider. Far too wide. And that laughing mouth was filled with far too many teeth.

Rudy screamed.

The shriek was torn from deep inside his chest, and it boiled out of him to fill the chapel. On the altar, the silver crucifix toppled and fell so that the dying Jesus landed on His face. The flickering lights of the candles were instantly snuffed out.

Rudy felt himself suddenly falling.

Backward, out of the pew.

Onto the floor.

His hand slipped free from the priest's burning grip.

His head struck first the edge of the seat and then the floor, each blow feeling as hard as a kick. Lights detonated in Rudy's eyes, and the whole of reality seemed to cant sideways and fall off its hinges.

He tried to call for Cowpers. He couldn't understand why the agent hadn't already burst into the room. But the man did not come. Instead, Rudy lay sprawled and helpless as the little priest bent over him. Those strange, strange eyes seemed to glow as if lit from within. Lambent and so wrong. The priest reached out and caressed Rudy's cheek with the familiarity and intimacy of a lover.

"Listen to me, Rudolfo Ernesto Sanchez y Martinez," the priest said in an accent unlike either he had previously used. This was the creaking voice of an old man. Dry and dusty and filled with malevolence. "We have met before, and we are ill met now. We will meet one more time, and it will be on the day of justice, when the conquerors are conquered and those who steal the blood of the earth are brought low by their own greed and hubris. Then I will come and take everything you love and leave you with bones and dust."

Rudy cringed back in horror. He beat at the priest's face and felt his hand bones crack and the skin of his knuckles split, but he did no damage to the man—to the thing—that crouched over him.

"What are you?" cried Rudy.

In answer, the priest bent closer still and, with his hot, wet tongue, licked Rudy's face. First his chin, then over Rudy's lips and nose, up his check,

over his one good eye, through the bristle of his eyebrow, and up his brow
to his hairline.

"The whore and the maggot are mine, doctor. Mine. There is nothing
you can do to save them."

Rudy Sanchez screamed.

The priest straightened and stood over him.

"They are mine."

He raised his foot, and, though Rudy tried to turn away to protect his
face, the heel filled his vision as the priest stamped down.

Everything went black, and Rudy felt himself falling.

He never felt himself land.

Chapter Fifty-six

Boyer Hall
University of California, Los Angeles
March 30, 5:33 P.M.

The president of the United States wanted to hit someone. Anyone. It didn't
matter to him. He sat in a stuffed armchair, fists balled in his lap, jaw
clenched, his people clustered around him as they all watched his political
world come crashing down.

Even though he had not been president when Osama bin Laden—
through his involvement with both al-Qaeda and the Seven Kings—had
sent planes into the Twin Towers and the Pentagon, this was on him. Even
though he had not been president when SEAL Team Six breeched the
compound in Abbottabad and killed the man everyone believed to be bin
Laden, this was on him.

It was all on him.

He was the captain of the *Titanic,* and the ship had just hit the iceberg.

The so-called Friends of the Truth had fired their shot.

They had released the video from the DMS hit on the Resort. Seventy-
one seconds that showed three big men in the distinctive black clothes of
covert special ops standing around the nearly naked and thoroughly abused
corpse of Osama bin Laden.

Already, news channels were using facial recognition software to confirm the identity of the dead man. The video footage was in ultra-high-definition, which allowed them to focus tightly on the smallest mole and scar. On the shapes of the nose, ear, eye, and mouth. On the precise distances between the landmarks of that hated face.

Experts were being added to the hysterical conversation. Everyone was on the same page.

This was Osama bin Laden.

They could see this corpse.

No one had seen the body of the man killed in Pakistan. The corpse had been mangled by gunfire, bagged, shipped, and then buried at sea. All of the conspiracy theories that had begun burning after Abbottabad now caught like brushfire, the flames driven by winds of doubt and what seemed incontrovertible proof.

The chief of staff and the top advisors were bent together in a cluster, firing verbiage back and forth, trying to construct a response that would not put them all on the public chopping block, not to mention the unemployment line.

"Fix this," muttered the president. Everyone looked up at him, and for a moment the only sound was the chatter from the TV. The president repeated it. Again and again. Whether he was talking to his staff or himself was unclear.

Chapter Fifty-seven

Over Nevada Airspace
March 30, 5:38 P.M. Pacific Standard Time

Boy sat alone in the cabin of the Boeing 747–8 VIP. The cabin was a demonstration of absolute excess and vulgar luxury on an aircraft with a sticker price over $230 million. Boy did not need or even enjoy such luxury. Her tastes were simple, but this was the closest Kings jet available at an airfield outside the Philadelphia no-fly zone. She'd driven to Virginia to catch this flight.

The jet had once belonged to Hugo Vox and was one of three different ultra-high-end aircraft that still remained in the inventory of the Seven

Kings. She looked around at all the wasted space. At the piano and winding staircase and heavy furniture. All of it requiring so much fuel to lift. Thirty thousand per trip, minimum.

Now the jet shot through the American skies.

There was an elaborate computer setup aboard the plane with a big high-end, flat-screen TV whose display was broken into several smaller windows. One window was a continuous feed from the ballpark in Philadelphia. Another looped the president's speech and the resulting hit of the full bin Laden video file. A dozen smaller screens showed the media firestorm that had resulted, including footage of riots in Saudi Arabia, Syria, and Lebanon. Another cluster of windows showed a burning house in Fort Myers, Florida, a townhouse in Brooklyn, a hospital in San Diego, a house in Chula Vista, and other locations. Some events were past tense. Others were in progress. Everything was running according to a timetable that no longer needed her oversight. No orders needed to be given. Not for this phase. From here, it was the great machine of the Seven Kings grinding away the old version of the world to make room for whatever was next.

After the fires and explosions.

After the deaths.

After the chaos.

The jet flew on through sunlight and clouds.

She wondered how long it would be before no planes flew over this country anymore?

Soon.

So soon.

Chapter Fifty-eight

27 Eighth Avenue
Park Slope, Brooklyn
March 30, 5:39 P.M.

"Will you need me, Auntie?" asked the DMS agent as he held the door open for his boss.

Aunt Sallie shook her head. "No, that's okay, Tank. Just want to grab a change of clothes. I'll only be a minute. Go wait in the car."

Tank, who was a tall, wide, muscular man with no visible neck and the cold eyes of a reptile, nodded. He was one of three agents on permanent detail to protect the woman who was second in command of the Department of Military Sciences. He'd worked for her since the DMS scouts recruited him from the army military police. Tank's partners, Colby and Kang, were on the street. Colby stood by the open door of the Escalade, her humorless face turned toward the foot traffic. Kang was looking at the traffic. Every few moments, they would shift position to check the other direction, overlapping their line-of-sight surveillance.

"I can carry the stuff for you," offered Tank.

"And I can carry it my own damn self," she fired back. Aunt Sallie was in her midsixties, short, heavier than she used to be, but still capable of pulling a suitcase. "Now go down to the street like a good dog."

Tank did not take offense. He was too practiced at working this detail. No one made the cut for Auntie's team unless they had thick hides, a balanced ego, and the ability to keep their opinions and reactions to themselves.

"Of course," he said.

Once, when he first joined the detail, he'd made the grave mistake of calling Auntie "ma'am." She had promised to kneecap him if he ever— *ever*—called her that again. Not only had her glare been convincing, Colby and Kang, who were already on the detail and who stood behind Auntie, shook their heads in warning and silently cut their hands back and forth across their throats. The look of alarm on their faces was eloquent, and Tank was quick-witted enough to jump in the right direction when he thought there was a land mine.

He waited until she was inside the townhouse, then retreated down the steps to stand on the pavement. He would not wait in the car.

INSIDE HER HOME, Auntie tossed her keys on the table by the door, picked up the mail from the rug and threw it in on the couch without looking at it, and headed upstairs. Her house was lovely, understated, nicely appointed, and virtually unused. Most of the time she slept in her suite at the Hangar, the main DMS headquarters buried under a hangar at Floyd Bennett Field in Brooklyn. But she'd been there for three days straight now, and she needed fresh clothes and a few of her prescriptions. Valsartan for her blood pressure. Celebrex for her arthritis. Extra syringes and insulin for her diabetes. It annoyed her to be a slave to both age and medicine, but there wasn't much she could do about either. Well, maybe she could cut down on the sweets and lose a few pounds. But, as she often said to her doctor, fuck it. Life was too short to live small.

She stood for a moment at the base of the stairs, listening to the quiet. It was nice. And for her it was rare. The DMS was a loud place. Hundreds of employees, lots of machines, conversation, videoconferences. This place, though somewhat sterile, was soothing and quiet.

She sighed, rubbed her tired eyes, and began climbing the stairs. With the mess in Philadelphia now tied to the Seven Kings, she knew that once she got back to the Hangar, she'd probably be living there for at least a week. She hoped she had enough clean clothes.

The wall beside the stairs was lined with paintings. All original— some valuable, some not. Each was important to her, though. Not in terms of the art—something she understood but didn't treasure—but because each piece reminded her of something. Or someone. The small Picasso litho midway up was bought after the death of her first husband. Simeon. Every time she passed it, Auntie remembered him and smiled. He'd been a man's man. And an agent's agent. An American version of James Bond. Suave, sophisticated, deadly as a pit viper. Great in the sack. He'd been part of one of the Deacon's early teams. Way back when. But, sadly, he'd been ambushed in Diyarbakir, Turkey. Forty-nine bullets and a closed coffin. Simeon had loved Picasso.

The piece above that one was a framed piece of Nigerian beadwork. Another memory. Callisto. The entire time they were lovers, she hadn't known his real name. She found out when the State Department told her he was dead. Anton Michael Gunn. A Scot who worked for MI6 and who died with a Russian bullet in his brain.

There were others. All tied to memories of people whose faces could never be put on her walls. Security, ethics, politics. They had to remain anonymous except inside her memories. The most bittersweet was the one at the top of the landing. A big framed piece with its own small light. A moody surrealist landscape in which nothing appeared to be present except dust blown by colored wind. To the discerning, attentive eye, however, there were shapes suggested by deft brushstrokes. Lions and prey animals, carrion birds and jackals. But you had to know how to see them. It was subtle and powerful. So powerful.

That piece was the only one that was not tied to a ghost.

The man was alive, but he was as unreachable as the surface of an alien world. A man who was layered in mystery, just as the theme of the painting was layered.

She paused, as she often did, and studied the painting, a faint smile on her lips that she was totally unaware of.

She did not speak his name aloud. Not even here. Not that she thought her place was bugged or that he was watching. No, her life was built around habits of good security. Repairing damage was not preferable when damage could be avoided.

So, she never spoke his name here.

Not his real name or any of the many names he used. Now and over the years. Instead, she sighed and reached out to touch the lion hidden by the swirling clouds of color.

She never heard the bedroom door open.

She never heard the silent footfall on the carpet.

She never knew how close to death she was until the point of the knife buried itself between her ribs.

Chapter Fifty-nine

Thomas Jefferson University Hospital
Philadelphia, Pennsylvania
March 30, 5:43 P.M.

I lay there like a lump while Church called Toys. Church put the call on speaker, and I heard both sides of the conversation. Toys's voice was subdued, nearly uninflected. I could imagine why. After the fall of the Seven Kings and the destruction of the Red Order, Church had taken Toys on as some kind of project. He gave him access to a lot of the Kings money and encouraged him to do some good with it. Maybe it was some kind of social-engineering project. Maybe the big man liked to study insects. Not sure, and I don't much care. If Toys stepped in front of a crosstown bus, I wouldn't much care, either.

Perhaps I need to learn to be more forgiving.

Perhaps I don't want to.

Toys represented the kind of human animal that was preying on the rest of the herd. I don't bond with predators. Never have. My life was ruined by a gang of predators who raped my girlfriend and nearly beat me to death. If that's made me unfair or intolerant, then fuck it.

Church had his own agendas, his own motivations. He thought Toys was worth trying to save.

Everyone needs a hobby.

On the other hand, some of what Toys was saying made me sit up and pay attention.

"I've been putting this all together. The drone attack at the ballpark in Philadelphia, the secondary set of bombs. That almost fits a pattern," said Toys.

"What pattern would that be, Mr. Chismer?"

"It was something Hugo Vox had put together years ago. He was working on a way to follow up 9/11 and one-up the game. He wanted a bigger hit, with longer-lasting effects on the U.S. and world stock markets. He wanted to essentially crash the American infrastructure. At the same time, he wanted to disable the DMS via a series of attacks that would have an emotional impact on the key players."

"You're saying you knew of this plan and have waited until now to share it with us. I find that very interesting."

"No," Toys said quickly, "you don't understand. This was something Hugo had wanted to do, but he'd shelved it because the rest of the Kings opted to go with the Ten Plagues Initiative instead. Hugo told us about it one night over brandy and cigars."

"Us?"

"Well . . . Sebastian and me. Hugo was thinking out loud. Being expansive, the way he liked to do. Showing how easy it would be to work a big con on the rubes. His words. Hugo laid out exactly how it could be done using drones. And that was before drones were as sophisticated as they are now. Hugo anticipated their development, even estimating a timetable for it. He was brilliant like that."

"Sing me his praises another time," said Church. "Right now, I'd like you to tell me what he said."

"Okay, but you need to understand that I don't think anything was ever put into play, because it wasn't long after that the Kings were torn down by your lot. And now Hugo and the other Kings are all dead."

"Understood."

"Well, Hugo said that a strike at a sports arena would be hugely successful. Security is never as good as they think it is. Materials and weapons could be brought in any of a dozen ways. Hidden in parts for an industrial air conditioner, for example. Like that. He said if you did it right and planned ahead, you could manage it quite easily. And then it would be a matter of picking the right event. Hugo favored baseball over any other sport because it's known as the national bloody pastime. It's more American than hockey. Even more than football, as he saw it. And opening day would mean a greater sentimental attachment and better media coverage. His second choice would be the World Series, but since you couldn't know which teams would be playing, it would be more difficult to plan ahead."

"I see," said Church. "And it's your opinion that someone has taken Hugo's idea and put it into play?"

Toys laughed. Short and ugly. "Junie told me what you think of coincidences. I never thought much of them, either."

"Is there anything else?" asked Church.

"Nothing specific, but . . . if someone's taken Hugo's idea, doesn't that mean they have access to Seven Kings' information? I mean, I know Hugo's island was destroyed, but Sebastian and the others were clever bastards, and they were bloody paranoid. They could have made duplicates of their records, contacts, research . . . Someone could do a lot of harm with even a fraction of that."

"Yes," said Church dryly, "that had occurred to us."

He glanced at me as he said this. I've spent a lot of the last few years of my life hunting down groups that had been using pieces of the Kings' science and fragments of their infrastructure. They're a bit like genital herpes. They never quite go away.

"Look," said Toys, "I'm sorry that I don't have something more concrete. I left that all behind, and Hugo shut the doors pretty heavily after the Ten Plagues Initiative. All I bleeding well have are suspicions and a few things I remember. Would you rather I *didn't* call?"

"Of course not," said Church mildly. "And we do appreciate this information. Truly. Did Hugo say how he planned to make that attack? Would he have used drones for this attack?"

"Not exactly. Not back then, anyway. Drones weren't that practical back then. The technology's come a long way since he told us about it, but he did say that one of these days drones would be the primary weapon of terrorism. He said that they'd be practical."

"Practical," echoed Church.

"His word."

"Thank you, Mr. Chismer. Let me know if you remember anything else." He disconnected the call.

I glanced up at him. "And you're absolutely sure Hugo Vox is dead?"

He didn't answer. A few years ago, Church said that he'd personally killed Vox. I doubted Church would make a claim like that unless he was sure.

Even so, I felt like Vox's ghost was standing just out of sight, laughing at us.

Chapter Sixty

UC San Diego Medical Center
200 West Arbor Drive
San Diego, California
March 30, 5:45 P.M.

"They're bringing him up!" shouted Lydia, and immediately Junie and Toys burst from Circe's room and ran to the elevators. The doors opened as they got there and a team of nurses and doctors came hurrying out, pushing a gurney on which Rudy Sanchez lay moaning and bloody. DMS Agent Cowpers was with them, his sidearm drawn but held down beside his leg. He stepped out and waved everyone back to clear the way.

"Rudy!" cried Junie, reaching for the injured man's hand. Rudy flapped his hand at her, clawing the air as if trying to tear through some envelope of pain in order to reach her. Their fingers met, entwined, and then she was running alongside the gurney, holding his hand. They rushed to the empty ICU room next to Circe's.

Lydia Ruiz and Sam Imura grabbed Cowpers and pulled him aside, and Toys was bemused to see that the agent was thrust against the wall with no more force than Lydia had used on him.

"What the fuck happened?" demanded Lydia. A nurse tried to tell her to watch her language, but Lydia fried her with a glare.

While Cowpers began recounting what appeared to be a contradictory story about an empty chapel and a surprise attack, Toys ghosted up to stand outside the ICU room. He watched as the medical team began examining Rudy. From what Toys could see, the injuries did not look too bad. Some cuts and bruises on his face and what looked like burns on his hand. But Rudy thrashed and moaned as if in great agony. It was clear that he was delirious and maybe on the edge of a psychotic break. His eyes were wild with shock or madness.

Junie tried to soothe him, and she had to fight to keep her place beside him. The nurses did not seem able to shake her. That amused Toys. He always liked Junie, but his respect for her strength was growing.

Fierce little bitch, he thought. A good match for that thug, Ledger.

Then his attention was torn away from thoughts of Junie, of Ledger, of anything. A word hung on the air as clearly as if it had been painted there. A word. A name. Something Toys heard only as an afterthought as Rudy Sanchez, in his delirium, mumbled it.

Toys reeled.

Rudy said it again.

And again.

That same name.

That dreadful, impossible name.

He watched Rudy's bloody lips form it again. Speak it again.

"Nicodemus . . . Nicodemus . . . "

Chapter Sixty-one

"What do you want me to do?" I asked.

"For the moment, nothing. Because of your concussion, the doctors want you here for at least another day."

"The doctors can kiss my—"

The door jerked open, and Brick hurried in without waiting. "Boss, turn on the TV. Shit is hitting the damn fan."

I snatched up the remote and hit the button. It wasn't necessary to ask Brick which channel, because there was only one story and it was on every channel. As soon as the screen came to life, we all looked into listless, dead eyes. The reporters were yelling. Actually yelling. They were that excited.

Brick and I looked at Church, expecting him to be as rattled as us. We should have known better. He sighed, removed his glasses, cleaned the lenses with a handkerchief, put his glasses back on, and then folded the handkerchief and tucked it neatly back into his jacket pocket.

"It is not generally my policy to say, 'I told you so,'" he murmured, "but I did advise the president to disclose this and make a full statement to the nation."

"Too late now," I said.

"Yes," said Church. "Months too late."

"What's going to happen?" asked Brick.

Church shook his head. "A witch hunt. And very likely criminal charges. The CIA in its present form will be finished. Done. There's no way they can recover from this."

"Will the president?" I asked.

Church gave a small shrug. "If he'd revealed this within hours of Echo Team hitting the Resort, he'd have come out of it as a hero. A sure thing for a second term. Now . . . his only chance will be to throw the CIA under the bus and hope that his delaying of this information doesn't result in impeachment."

"Will it?"

Church nodded. "Oh yes. He's done, too. And the previous administration may face criminal charges. Some members certainly will, though some people may fall on their sword to keep the former president from having to take any direct blame. Plausible deniability is elastic."

"Damn," said Brick.

"What's our play in this?" I asked.

He looked at me. "Our play? We have no play, Captain. We did a very specific mission, we accomplished as many of the goals of that as were possible, and we turned all of the evidence and materials over to the White House, the NSA, Homeland, and other relevant authorities. We were out of it once your team left the island. We have no part in this. And, quite frankly, I can't waste much time on it. I made my recommendations when there was time to do this all the right way."

He said it with a note of inflexible finality. Brick and I looked at each other, eyebrows raised. He mouthed the words, "Oh boy." Shaking his head, he went back out into the hall.

"Got to ask, though," I said to Church. "What do you think of the timing of this? The video being released today, while all this is going on."

"Seven Kings," he said. "Without a doubt."

"Is this the other shoe you thought they were going to drop?"

"Hard to say. It's a considerable punch. There will be shock waves around the world. Embassies will need to be put on high alert, and some will probably need to be evacuated. We're fortunate that the attack at the ballpark happened on a Sunday rather than a business day. The president was able to keep the market from opening. I only hope POTUS is cautious enough to keep the stock exchange closed for the rest of the week. This could crash the economy."

I nodded. "But is this it? Is this the endgame for the Kings and does that mean we've lost the whole damn fight? The attack in Philly and then this to take down the president. I mean . . . this is bad. This could do more damage to the economy, world opinion, and our standing in the global community than the fall of any dozen towers. I've got a bad case of the shakes happening here because it looks like the Kings picked the kind of fight the DMS isn't set up for."

As if in answer, Church's phone rang again.

He looked at the display and walked out into the hall to take the call. I could see him stiffen as he listened. Then he spoke very quietly for several minutes. His body looked incredibly tense. Beside him, Brick looked on with growing concern. Brick shot me a brief, worried look.

Few things worry Brick.

Church ended his call and spoke with Brick for a moment. Then the big soldier went hurrying off. I watched Church take a moment to compose himself before reentering my room. He is not a man who rattles easily. Or, like, at all. But he looked rattled now. You had to know him to tell, though. He came in and sat down, crossed his legs and drummed his fingers very slowly on his thigh. That's his tell. He only does that when he's been pushed out of his calm space. He does it very slowly and deliberately, as if each tap hammers another nail back into his calm. I said nothing, waiting him out, and dreading what he was going to say.

Finally he took a breath, exhaled, nodded as if agreeing with a thought. "That was Chief Petty Officer Ruiz. There has been an incident at UC Medical Center in San Diego. Doctor Sanchez has been attacked." He held up a hand to stop me from jumping out of the bed. "Hear me out. Doctor Sanchez is alive and is not in danger. He has a concussion."

"How's that possible?" I demanded. "You told me you had a man on Rudy. Cowpers, right?"

"Agent Cowpers escorted Doctor Sanchez to a chapel at the hospital where Circe is staying. He cleared the chapel before letting Doctor Sanchez enter. However, he heard the doctor cry out. And when he went back into the chapel, he found Doctor Sanchez unconscious on the floor between two pews. He had been beaten by a man dressed as a priest. He has a head injury and some burns."

"Burns?"

"On his hand."

"Who did this?" I demanded. "Who the hell is this priest?"

"When he was brought upstairs, Doctor Sanchez was semiconscious and murmuring a name." He paused to take a steadying breath. "Nicodemus."

Chapter Sixty-two

The little camera on the wall of the black woman's townhouse captured everything.

The silver flash of the knife as it moved.

The intense and lovely red of blood. Always darker than people expected. Rich.

The slithery sound of steel stabbing through clothes and deep into muscle and organs.

The piercing shriek of pain.

Boy watched it all and felt her pulse quicken. She felt herself get wet and ached to touch herself, to stroke herself to orgasm as the murder unfolded before her on the big-screen TV.

Chapter Sixty-three

"Taking a long time," said Kang. "She's usually in and out."

"You want to tell her she's wasting our time?" asked Tank.

Kang snorted. "No thanks. I like my nutsack attached, thank you. I was just saying—"

They suddenly turned at the sound of shattering glass. Tank's gun was in his hand before he completed the turn, and he looked up to see the bloody figure fly outward from the second-floor window. It fell, trailing a comet's tail of glittering fragments and shreds of curtain as Kang and Colby both cried.

The body slammed down on the roof of the Escalade with enough force to blow out the windows. Tank spun away, shielding his eyes from the safety glass.

"Auntie!" he bellowed.

The body had landed solidly and was sprawled like a broken doll in a crater of black metal. The head hung down over the cracked windshield. Eyes vacant, mouth open. Throat cut.

It was a man.

Had been a man.

Now it was meat.

Through the open second-floor window, Tank heard a shriek of terrible agony. And then two gunshots.

Tank charged up the steps and threw his shoulder against the door, which splintered inward with a huge crash. Colby and Kang were right behind him.

They almost tripped over the body at the foot of the stairs.

This one was a woman.

She wore black clothes and a ski mask. Her broken right index finger was twisted inside the trigger guard of a .22 automatic pistol. A knife was buried to the hilt in her eye socket.

There was a third shot from upstairs.

A fourth.

"Federal agents," bellowed Colby, but Tank saved his breath for running. He jumped over the corpse and took the stairs three at a time. The entire second-floor landing was painted with blood. On the floor, on the walls, splashed over the big painting at the top of the steps.

There was a third body there. His arm jagged to the right, and a vicious compound fracture had sent the ends of his humerus through the meat of his biceps. His throat looked wrong. Flattened. As if the entire trachea and hyoid bone had been crushed.

The left-hand hall was empty. But a trail of blood led to the front bedroom, and inside were the sounds of a violent struggle. Screams and curses. Tank and the others barreled down the hall and burst into the master bedroom. Two figures stood locked in a deadly struggle. A man dressed in the same dark clothes as the other assassins, and Aunt Sallie.

Both of them were hurt. Both were bleeding. The handle of a knife protruded from Auntie's lower back, and blood streamed from both nostrils and bubbled over her lower lip. She had one hand locked around the wrist of the man, and his hand held a smoking pistol; his face was a torn mask of ruined flesh. One eye was gone, burst and dripping, and his nose was shattered, but he had Auntie's throat in his other hand and was driving her toward the smashed-out window. The figures were locked in a terminal dance.

Tank reached the man in two long strides. He grabbed the wrist of the gun hand and tore it out of Auntie's grip, clamped another hand around the back of the man's neck, and, with a savage grunt, dragged him backward. Tank lifted him into the air and slammed him down as he quickly knelt. The man's spine struck Tank's knee and broke with a sound as loud as any gunshot.

With a grunt of fury, he shoved the man aside just as Colby and Kang were lunging to catch Aunt Sallie before she fell out the window. Kang muscled in between them and scooped her up.

"*Call 911!*" he roared.

In his arms, Aunt Sallie's face was knotted with pain.

Then her eyes rolled high and white and she went totally slack.

Chapter Sixty-four

Thomas Jefferson University Hospital
Philadelphia, Pennsylvania
March 30, 6:31 P.M.

The day was far from done with us. Just as Church finished telling me about Rudy, his phone rang again. I could tell that he didn't want to answer it. His face was a stone mask.

He listened, and I saw the color drain from his skin.

It was bad. Worse than bad.

"Is she alive?" he said.

Those are not good words, no matter who they're attached to.

She.

There are a lot of women in my life. In Church's. All of them are precious. All of them, in one way or another, are family.

There was pain on Church's face, in his eyes. He listened.

Then he said, "I am initiating a Level One-A-One security protocol. Alert all stations. Activate the Red Blanket. Do it now. Call me when it's done."

Church lowered the phone and sagged back.

"Christ," I said, "what happened?"

He had to take a moment to collect himself. Whatever the news was, it was hurting him. "There has been another attack on our people," he said in a ghostly quiet voice.

I tensed, actually gripping fistfuls of the sheets as if they could keep me braced for what was coming.

"Aunt Sallie is in critical condition with a knife wound to her right kidney," he said slowly. He paused and pinched the bridge of his nose, squinting, getting a grip on his emotions. "The emergency surgeons are not optimistic."

Chapter Sixty-five

Tanglewood Island
Pierce County, Washington
March 30, 6:33 P.M.

"Your daughter," said the Gentleman. "You know she's totally daft, right?"

Pharos shrugged. "Look at us. How many people do either of us know who could be cited as a paragon of mental stability?"

The burned man thought about it. "Fair enough."

After a moment, the Gentleman added, "She's good, though. I'll give her that. Mad as the moon, but she's bloody good."

Pharos smiled, his heart swelling with pride.

They watched the news stories tumble and spin.

A few small windows on the big screen were data feeds that provided text-message updates from field agents. Some of them even included digital images. They were every bit as entertaining as the news stories.

Below the cluster of windows was a stack of news crawls, each showing information from different markets. Not the American stock market, of course, which had been closed following the ballpark bombings, but real-time feeds from commodities markets around the world. Asia, the EU. Elsewhere. Even smaller markets controlled by China and Russia. Gold, wheat, pork bellies, orange juice, rice, technologies, pharmaceuticals. Many others. And oil, of course. Always oil. With each new story, each update from reporters who shared the latest death tolls, the prices shifted. Up and down, up and down.

Doctor Pharos and the Gentleman owned hundreds of people in the world markets. Commodities buyers and sellers who scrambled to find the profit foothold. Many people were panicking, thinking that another 9/11 was happening. Pharos had primed the pump with the release of the partial video; and now they let that engine run wild. The machine purred, and the product it manufactured was fear. No one wanted another Iraq, another Afghanistan. Not America or its allies. Not the Taliban or al-Qaeda, who, despite their bluster, had been devastated by the wars. America had withdrawn the bulk of its forces from Afghanistan and ended the thirteen-year-long war. No one wanted them to rearm and return. Especially not with their new generation of autonomous UAV weapons of war. Shooting down a drone doesn't make the same kind of emotional statement.

So, the market shuddered and jerked as if continually punched.

With every staggering step, the brokers and bankers, buyers and sellers working for the burned man and Pharos made a profit. They bet on rises and falls, or steep swoops and terrified plummets. It was all a matter of being positioned long before the first tremor.

"As the American expression goes," said Pharos, "buckle up. It's about to get bumpy."

There was a small sound from the other side of the room. A soft gagging sound. They turned.

Doctor Aaron Davidovich sat on a metal folding chair. Two broad-shouldered Blue Diamond Security men flanked him. Davidovich had one hand over his mouth and the other flat against his chest.

"Christ," growled the burned man, "if you're going to vomit, don't do it in here."

Davidovich's face was the color of old milk, but he shook his head. The only sounds he made were tiny squeaks as his eyes darted from screen to screen to screen.

Pharos and the Gentleman exchanged a glance.

"I told you," said the Gentleman. "I bloody well told you."

Pharos raised both hands and made small pushing motions with his palms. "Wait, wait, let's give him a chance."

He got up and walked over to the scientist. Davidovich flinched back, but one of the guards clamped a steadying hand on his shoulder.

"Shhhh," said Pharos, holding a finger to his lips, "shhhh, it's all right, my friend. You have absolutely nothing to fear from us. Nothing at all."

"I—I—I'm not af-afraid," stammered Davidovich.

"No, of course not. We're all such good friends here. Everything is perfectly fine."

Davidovich said nothing. He was sweating heavily and smelled sour and stale.

Pharos squatted down in front of him, still smiling warmly. He pivoted on the balls of his feet and looked at the screens behind him, then turned back to the scientist.

"Does all of that bother you?"

Davidovich said nothing.

"Does it?" prompted Pharos.

"N-no . . . "

"Doctor, please . . . if we can't be frank with each other, then what do we have? Nothing. So, come now. There is absolutely nothing you can tell, nothing you can say that would offend or upset me. Truly, nothing."

Davidovich said nothing.

"Doctor . . . listen to me and, please, hear me. I do understand what you're going through. I am also a scientist. A doctor, not of computers. Of medicine, but even so. We are men of science. We were not trained for this. When we began our schooling, we did not have this in mind. I did not, and I'm sure you didn't, either. Can we agree on that?"

Davidovich paused, then nodded. A small nod.

"We can also agree, I'm sure, that the view we held of the world when we were younger was much different from what the world actually is. Yes?"

Another small nod.

"Over the years, I became much less naive about the way things work. I looked at the play of politics. Right and left, one party and another, and I'm sure you know what I discovered when I stepped back to view it with perspective. There is no difference. Liberal and conservative, capitalist or socialist, first world or third. All of the rhetoric amounts to something less than a pile of old shit. We can agree on that. The promises of politicians has value only to them and the people who expect to benefit from seeing them get into office. The policies of governments are never actually for the betterment of anything but are truly only grunts of effort as they jockey for position and advantage in a giant global polo match. Even the so-called nonprofit organizations are either covertly funded by governments who want to exploit their access or resources, or they are even more naive than I was and are therefore inconsequential."

Davidovich was listening. There was even a trace of a nod once or twice.

Pharos remained in a squat, positioned so that Davidovich was higher than him, ceding the nominal power within their shared envelope of confidence. It was a very useful trick. That and making statements laced with truisims tailored to encourage Davidovich to agree. It trained the scientist like a dog to agree and to feel powerful, moment by moment, because of those agreements.

"I did not set out to become a criminal, doctor," said Pharos. "Truly I did not. Even now I don't think of myself in that way. I don't look into my shaving mirror and say, 'You're evil.' Who does? A madman, perhaps? Or someone in a movie? No, what I see when I look in the mirror every single day and night is a man who has come to understand the way in which the world works, the structures that underpin what we call society, and the true meaning of our existence here. I know for a fact, from your reports, from what Boy has told me, from what you've done for us, that you see the same things when you look at yourself. You do not see a weak man. You certainly don't see a failure. What you see, Doctor Davidovich, is a man who has awakened into the reality of this world. A man who has studied the systems, the blueprints, the schematics of society and decided that he would rather be a master of this game than merely a factor. You are not a subroutine of someone else's game, Doctor. You are the game. You see that in the mirror. You look at that face, into these eyes, and you know the secret to winning this game. Because, oh yes, men like us have in fact discovered that secret. We know it and we act upon it. That secret, doctor, is power."

Davidovich probably did not know he nodded. But he did.

"Power is what it's all about. Money, of course, is the fuel that runs the great generator of power. Money protects us, it empowers us, it provides for us and those we love. Money is also the great truth serum. It opens hearts and minds. They say that everyone has a price. They do, that's an old, old truth. If they have that price, then the so-called values and morals that they claim to prize are meaningless. If morality was a genuine and powerful thing, then there would be no price at all to make men turn away from it. And yet every man and woman knows that they would if the price was high enough. I did. Boy did. The Seven Kings did. Everyone who works for us and with us did. Just as you did, doctor, when you realized that you were not a captive . . . no, hardly that. You realized that your brain, your talents, your insight were all demonstrations of the vast power waiting within you."

Pharos touched Davidovich on the chest and then on the forehead.

"In here and in here. So much power," said Pharos, shaking his head as if in wonder. "So much more than anyone else you've ever met. Until now. Until you met my daughter, Boy. Until you came here to this island. Until you met the Gentleman and met me. And what does that tell you? What does it say that you are here with us? With us, you understand? Not a prisoner. Not some lackey. You are here, at this time, in this place, at this moment, with us. With the last of the Seven Kings and with the man who runs their entire operation. Two giants. And you . . . a giant as well. A towering intellect. A person who should not ever allow his genius to be contained or marginalized by lesser, jealous, weaker people."

Davidovich was listening. And panting. His eyes were fever bright.

"Tell me I'm wrong," said Pharos. "Tell me I'm wrong about you."

Davidovich said nothing, but his lips were wet and parted.

"Tell me that you're a small man, a lesser man, a weak man. Tell me that you're incapable of embracing power. Tell me that you are unwilling to taste it. Tell me that you are not a giant. A legend." Pharos bent closer. "A King."

Davidovich's fists were clutched into white-knuckled hammers on his lap. His mouth worked and worked and finally spoke a single word.

Pharos loved that word.

It was the only word he could hear, the only word he wanted to hear, the only word that he would allow. And so, to his ears and to the Gentleman's, it was a word of beauty.

"Yes," said Davidovich.

Chapter Sixty-six

DeNeille Taylor-Williams was on her exercise bike but her mind was racing far away from her house in Fort Meyers.

The bike, like the other gym equipment, the big-screen TV, and the whole house, was a gift from her son, Jerome. Known as Bug to her and everyone. He'd moved her out of the small house in which she'd raised Bug, asked her where she wanted to live, and then handled all the arrangements to move her to Florida. Bug's stepfather, Terrence, had moved down here with her, though his health was bad and the good Lord took him last summer. DeNeille had grieved for him, but there were so many widows here in Fort Myers that she had a flock around her nearly all the time.

Bug, though, was rarely with her, and she missed him. Her son worked for the government doing something important and secret with computers. She didn't know what it was, but the government must pay him very well. DeNeille never had to pay a bill, and Bug's sisters were working on their advanced degrees on scholarships she was certain Bug had arranged.

The house, though, was quiet. DeNeille missed her husband, missed her daughters, missed her son.

As she pedaled the recumbent bike, she watched the travel channel and thought about where she would like to go. She'd never traveled with Terrence. He'd been a hardworking man who ran a dry-cleaning store, but right around the time he'd begun talking about retiring and going overseas with her, or on a cruise, the cancer had taken him. So fast. Too fast. The chemicals from the dry-cleaning. In May of last year, he was a two-hundred-pound man. Tall and proud. In August he was a stick figure who didn't even know her name. Now his ashes floated on the waves, and DeNeille was alone with memories, money, and an empty house.

The show currently running was about the Viking Cruises. There was a woman at the hair dresser who'd been talking about taking one. Another widow. What would she think about taking a cruise together?

That's when DeNeille heard glass break in the other room.

You get so you know what something is from the way it breaks. A falling vase sounds different from window glass.

This was a window.

She got off the bike and listened, but she did not immediately run into the other room. She'd spent too much of her life in neighborhoods where drive-by shootings were a fact of life. Her hand strayed to the locket she always wore. It was an Eye of Horus that Bug had given her a few years ago. Very pretty, very expensive, and very deceptive. The central jewel was actually a button. Like one of those "I've fallen and I can't get up" devices, except this sent a signal to the people Bug worked for. He told her that it was a standard security precaution, though DeNeille knew plenty of other people who were family to government employees. None of them had something like that. Normally she scoffed at it even while making sure to wear it, but now . . . Her fingers closed around the pendant.

There was no sound now. No sound of gunshots. None of the shouts or laughter of gangbangers. Nothing.

She relaxed only a little bit.

What was it, she wondered. Had a bird hit the window? There were certainly no street gangs here in Fort Myers. No one who would throw a rock.

The gym was in the back of the house in a big Florida room that looked out over a large garden of palms, ferns, and succulents. This noise had found her all the way down the hallway. It sounded to her like it had come from the living room?

"Come on, woman," she murmured aloud.

She nodded to herself and hurried along the hall, past open and empty bedrooms filled with boxes she had never bothered to unpack. She saw the glass glittering on the carpet before she'd even reached the living room.

She felt the fresh breeze from outside.

The window, for sure.

DeNeille came quickly into the room and saw that the big picture window was gone. Pieces of glass covered her couch, the coffee table, the rug, the side tables. It was everywhere. Only pieces stuck out of the frame like jagged teeth.

"Oh God . . . "

She did not enter the room any further, fearful of the glass. It was going to be a hell of a job cleaning it all up. Especially little splinters in the fabric of the sofa.

Thoughts of what to do and why it happened suddenly stalled as she saw something lying on the floor across the living room, jammed up against the TV cabinet. At first she thought it was a toy of some kind. A kid's remote-controlled airplane. That's what it looked like. She glanced out the window, looking for the kid who owned it. The kid whom she would be dragging to his parents in about five minutes.

The street was empty.

No kids.

"Ran away, the little bastard," she concluded.

DeNeille stood there, angry and indecisive. Her hand fell away from the Eye of Horus. She didn't call for help. She didn't call Bug to tell him about this. It could wait until some other time. Her son worked for the government, and there was so much going on right now. That horrible thing in Philadelphia yesterday. More terrorists. She shook her head.

No, there was no need to tell Bug about this.

Except . . .

The news stories said something about the bombs yesterday being inside little machines. Like birds. Pigeon drones. That's what Anderson Cooper called them.

This wasn't one of those.

This was a little airplane.

But . . . even so.

She stood there, confused, trying to decide whether to worry or simply start looking for some kid in the neighborhood.

DeNeille Taylor-Williams was still fretting about it when the crumpled little airplane exploded.

Chapter Sixty-seven

Thomas Jefferson University Hospital
Philadelphia, Pennsylvania
March 30, 6:55 P.M.

I got out of bed and began pulling on clothes. The only thing available was a set of scrubs, so I put those on. I could change later.

"I think I should head out to San Diego," I said. "Two attacks out there, and Nicodemus is on the loose. I want to bag him and have a meaningful chat. Unless, of course, you think I'd be more useful at the ballpark?"

"No. That part's over. Jerry Spencer and his team are doing good work. I'd rather you followed your instincts and went to California."

I nodded and pulled on the cheap hospital slippers.

Church said, "Not sure if you caught Bug's passing reference to the QF-16 program."

"Didn't want to interrupt him at the time. What is it?"

"The air force has been experimenting with AI and various software and hardware upgrades to retrofit decommissioned F-16s and turn them into drones."

I stared at him.

"The initial idea was to have them remote-piloted so that more advanced fighters could practice aerial maneuvers against real aircraft. That part's a good idea. The part we don't like is that there is a deeper level to the project involving armed-combat fighter drones."

"Armed but remote-piloted, right? I mean, they wouldn't be that stupid . . . "

Church's wordless look was enough.

"I hate this job," I said. "What do we do about that?"

"There's a unit testing them down at Eglin in Florida. Sending Top and Bunny down there to observe the test. They're both sharp. If they see anything amiss, we need to know about it immediately."

"You think the Kings would try and hijack some drones while every eye is on them during a testing phase?"

"These drones have the full Regis package." He stopped me before I could say anything. "I'm not saying Regis is corrupt. So far, we don't have any genuine proof of that. However, Regis is becoming a common factor. Due diligence and common sense require that we have eyes on this."

I didn't like it, but I made the call. Top and Bunny didn't like it either. They were downstairs, and we'd all go the airport together.

Church nodded gravely. "I'm going to Brooklyn. Then, depending on how things go, I'll meet you in San Diego."

"Who's running the Hangar?"

"I pulled Juan Esposito from Boston."

I nodded. Juan was a good guy who ran three teams out of Beantown. Former Army Intelligence. Very solid.

Church started to go, but I touched him on the arm.

"Church," I said, "I know the world's on fire, but take a moment. If Rudy was here, he'd tell you to—"

"Let me head you off at the pass, Captain. I am well aware that all of this puts a great deal of stress on me. I know that there is a danger of my judgment and clarity of mind being compromised by what's happened to Circe and Aunt Sallie. This is not my first rodeo. This is hardly the first time I've had to deal with personal issues while still working a case. It would be nice to say that I am inexperienced at this sort of thing, but we both know that's not the case."

"Okay, so you got that part. Rudy would approve. But here's the other thing. Circe is down, Rudy is down, Aunt Sallie is down. I was down for a day. This is more than a matter of us having to function under stress. I think that is part of the point. We know how devious the Seven Kings are. I see all this stuff happening, and I have to look at the timing. It's more than a series of punches. They know we can take punches. Who better? No, this is like dodging punches while somebody is throwing firecrackers into the ring. It's shock an awe."

Church went over and sat down on the edge of the bed. "You think this is more than an attack on us?"

"I damn well do. Everything we know about the Kings' MO is that they always have a hidden agenda. They love misdirection. They love coercion, and even though they aren't strapping us to chairs with electrodes on our nuts, this is coercion. They're hurting us by hurting the people we care about, and they know it has to have an impact."

"Get to your point," he said. "You're drifting."

"Maybe I'm not. I think they are trying to take us out of the game so that whatever they're planning is something we won't be ready or able to stop."

Church nodded, and for a moment he seemed to go into his own head. I know that he would never admit to being shaken, but he was. So was I. Finally, he nodded to himself and stood, and he stood very tall. His energy seemed to fill the room, and the look in his eyes was as vicious and inflexible as a knife to the heart.

"Captain Ledger, if their intention was to remove us from the chess-board," he said mildly, "they have failed."

"Then let's go kill the evil sons of bitches."

"Yes," he said quietly. "Let's."

I offered him my hand. "Good hunting," I said to him.

He took my hand and shook it, and held it for a moment. "This is a time for clarity of purpose," he said. "Not for mercy."

He gave my hand a final squeeze.

With that, he left.

Chapter Sixty-eight

Tanglewood Island
Pierce County, Washington
March 30, 6:56 P.M.

"I need to go to the bathroom," said Doctor Davidovich.

The Gentleman ignored him; however, Pharos turned and smiled. They were sitting in a row—the burned man on the far end, swathed in bandages and connected to his wires and tubes, and Pharos and the scientist on his left. The two mercenaries stood fifteen feet behind the row in postures approximating parade rest. The screens on the walls were alive with noise and movement as the day continued to crack apart.

"Do I go by myself?" asked Davidovich. "Or ——?"

Pharos allowed a slow smile to form on his face. "You're one of us now, doctor. You don't need to ask permission. Merely directions." He gestured to the door. "Go out and left. Third door along the passage."

Then he turned back to watch the screen.

He did not see Davidovich, but he could imagine the uncertainty, the fragile trust warring with horrible doubts on his face. That was fine. This was a teaching moment.

Pharos heard the scrape of the scientist's chair, the hesitant footfalls as the man walked toward the door. The steadier, more confident pace as no one said anything or did anything to stop him. The door opened and closed.

After a moment, the Gentleman said, "You think he's actually buying it?"

"Certainly," said Pharos. "And why should he not? He is one of us."

The Gentleman snorted. "Whatever that means."

"Exactly," agreed Doctor Pharos. "Whatever that means."

They smiled at one another for a moment, both of them in perfect agreement for once. Then they turned back to watch the drama.

Chapter Sixty-nine

Thomas Jefferson Medical Center
Philadelphia, Pennsylvania
March 30, 7:02 P.M.

Church wasn't halfway down the hall when I saw him stop to take another call. He looked at his phone like it was a friend who was betraying him.

He listened and then lowered the phone as if unable or unwilling to hear the rest of it. He stood that way for a long two seconds, then finished his call.

Finally, he turned and came walking back, his steps heavy, his face stern and sad.

"There's more," said Church.

"Circe—?"

"No. And not Junie, either."

"Then—?"

"A bomb went off at the home of Bug's mother," he said. "She's dead."

I stared at him.

What do you say to that?

What can you say? Church told me what he knew. It wasn't much, but it was too much. The most telling part was that one of the neighbors saw something fly in through her window. It wasn't a bird. A model airplane.

A goddamn drone.

"Does . . . Bug know?" I asked.

Church shook his head. "I have to tell him."

He stood up slowly and walked into the hallway again. For a moment he stood there, looking at his cell phone like it was something hateful. Something he wanted to smash and grind underfoot. Then he leaned one hand against the wall and made the call. I watched him, watched how pain and a shared grief changed his posture. He was the strongest person I knew, but no one is really Superman. No one. Aunt Sallie was his closest confidante and oldest friend. I didn't like her at all, but at that moment I was feeling pain, too. I could only imagine what Church was going through. The doubt, the fear, that clenching of the soul as you prepare for the worst.

And Bug.

Christ.

We all loved Bug. He was the kid we all wished we could still be. He was the innocent heart and soul of the DMS. This was going to kill him. Crush him. Maybe extinguish the light that burned in him. The light we all hovered next to in order to rekindle our own optimism.

I'd only met his mother once, briefly, at his sister's wedding. His mom kept getting my name wrong. Called me Jim. It didn't matter. She was a sweetheart. She loved her son but had no idea how much he had contributed to a nasty war. Bug's genius had helped save the lives of every field operative in the DMS, which meant that we were able to go save the world. Over and over again. Bug owned a major piece of that. His mother had died without really knowing what kind of a hero her son was.

I had no cell phone and no earbud. No way to reach out to anyone. Then I saw Bunny in the hall, and I waved him in. From the look on his face, it was obvious he already knew.

"How's Bug?"

Church sighed. "Hurting. That poor . . . poor young man." He shook his head. Even for him this was getting to be too much. "He wanted to stay on the job, but I told him to fly to Florida. Yoda and Nikki can handle things."

"Not to be a prick, Boss, but can they? With everything falling apart . . . "

His look and, I suppose, my conscience stopped me from saying the rest of that statement and thus from showing how insensitive and stupid I can be. Church shook his head, dismissing it.

I said, "Are you sending someone with him?"

"Of course. We take care of our own." He paused. "Except when we can't."

"Church, about what I said earlier, about the Kings targeting us on a personal level? This is proof of that. But there's something else. Hugo Vox had the list of DMS employees and their families from back when he used to be a good guy. Or pretended to be a good guy. Whatever. He was willing to give that list to the Red Order and their Red Knights. We have to go on the assumption that the list is now in the hands of the Seven Kings. They know they can't take us in a stand-up fight . . . so they're doing this instead. Hurting us."

Church nodded. "I've already initiated the protocols to protect our families, but—"

I knew what he was going to say and cut him off. "I know. The resources. We have how many people in the DMS now? Eleven hundred?"

"Closer to twelve."

"And all their families. That's a lot of people they're making us spend on protection. It's taking most of our chess pieces right off the board."

He nodded. "Local law can handle some of the protection, but we have to face the possibility that we might not be able to protect everyone. There is a national crisis and we're already hurt, Captain. I don't yet know what this will do to our operational efficiency."

"The hit on Auntie didn't involve drones, but they used one to kill Bug's mom. Drones are at the heart of this. It's got to be Regis. Can we shut it down? I mean, is that even possible?"

"I doubt it. There is a reset code built into the system, but to shut it down would mean shutting down more than three-quarters of our mechanized military."

"Why? It's just one program—"

"It's one program built to oversee them all. To uninstall it means shutting down each piece of equipment—each ship or plane—while the software is stripped out. And then some kind of other software would need to be installed as a placeholder."

"Christ."

"This is why some of us advised against using Regis at all."

"Okay," I said, "but even with all that, we're going to have to do something, right?"

Church gave another shake of his head. "The Department of Defense committed itself to Regis with a will. It is universally viewed as the central solution to our military problems. Even now, we only have a suspicion that it might either be infected or vulnerable to outside manipulation. We have no solid proof, and no one is going to act on a suspicion."

He turned, and I watched him square his shoulders slowly, take a breath, and go out. I wondered if he was dreading the ringing of a phone as much as I was.

Probably.

More so, I suspect.

Chapter Seventy

Tanglewood Island
Pierce County, Washington
March 30, 7:03 P.M.

While Davidovich was gone, Doctor Pharos had the Gentleman wheeled out onto an enclosed patio where they could sit together and watch the shorebirds. The wind was cool, but the nurses had bundled the burned man up nicely, and one of Doctor Rizzo's cocktails was buzzing its way through his bloodstream.

The Gentleman even smiled.

If the twist of mangled lips could accurately be called a smile. Pharos had his doubts, though he gave the burned man points for effort.

They watched a brown gull float on the wind.

The burned man started to say something, stopped, tried again, stopped again. Pharos waited for him to get around to it.

"About our new 'family member,'" said the Gentleman. "About Davidovich . . ."

"Yes."

"Maybe you were right about him after all."

Pharos turned, always suspicious of anything that sounded like a compliment. Few things coming from this man were. But this time the Gentleman seemed in earnest.

"You said he would turn."

"I thought he might," Pharos gently corrected. "I hoped he would. There was enough of a tendency toward sociopathy in his psych profiles to suggest that he was not welded to his moral compass."

"Apparently not."

They watched the gull. A second shorebird drifted on the same current half a mile beyond it. They seemed frozen against the sky.

"Your, um, daughter," began the Gentleman. "Boy. How much do you trust her judgment?"

"Quite a lot. She's turned other hard cases before."

"Mmm. No one of Davidovich's intellect, though."

"There are very few people in the world of Davidovich's intellect. But intelligence, even genius, doesn't necessarily come with a high emotional IQ, and it certainly doesn't automatically come with built-in loyalty or iron-clad ethics. History tells us that much."

The burned man nodded. Pharos made a mental note to give Doctor Rizzo a bonus. The latest cocktail seemed to have balanced the man out nicely. This was the most genial conversation they'd had in five or six months.

"What about his family ties? He had a wife and son. A mother, too."

Pharos smiled. "Ah, but that's where Boy shows her genius. She's made sure that good things happen to Davidovich's family. The mother is in a very expensive retirement community in Boca Raton. She has many friends, and even some suitors."

"How many of them do we own?"

"Nearly all of them. Though she's an attractive woman for her age, and she appears to be moneyed, so some of the suitors are genuine. Possibly gold diggers, but nonetheless genuine."

"Nice. The son . . . ?"

"Matthew's GPA has improved, thanks to some computer hacking and a little money shifted to the right bank accounts. Teachers are poor, and some of them can be purchased for far less than you'd think. The same goes for sports coaches. His son has become a starter in two sports and gets a lot of extra coaching, which also gives him good male role models. He's prospering. The boy is prepping for college, and will be accepted into any college to which he applies. That's been taken care of. He thinks his father is dead, so he's completed his grief process and is very well-balanced. We steer some girls his way, and he has earned a reputation as a ladies' man."

"Teen hookers? I thought that wasn't your thing."

Pharos sighed. "It's not. Each of these girls looks like a teenager but is actually older. One is twenty-six but can pass for seventeen."

The Gentleman chuckled. "You have that ridiculous soft spot. Bloody silly, if you ask me."

I didn't ask, you poached asshole, thought Pharos. *Fuck off and die.*

"And the wife?" asked the burned man.

"We corrupted her, of course. Lovers and pills. She's a train wreck, and that seems to be a comfort to Davidovich. He likes to watch videos of her throwing up or lying passed out in her own piss."

The Gentleman grunted. "Even so, Davidovich has to remember that we kidnapped him and threatened to murder his family if he didn't—"

"He remembers. But he also understands," said Pharos. "He's come to embrace our philosophy. And he has more than demonstrated his willingness to participate in his own corruption. He has not only done more than he was asked, he made improvements on the project without being told. He made suggestions for ways to increase operational efficiency. He's been innovative. He's clearly taking pride in our version of his Regis project. You can track his progression in the interviews and transcripts of the conversations Boy taped, including those done when he didn't know he was being taped. Casual dinner chatter. At first he referred to it as 'that thing you want me to do.' Then it was 'your project,' then 'the project.' Then 'this project'—a change that suggests a connection to something immediate. Last summer, he began slipping, calling it 'our project.' That was a major jump forward. Major. But the real change began occurring around the first of this year, when he several times called Regis his project."

"Well, technically, it is . . . "

"Only technically. On one hand, he built it for DARPA, and on the other, he knows that we hijacked it. It was taken away from him. What he's proved, though, is that he not only wants back in, he wants to remain lead software engineer. Permanently. I think it's clear the man has crossed his own personal Rubicon, that he's embraced a new life. That he's accepted that he is a part of this."

"Even though he's still a prisoner?"

"Yes," said Pharos. "Though I think he hopes that our bringing him here is a step toward changing that relationship."

"Even though he knows that if he betrays us even now his family will suffer?"

"Even so. He's at that stage of acceptance and rationalization when he views this as protection for them rather than a threat."

The burned man shook his head. "Bloody hell."

They sat and watched the birds, sipping tea, enjoying each other's company for the first time in a very long while.

"So," said Pharos, "what do you think about bringing Davidovich into the family? To let him become an employee rather than a caged bird?"

"If we did, I would still want him watched."

"Of course he'll be watched. And even if we tell him that his family is no longer in immediate threat, he's smart enough to know that it won't mean they're safe from us. By now he has to have an excellent sense of the kind of power, the kind of reach, we have. A man as smart as him would make sure that he is always of use, always valuable, and therefore his family, by extension, is too valuable to hurt. Just as he'll know that a member of our group, rather than its victim, would be able to do more direct and obvious good for his son and mother."

"And the wife—?"

"How much would you like to wager that within a year of joining us Davidovich would ask a special favor of Boy?"

"What? Have her killed?"

Pharos spread his hands. "We've seen that pathology before."

The Gentleman nodded. A nurse came and refilled their cups and brought a plate of nutrient-rich cakes. Pharos knew that the Gentleman's cakes were laced with more of Doctor Rizzo's cocktail.

It was the Gentleman who finally broke the silence.

"It's all going to start soon," he said, and then a moment later amended that statement. "It's all going to end soon."

Pharos said nothing. He nibbled a cake.

"When I go," continued the burned man, "I want to leave something behind. A legacy."

"What kind?" asked Pharos.

"A changed world."

"Ah. I can pretty well guarantee you'll have your wish."

The Gentleman looked at him, and there was an honest, clear light in his remaining eye. "Listen to me, Michael," he said. It was maybe the second time since they'd known each other that he'd used Pharos's first name. "Listen to me. I know I'm a monster. I know that in a lot of ways I'm a parasite. You tolerate me because you want the banking codes. No, don't deny it. We both know it's the truth. Just as we know that as long as I hold on to them, I get taken care of and washed and drugged. Let's be effing adults and leave that on the table."

Pharos said nothing.

"We both know that I'll never live long enough to see the whole project come to fruition. This is too big, and it will go on for a long time. This is the machine that you used to talk about with Hugo. The well-oiled perpetual-motion chaos engine. Once it's fully engaged, then it's going to grind a hole through the heart of this sodding country, and when America goes down, then a whole lot of the rest of the world will go down with it. Chaos for sure, which should please Hugo—whether he's in Valhalla or the Pit."

Pharos said nothing.

"But you, Michael, are going to outlive me. You're going to be there when it all falls down, and you're going to live a long time in whatever world will come after this one. You know that most of the currency in my accounts will be worthless. Only those currencies tied to moderately stable nations and international banks will be worth something, and even then it'll be pennies on the dollar. Which doesn't really matter to you if you get those codes, because pennies on the dollar still adds up to more money than you can ever spend when you're talking about more than a hundred billion dollars. I've seen projections that could put that figure at four hundred billion. You could walk away and retire with fifteen to twenty billion. You'd be able to buy an island, hire an army, and live like a king for the rest of your life, while all around you the world tries to find the reset button."

The burned man leaned slightly forward in his wheelchair, wincing at the pain. "I want to make you an offer, Michael," he said. "I want to make a deal."

Pharos cleared his throat. "What kind of deal?"

"Care for me. Treat me with respect, treat me like a friend, make sure I'm comfortable until I'm ready to die. We both know it's a temporary job. A few months at most. Maybe only a few weeks."

"I do that now . . . "

"No, you go through the motions in the hopes that I get soft in the head and tell you the codes. I'm asking you to be my friend, my last friend, for whatever time I have left. Give me that, and in return I will make sure that you get all of it. There's more than you think, Pharos. There's more than currency in numbered banks. There's gold, too. Do you understand what the value of gold will become when paper currency and electronic banking collapses? This morning, gold was twelve hundred ninety-two dollars and forty-two cents per ounce. In a collapsed economy, gold would be worth five times that. Ten times. More. Do you know how much gold I have? How much I inherited when I became the last surviving member of this organization? Want to take a guess?"

Pharos shook his head.

"I can tell you where you can find three and a half tons of it. In bars. Untouched. Do the math."

Pharos didn't need to. His heart was beating so fast, he thought he was going to faint.

"Now listen to me, Michael," said the Gentleman, his voice hoarse and low. "I will give you the banking codes before I die. I promise. If you're kind, I promise that. All those billions. But if you swear to me, right here and now, that you will take care of me, be a friend to me, protect me until then . . . I will give you the location and access codes to the gold vault right now."

Pharos could not speak.

He absolutely could not.

The Gentleman smiled and held out his one remaining hand. Wizened, scarred, twisted.

"Tell me if we have a deal," he said.

Chapter Seventy-one

UC San Diego Medical Center
200 West Arbor Drive
San Diego, California
March 30, 7:05 P.M.

Toys stood apart from the group, feeling small and useless and alien.

He listened as Lydia told her team and Junie about the murder of Bug's mother and the attack on Aunt Sallie. Junie wept. No one else did. Toys looked at the faces of Lydia and Sam Imura, Montana Parker and Brian

Botley. And at other soldiers he didn't know. Their faces were hard. Not without emotion, but completely without mercy.

He expected to hear trash talk, threats, the kind of threats and promises all soldiers make when they learn about a fallen comrade. There was none of that. When Lydia was done relating the news, they all stood there. Toys wasn't even sure they were looking at each other. They were just—there. As tall and straight and silent as chess pieces.

Without saying a single thing, the DMS agents turned and went back to their posts. Junie stood alone, weeping openly into a crumpled tissue. Toys wanted to say something to her, to offer comfort to her, but he did not have the courage to approach. Not in a moment like this.

After all, what comfort could a monster give when human hearts were breaking?

Chapter Seventy-two

Thomas Jefferson University Hospital
Philadelphia, Pennsylvania
March 30, 7:06 P.M.

Mr. Church exited the hospital and got into the Cadillac waiting at the curb. Brick shot the locks, lit up the lights and sirens, and bullied his way into traffic. Two city police cars fell into place fore and aft, and they headed toward I-95 and the airport.

"Sorry about Auntie," said Brick. "But she's a strong old vulture. No way this is canceling her ticket."

"When she recovers, I'll tell her you called her a vulture."

"If she wants to kick my ass, she'd better recover. But give me warning so I can get out of town."

He smiled at Church in the rearview mirror. Church gave him a small smile in return. Neither smile was any more real than the banter.

Church's phone rang, and when he looked at the display, it showed a symbol rather than a name. A poppy. Deadly and cold. The signature of a very specific person.

A woman of great power. Not exactly a friend. Nor always an ally.

He smiled faintly as he answered the call.

"Hello, Lilith."

"I heard about the attacks," said a stern female voice. "They killed a civilian? Your computer man—Bug, is it? They killed his mother?"

"Yes."

Her reply was a vile curse in an old language known for its eloquent obscenities. "And Auntie? They tried to kill her."

"They tried." He didn't ask how she knew. Neither Aunt Sallie nor Bug was named in any of the news stories, but Lilith had her sources.

"Who did it?" asked Lilith.

"Five-man team," said Church. "Almost certainly a Seven Kings hit."

"Kingsmen?" she asked.

"Likely. They were tough."

"Interrogation?"

"Sadly, no longer an option."

"Pity," said Lilith. "Will she die?"

"I don't know."

A pause. "I never liked her, you know," said Lilith.

"There was never love lost between you two."

"Even so, it's better to have her in the fight."

"Yes," said Church. "It is."

"And . . . Circe? I heard about that, too. No suspects. No apparent cause. But the timing is suggestive. So the Kings are targeting the DMS and their families?"

"Apparently."

"If they're after Circe, then they know too many of your secrets."

"Of course."

"Them hitting you now, while the stadium in Philadelphia is still burning, that's no coincidence. They're trying to weaken you or distract you, or both, while they make their play."

"Of course," he said again.

Another pause. "I've got people on this, Saint Germaine."

"That isn't my name."

"It was."

"And I left it behind."

"As you left so many things behind. When you're done with them. When they're of no use to you."

"Did you call to try me for old crimes? Your timing is questionable."

"No," barked Lilith. Then she sighed. "No . . . I did not. So, what should I call you? Deacon? Does that still work?"

"It will do," said Church. "Why are you calling?"

"I don't want to bore you if it's something you already know."

"You are many things, Lilith," said Church, "but you are never boring."

"Charm? And a compliment? From you? Pardon me while I faint."

"Do it later," he said. "I'm on the way to the airport."

"Ah. I heard a rumor about the doctor who works for you. Sanchez. My people say he was attacked by a priest. Sanchez was overheard saying a certain name."

"Yes."

"If he's involved in this, then you are all in trouble. But . . . you already know that. Who's guarding your people in San Diego, then? That thug Ledger?"

"His team. Ledger was injured in the attack on the stadium."

"Mmm, I heard. Didn't die, though. Ah, well," Lilith said, then added, "Violin is in California. She's on a job for me, so I can't station her at the hospital, but she has Banshee with her."

"Banshee? Who is that?"

"She's the great-granddaughter of an old friend. Do you remember that cave we found in the Hoia Baciu Forest in Romania? Do you remember who was with me?"

"Everyone who was with you died."

"Not everyone."

Church said, "Ah. Strega."

"So," said Lilith, "you do remember."

"I was always very fond of Strega. This is her great-granddaughter? Banshee?"

"Yes."

"She's with Violin?"

"Yes. And I can have my daughter leave Banshee to guard Circe. And, just to be clear, Deacon. I don't make this offer for you. This is only for Circe. Not for you."

"I understand that."

"Circe's pregnant, I hear. Near her time."

"Yes."

"Let me help her."

Church closed his eyes. "Thank you, Lilith."

The line went dead.

Chapter Seventy-three

Tanglewood Island

Pierce County, Washington

March 30, 7:13 P.M.

Doctor Davidovich was in the bathroom a long time. Longer than he knew was wise, which was the point. He was waiting to see how far this new trust would stretch. How long before Doctor Pharos and that burned freak in the bed would send men looking for him?

He sat on the closed lid of the toilet and stared at the wood grain of the stall's door. The bathroom and all of its fittings were of the highest quality. Expensive wood, polished brass, imported marble. Incense burning in a discreet niche. Egyptian cotton hand towels.

The degree of conspicuous wealth just in this bathroom was impressive. Everything that he'd seen so far at Tanglewood was designed to overwhelm ordinary senses. Pharos seemed to disregard it, which, Davidovich believed, was a sign of privilege. To be so rich that luxury was ordinary . . . that was very appealing. He was aware that his level of genius would ultimately bring him to this point. That was inevitable in a technologies-rich market. He had insight and ideas that no one else had. His QC computer was years in front of the competition.

Years.

His fault had been signing that contract with the Department of Defense to work exclusively for them for six years.

Six years.

He'd been four years into that stretch when he'd been abducted by Boy. Four years during which his paycheck wasn't worth lining his cat's litter box with. Sure, it was six figures, but it should have been eight. Or nine. Maybe the high nines. Ten was not out of the question. Ask Bill Gates.

The QC was the personal computer of this century. It was the new direction.

Even his software was radical. God, if he'd developed Regis in the private sector and then sold it to the military . . .

Shit. He'd be worth billions now.

Instead, where was he?

Sitting on a toilet on an island somewhere, while absolute fucking madmen waited for him. While maniacs used his software and quantum technology for what? A stock market and commodities scam? Okay, sure, it was on a global scale, but still. It was a scam. Doctor Pharos was basically a bureaucrat turned big-time con man. Somewhere on the larceny scale between Bernie Madoff and the old robber barons. White-collar thieves. Diamond-cuff-link gangbangers.

Which made him—what?

An accomplice?

A tool?

A lackey?

The speech Pharos gave him back there was impressive. So impressive that Davidovich was tempted to buy the con. But the man was really a bureaucrat and not a salesman. He was good at pitching, but he wasn't great at it.

And Davidovich knew that the man wasn't as smart as he thought he was.

Pharos believed the hook was set, that all he had to do was jerk the line to reel Davidovich in.

The scientist got up and washed his face. Thoroughly. Then he wet his fingers and ran them through his thinning hair. He leaned on the edge of the expensive sink and looked into the eyes of a man he did not truly know. An absent father. A husband who despised his wife. A failed son.

A brilliant scientist.

An innovative genius.

A captive.

A slave.

All of those things.

And people were dying because of him. He looked —as he had looked so many times since Boy captured him—deep inside his soul for some faint flicker of conscience. That inward look had always been like looking through black glass. There was never any light to see.

Never.

Never.

He sank to his knees and wrapped his arms over his head.

Why the fuck was there nothing in there to see?

Chapter Seventy-four

UC San Diego Medical Center

200 West Arbor Drive

San Diego, California

March 30, 7:17 P.M. Pacific Standard Time

The woman entered the hospital wearing a hat with a floppy brim and oversize sunglasses. Not at all unusual in Southern California. She was tall and slim, with an olive complexion and good bones. Men noticed her, even wearing a belted trench coat. She was the kind of person who got noticed. She was aware of it, and she used it.

At her side walked an enormous dog. An Irish wolfhound. Forty inches at the shoulders. Two hundred pounds of muscle and bone covered in wiry smoke-gray hair. Eyes that swept left and right and missed nothing.

The dog wore a blue vest belted with Velcro and printed with the words SERVICE DOG—ALL ACCESS in friendly letters. A caduceus was embroidered on the top.

The woman and the dog crossed the lobby, and every eye was on them. The security guard looked first at her, then at the dog, then at the vest, then at the woman's legs, and then back to the dog. He moved in to intercept her before she got to the reception desk.

"Excuse me, miss? Is your dog registered?"

The woman turned slowly toward him. She smiled a faint, tremulous smile. A cautious smile.

"Yes, she is," she said. "Do you want to see her license?"

"Please."

The woman fumbled in her pocket, and as she did so she became less of an exotic beauty and more of a woman with clear disabilities. Not blind, but vision impaired. She went through several pockets of her trench coat before producing the proper license issued by the state of California. The guard barely glanced at it. He already felt enormously awkward, a reaction triggered by the woman's obvious discomfiture.

The dog sat and waited with quiet patience, her dark brown eyes seeming to take in everything in the lobby without appearing to react to anything. Like a good service dog is trained to do.

"That's okay, miss," he said quickly. "Can I be of assistance?"

"Oh," said the woman, "I—I'm here to visit a friend of mine. She was brought in yesterday."

"I can help you with that," said the guard, taking her elbow—the one farthest from the dog—and guiding her to the reception desk. The dog, prosaically, stood and followed. People in the lobby pretended they weren't watching.

"Thank you," said the woman. She had a soft voice and a mild Italian accent.

"Carol," said the guard to the receptionist, "could you help this lady?"

"Sure," said a bright-eyed Asian woman. "Who did you want to see, miss?"

The woman smiled a warm and grateful smile. "My friend's name is Doctor O'Tree-Sanchez. She was brought in yesterday. She's pregnant."

The receptionist's smile flickered. "I'm afraid Doctor O'Tree-Sanchez is not allowed to have any visitors."

"Is Ms. Flynn with her?"

"Um . . ."

"She called me this morning and asked me to come by. Junie Flynn," said the woman. "Could you contact her and say that I'm here?"

The receptionist and the guard exchanged a look. The woman, behind her big sunglasses, appeared to be staring in the wrong direction. The dog looked bored.

"Okay," said Carol. "But I can't promise anything. We have strict orders."

"I understand."

"Who should I say is here?"

The woman said, "Maria Mandocello."

The receptionist nodded and made the call. She spoke to the federal agent guarding the patient and was surprised to have the call passed to Junie Flynn, who was some kind of liaison to the agency overseeing Doctor O'Tree-Sanchez.

"Put her on, please," said Junie Flynn. Carol handed the phone to the guard who placed it carefully in the blind woman's hand. There was a brief conversation that Carol couldn't quite hear, and then Ms. Mandocello handed the phone back to Carol, though she extended it in the wrong direction. Carol, tolerant and experienced, reached over to intercept it without comment. She put the phone to her own ear.

"Is everything okay, Ms. Flynn?"

"Yes. I'll be right down," said Junie Flynn, and disconnected the call.

They waited there for almost three minutes. Saying very little. Talking nonsense stuff. The weather. The terrible events in Philadelphia. Like that. Then the elevator doors slid open and two figures stepped out. A Japanese man with a hard, flat face and eyes that appeared to be absolutely lifeless, and a woman with wild blond hair and blue eyes that were filled with light.

And with pain.

The blonde spotted the woman at once and immediately rushed toward her. She saw the dog and her stride faltered, but the blind woman held out her hands and took the other woman into her arms. They embraced like friends who loved each other but had been apart for far too long. It was so genuine a thing that Carol the receptionist and Myron the guard smiled at each other. The dog sniffed the blonde and turned away, as if to say, "Noted and filed away."

"God!" said Junie, "it's so good to see you."

"Sorry it's for this reason."

"I know. But thanks for coming. It means a lot."

"Anything for the family." She glanced toward the elevator. "I can't stay long—I'm in the middle of something that won't wait—but I brought a friend. This is Banshee."

Junie bent and ruffled the head of the gigantic dog. Most people would never dare do something like that. Not to a dog who looked like she would not enjoy that sort of thing from strangers. But the big wolfhound gave a couple of brief wags of her tail.

"She likes you," said Ms. Mandocello.

"I like her. She has a big spirit."

"She does."

"There's a lot of light around her."

Ms. Mandocello only smiled at that.

Junie turned to the receptionist. "It's okay, Carol. I'll take her up."

"She's not on the list, Ms. Flynn," said Carol hesitantly.

Junie flashed her a big smile. "Check again."

"Don't bother," said the Japanese man. He opened his identification wallet and flashed a National Security Agency badge. The name on the adjoining card read SPECIAL AGENT SAMUEL THOMAS IMURA. "Ms. Mandocello is approved."

Carol nodded. The security guard relaxed.

Agent Imura shook hands with the visitor, then held his hand out to the dog.

"What was her name again?" he asked.

"Banshee," said Ms. Mandocello.

"Nice."

"She isn't."

Sam smiled. "I mean the name."

Ms. Mandocello smiled, too. "It's good to see you again, Sam."

"Good to see you, too, Violin."

He did not say that name loud enough for anyone but Junie to hear.

The two women, the DMS agent, and the Irish wolfhound named Banshee headed over to the elevators.

Chapter Seventy-five

Thomas Jefferson University Hospital
Philadelphia, Pennsylvania
March 31, 9:14 A.M.

I tried checking myself out of the hospital, got as far as the nurses' station, and then the shakes hit me. I staggered, dizzy and sick. Nausea was like a fist to the gut, and when I opened my mouth to tell the nurse I wanted to leave, I vomited all over the counter.

The nurses hustled me back to bed, cleaned me up, and, despite every protest I could make, shot me up with something that dropped me into a big, dark hole.

I slept badly and dreamed of monsters. Of fleet-footed scavenger animals that ran wild through the brush. Of a man with the body and clothes of a priest and the laughing head of a demon.

I dreamed that everyone I loved was dead. Not dying . . . already gone.

I woke in the dawn's early light, shaken and afraid.

When I got out of bed, I expected to fall down, but even though the floor did an Irish jig for a wild moment, the world steadied. My stomach no longer felt like it was filled with greasy dishwater.

So, I found fresh scrubs in a hall closet and this time managed to convince the nurse that I was leaving. They can't legally keep me. They tried, though. Got to give them that.

I grudgingly accepted a wheelchair ride to the front door, then tottered to the front door like an old man who'd lived a hard life. Every single inch of my body hurt. My hair hurt. My shoes hurt.

My heart hurt.

Top was waiting in the lobby, scowling and chewing on a wooden matchstick.

"Bunny's bringing the car around," he said, then gave me a sour up-and-down appraisal. "You up for this, Cap'n?"

"Sure."

"You lying to me?"

"Sure. Still going, though."

"Okay. But if you look like you're going to fade on me, I'm going to put you on the bench, you dig?"

"Yes, mother."

Top showed me his teeth. Not sure if you'd call it a smile.

He smile faded as he studied my face. "What is it?" he asked. "Did something else happen?"

It was a simple question with a terribly complex answer.

"Not here," I said. "In the car."

Black Bess pulled up outside and Top helped me into the back. He climbed into the shotgun seat.

"You guys have your go bags?" I asked.

Bunny ticked his head to the back bay. "Always. Where we going?"

"Airport first, then Florida." I licked my lips, which were as dry as my throat. Then, as Bunny pulled away from the curb, I laid it on them. Rudy and Nicodemus. Aunt Sallie. Bug's mother.

Regis.

My fears about Davidovich and the Seven Kings.

All of it.

They're good friends, and this was a bad thing to do to them. I watched what it did to their faces, how it changed them. Bunny's face fell into sickness; Top's turned to stone. We all have our own ways of processing hurt and anger.

Top, Bunny, and I—we were all feeling it. We grieved for Bug and feared for Auntie, but none of us knew what we could do to help them. We were killers, not healers. And as much as we wanted to, we couldn't raise the dead.

They asked a lot of questions as we crept through traffic. I gave them what few answers I had. Then we fell into a bitter silence that lasted from when Bunny got onto I-95 in Old City to when we pulled into the security lot at the airport. I saw my jet on the tarmac and a smaller one standing apart, waiting for Top and Bunny. I saw Birddog standing by my ride, and there was Ghost sitting beside him. Battered and bandaged but alert.

Bunny killed the engine and we sat for a moment longer, saying nothing, thinking bad, bad thoughts.

Nobody wanted to say it, so I said it. "We're going to find these sons of bitches, and we are going to wipe them off the face of the earth."

Bunny grunted. A low, dangerous sound. "For Bug, for Aunt Sallie. For Circe and Rudy. For everyone at the ballpark."

Top said it best. "We been sidelined watching the world burn, Cap'n. That shit's got to stop."

"Hooah," I said softly.

"Hooah," they echoed.

"Nico-fucking-demus?" said Top slowly. "Shee-e-e-e-et."

"How'd he get to Rudy?" said Bunny. "Cowpers said he cleared the chapel?"

"That's what he said," I said. "Our guys are reviewing the hospital security footage. So far, nothing. He slipped past us."

"I'm going to have me a long and meaningful chat with Cowpers," Top said. "I'd like to know how the fuck he could miss someone hiding in a room as small as a hospital chapel?"

"Cowpers is pretty sharp. Wouldn't be like him to miss something like that."

"All I'm saying," muttered Top, "is he better have a damn good explanation, or I'm going to put my whole foot up his ass."

We got out of the car. They took their gear and headed toward their jet. I leaned against the fender and dug my cell phone out of my pocket.

Called Junie.

I needed to hear her voice. Not only to know that she was okay, but because she was my tether to hope and optimism and all the things I fight for.

"Joe!" she said as she answered. I could tell from her voice that she'd been crying. "I just called your room, and they said that you were discharged. What are you doing?"

"It's okay, baby," I soothed. "I'm fine. Dented but that's all. Look, Junie," I said, "Church told me about what happened to Rudy."

"Oh God, I know. Poor Rudy!"

"How is he?"

She told me everything she knew, but it didn't add much to what Church had said. The same with Circe. No changes. No news.

No goddamn answers.

Junie started to cry again. Deep sobs that threatened to break my heart. Unlike me, Junie got along with Auntie. They often spent hours talking on the phone. And, like me, she loved Bug.

"I'm coming out there," I told her. "Until I do . . . who's there with you? I mean right there, right where you can see them?"

"Montana's here. And the rest of the team is patrolling the hospital," said Junie, sniffing. Montana Parker was the second woman on Echo Team. She'd joined a year ago during the Mother Night operation. A former member of the FBI's hostage-rescue team. Tough as nails. I trusted her to look after Junie, and felt relieved that she was on the clock.

"Good. You don't go anywhere without Montana, you understand? Not even to the ladies' room. Nowhere."

"I know how this works," said Junie.

I had to smile. Junie looked like a throwback to the era of flower power and love beads, but she had a complicated history that had made her neither naive nor weak.

"Okay, okay," I said. "Tell Rudy that I'm coming out there, too. Let him know."

"I will, Joe."

When the call was over, I limped toward my jet. Ghost broke from Birddog's side and came limping toward me. I knelt and hugged him to me, buried my face in his fur, and tried very hard not to weep like a child.

Chapter Seventy-six

Third and E Streets

Chula Vista, California

March 31, 11:44 A.M.

Jorge Quiñones dug a fresh beer from the fridge, used his retro Star Trek *Enterprise* bottle opener to pop off the cap, took a long pull, and sighed. Life was good. So good.

He opened the sliding screen door and stepped out onto the concrete pad that served as a deck. His girlfriend, Jill, was stretched out on a chaise lounge, earbuds in, sunglasses on, little rubber things separating her freshly painted toes. Jorge turned around and went back inside to fetch her a beer, too. He came up on her blind side and began to move the icy bottom rim of the bottle down onto the bare brown skin of her thigh.

Jill had great thighs. She had great everything. She was far and away the best-looking girl he'd ever dated. Maybe the best-looking girl he'd ever spoken to. All the goodies in front and in back, eyes as black as coal, and lots of wildly curly hair. Greek-Spanish. Real Spain Spanish, too. Not the Mexican Spanish in his genes, which was probably half Indio anyway. She was fine.

He tried to see through her sunglasses to tell if she was asleep or not. If she was asleep, then she'd jump ten feet in the air when the glass touched her. It was hot for late March. Some kind of global-warming thing, according to the news. Eighty-five degrees, and tomorrow was supposed to be eighty-seven. Nice.

Jill wore white short-shorts and a bikini top that was so skimpy he could see the little ladybug tattoo she had near her right nipple. He loved that tattoo. She had a hummingbird on her lower back. Jorge would never call something so delicate a "tramp stamp," though sometimes Jill joked around and called it that. He loved that hummingbird, too. He stared at it when she was on all fours and he was kneeling behind her. Her skin flushed when she was ready to come, and that changed the colors in the hummingbird's wings.

Thinking about those two tattoos made him hard, and he paused in the act of commission, the bottle not yet touching. She would be furious with him. No doubt about that. Yeah, he could charm her and they'd laugh about it, but was the laugh worth the yelling?

Nah.

He began to lift the bottle when Jill spoke, "And now I don't have to cut your balls off while you sleep."

He jerked backward. "Oh. You're awake."

She raised the sunglasses and squinted up at him. "You know I'd kill you, right?"

"I wasn't going to do it."

"Yes you were, *bastardo*."

"I swear," he protested. "I changed my mind."

"Mmm-hmm." She glared at him, but she was smiling, too. "*Anda que te coja un burro.*"

"Hey, you kiss your mother with that mouth?"

"That's not all I do with that mouth," she said, and darted out a hand, hooked a finger in the elastic waistband of his sunflower-pattern swim trunks, and pulled them down far enough so the tufts of his pubic hair popped out. He danced backward, pulling them up, flushing red, spilling a little beer down his thighs.

"Crazy bitch," he said, but now they were both laughing. "This is a family neighborhood."

She batted her eyelashes at him. "How do you think families are made, Romeo?"

Jorge shook his head and circled the chaise so he could sit down on his. He handed her the beer, tapped his bottle against hers, and they drank.

"I'm hungry," she said.

"I know. Me too. I ordered some stuff, though."

"Oh?" she asked, interested. "Did you try that new place?"

"NachoCopter? Yes, ma'am. Couple of beef and bean burritos, nachos and salsa, and four fish tacos. Got two wahoo and two tilapia."

"Jeez, are you trying to get me fat?"

"More cushion, less pushing."

"Ugh. That's crude."

"Says the chica who tried to pants me in my own yard."

There was a buzz high away and to their left, and they both turned, shading their eyes with their hands, looking for the delivery drone. It came wobbling through the sky on four small rotors. It was an ungainly device, but it buzzed along at a good pace.

"It's stupid-looking," said Jill. "Looks like a lawn mower had sex with a helicopter and this is what came out."

"Can't argue with that," agreed Jorge. "But it's bringing us our lunch. We don't have to drive anywhere."

"Works for me. Now if you can get one that delivers ice cream, I wouldn't care if it looked like a Decepticon."

He grinned at her. "You made a pop-culture reference. You made a correct pop-culture reference. I think I love you."

She snorted. "You love me for my tits."

"You have great tits."

"I do."

"Great tits on a gorgeous girl who can drop Transformers references while wearing a bikini . . . that's pretty much my definition of heaven on earth."

She returned his grin, looked around for a moment, then hooked her fingers in the cups of her top and flashed him. Just for a second. Two beautiful brown nipples.

"Oh, mama!" he said as he set his beer down and leaned over to kiss her on the lips and the side of the throat. "You are in so much trouble."

"I'd better be," she purred.

The NachoCopter soared toward them. Jorge's cell phone buzzed to indicate a text. It read:

NACHOCOPTER™ IS HERE!

Please wait for the NachoCopter™ to land and release the package.

Do not approach the package until NachoCopter™

has taken off and is at least fifty feet in the air.

Your credit card has been billed for $32.18.

Reply if you received this message.

Enjoy your food and dine with us again!

It was the same every time. The little drone began flashing red lights on each of its four whirling blades. It hovered for a moment until Jorge replied.

Jorge did exactly as requested. He waited until the machine descended to the grass on the far side of the yard, released its clamps on the canvas carry bag, then rose slowly, exposing the cardboard delivery container. With the empty canvas flapping, the drone rose into the air, buzzing like an overgrown bee, and headed back to the store ten blocks away.

Jorge retrieved the food, which was so fresh that the cardboard was almost too hot to touch. He carried it to the picnic table, and when Jill joined him, they clinked bottles again and dug in. They ate almost all of it.

They slept in the sun for a while.

Then they went inside and made love for a lazy twenty minutes before falling asleep.

It wasn't until the sun was sliding down over the western horizon that the convulsions began.

Jill fell out of bed, naked, shivering, her body covered with furious red welts. She tried to scream, to call out his name, but the only thing that came out of her mouth was a torrent of dark red blood.

Jorge could not help her. He couldn't reach her. All he could do—the very last thing he could do—was to dial 911.

He said one word, "Help."

It was wet and thick and nearly unintelligible. But it was enough to get the machinery in motion.

However, when the police arrived, there was nothing to do but wait for the EMTs.

When they arrived, the EMTs immediately backed out of Jorge's house and called their supervisor, who called the doctor at the local hospital. And it was the doctor who called the Centers for Disease Control. He forwarded a cell-phone picture of the two bleeding, nearly shapeless lumps that had been Jorge Quiñones and Jillian Santa Domingo.

Chapter Seventy-seven

Philadelphia International Airport
March 31, 2:07 P.M.

Top and Bunny flew out, but I had to wait several hours for my pilot to replace some pain in the ass little part and then get the jet fueled.

I watched it roll along the tarmac. It wasn't a fighter, but it looked sleek and somehow dangerous.

Being the Big Kahuna of the Special Projects Division came with perks. I now had my own personal jet, a sleek Gulfstream G650. It could carry all seven members of Echo Team, along with two logistics guys and the flight crew. It had a range of seven thousand nautical miles and could hit a maximum speed of Mach 0.85. It was soundproofed and had leather seats, and the interior looked like a yacht that might have belonged to a porn-industry mogul. Gold filigree, expensive paintings bolted to the walls, a full-sized toilet stall.

It had once belonged to a Colombian billionaire who ran a bioweapons shop in the same lab he was using to make coke and heroin. He'd begun providing drug cartels with weaponized pathogens designed to kill ATF and Border Patrol agents and their families. Despite the fact that so many people flew high on his drugs, the billionaire plummeted like a rock when I threw him out of the forward hatch. We'd had a disagreement over whether he needed to remain alive. Apparently, the world could still turn without him. Imagine that.

I loved the jet. I named her *Shirley*. Don't ask why.

Usually being aboard her made me smile. Not today, though.

As I climbed the stairs to the hatch, I heard a voice in my ear.

Small.

Distant.

Lost.

So lost.

"Joe . . . ?"

I stopped what I was doing and sagged back against a burned wall.

"Bug," I said, and tapped my earbud to bring up the volume.

"Joe?" he repeated.

"Jesus, kid, I'm so goddamn sorry."

It was true, but it was lame. Though, really, what part of the human vocabulary has words that will make a moment like this make sense? Which words, which phrases, actually help? How can sounds pull the knives out of the human heart? What clever catchphrases or wise aphorisms can address in any adequate way the unchangeable reality of death?

Go farther. What can you say to a friend whose mother has been murdered?

Tell me.

What can you say?

He wept. A voice in my ear.

I sank down in one of the leather seats, put my face in my hands, wept for him and with him.

Chapter Seventy-eight

Eglin Air Force Base
Boatner Road
Near Valparaiso, Florida
March 31, 4:46 P.M.

Top and Bunny leaned against the side of a Humvee parked on the grass at Eglin Air Force Base. They had cups of coffee provided by one of Top's oldest friends, Chief Master Sergeant Dilbert Howell of the Ninety-sixth Test Wing. The sky above them was a flawless dome of dark blue. Around them, the trees of spring were coming alive after a hard winter. The temperature was in the midseventies, and there was a breeze filled with the mingled scents of pine and flowers.

It was the kind of day that could put a smile on a sad man's face, but none of the men were grinning.

Top had explained why they were there. Even if the ties to Philadelphia were tenuous at best, it soured the day.

Howell sipped his coffee. "Your captain," he said. "Ledger? He seems like a good man."

Top nodded. "He'll do."

"From what I've heard," continued Howell, "he really got into the thick of it at the ballpark. Took out several hostiles without backup? Is that right?"

"He's not afraid to get his hands dirty," agreed Top. Bunny snorted.

Howell nodded. "You guys been with him for a while now?"

"For a bit, Dil," said Top.

"Aren't you getting a little old for that kind of stuff?"

Bunny was in the middle of taking a sip, and a single laugh exploded out. He tried to hide it with a fake cough.

Top pointed a finger at him. "You secure that shit right now, Farm Boy."

Bunny held up his free hand in a no-problem gesture. "I just swallowed the wrong way."

"I'm just saying, Top," Howell went on. "You're almost as old as me, and I stopped doing that yee-haw crap a while back."

"You ain't that old, Dil."

"You know what they say. It ain't the years, it's the mileage. These knees can't take the jumps anymore. Lower back's a bitch ever since Iraq. And those early mornings? Nah, not for me anymore."

"Which is why you're getting fat," observed Top.

Dilbert Howell had a stomach as flat and hard as boilerplate. He slapped his gut. "Yeah. This is me getting soft."

"The waistline's the first thing to go," said Top, shaking his head. "Then it's the hair, man boobs, and suddenly you got no barrel left in your long gun. Keeping in the game is the way to keep Father Time from bending you over a—"

"Hey! What's that?" interrupted Bunny. He straightened and squinted toward the water tower on the other side of Boatner Road. The others looked, too.

There was a speck in the sky. Bigger than a bird. Much bigger. Nearly airplane-sized. Sleek and silver-gray. It was coming toward them fast.

"That," said Howell with obvious pride, "is what you boys came here to see."

258 | Jonathan Maberry

"Oh shit," sighed Bunny. "Tell me that's not another goddamn drone?"

The drone flew past the water tower and resolved itself into a machine they all recognized. Forty-eight-foot wingspan and a twenty-seven-foot body that was smooth and bulbous and sinister.

"Fuck me," murmured Top

"Modified MQ-1-AI Super Predator," said Howell. "We got six of them in last week. Same hull design as the old MQ-1s but with upgraded avionics, an advanced aerial-evasion package, a new generation of the Multi-Spectral Targeting System, that new Robinson-Landau targeting radar. All sorts of goodies."

"And the Regis-integration software package," grumbled Top.

"Sure. Which is why it works so damn well," said Howell. "Only downside is that by using the old hull design, they had to more or less keep the speed the same. It buries the needle at one-three-seven miles per hour. But that more or less works in our favor. Anyone spots it, they think it's one of the older birds, until this flies right up their ass."

"Man's in love," said Bunny. "Hope you'll both be very happy."

Howell ignored him. "All this week we're testing the AI guidance system."

Top nodded. "It's science fiction bullshit."

"It's the future of warfare," Howell said, and seemed to swell with pride. "Artificial intelligence is at a breakthrough stage. These new models are designed for independence and coordinated action, largely without human interaction or remote piloting. You should see them work as a team, communicating with each other at ultrahigh speeds. Sharing tactical data with reaction times that make us look like cavemen. DARPA's got these birds doing everything but keeping diaries and braiding each other's hair. They have these things picking their own targets, making decisions to change their own mission protocols."

The predator did a circle around the water tower and then flew up and over the trees.

"Nimble little minx," observed Bunny.

"Very. And what you're seeing is a UAV teaching itself to fly in unpredictable patterns in order to make maximum use of the terrain."

Bunny looked at him. "Wait, you're saying there's no remote pilot at the controls of that thing?"

Howell chuckled. "Settle down, son. This isn't the movies. It's not going to suddenly develop a personality and decide that all humans must die. AI isn't like that. It's a program."

"Self-learning," said Top.

"Sure, but that's not the same thing as actual consciousness." Howell nodded at the Predator, which had reappeared sixty yards over the field that ran alongside the road. "There are limits written into the software to keep it from making mistakes. And they installed subroutines that will always give active control back to human remote pilots. And, just in case your nuts are up in your chest cavity, boys, there's a whole team sitting in a command truck right now, hands on the controls, ready to throw the right switches. They can remote-detonate it, force it to land, or even cut its engines off and make it ditch into the water."

"Still scary as hell," said Bunny.

"Only if you're the bad guy," said Howell. "No . . . these things are safe. You can tell your captain that. He may have a bug up his ass about Regis, but I think he's looking in the wrong direction. Regis is rock-solid. And the UAV program is going to save American lives. The whole point of using them is to reduce the risk to human life. To make warfare safer." He turned and pointed to a truck parked on the field. A complex array of antennae sprouted from it. "Mobile command unit. Everything needed to support and manage the Predator fits into four suitcases. Not counting missiles."

"It's not carrying missiles now, is it?" asked Bunny. "'Cause I am going to leave a mile long shit stain getting out of here."

Howell shook his head. "It has dummies. Same weight as four AIM-92 Stingers and six Griffin air-to-surface missiles, but no warheads. And even the dummies are bolted on so they won't drop during testing. Ditto for the guns. Ammunition is deadweight, nothing hooked up to fire. They're testing aerodynamics with simulated full weight of armament but with zero threat in case of error. Hey, I'll never claim that the air force is sane, but we're not so crazy we arm self-guided drones on a test flight. Not yet. And when we do, we won't let them fly around like this. It'll be a test range with no one loitering around where they can get their wieners blown off."

"And this sort of thing will never slip the leash and bite us on the ass?" said Bunny with obvious skepticism.

"Could be worse," said Howell. "They're retrofitting a bunch of F-16s to turn them into UAVs. They call 'em QF-16s. You heard about that?"

Top nodded. "Sure. Back in 2013."

"Still doing it. Got a mess of them. They're doing that down at Tyndall."

Top nodded. He'd been to a demonstration of the F-16 drones at the air base near Panama City. "I thought they were using those birds for target practice. So pilots could fight real jets but without anyone getting killed."

Howell gave him a knowing look. "Don't believe everything you read on Wikipedia, Top. The QF-16s are aerial targets, but the QF-16Xs are what we're calling superdrones. It's a new class. They call them Pterosaurs. You boys know what that means?"

"Sure," said Bug. "Flying dinosaurs."

"Don't confuse flying dinosaur with something old and clunky. These Pterosaurs can fly right up your colon and deliver air-to-air, air-to-ground, and air-to-ship missiles and then drop Paveway IIIs and Gator mines. And they have M61 Vulcan six-barrel Gatling cannons."

"You don't need to sell us, Dil," said Top. "We're not shopping for Christmas presents."

"Just making a point, fellows. Everyone hopes that we can put these birds in the air as fully functional, totally autonomous frontline fighters."

"Jeeee-zus," said Bunny.

"We got a bunch of them ready to go into actual combat," said Howell with pride. "Some at Tyndall and a whole flight of them up at Beale in Marysville, California. They're running tests around the clock up there."

"Even today?" asked Bunny, appalled.

"Especially today," said Howell. "If this is going to turn into another 9/11, we need a response that delivers a new kind of shock and awe. And one that doesn't put a lot of U.S. servicemen in the fucking ground. We want the bad guys to start digging graves, because we're going after them with a fully armed, automated response."

"Yeah," sighed Bunny. "I know. Not a fan of that, either."

"What's wrong with you, son?" asked Howell. "Would you rather put American pilots and ground troops in harm's way instead of a couple machines?"

"Oh, don't get me wrong," said Bunny. "I'm all for the drone program. Predators and Reapers have saved my ass more than once. I have friends who are alive because drones were in the air. There are a lot of bad guys who have been sent to the showers because of drones. And don't get me started on surveillance, low-risk intel acquisition, and using them to find lost troops. No, I'm good with drones. I loves me some drones."

"So . . . ?"

"I just don't want to be a day player in the next Terminator film. That whole self-guided, self-determining thing? Not a fan. I'd rather see Uncle Sam offer employment to a whole shitload of remote UAV pilots. Keep a human being at the stick. At least on anything flying around with fucking missiles on it."

Howell shrugged. "Opinions differ. Case you haven't checked, we're more than halfway through the second decade of the twenty-first century. Science marches on."

"Yeah, yeah, wave of the future," Bunny said, shaking his head. "I get it. But I don't like it. There are too many things that can go wrong." Howell began to say something, but Bunny added, "And before you tell me that I don't know what I'm talking about or I'm behind the learning curve of military science, trust me when I tell you that we've"—and here he jiggled his cup to indicate Top, and by association all of the DMS—"seen what happens when this shit goes off the rails. That's our day job, and it is not pretty. Worst-case scenario is pretty much our job description."

"Put it in park, Farm Boy," said Top quietly.

"No," said Howell, "it's okay. I don't entirely trust this stuff myself. That's why we're here to test it. We're going to put these birds through the wringer to make damn sure that they work exactly and only as intended."

"Hey," said Bunny, "I didn't mean—"

He stopped as the faint buzz of the drone's engine suddenly changed. They all turned to look at it.

"Uh-oh," said Bunny. "Is it supposed to be doing that?"

The drone was accelerating and was now flying toward them at a much higher rate of speed. It whipped over them at nearly a hundred miles an hour. Forty miles short of its top speed, but fast enough to drag a lot of air behind it. The gust fluttered their clothes, and three of the four men ducked. Only Howell didn't move, though his grin dimmed a bit. The Predator hurtled off into the distance, diminishing to the size of a condor, then a hawk, then a sparrow, and then it was gone, circling wide and low behind the trees.

"Christ!" gasped Bunny. "Is it supposed to buzz noncombatants?"

"Does that fancy AI software give it a smart-ass personality?" asked Top.

"Nah," said Howell. "It wouldn't buzz us unless someone in the control vehicle took over and is deliberately screwing with us."

"Cute," said Top. "I'd like to deliberately kick that person's ass."

"Hooah," agreed Bunny.

"Oh, don't get your panties in a bunch, big man," said Howell, "that's not SOP. Don't worry, I'll find out who the joker is, and I'll kick his ass for you."

"I'd appreciate it."

"Not 'cause of making you shit your pants," continued Howell. "He's flying too close to the road. Big no-no. I expect someone in that truck is telling him about that right now. They're just messing with the hotshot special ops pistoleros. But . . . have no doubts, he will get read the whole riot act. That bird will be heading over to the test range to fly an obstacle course."

"Really?" asked Bunny, pointing with his chin. "'Cause here it comes again."

Howell was smiling when he looked up to see the Predator circling back toward the road. It dropped down to fifty yards and leveled off, cruising right over the centerline on the blacktop. His smile faded slowly and, like a burned match, went out.

"What the hell . . . ? It's not supposed to be over the road."

Suddenly the air was split by the shattering blare of warning sirens. Doors burst open, and people erupted from half a dozen buildings. The rear hatch of the big mobile-control vehicle flew open, and an officer jumped out. He pointed up to the drone while yelling over his shoulder at whoever was inside the truck.

"What's happening?" shouted Bunny.

"Nothing good," replied Top, unsnapping his sidearm.

Chief Master Sergeant Howell glanced up at the drone, back at the vehicle, at the people running out of the buildings, and back at the drone.

"Stay here," he snapped, and then bolted across the road toward the command vehicle.

The drone accelerated, its motor buzz rising to a scream.

"Oh . . . shit," said Bunny. "It's coming right at us."

They started to disperse, but Top stopped him with a hand on his arm. "No, it's turning."

He was right. The drone veered sharply from the road and rocketed above the lawn. Howell was pelting across the field toward the truck.

"It's following Dil!" he shouted. Top drew his M9 Beretta and brought it up.

"You can't hit it from here," warned Bunny, though he brought his gun up, too. The drone was forty yards above him and three hundreds yards behind.

They began running.

Hard.

Tearing across the field. All of them yelling, even though their cries were lost beneath the crushing weight of the alarm sirens.

Across the field, the officer who had exited the truck stood frozen in horror.

Howell turned and looked up as the drone closed the distance in mere seconds.

The Predator could not fire on Howell. It could not launch missiles at the truck. It carried no live weapons.

What it did instead tore screams from Top and the others.

It swooped down to the field so that its landing legs were five feet above the grass.

Top could not hear the sound of the drone's engines firing to maximum speed as the machine came up behind his friend at 135 miles an hour.

But he could see the effect.

It was sudden.

It was red.

And it was unspeakable.

The front landing leg hit Dilbert Howell in the back, directly between the shoulder blades: 2,250 pounds of mass traveling at high velocity impacted two hundred pounds running at eight miles an hour. The body of the running man seemed to fly apart. To become inhuman in a terrible instant.

The wheel strut crumbled and folded back, and the shock tilted the drone downward. The onboard avionics did their best to correct the pitch, but there wasn't time before the drone slammed into the second figure—the yelling officer—and then the truck that was four feet behind him.

The sirens did not stop blaring.

Top did not stop screaming all the way across the field.

Chapter Seventy-nine

Tanglewood Island
Pierce County, Washington
March 31, 4:13 P.M.

Doctor Pharos stood in front of the wall of TV screens, arms held wide. He turned slowly toward the Gentleman. On the screens there were reporters speaking from outside a collapsed house in Fort Myers. Other reporters speculated as to the nature of a violent confrontation in Brooklyn. News feeds from Chula Vista showed men in hazmat suits removing two body bags from a small house. The rest of the screens showed views of the mourners, police, and emergency workers at Citizens Bank Park. The bulk of the news was now an even split between the drone attack at Citizens Bank Park and the video of Osama bin Laden.

The digital crawls along the bottom of each news feed asked hysterical questions and made bold statements.

America Under Attack?
Is This the Return of Mother Night?
Osama bin Laden—They Lied!
Who Knew and When Did They Know?
Terrorism in America. What's Next?

"And that," said Doctor Pharos, his arms still wide as if he could embrace the whole of the pain and suffering, "is what magic looks like."

On a metal folding chair placed a dozen feet from the hospital bed, Doctor Aaron Davidovich nodded and smiled.

Nodded and smiled.

Nodded and smiled.

If Doctor Pharos took note of the fact that the scientist's hands were clutched into fists in his lap, he did not care to comment.

Chapter Eighty

NewYork-Presbyterian/Weill Cornell Medical Center

525 East 68th Street

New York City

March 31, 4:13 P.M.

Mr. Church spoke with the medical team for a long time. He was not given the usual soft-soap responses common with family or friends of someone undergoing surgery. Even though he did not flash credentials, the doctors responded to him as if it was right and proper to disclose everything. Nor did they give him the layman's version. The content of his questions set the tone.

When they were finished with their report—which was guardedly optimistic but in no way enthusiastic—Church outlined several resources he was willing to make available to them. Protection, of course, but also access to advanced technologies and top specialists from around the world.

"Whatever you want or need will be made available," he said. "No questions and no red tape."

The doctors accepted this. Some people boast and make dramatic statements in stressful moments. Others simply set a higher bar for the truth.

Church shook hands with them and gave them each a card with his private cell number and a second number should he be unavailable. That other number, he assured them, would be answered twenty-four hours a day.

Then he went with Brick up to the hospital helipad, where a bird was waiting. Within forty minutes they were on a private jet heading west.

Heading to Circe.

All the way to the airport and throughout the entire flight, Church's phone kept ringing. Not from the doctors he'd just left. These were calls from the president, the chief of staff, generals, the NSA, Homeland, the CIA, the FBI, the ATF, the Centers for Disease Control, the National Institutes of Health, and a dozen other groups.

Brick took some of the calls, triaging them, responding to some, connecting callers with resources, providing access to teams and assets, sharing the workload with Church. Brick did not like the way his boss looked. Pale and strained. Tense. He wondered how much more of this even Mr. Church could take.

The attacks kept coming.

Eglin Air Force Base was the latest. That one alone would have poisoned any given day.

But the day had so much more to do.

One call in particular made Brick stiffen. He immediately handed the phone to Mr. Church. "You better take this one, Boss. Something weird just happened in Chula Vista."

Chapter Eighty-one

UC San Diego Medical Center
200 West Arbor Drive
San Diego, California
March 31, 4:37 P.M.

Lydia Ruiz saw the dog first and stiffened, her hand going immediately to the handle of her holstered Beretta. Then she saw Junie and Sam. And then Violin.

She did not exactly relax at the sight of the strange woman she'd first met during that mission in Iran. Lydia liked Violin, but she was also afraid of her. Genuinely and, she felt, justifiably afraid. Violin was not normal. Not in any way that Lydia reckoned. Violin was undoubtedly the second most dangerous woman Lydia had ever met. The first most dangerous being Violin's mother, Lilith. A demon if there ever was one.

Which made Violin . . . what, exactly?

There was a lot of debate about that among the members of Echo Team. Never, though, when Captain Ledger was around. Violin was more or less the captain's ex, and he considered her part of the family. His own family and also the extended family of Echo Team.

And she was here to help.

With the insanity of what had happened in Philadelphia, it was difficult even for Mr. Church to keep his top-tier team working guard duty. The captain was banged up from the attack on the ballpark, but Lydia knew it wouldn't matter much. It was hard to keep Captain Ledger out of the fight. And he'd absolutely want to be in this fight. In this hunt. If the man had two broken legs and was stepping on his own intestines, he'd want to be in this fight. He was that kind of guy.

It was why Lydia Ruiz would have walked through fire for him.

She stepped outside Circe's room to intercept the party at the door. Violin offered her hand, and Lydia took it. The Italian woman's grip was always so much stronger than it should be. Always a surprise. Hard, dry, and holding within it the promise of a great deal more strength. Never, however, a challenge. It wasn't a bully handshake; she wasn't trying to prove anything. The power was simply there.

Toys gaped at the dog. "Bloody hell."

No one acknowledged his remark.

"Lydia," said Violin.

"Hey."

Violin looked past her to where Circe lay amid a cluster of arcane machines. She glanced at Toys and then away, as if noting but otherwise dismissing him. She took a step toward the comatose woman.

"May I?"

Lydia flicked a glance at Junie, who nodded. Lydia was nominally in charge of this room and this detail, but somehow Junie Flynn seemed to be in actual charge. Nothing was ever said; no orders were given to that effect. But it was the case, and everyone knew it.

Lydia looked from Violin down to the dog and up again. Then she stepped aside. Toys gave the dog a very wide berth, retreating all the way to the nurses' station. Behind the desk, the nurses and a doctor gaped at the dog, but the day had already changed it's frequency so completely that they no longer tried to impose rules and restrictions on anything that happened. And all other patients had been moved from this floor.

The Italian woman entered the room with Banshee following silently behind. For so large a dog, it made no sound. Not even the click of nails on the tiled floor. Violin went over to the bed, picked up the chart that was hung on the end, read it, replaced it, and then bent and kissed Circe's forehead. Then she did something Lydia did not understand at all. Violin then turned, bent, and kissed Banshee's forehead in exactly the same way. She spoke very softly and slowly to the dog, and Lydia would later swear to Bunny and anyone else who would listen that the damn dog actually nodded.

Then Violin turned and walked out of the room, shepherding Junie out as well. The dog, however, did not follow. It suddenly raised up and placed both front paws on the side of the bed.

"Bloody hell," Toys said again.

"Whoa!" growled Sam.

"Get her down," snapped Lydia, starting forward, a hand on her sidearm.

Violin merely shook her head. Junie shifted to block the two soldiers from entering the room.

"Wait," she said. "It's okay."

The dog stood there, looking down at Circe with dark, intense eyes. It did not try to lick her. It didn't even sniff her. All Banshee did was stare at the comatose woman as the seconds peeled off the clock and dropped slowly to the floor.

Banshee abruptly pushed off and dropped to all fours. She gave Lydia and Sam a long and penetrating stare. No one spoke. Then the wolfhound walked over to the corner of the room and sat.

She remained there, as still and silent as a statue.

Violin touched Junie's arm. "I have to go. I have a team waiting for me. Banshee will stay here."

"Thank you," said Junie. She kissed Violin's cheek. "Please be safe."

A troubled look flickered on the Italian woman's face. "There is something very bad coming."

"What have you heard?"

"It isn't anything from our sources, nothing like that. This is more of a feeling." She paused. "There is evil abroad in the land, Junie. That is not melodrama. Real evil is out there, and it's coming for all of us. It hurts me that I can't be here to stand with you. Look to Banshee. She was born on the night of new moon when the doorways between worlds are at their thinnest. She can see through shadows. Do you understand?"

Junie chewed her lip for a moment, then nodded. "I think I do."

Violin nodded. "If my team and I finish our job, I'll try to get back here. Until then, stay vigilant and stay safe."

With that, Violin turned and left

After a moment, Junie went into Circe's room and closed the door.

Outside, staring through the glass, Lydia and Sam stood together in a pool of profound confusion.

"What," said Lydia slowly, "the hell was that all about?"

Sam Imura shook his head. "I really do not know."

Before either of them could say anything else, Lydia's phone rang. It was Mr. Church.

Chapter Eighty-two

Tanglewood Island

Pierce County, Washington

March 31, 4:45 P.M.

Doctor Davidovich followed the guard back to his room.

The guard said nothing at all, even when Davidovich asked casual questions. The halls of the island resort were immaculate and lifeless. The dark hardwood wainscoting had been polished to a high gloss, the runner carpets were the very best quality, the Tiffany shades on the wall sconces were lovely. But there was absolutely no personality to the place. It was like stepping into a catalog page. Attractive down to the last detail, but unreal and unrelatable.

Like so many other aspects of his life.

Like the two men he had just spent the last hours with. Doctor Pharos and the cripple. A mad doctor and a freak. That's how he thought of them. Both hideous in their way. Both of them claiming to be part of the same family as him. Both of them believing that he was part of their world, that he was as corrupt, as demented, as vile as they were.

Two monsters.

Two, or three?

That was such a terrible question.

While he'd been in the bathroom, Davidovich had despaired over finding no faint sparks of conscience or morality in his own head or heart. Now, realizing that they were gone, that he had participated in the extinguishing of that heat, it left him feeling strange.

It should, he knew, have made it easier to step completely out of the world as he'd known it, even out of the capsule world in which he'd lived for the last few years. It should have made it a snap to become one with the darkness. As those two men were in tune with it.

That should absolutely have happened.

In the absence of conscience, there can be no genuine regret.

None.

As he walked, Davidovich wondered how sane he was. Because, despite the absolute darkness within, he felt an acid burn in his esophagus, right behind his heart.

Chapter Eighty-three

Over Ohio Airspace
March 31, 5:01 P.M.

I keep several sets of clothes aboard *Shirley*. I changed from the borrowed hospital scrubs into jeans, a tank top, and a Hawaiian shirt with sailboats on it. Usually, those shirts remind me of happy, peaceful times. Today, I felt like I was wearing a clown suit to a funeral. But it was the most sedate thing I had.

Then I got the call from Top.

Jesus.

I spent some long, bad minutes on the phone with Top and Bunny. Mostly Bunny. Top was hurting. Dilbert Howell had been a friend of his for many years.

"Has to be the fucking Seven Kings," he said.

"Has to be," I agreed.

I next called Glory Price, the top kick of the Miami field office. She and her people were already on the way in a couple of Black Hawks. We discussed the matter at some length, and I filled her in on my conversations with Bug and Church. She already knew about the rest. About the Kings targeting the DMS.

"I knew it was going to be a strange day from the jump," she told me.

"Why, because of Philly?"

"No," she said. "Because this morning on the way into the office I hit a dog. Or . . . I hit what I thought was a dog."

"You okay?"

"Me? Yeah, just shook up. It really rattled me. The thing came darting out between two parked cars."

"What kind of dog was it?"

"That's just it," said Glory, "it wasn't a dog at all. Not really. When I took a look, I thought maybe it was a coyote. But it wasn't that, either."

"I'm not following you."

"Joe," she said, "the thing I ran over was a jackal."

"A what?"

"A jackal. A fucking jackal. The animal-control guys had to send a picture of it to a zoo to get a proper ID. It was a *Canis adustus*, a side-striped jackal from southern Africa. And, get this, there aren't any in any zoos closer than Philadelphia. None known to be in private collections, either. So weird."

"Yeah," I said, "and I'm not really in the mood for today to get any weirder."

"Well, buckle up," she said, "'cause there's one more thing. And that's what really has me freaked out."

I didn't want to hear it, but I told her to tell me anyway.

"When the animal-control guys loaded it onto their truck, one of them spotted something. A dark mark on the jackal's gums."

"What kind of mark?"

"A tattoo. Two letters and some numbers: I, S, period. Then, thirteen, followed by a colon and twenty-one. At first we all thought it was some kind of identification tag, like they used to have on racehorses before they started using RFID chips. But it wasn't. I had Nikki run it for me, and it came back as a Bible reference. Isaiah 13:21: 'But desert beasts will lie down there, and their houses will be full of howling creatures; there owls will dwell, and goat-demons will dance there.'"

"Well . . . shit," I said.

"I know. So freaky. I mean . . . this has to be tied to what happened to Rudy. This has to be tied to that guy Nicodemus, right?"

"I'm afraid so," I said.

Operative word: "afraid."

My next call was to Church, but I couldn't get through. So I called Yoda at the Hangar. He was Bug's second in command.

"We're, ummmm, all over this." He is one of those people who always makes some kind of noise. Mostly a strange little humming sound. He always sounds like a pedantic bumble bee. Charming for about half a minute and then intensely irritating thereafter.

"I want more than that, Yoda."

"Mmmmm, meaning what, mmmm, exactly?"

"I have two guys heading to the airport for a direct flight to Eglin. They're taking a MindReader station with them, and we're going to take over control of the investigation. At least as far as the software and hardware goes. Mr. Church doesn't want us to interfere with the military's investigation."

"Top will oversee that," I said, but Yoda told me I was wrong.

"Mmmmmm, Mr. Church ordered Top and Bunny to, ummmm, head to San Diego."

"Why? They're needed at Eglin. I was just talking to them an hour ago."

"They're already on a, ummmm, plane."

"What's happening?"

He took another breath. "We have another, ummmm, drone thing," he said. "I, ummmm, think the Kings are using food-delivery drones to target citizens."

Chapter Eighty-four

Tanglewood Island
Pierce County, Washington
March 31, 5:09 P.M.

Doctor Davidovich sat in his room and stared at nothing. The room's lights were off, and he sat in an envelope of darkness.

Without and within.

He was trying to detach his mind from the strangeness of the moment, from the bizarre theatrics of his encounter with Doctor Pharos and the Gentleman. The lights were off so that his attention could not be pulled toward his computer or the stacks of notebooks that had come with him from his years in captivity.

He wanted to think. To take stock. To lay out the chronology of his personal descent from the man he thought he'd been to the man he clearly was. Aaron Davidovich was neither religious nor sentimental enough to view this process as his "long, dark night of the soul." That was a laughable thought.

A dark few hours in a posh resort on one of the outer rings of hell. It would make a good reality show. *Life in Hell,* with Aaron Davidovich.

The truly sad thing was that he would probably watch that show.

He wished he had it on DVD now so he could binge watch it. He wanted that kind of telescoped perspective. All of the seasons of his life. Teen nerd. College wunderkind. Hot prospect scouted by top universities. The man *Scientific American* called the "Computer Einstein." Then, the DARPA years. The government's excitement about Regis.

Then Boy.

Then the years as a prisoner.

The new work. Regis. The master-control program. The masterpiece of the quantum computer.

Boy.

Those days with her. The nights.

There were such tangled memories there. Horrible and . . .

And what?

His mind had been going for alliteration.

Horrible and . . . hot.

So hot.

Those nights when she came to him in the blank hours between a dying midnight and a mysterious new dawn.

The first time was after a meal with Boy. She'd made quinoa pasta with turkey-meat sauce, broccoli, and crusty whole grain bread. They washed it down with a good Italian red, and all during the meal Boy sat close to him, her knee touching his thigh. They'd listened to Cambodian music and talked about the scientific and artistic requirements of performance. Sometimes they laughed. They never talked about work over meals. Never.

That night, she crept into his bed and made love to him. If "love" was a useful word for what happened. Boy never spoke when they were in bed. The lights were always out, the room in total darkness. She never let him touch her. He had to lie there and experience what she did with her small, clever hands, with her mouth, with her skin, with her wetness. Over the years, she'd come to him seven times.

Seven.

That first time, it seemed utterly random, a product of too much wine and the enforced closeness in the apartment. But then Davidovich realized that it had to be a response to what had happened earlier that day.

Had to be.

That was the day he'd cracked the encryption that DARPA had put on Regis in the days following his abduction. Davidovich cracked it and used one of several back doors he'd built into his system to intrude and access passive programs hidden within the code. The fact of those back doors and the passive codes were something the Seven Kings seemed to already know about. Or maybe they presumed they would be there. Davidovich was known for being possessive. It was a character trait they had clearly expected to exploit when they'd taken him. It might have been as important to them as the nature of his genius. Though it was also well known in the world of advanced software design for the creator to build such deliberate portals into their work. Partly as a way of accessing the system should there be a failure in the primary control software, and partly because they could. The only real trick was to design a back door that could not be discovered by the aggressive security software used to find such things.

Davidovich found even the most belligerent hound-dog security programs to be both a personal affront and a challenge. He was absolutely positive that no one—not even the top tier of computer experts like Bug at the DMS, even with MindReader—could find his escape hatches.

On that day, when he'd cracked the encryption, Regis lay back and spread its legs for him, welcoming him like a familiar lover. Davidovich had gone into the system, touching subroutines with knowing hands. This was his. It did not matter to him that it was a work for hire for the Department of Defense. Who were they? At best, they were patrons. How many people could name Da Vinci's patrons? One in ten thousand? How many knew Da Vinci? Everyone.

That night, Boy had come to him and did things to him that Davido-vich's wife never even did with her dentist lover. She'd left him sprawled on the floor, one leg hooked on the edge of the bed, the sheets soaked and torn. The next morning, when he tried to talk about it, Boy did not respond. After he tried several times to engage her in playful next-day postcoital banter, she'd kicked him in the groin. Very fast, though not very hard. Enough to bend him over and make him nauseated for hours.

After that, he learned his lesson.

It was four months before she came to his bed again.

That time, and every time thereafter, he followed her unspoken set of rules. Not merely because he was afraid of her beatings. And not entirely because he hungered for her touch and all the physical mysteries she shared with him on those dark and silent nights.

No, what he wanted was her approval. He knew that about himself; he understood it. He wasn't proud of it, but he accepted it.

Sex wasn't the only way she showed her gratitude and approval. Eigh-teen months ago, after he'd devised a simple hacking virus that would allow Regis to infect any autonomous automobile program with a new ver-sion of Enact, Boy gave him a DVD to watch. On the DVD, Davidovich saw surveillance footage of two people being mugged. His wife and her lover. The attack happened in a parking garage. One man came out of the shadows, clamped a hand over his wife's mouth, and wrapped an arm around her throat, while two other men—both of them in black clothes, gloves, and ski masks—systematically beat the dentist into a red heap. They didn't kill him, but they paid particular attention to his groin, his hands, and his knees. And they knocked out every one of his teeth. They did not injure Davidovich's wife, but she was a screaming wreck when they finally released her and melted away.

Davidovich was positive that the two men doing the beating were Mason and Jacob.

Davidovich wanted to be shocked, horrified, appalled.

Instead, he watched it again.

Then he went into the bathroom and masturbated.

Afterward, he threw up and sat in a hot shower for an hour, boiling away his shame. He never commented on the DVD, nor did Boy.

Another time, after he had presented the schematics for a miniature version of the QC he was building and explained that it could be used in drones as small as a common pigeon, he'd received another gift. An extremely pretty girl asked his son to the dance. It did not matter to Davidovich if the girl was actually a twentysomething passing for a teenager. It didn't matter that she was a Seven Kings employee, probably a prostitute, who was part of the team keeping tabs on Matthew. All that mattered was the sheer joy on his son's face.

Davidovich was certainly smart enough to know that he was being manipulated. Threats first, then a show of consideration. Then sex. It was all part of a careful but—to him—obvious plan of corruption. He had, in fact, been corrupted by it. He was thoroughly corrupt now. His postabduction work with Regis, the other software he'd written over the last few years, the QC, the drones, the takeover of autonomous vehicle software—all of that proved that he was every bit as much a monster as Pharos and the charcoal briquette. Each of those things was another drop of water onto the smoking embers of his soul. Absolutely. No doubt about it.

And yet.

As he sat there in the dark, he thought of two people.

The first was Boy. He wanted her. He ached for her. Even though he was only ever a passive lump of flesh to her. Although he was never allowed to touch her, not even in the fiercest moments of their coupling, he wanted her. He felt something suspiciously like love for her. And it did not ameliorate it one whit to know that this was some perverse spin on Stockholm syndrome. Understanding a thing did not necessarily mean that you were free of it. Ask any addict. Ask an alcoholic who has been ten years dry but who reaches for a bottle after a few consecutive personal setbacks. They understood.

He thought of Boy and wondered how far into hell he would go if he knew that she would come to his bed one more time. Just once.

Davidovich knew that he would shovel coal into the devil's furnace for one more touch.

In the darkness he shook his head.

Then, in the next moment, he thought of the other person who was never far from his thoughts.

Matthew.

His son.

"Goddamn it," breathed Davidovich. In the darkness, he spoke his son's name.

"Matthew."

Matthew.

The tears started then.

"I did it for you," he told the image of his son that he kept safe in his mind. Not the teenager, not the college-bound young man. The picture in his mind was his son as he had been on the day he was born. A tiny thing. Pink and helpless. Crying because he had no power at all in the world. Crying because everything was strange and new and he didn't understand anything.

Davidovich had taken him from the nurse and kissed the squalling face. Each cheek. The forehead. The little heaving chest, over the fluttering heart. Then Davidovich had cuddled the infant to his own chest and soothed him and whispered to him. Promises of love. Promises of protection. Promises of always being there.

Promises.

Gone, now. Cracked by Boy and her thugs, but comprehensively ground into dust beneath Davidovich's own feet. Month by month, day by day since the CIA safe house.

Maybe before.

"Matthew," he said. Davidovich did not recognize his own voice. He was certain it was not the same voice that had whispered those promises to a newborn a million years ago.

Part Four
Solomon's Minefield

There is a sufficiency in the world for man's need but not for man's greed.

—MAHATMA GANDHI

Chapter Eighty-five

UC San Diego Medical Center
200 West Arbor Drive
San Diego, California
March 31, 5:42 P.M.

Toys felt as if he'd lost any contact with the real world.

He'd been at the hospital for a full day, and so far, except for that one call with Mr. Church, he felt as if the full sum of his usefulness was a few ticks below zero.

He sat on the floor outside Circe's room. The massive dog, Banshee, lay on the other side of the wall. Inside the room. Junie was in there, too. Everyone else was outside in the hall. Lydia was pacing incessantly up and down a twelve-foot line in front of Circe's door, her booted feet making soft sounds as she passed within inches of where Toys sat.

Toys closed his eyes, unwilling to endure the vile looks the DMS agent threw him on every turn. He went into his head and thought about the wild stories Hugo Vox had told him about Nicodemus. Impossible stories. Mythical fantasies and outright horror stories. All of which Hugo swore were true. Since he'd heard Rudy Sanchez speak the name of the monstrous little priest, Toys had felt as if the world was cracking and falling apart around him.

Toys had even seen the little priest at Hugo's estate in Iran, though he had begged off from an actual introduction. He'd heard too many tales about how those introductions often went. Nicodemus liked to make a lasting impression on a person. Some people never quite recovered from those encounters. There were rumors of at least two suicides directly following private meetings. In those days following the fall of the Kings, when Hugo and Toys lived in Iran, Toys had begun his downward slide into regret, shame, and self-hatred. Even at his worst, though, he was too clever to risk an encounter with someone for whom the word "chaos" seemed to have been deliberately invented. The priest was a trickster. A monster in every sense that Toys could imagine. And Toys was not entirely sure he was human.

So, no, he had chosen not to shake the man's hand or stand in his company.

Even now, with nothing more than the sound of his name on the air, Toys felt filthy, diseased, leprous—as if that name could taint the hearer.

Toys suddenly felt something, and it pulled him out of his terrified musings. It was more of a sensation rather than a noise. It was a something. A feeling, or an awareness. He straightened and looked around and immediately understood what it was.

A disturbance in the bloody Force, he mused, getting to his feet.

A big man came out of the elevator, flanked by soldiers with weapons in their hands and grim faces. The big man carried no obvious weapon and wore a dark suit of the best quality. His face was equally grim, though. His eyes were hidden behind the lenses of tinted glasses.

Mr. Church.

Behind him was an even bigger man. Brick. When Toys encountered Brick in the past, he'd tried—and failed—to strike up casual conversation.

Toys scrambled to his feet but stayed where he was, uncertain what to do.

As he approached, Church glanced at Rudy Sanchez's room and nodded to the soldier who stood by the door but walked directly toward Circe's room. Junie came out to meet him, and she gave him a powerful hug that the big man—after only a slight hesitation—returned. Then he gently pushed her to arm's length and looked past her to where Toys stood.

"What are you doing here?" he asked. There was no reproach, no accusation, no hostility. But there was also no room to sidestep or evade the question, even if Toys had wanted to.

"I came to talk to Junie, and stuck around after things started happening."

"He's been keeping me company and—" began Junie, but Church cut her off.

"Has he been in here alone at any point?"

"No, I haven't," said Toys. "You don't need to worry about me."

Church's mouth was a hard, unsmiling line. "If I thought I should worry about you, Mr. Chismer, you would not be here."

From the way he said it, Toys chose to take it as a threat to his general existence rather than merely to his being present at the hospital. He nodded, accepting any meaning Church wanted to imply.

"Toys is a friend," said Junie, shifting her body as if wanting to put herself between the young Brit and the head of the DMS.

There was a movement, and they all turned to see Banshee come and stand in the doorway. The massive dog looked at Church.

"Violin brought her," said Junie. "She wanted to stay but couldn't. She left Banshee here for Circe."

"I know," Church told her. He walked toward the dog, which held her ground and watched him. Church stopped and held out his hand to be sniffed. Banshee paused for a moment and then took his scent. Then Church bent close to the dog and spoke rapidly but softly to it in a language Toys did not recognize. The dog licked his hand, turned, and went back into the room. Everyone stared at her and then slowly shifted their eyes to Church. To Junie, Church said, "I'll be a few minutes."

Church entered the room, closed the door, and drew the heavy curtains.

Chapter Eighty-six

Tanglewood Island

Pierce County, Washington

March 31, 5:46 P.M.

Doctor Aaron Davidovich opened his bedroom door and walked into the hall. There was a guard stationed ten feet away, and he turned toward the scientist with crisp military precision and natural suspicion.

"Sir," he said, "may I help you?"

Davidovich smiled. "I want to take a walk. Get some air. Am I allowed?"

The guard hesitated, and Davidovich watched several emotions flicker on the man's hard face. Davidovich was sure he could catalog them. He was sure that the man had been given what would feel like conflicting orders. Until today, Davidovich had been a prisoner; after all, he'd been brought to the island with a black bag over his head. This guard might even

284 | Jonathan Maberry

have been part of the escort detail. At first Davidovich had been locked in his room with strict orders to stay there. The guards would know about that restriction. Then were was Pharos's big speech about how Davidovich was now part of the family. An equal. Blah, blah, blah. All bullshit. Manipulative and clumsy. The guards would know some of that, too. Being allowed to spend so much time in the bathroom before had been a test of the supposed tolerance and freedom. Everyone would know that. Pharos, the Gentleman, all the guards.

Exactly as they should have.

Just as Pharos would probably expect Davidovich to further test that freedom in some way. A stroll around the building would be one predictable way. A stroll on the grounds would be another.

How would the guard react? How were the orders phrased?

The guard took a step back, thereby increasing the subjective control that a guard would have over a prisoner.

"Of course, sir."

"So," pushed Davidovich, "I'm allowed to go outside?"

The little muscles at the corners of the guard's face tightened, but otherwise his face showed exactly zero emotion. It was a very "soldierly" thing for him to do.

"Absolutely, sir," said the guard.

Davidovich smiled, but he exhaled, too. To show relief. Everything here was theater, so he felt it important to run with that. To play his role.

"Which way is it?" asked Davidovich. "Can't seem to remember the way."

He laughed as he said that. Reminding the guard about the black hood. Making a joke of it. Sharing the joke.

There was the slightest flicker on the guard's lips. "Let me show you."

No "sir" this time. A more human response.

Good, thought Davidovich coldly. That will make it easier.

The guard led him to a closed door, unlocked it with a keycard, pushed it open, and held it for him. There was a set of stairs, and the guard followed him up, through another door, along a corridor that looked identical to the one downstairs, and then out into the humid, misty day.

The sound was covered by a writhing layer of mist that flowed like pale snakes under a thin blanket. High above them, pelicans glided in formation. Boats swung at anchor across the water, and, far out toward the horizon line, an oil tanker lumbered its relentless way from Alaska to some port in California.

Davidovich did not know which island he was on, but during the trip he'd overheard enough bits and pieces to know they were in Washington State and that this was very likely Puget Sound. Collecting disparate data and assembling them into cohesive information were nothing to him. And since being in captivity, his survival depended on observing and assessing every fragment of data. About everything.

Every single thing.

There was a wide wooden porch with a slat rail built completely around the hotel. It was painted a rather bland tan color. Artless. Darker brown benches were bolted to the deck against the wall at regular intervals. Beyond the rail the terrain varied. In some spots there were lush flowerbeds, in others patches of neatly mowed grass. They passed another guard, who stood watch at the entrance to a finger pier. Davidovich nodded to him. The sentry didn't even look at him but instead cocked an eyebrow at Davidovich's guard.

"Taking a walk, Max," said the guard.

The sentry responded with a single curt nod.

They walked on. In a few places, the rail overlooked stretches of a rock shoreline, where boulders were continually splashed with foamy seawater. Crabs scuttled over them. The rocks were patterned with overlapping splashes of new and old gull droppings.

"Can we go down to the water?" asked Davidovich. "God, it's been so long since I smelled the ocean."

From the guard's expression, he clearly wanted to say no. His smile was entirely plastic. "Sure. But you have to be careful."

"Oh, I'm not going in," laughed Davidovich.

There was a latched waist-high gate nearby, and Davidovich waited while the guard opened it. The scientist nodded thanks as he stepped through and then followed a short, winding path down to the soft, muddy sand. Davidovich stood for a moment and took several long, deep breaths of sea air.

"It's wonderful," he said, grinning.

The guard nodded. "I guess."

Davidovich squatted down. "Oh, look. Those stones look just like dinosaur eggs."

The beach was strewn with many fist-sized black and charcoal-gray rocks that had been polished to smoothness by ten million waves as they rolled and tumbled through the Pacific. Davidovich picked up a couple of them and studied the pores and curves.

"They really do look like eggs," he said. "Don't you think?"

"I guess," repeated the guard. The man was already deeply bored.

"You know," said Davidovich, "I almost went into paleontology. Loved dinosaurs when I was a kid. Well, when I say I almost went into it, I mean I thought about it. *Jurassic Park* came out when I was in high school. Great flick, even thought Michael Crichton got most of his science wrong. You can't really clone a dinosaur from blood in a mosquito. Everyone knows that. And using frog genes to patch gaps in dinosaur DNA? Don't get me started on that." He weighed one of the stones and then pitched it out into the surf. "Most people don't really understand dinosaurs. They didn't evolve into crocodiles or Komodo dragons. No, the chicken has a lot more in common with velociraptors. Think about that next time you're eating Chicken McNuggets."

He stood up with several stones in his hands and spent a few minutes throwing them out to sea, scooping up more, throwing them. One of the stones clanged off a buoy and rebounded, skipped along the top of an incoming wave, and then plopped down out of sight.

"Whoohooo!" shouted Davidovich. "You see that?"

"Nice throw, sir."

Davidovich held a stone out to the guard. "How's your arm?"

The guard shook his head. "That's okay, sir."

"Oh, come on. Have a little fun. See if you can hit that buoy?"

"Really, I'm not supposed to—"

"Not supposed to have a little fun? I don't believe it. I will not believe your orders specified that you can't lighten up and fuck around a little. What's your name?"

"Steve."

"Come on, Steve. Just throw one. You're not going to tell me that you can't outthrow a computer geek, for God's sake."

"It's not that," said Steve.

Davidovich held out the stone, still grinning. "Won't take no for an answer. Just one throw."

"I—"

"Steve . . . "

The guard looked up and down the shoreline as if expecting to see his fellow mercenaries or maybe Doctor Pharos standing there watching. He shook his head.

But after a moment he took the stone.

"Just one," he said.

"You have to hit the buoy."

Steve managed a small smile. A real one. "No problem."

He tossed the stone up and caught it, fitted his fingers around it like a ballplayer, raised his arm, and threw.

It was a good throw, but at the instant he threw it, a wave picked the buoy up and canted it to the left. The stone missed by an inch.

"Ha!" cried Davidovich. "You missed."

"It moved."

"Doesn't count. My turn." He picked up three more stones, switched two to his left hand, and with his right threw the other. It whistled through the mist and caught the buoy on the rise. The clang echoed back to them. "Got it!"

"That was a lucky shot," said Steve.

"Talk's cheap. Money where your mouth is," said Davidovich as he held one of the remaining stones out.

"I got this," said Steve, taking the stone. He was grinning, too, as he set himself for the throw. "I fucking got this."

He put a lot into the throw. Raising his left leg and stepping into the throw to put body weight behind a fastball pitch, he whipped the stone above the waves, and it hit the buoy dead center mass. It struck a massive clang from the metal that was three times as loud as the sound Davidovich's rock had made.

Steve laughed out loud and spun around, delighted that he'd won.

His broad, happy grin broke apart as Davidovich smashed the remaining stone into his face. The guard's head snapped back, and he immediately fell backward. Davidovich followed with desperate speed, hammering over and over with the rock as the man collapsed back onto the beach.

Over and over and over again until there was no trace of the smile, or the face, or the man. Only red horror. Blood leaped up around Davidovich as he continued to hammer at the man until there was no longer even a head shape.

Davidovich heard a sound. A high, shrill whimpering noise. When he realized that it was coming from his own throat, he reeled back from what he was doing. The rock fell from his hand, and for a moment he stared at the intense red that was smeared all over his it.

He could feel the warmth of it. Smell it.

Drops of it burned on his face.

It was the first time he had been this close to real blood since that day when Boy had strapped him to a chair and made him watch Mason and Jacob as they systematically dismembered and dehumanized a stranger back in Ashdod.

He fell backward and then scuttled away from the corpse like an upside-down crab.

Then a word exploded inside his head.

A name.

Matthew.

He stopped whimpering, stopped retreating.

Matthew.

Davidovich made himself look at Steve. Once upon a time, Boy had threatened to have Matthew picked up. Threatened to have his testicles and eyes mailed to where they were keeping him. So Davidovich could see the proof of his son's dismemberment. There was no way to know if Steve would have been part of that, but he worked for the Seven Kings. He might have participated. Maybe he would have held the boy down. Or handled the knife. Or shipped the package.

It didn't matter.

"Matthew," he said aloud. Then he summoned the rage that was almost drowned beneath the ocean of fear. He used it the way it should be used. He pumped it into his muscles. Into his tendons and bones.

Get the fuck up, he told himself.

And he got up.

Beyond the dead man were the waters of the Puget Sound.

Beyond them was the mainland.

Somewhere out there was his son. Maybe the Kings would still kill his boy, but Davidovich didn't think so. Not right away. No, they would place all of their resources into finding him. Into getting Davidovich back. Into silencing him.

"Try and catch me, you sick fucks," he said, and then he waded out into the cold water and struck out as hard and fast as he could. Boy had helped him get fit and strong. To have stamina.

Yeah, and fuck you, too, you little psycho bitch.

He tried not to think about those nights with her. All he allowed himself to think about was his son. And the phone number that his handler in the CIA had made him remember all those years ago.

Chapter Eighty-seven

UC San Diego Medical Center
200 West Arbor Drive
San Diego, California
March 31, 5:47 P.M.

Toys looked up sharply as the door to Circe's room opened and Mr. Church stepped into the hall. Lydia and Junie instantly began moving toward him, but Church shook his head and walked into Rudy Sanchez's room. Brick went and stood outside, arms folded, chest massive, expression unapproachable.

The big dog, Banshee, stood in the doorway and watched him with calm, dangerous, strange eyes. Junie walked past the door and went into Circe's room.

Doors closed.

Toys remained seated where he was.

"Whatever's going on," said a voice, and Toys jumped and looked up to see Sam Imura standing nearby, "it's way the hell above our pay grade."

Toys looked up at him, said nothing, and nodded.

Chapter Eighty-eight

UC San Diego Medical Center
200 West Arbor Drive
San Diego, California
March 31, 5:48 P.M.

"Doctor Sanchez," said Mr. Church, "can you hear me?"

Rudy Sanchez's eyes fluttered for a moment, then opened slowly. His pupils were dilated and the sclera was shot with red. There was a dark purple bruise in the center of his forehead. A half-moon shape. A heel shape.

Rudy licked his lips and tried to speak. Could not.

Mr. Church took a plastic sponge that had been provided by a nurse, dipped it in cool water, and pressed it gently to Rudy's lips. He let the man suck moisture from it, then set the sponge aside.

"Th-thanks . . . " Rudy's voice was hoarse, his voice cracked.

"Do you know who I am?"

"Yes."

"Who am I?"

"Mr. Church."

"Do you know who you are?"

"Yes."

"What is your name?"

"Rudy Sanchez."

"Good. Do you know where you are?" asked Church.

Rudy's eyes turned glassy, then wet. A tear broke and rolled from the corner of his eye, along his temple, and into his hair. He looked away and then squeezed his eye shut.

"I am in hell," said Rudy.

Chapter Eighty-nine

Over Indiana Airspace
March 31, 5:49 P.M. Eastern Standard Time

With Top and Bunny on a separate jet to take over the crime scene in Chula Vista, I decided to maximize the flight time to try and map out what we knew about this case. I used several packs of Post-its to paper my jet's interior walls. I called Top, and after consoling him on the loss of his friend, I told him that I wanted to make this a joint project. We kept an open line via earbuds and laptops and worked it through together.

The process filled the rest of the flight time.

"I think we have it mapped out," said Top. Our computers were synched to share data and we have the videoconference function thrown onto the big screens mounted inside of each aircraft. It was the closest we could get to being in the same room. This allowed us to see the notes we'd all taped to the walls. My high-def screen was the only part of *Shirley*'s interior that wasn't covered with little colored paper squares.

The three of us looked at what we had. The port side of *Shirley*'s cabin was covered in Post-it notes and larger papers taped to walls, windows, and seats. Both jets had onboard printers, and we'd printed out every news report that involved drones or autonomous computer systems.

I expected to find six or seven incidents. That would have been enough. That would have been truly frightening.

There were dozens of them.

I didn't even know what to call this.

We'd tagged more than ninety incidents that could be related to the Kings' experimention with UAVs and the Regis control software.

"There are clear patterns here," said Top, pointing. "You can see their whole damn rollout from day one. It started with this." He stepped up and tapped one Post-it on which was written

Aldus Binoche
Camera Crew
B-Unit Camera UAV
Lake Superior, WI

The date was one year ago from yesterday.

"Remember that?" asked Top. "The guy who had that Cajun-cooking reality show? Something happened and the whole crew died? Local law said a generator blew up, overheated the ice on the lake where Binoche was fishing, and the whole team went into the icy water. Died right there. Only thing is, there was a camera drone doing—whaddya call it when they have someone else take scenery shots and shit?"

"B-roll?" I suggested. "Second unit?"

"Right. They had a UAV camera doing that. A production assistant reported it going missing, then said it was back and heading their way. That was the last transmission."

"So, what are you saying?" asked Bunny. "Someone hijacked it and put a bomb on it?"

"That's exactly what I'm saying."

"Why?"

"Test drive," he said. "Can't prove it, but think about it. Remote spot and a way to completely hide the evidence? That sound like those Kings ass-fucks to you?"

"Okay," agreed Bunny, "but who the hell's Aldus Binoche. I mean, sure, he had that TV show, but he has no connection to the Kings."

"Figure it out, Farm Boy."

Bunny sighed. "Right, right, they picked someone with no connections to test-drive their thing. But . . . what thing were they test-driving. This isn't Regis."

"Actually, it is," I said. "The UAVs leased by the network all have Safe-Zone. The manufacturer of the software even had to do a big payout to prevent a lawsuit."

Bunny leafed through some pages on the floor of their jet. "So how come it didn't show up in the field-test stats? No, wait, I'm being slow again. It doesn't show up because this is the civilian version, and it's already sold, so why would the vendor report it? There's—what?—one of those legal things where they pay money but the other side has to sign something that says no one is actually accepting responsibility or admitting fault?"

"Brain finally switched on?" asked Top.

"I need more coffee. Can't remember the last time I slept."

We scanned our notes.

"Looks to me, from what we have here," said Top, "that the Kings can hack the GPS and controls of commercial UAV and maybe autonomous drive systems. That seem like a fair assessment?"

We thought about it, nodded. There were several incidents of wayward drones whose misbehavior had no known cause. Unless you consider the hacking and hijacking angle.

"You know, Boss," said Bunny, "this makes me think a little harder about your theory that they have either Davidovich or his research."

We looked at the other notes.

"Then there's this from ten months ago," said Top, taking a matchstick out of his mouth and pointing to another. "Four serious accidents involving self-parking cars. One fatality in Saint Louis. Girl gets killed when her car suddenly pulls out into traffic. Statement from her friend inside the salon and witnesses on the street confirm that the girl was fighting to get out of the car but was killed. That's number two."

"SafeZone?" asked Bunny.

Top nodded and pointed to more than thirty other accidents, including some fatal crashes, involving autonomous driving systems. The accidents were random, scattered across the country, across economic and social demographics, across age groups. There was a pattern, but it wasn't easy to see.

We saw it now, though.

"Again, they're hacking SafeZone software and causing it to malfunction," said Top. "All of which led up to Cadillac One going ass-wild a little while back."

The Beast, the president's armored car, had indeed malfunctioned, causing some minor injuries. Linden Brierly, a close friend of Mr. Church, had had his face dented.

"Wait," said Bunny, "so they had this same software in the president's car? Is it still there? I mean, if so, we need to make a call."

I shook my head. "No. As soon as it malfunctioned, it was stripped out and replaced by a different system. Solomon, I think. Different manufacturer altogether and it isn't tied to Regis. Bug ran a check on that for Church after it happened. No one who was anywhere near Regis was involved with Solomon. It has no DARPA or DoD connection, and it has no military application of any kind."

"Sure, okay," said Bunny, "but does that mean we trust it?"

"Right now," I said, "I don't trust the timer on my Mr. Coffee."

"Hooah," agreed Top.

"We'll forward all of this to Nikki and Church. And to Linden Brierly." I looked at the wall. "What's next?"

Top looked at his laptop. "El train in Chicago. Autodrive system on two trains went ape-shit four months back. Engineers couldn't control the trains, and they crashed."

"Geez," said Bunny, "I remember that. Something like eleven people dead."

"Twelve," said Top. "Put down to computer error."

I stepped closer to the wall. "That's a bigger system to take control of. With each step, the Kings have been flexing their wings. Testing SafeZone, proving to themselves that they can take it over." I turned to the others. "What questions does this raise? Hit me."

"Right out of the gate," said Bunny, "what about BattleZone? We have the Eglin thing, but there's nothing else here that says they can hack into the software packages the Department of Defense has been installing. No ships have launched missiles, no fighters have gone crazy. What's that tell us? Do they not have access to the military version of Regis? Is it only Safe-Zone that they can control?"

"Eglin," said Top.

"Sure, Eglin," Bunny agreed, "but what about it? That Regis stuff's in everything. Why aren't there missiles in the air? If they had control over BattleZone and all of Regis, they could launch all their shit and that would be game over. The fact that they haven't makes me think that what happened to Dilbert Howell was actual computer error. Sad, tragic, sure, but I'm not sure we can make a case to connect that to the Kings."

"You're saying you don't believe it?" I asked.

"What I'm saying," insisted Bunny, "is that we can't prove it. Eglin could be bad timing and a tragic accident."

Top gave him a long and withering look.

"We can't take Eglin off the board," I said slowly. "I mean, if it was the Kings, it's a big win for them. It might have told them everything they need to know if they're planning something really big."

"Like a major launch?" asked Bunny.

"Like a major launch."

"Shit."

"Which puts us exactly where, Cap'n?" asked Top. "Do we recommend to the entire United States military that they flush a few billion dollars and pull the software out of every plane, tank, and warship? They would burn us at the damn stake."

"In a heartbeat," said Bunny.

"Got to file a recommendation of caution," I said. "And we have to hope that Eglin wasn't part of this."

From the looks on their faces, I knew they didn't buy that any more than I did.

"Other questions?" I asked.

"Drones in general," said Bunny. "Aside from being able to hack other people's drones, the Kings have access to their own. The one at the Resort. Two different kinds of drones in Philly. And the one that killed Bug's mom. Where are they getting them?"

It was a good question with, unfortunately, a disappointing answer. UAVs are everywhere now. More than 320 companies based in the United States manufacture drones or drone parts. Thousands of stores sell kits to build them. Plus, there are imports. Canada and Mexico have factories, and everyone in Southeast Asia who could retool a plant are turning them out.

I called Doctor Hu to see if he had anything, but he transferred me to Yoda without actually responding to my question. He does that sort of thing. Hu's a dick.

When Yoda came on the line, I explained what I wanted.

"Hmmmm. Well, the, ummmm, drone from the ballpark isn't standard. It's, ummm, a variation on a design used by the Russians. Though, ummmm, we've seen an almost identical model in North Korea. Built to look like a regular pigeon. I think, mmmm, Nikki told you that it had some kind of radical QC CPU. Mmmmm-hmmmm, that's kind of delicious, and we're picking it apart to see, ummm, how it works. Or why it works, because it's so small. Nothing like it anywhere. I, ummmm, dream about tech like this."

"Okay," I said, and damn near followed it with an "mmmm." "Does it tell us anything? Does it lead us anywhere?"

"Ummmm, no. Not really. Just, mmmm, tells us that they're smarter than us."

296 | Jonathan Maberry

"Not really what I want to hear, Yoda."

"Not really what I, ummmm, ever want to admit."

I ended the call. Then I thought about it and called Nikki. She didn't hum, and she worked in a different part of Bug's group. She was a superstar in research and hacking.

"Nikki," I said, putting the call on speaker, "I want to describe something to you, and I want your reaction. Okay? Let me outline it without commentary."

"Sure, Joe. Go for it."

I told her what Top, Bunny, and I had come up with. The yearlong pattern of what appeared to be field tests of the ability to hack and subvert autonomous driving systems and commercial drones. When I was finished, I could almost hear her frown.

"This can't be right," she said.

"Tell me why."

"What you're describing is a pretty clear pattern, Joe. I mean, sure, they hid it pretty well by spreading it around and making it look like either random accidents or, in the case of the TV drone, some kind of domestic terrorism."

"Right, but . . . ?"

"But if this pattern actually exists, then we should already know about it. I mean . . . that's what MindReader does. It's what I do. We look for patterns in the big jumble of events, news stories, incident reports, police reports, and everything filed by the FBI, Homeland . . . It's just that this has to be wrong."

I took a breath. "Or . . . what's the alternative, kid?"

She didn't want to say it, and—let's face it—we didn't want to hear it. She said it anyway.

"Or they kept this from us. They hid it. Which means someone's learned how to block MindReader."

Bam. There it was.

Nikki put a button on it, though. "Setting aside how they did it, if they have something like this . . . what else are they hiding?"

Chapter Ninety

Aaron Davidovich washed ashore like a piece of trash. Rumpled, broken, filthy, and cold.

So cold.

His clothes were soaked. He'd kicked off his shoes in the water, and his feet were bruised and cut. Every muscle he owned ached like he'd been beaten. He lay on the beach, half covered by muddy sand, chest down, face turned sideways so he could breath through the little gap between the bunched fabric at the shoulder of his torn and sodden suit and the angle of his forearm. His cheek rested on his hand, but the hand was like a block of ice that didn't seem to belong to him anymore.

"God," he gasped. "God . . . "

Davidovich felt like he was welded into the sand. Part of a desolate landscape. Maybe he would die here and truly become part of this place. The sand fleas and worms would consume his skin and organs. His blood would drain away into the sluggish surf. If no one found him, his bones would dissolve beneath the relentless assault of parasites and bacteria. He would cease to be. He would fade into nothingness.

All that would be left was the memory of him.

A hated man. Despised. Reviled.

Maybe damned.

Damned.

He believed that Matthew would continue to love him for a little while, but after the full extent of his crimes were known and endlessly dissected in the press, that would change. A son's love for his father would change into bitter hate and disappointment. And that would pollute the life of a child who should have been allowed to grow up with no emotional scarring, no trauma that might twist him into some ugly adult shape.

A father who was a traitor, a terrorist, and a mass murderer?

Yes. That was going to ruin the boy.

It would definitely kill Davidovich's mother. She was holding on by a thread as it was. This would snap that slender filament and send her plunging down into the pit.

He wished he would die, too.

Right here, right now.

He prayed that there was no god, and he was aware of the absurdity of that. He wanted death to be a big black doorway that led nowhere. If there was nothing, there was no shame. There would be no memory of the harm he'd done—and would continue to do—to his son.

A wave broke over him, pushing stinking seawater up to his shoulders. He turned his face to keep it from filling his slack mouth. The action was too slow, and he gagged on a mouthful of brackish water and fish excrement.

Davidovich tried to spit it out, failed to do it the right way, and gasped in half a pint of water. Into his throat, into his lungs.

The coughing fit was immediate, and it was terrible. His lungs felt like they were exploding as he coughed and spat and choked. His body convulsed, tearing itself loose of the sand until he was a tiny ball on elbows and knees, his chest pulsing with the deep, braying coughs. Pain detonated in his chest, in his lungs. The world fragmented into fireworks of pure white and midnight black, with a fringe of red around the edges.

"Please," he gasped between fits.

That word was worse than the pain of the spasms. It tasted more disgusting than the seawater in his mouth.

Please.

It was what he had said to Boy years ago. When she'd first come to him and beaten him, and humiliated him. It had been the thing he'd said when she made him watch the degradation and evisceration of the man Boy had killed on that day she made him her slave. It was what he had whispered in the nights when she came to him and touched him and drew him to the top of a swaying tower.

Please.

Such a weak word.

Such a terrible word.

He said it again. Meaning so much.

"Please . . ." he said.

The coughing fit faded. Slowly and reluctantly, as if his body would have preferred to continue punishing him. He remained on elbows and knees.

For a long time.

And then he gathered together everything that he had and everything that he was. Scientist, father, husband, son, man, traitor, murderer, monster.

Each of those aspects had a part in making him get up off his knees. Get to his feet. Orient himself. Take a step.

And another.

Walking up the sandy slope toward the lights.

Across the water was the dark bulk of the hotel on Tanglewood Island.

Beyond the trees in front of him, rising like the promise of heavenly retribution, was the snowcapped bulk of Mount Rainier.

For reasons he could never explain to himself, not even in that moment, Davidovich spat toward the mountain and muttered, "Fuck you."

He kept moving up the beach, angling toward the Fox Island Bridge. Limping on his battered feet. Leaving smudges of blood behind him with every footfall.

Walking away from the edge of the abyss, one trembling step at a time.

Chapter Ninety-one

UC San Diego Medical Center
200 West Arbor Drive
San Diego, California
March 31, 6:02 P.M.

"The prognosis is encouraging," said Mr. Church. He had his briefcase open on the wheeled table beside Rudy Sanchez's bed. An open package of Nilla Wafers sat atop a stack of folders. Church selected a cookie, tapped crumbs from it, bit a piece, and chewed quietly. Rudy watched him. "The concussion was mild. There are no fractures."

"You're ignoring what I said."

Church studied the cookie for a moment, then set it down. "Ignoring? No, doctor, I am not."

"Aren't you going to say something?" asked Rudy.

"What would you expect me to say? You're in great distress. Understandably so, given your devotion to Circe and concerns for your baby. You were attacked and have sustained injuries. The nation is under attack, and you likely feel torn between wanting to be here and needing to be out there doing what you can."

"No," said Rudy.

"No—what?"

"That's not it."

Church nodded and settled back in his chair. "Then tell me what it is."

"The man who attacked me . . ." Rudy's words trickled down, and for several long minutes he lay there, not looking at Church. Not really looking at anything in the room. His gaze drifted upward to the acoustic tiles fitted into their aluminum frame in the ceiling. He stared at them as if they were windows into his own thoughts. Church said nothing. He ate the rest of his cookie. Drank some water from a bottle of Arrowhead. Ate another cookie. Waited.

The room was very still, very quiet.

Finally, Rudy took a ragged breath. It was loud, like a drowning man breaking the surface to drink in his first lungful. His body trembled, and he dabbed at fresh tears in his eye.

"I—I'm afraid," he began slowly, "that you won't believe me. That you'll think the details of my attack are the product of cranial trauma."

"Would you allow me to be the governor of my own credulity, Doctor Sanchez?"

Rudy glanced at him. "What I have to say won't seem rational. You won't be able to believe it."

Mr. Church gave him a small, weary smile. "Doctor, over the last six years, we've come to know each other very well. I believe I can accurately state that the understanding we share exceeds the bounds of what has actually been spoken between us. You possess insight, and I've been more candid with you than with most. Do you honestly believe that I would sit in close-minded judgment of anything you would have to tell me?"

"I don't know."

"Doctor . . ."

"I don't think so, but this is difficult for me to even think about, let alone say. I don't know if I believe it."

"Then," continued Church, "perhaps we can help each other come to a level of understanding and acceptance."

Rudy almost smiled. "You say that like you've been in this situation before. With ordinarily reliable witnesses who have extraordinary things to say."

"More times than I care to recall, doctor. Before and after Captain Ledger came to work for me."

Rudy closed his eyes for a moment and repeatedly licked his lips. Then he opened his eyes and stared up at the ceiling. Not at Church.

"There was a priest in the chapel," he said. His tone was soft, almost hushed. "Even though Agent Cowpers had cleared the room, he was there."

"This man was not a total stranger to you?" asked Church. "Was he?"

"I don't . . . "

"Doctor, now is not the time to be coy. If you have some suspicion, then please share it. This man is a threat to you and to Circe."

Rudy thought Church almost said "to my daughter." There was the slightest hitch in his words, but Church was too skilled to let himself make that kind of error. The truth—and the urgency of it—hung in the air, though.

So, Rudy took one more breath and blurted it out. "I think I know who it was."

"Who was it?" Church asked.

"You won't believe me."

"Try me."

Rudy paused. "I think it was Nicodemus."

"Ah."

"You . . . don't seem surprised. Why? Do you know something?"

Church nodded. "You were overheard speaking that name when the staff brought you up here."

"Then, you already heard? Good, but know this . . . he doesn't look the same."

"Meaning what? Was he in disguise?"

"No. I saw him at Graterford Prison several years ago. I sat with the man, spoke with him. And although the man who attacked me looks a bit like him, speaks like him, knows what he knows, he's also different. It's almost like he was in another body. Like he was wearing someone else's skin." Rudy paused again. "I am aware of how this sounds, and I'll accept that blunt-force trauma is a factor here. However . . . "

"Go on."

Rudy's hands were shaking as he reached up to run fingers through his hair. "Dear God and the Virgin Mary protect me," he said in a small and frightened voice, "I think the thing I met in the chapel wasn't human. I think it was a monster."

Chapter Ninety-two

UC San Diego Medical Center
200 West Arbor Drive
San Diego, California
March 31, 6:11 P.M.

Toys wondered if Junie Flynn knew about Church's connection to Circe. She seemed to be on the inside track of a lot of things, but that secret was huge—and she was, after all, a civilian. Toys knew about Circe from Hugo, and he'd had one very uncomfortable conversation with Church about it after finding out.

Church had said, "You understand that very few people in the world know that Circe is my daughter. It complicates things that you know it, that Hugo told you. It would be easier for me, and safer for Circe, if I put a bullet in you now. Do you understand that?"

"I do," Toys had said. "And if you need to do that, then go ahead."

Church had been a long time considering his next comment, and it had taken Toys off guard. "In my life," he said, "I've met several people with complicated histories who claimed to be on the road to redemption. Some of them, in fact, made their journeys. A few—a very few—of those people are friends of mine. The majority of them are not. And a fair percentage of those who are not are now dead."

"You really think you need to threaten me?" asked Toys.

"That's not what I'm doing," Church replied. "Should I ever feel the need to threaten you, there will be little doubt as to what's happening. What I'm doing is establishing the parameters of our shared understanding. Protecting the connection between Circe and myself matters more to me than almost anything else."

Toys remembered that Church had said "almost." The man had interesting priorities. Then again, the scary old bastard was saving the world. Pretty often, too. So there was that.

That conversation had happened years ago, and for the most part Toys had shoved the knowledge that Circe was Church's daughter into the very back of his mental closet. Even now, he could hardly connect the woman he'd worked with so often at FreeTech with this hard, unemotional, dangerous man. They barely seemed like they belonged to the same species, let alone the same family.

After more than half an hour, Church pulled back the curtains and opened the door. For once, his legendary cool seemed shaken. He was pale and looked much older than the sixty-something Toys figured him for. Church walked past him without comment and spoke quietly with a trio of doctors. He shook their hands and then went and consulted with his agents. Toys waited him out. He had nowhere else to be.

Finally, Church glanced at him, nodded briefly, and walked toward an empty corner of the ICU. Toys dutifully followed.

"Junie told me about what happened to Aunt Sallie," said Toys. "How bad is it?"

"Bad enough."

"Pity. I mean that, really. I mean, sure, she hates my sodding guts, but she's a character. She's an interesting woman. Hugo was afraid of her."

"That's not an unreasonable feeling. They sent a team of Kingsmen after her, and they're all dead," said Church, then switched the subject. "Per our earlier conversation, is there anything else you wanted to tell me?"

"No. Nothing of use other than to warn you to be careful of that psychotic son of a bitch Nicodemus. Sebastian and Hugo all but worshipped him, and everyone else was terrified of him. I know I was. I . . . "

"What?"

"No, you'll think I'm daft."

"Try me."

"I . . . I don't think Nicodemus is exactly what he appears to be."

"And what does he appear to be?"

"Human."

Chapter Ninety-three

Aaron Davidovich knew that hitchhiking was out of the question. He had no money, no shoes, no chance of being seen as anything except a vagrant or a threat. By now, the Kings would have people out looking for him. They would be driving the roads, listening to police reports.

He needed to stay off the grid.

The biggest problem was that this part of Fox Island was upscale. Big homes. Money. And with the money came the domestic security systems. He knew he could bypass anything, but he lacked even a basic set of tools.

He was scared, cold, desperate, and wild.

All of that was what made people make stupid mistakes. He could not afford to make a single mistake. Not one.

It would get him killed, and it wouldn't help Matthew.

It would also guarantee that the world—the whole damn world—would fall apart. There were only hours left until the Kings used Regis and the other programs to change the world.

To destroy it.

To destroy Matthew's world.

"No," he told himself as he staggered along a service alley between estates. It was the kind of passage used by meter readers and landscapers. He was shivering badly, and the pain in his feet was awful.

Then he saw it. Fifty feet ahead. Just standing there as if planted in his path by providence.

An open gate.

A goddamn open gate.

How or why it was open didn't matter. A utility-company man who didn't care. A lawn cutter who wasn't doing his job. What did it matter?

Davidovich approached it cautiously, ducking down to use the cover of a thick row of hedges. As he approached the gate, he knelt down and crawled the rest of the way on hands and knees, then cautiously peered around the gatepost. Beyond it was a half acre of green grass, flowerbeds, a swing set, and a toolshed.

A toolshed.

A fucking toolshed.

It would be locked, of course. But no one puts an alarm on a toolshed.

A sob broke in Davidovich's chest as he crawled through the gate and onto the soft, cool grass. He stumbled getting up and ran most of the way on hands and feet, hunched over like a dog.

Chapter Ninety-four

UC San Diego Medical Center
200 West Arbor Drive
San Diego, California
March 31, 6:28 P.M.

Toys knew he should leave the hospital. He'd shared his information with Church and showed his support for Circe and Junie. But now he was doing nothing more useful than being a gofer. He fetched coffee, did a run to the nearest sandwich shop, and read a lot of magazines.

Church had somehow commandeered a doctor's office and turned it into a situation room. Technicians arrived with portable computers. More armed guards showed up, too. The whole hospital was becoming an armed camp, though if anyone in administration had a problem with it, Toys didn't hear them complain out loud.

Junie and Banshee were camped out in Circe's room with Lydia Ruiz standing outside.

Toys was sipping a diet Dr Pepper when he heard a sound and turned to see a pale and shaken Rudy Sanchez limp slowly out of his room. Rudy wore a hospital gown and a troubled look. When he spotted Toys, he beckoned him over and retreated back into his room.

"Are you sure you should be out of bed?" asked Toys as he came into the room.

"I'm certain I shouldn't be," said Rudy. "Why are you here?"

Toys explained. He'd met Sanchez a number of times, and, unlike Joe Ledger and some of the soldiers, Rudy never showed him disrespect or hostility. Rather, the reverse. The doctor was always gracious to him. Toys wasn't sure if that was good manners or if Sanchez believed in Toys's reformation. Not that it mattered, but it was nice not to see open contempt in someone's eyes.

"Can I get you something?" asked Toys awkwardly. "A nurse, some food . . . anything?"

Rudy attempted a smile. It was appalling and false. "You can go find me some clothes. Hospital scrubs will do. I still have my shoes, and my walking stick is somewhere around here . . . "

"Clothes? Why?"

"So I can get out of here. I want you to help me."

Toys shook his head. "Uh-uh, no way am I helping you do that. Mr. Church will have my guts for garters."

Rudy shook his head. "Not if we don't tell him where I got the clothes. Come on, Mr. Chismer. As I recall, you have a reputation for accomplishing anything asked of you. This is asking very little. See what you can do."

Chapter Ninety-five

Over Illinois Airspace
March 31, 6:41 P.M. Central Time

I forwarded all the information to Church's computer. It took a dozen tries to get the big man on the phone, though. He was a busy man at the best of times, and right now he was like one of those circus performers who puts spinning plates on the top of slender wooden sticks and keeps adding more until he has a lot of plates spinning. Every few seconds, the performer has to shake one pole to keep a plate from wobbling and falling, then spins another and another. Soon, his entire life is nothing but going from one near disaster to another.

Church was very good at it, and today he had a lot of crockery up in the air.

When we spoke, he was already reviewing the notes I'd sent. He wasn't happy.

"I think you've found the back-trail," he said. "Congratulations on that."

"Top and Bunny did more than their share."

"No doubt. It's troubling—but not entirely surprising—that the Kings have found a way to block MindReader."

"You thinking what I'm thinking?"

"Of course. They have Davidovich, and he built a quantum computer for them."

"Can I quit now and go live in a monastery?"

"Save me a seat," said Church.

"It's pretty clear why they targeted Bug's mom," I said. "They wanted him out of the game."

"At the same time," added Church, "they wanted him to be a witness. They wanted him to see the failure of MindReader."

"It's a kind of torture, isn't it?" I said. "What they're doing. Hurting those we love. Scaring us."

"Are you frightened, Captain?"

"Sure."

"Is it likely to stop you?"

"Of course not. Nothing's going to stop me. No way in hell."

"What does that tell you?"

I thought about it. "Either they're underestimating us . . . "

"Or?"

"Or they don't need to stop us. Just slow us down. Make us react wrong."

"Why?"

"It would have to be a timing thing. It's like a magic trick. The magician shows you the inside of his hat, let's you look up his sleeve, and all the while the bunch of flowers is stuffed into a hidden pocket."

"Yes," he said.

I sighed. "Does that mean Regis is only a distraction?"

"Impossible to say in the absence of more information. However, even as a distraction, they are doing considerable damage with it."

"Which leaves us where? Do we keep following Regis and the drones? Or should we be looking somewhere else?"

"And where would that be?" asked Church.

I said nothing because there was nothing to say. The Kings were giving us one trail to follow and then abusing us for following it.

Church changed the subject and brought me quickly up to speed about what was going on at the hospital, which was mostly a goddamn frustrating holding pattern.

"I'm leaving San Diego in a few hours to meet with the president in Los Angeles. This reaction to the Resort tape seems to have leveled off at a high boil but hasn't gotten worse."

"Can it actually get worse?"

"It can, if Congress decides to impeach."

"Will they?"

"Many will want to, but cooler heads realize that we're in the middle of a national crisis. The timing might work for the president. If he can respond effectively against the Seven Kings, then he'll likely save his presidency. This term, at least. I wouldn't bet heavy money on a second term at this point. In either case, the hit in Philadelphia has given him some room to maneuver. I want to make sure that he uses that time to act intelligently and not politically."

"Ouch," I said.

"We need to be adults about this," he said.

"No argument."

"About the material you sent. Unfortunately, I have to agree that there is a definite pattern, but that means I need to agree with Nikki as well. The Kings have found a way to block MindReader."

"I can take a wild guess how. With that quantum computer thingee?"

"Clearly. Yoda is working on it, but I'm afraid he's out of his depth."

"I hate to be a total prick here," I said, "but what about Bug? Could he figure something out? I mean . . . if he knew about the QC. With that in mind, could he find a way to either block the block, or remove it, or whatever you'd call it?"

Church took a long time with that.

"Perhaps. Bug is a genius, but he would be the first to agree with me that he is not in the same league as Aaron Davidovich."

"Is anyone?" I asked hopefully.

"No. That is the problem with radical supergeniuses. The world always catches up, but the lag time is problematic."

"What can we do about it?"

"About things like autonomous drive systems in cars and public transit, I doubt there is anything that anyone can do. Not in the short term.

We can hardly have the president tell the nation to abandon their cars and avoid all public transit. The country would grind to a halt, and there is no infrastructure prepared to address or correct the situation. We are talking several million cars with some version of SafeZone. And virtually every commercial airline."

"We have to do something . . . "

"We can advise caution. We can advise the FAA to instruct all pilots to keep autopilot systems off."

"Which will result in a backlash. Pilots will go on strike."

"Or try to," agreed Church. "The same for inner-city rail."

"So far as I see it, the only break we caught was the fact that the ballpark hit was on a Sunday when the market was already closed."

"It's a break, Captain, but I would hope you're as suspicious of it as I am. It would be too catastrophic an error for the Kings to make to choose the wrong day for their attack."

"Yeah, damn it . . . " I sighed. "Damn, I wish there was something or someone I could hit. Or shoot. Shooting would feel good, too."

"For once, I reciprocate the sentiment."

I believe he meant it, too.

"Any new disasters?" I asked.

"The biological attack in Chula Vista is on the front burner. I'm waiting for the lab analysis of the pathogen."

"It's viral?"

"General term. It could be any of a number of things. Viruses and bacteria are at the top of our list, though. You'll take charge of that once you're on the ground. If any fresh intel comes up before you're wheels down, I'll let you know."

He ended the call.

I put my phone away and went to look at the wall again. Lots of disasters, lots of deaths. It was clear to all of us that the Seven Kings were not only playing a game whose rules were unknown to us. They were winning hands down, too.

Chapter Ninety-six

Rudy used his cane to knock on the door of the room Church was using as his command center. Church glanced up and waved him in.

"Did your doctor clear you to get out of bed?" asked Church.

"No," said Rudy, "and we're not having a conversation about my going back to bed."

Church leaned back in his chair. "What would you prefer to talk about?"

"I want to help."

"How?"

"Doing anything that you'll let me do."

"How are you feeling?" asked Church. "Accurate assessment, if you please. I'm not in the mood for games."

"Nor am I," said Rudy with asperity. "I'm useless lying in a hospital bed. Someone has attacked my wife, my friends. You are pressed for resources right now. I'm a resource. Use me."

There was a plate of cookies on Church's desk. Mostly vanilla wafers but also some Oreos and animal crackers. He pushed the plate toward Rudy.

"Have a cookie."

Chapter Ninety-seven

Aaron Davidovich crouched beside the toolshed and watched the house for almost twenty minutes, fighting to keep his teeth from chattering. The curtains were drawn. There were no toys in the yard. No dogs barked.

He snuck around the side of the house and looked at the big front yard and the strong, high security fence. It was closed. No cars in the gravel turnaround. When he peered through the garage, he saw a single car in there, but it was covered by a big tarp. There was a spiderweb strung between the mailbox and the light pole beside the front door. The web looked old, abandoned.

When he opened the flap of the mailbox, there was nothing inside. If no one was home and there was no mail in the box, there was a good chance whoever lived here had stopped mail delivery.

That was a blessing.

There were small metal signs on the lawn and stickers in the window from a well-known and highly respected security company. Davidovich almost laughed. Home-security systems could costs thousands, sometimes tens of thousands. But even the very best of them relied on technology that a first-year computer-engineering student could bypass in his sleep. Davidovich had designed the world's most sophisticated software and hardware systems. Regis and the QC. This kind of security wasn't a challenge. It was a gift.

Returning to the yard, he used a decorative rock to break the hasp and remove the lock on the toolshed. Inside, he found a lawn mower, rakes and shovels, bags of compost, stacks of empty clay pots, weed killer, and a yellow plastic toolbox. Inside the toolbox were beat-up old tools. Screwdrivers and hammers, an odd assortment of screws and nails. Wire cutters, a socket-wrench set for fixing the mower.

He selected the tools he'd need and hugged them to his chest.

Davidovich said, "Thank you."

He did not, however, know exactly whom he was thanking.

Chapter Ninety-eight

San Diego International Airport

March 31, 8:03 P.M.

I landed in San Diego and was met by Mike Harnick, the head of the motor pool and vehicles design shop at the Pier. He was actually polishing the hood with a rag when we came out of the terminal. Mike has something of an unhealthy relationship with the cars and trucks that he oversees. He kind of hates that he has to turn them over to guys like me who might, in the course of a day's work, get them blown up.

Ghost saw him and began wagging his tail. Mike usually has treats in his pocket. Totally outside combat-dog protocols, but I have so far not been able to get that point across to him.

When Mike spotted us, he tucked the rag in his back pocket and came over to shake hands. Mike was one of several key players from the Warehouse whom I'd coerced into moving to Southern California. Unlike some, who were dedicated East Coasters, Mike had embraced the change. He wore a Hawaiian shirt with a pattern of classic cars and Route 101 signs. He wore shorts and sandals and had a pair of Oliver Peoples sunglasses pushed up on his hair. Ghost went running to him, tail wagging, and I made sure I didn't see the Snausages Mike covertly slipped him.

Mike's smile, though, looked a bit like it was hammered in place with roofing nails.

"Hell of a day," he said as we shook.

"Hell of a day," I agreed.

He turned and swept an arm toward the car. "Say hello to Ugly Betty."

Ugly Betty was a brand-new Escalade with a lot of aftermarket work. I believe Mike prays nightly in a church dedicated to Q from the James Bond flicks. The car looked like every other black Escalade, but I knew that it was reinforced like a tank, weighed an absurd amount, and had an engine that could push all that weight up to about ninety and hold her there all day. Oversize armored gas tank with battery backup. Wi-Fi with satellite uplink. Machine guns, fore and aft rocket launchers. Everything.

"How's it take a curve?" I asked suspiciously. "Black Bess looked pretty and all, but she steered like a damn cow. This one any better?"

Mike grinned. "Depends on whether you know how to drive."

I showed him a lot of teeth. "I get into a wreck with this 'cause it's a slow piece of unmaneuverable elephant shit, you and me are going to have a long conversation. Knives may be involved. Warning you ahead of time."

"Damn, Joe, you're getting cranky in your old age."

"Keep talking, Doctor Truckenstein, but don't come crying to me if you wake up dead one morning."

Harnick's grin never faltered, and he mouthed the word "Truckenstein." I suspect it was going to be his new nickname.

He handed me a set of keys. "She's gassed and ready. GPS is programmed with the crime scene and the hospital where they took the bodies."

I thanked him and climbed in. The vehicle was absurdly comfortable, which felt good on all the parts of me that still hurt from the ballpark disaster. I saw that Mike had gone the extra yard and left a bag of extra-large dog biscuits. Ghost jumped into the back seat and came to point staring at them like he'd just discovered the Holy Grail. I gave him one, and he retreated into the back bay with his booty.

I wasn't sure I was up for a lot of driving. The scalpel cut on my forearm was beginning to itch under the bandage, my head hurt, and all of those other little aches and pains were still loitering around. I'd popped a couple of nondrowsy painkillers on the plane, but they were accomplishing exactly nothing. So I winced and cursed and damned Mike and everyone I ever knew to hellfire as I buckled up and adjusted the mirrors.

Mike stepped back and waved at me while I headed out of the airport. I wasn't even on Route 5 yet when I got a call from Rudy.

"Hey, Rude," I said, relieved to hear his voice, "how the hell are you?"

"A borderline mess, Cowboy," he admitted. "As, I suspect, are you."

"Not what I meant, Rude. I know who jumped you. How are you?"

"My answer holds."

"Okay," I said. "Got it. And . . . Circe?"

"No change." There were miles and miles of hurt in his voice. And twice as much fear. If that was Junie lying there, I'd be out of my fucking mind.

"Damn," I said. "I'm heading over there now and—"

"Listen, Joe," said Rudy, cutting me off, "Mr. Church doesn't want you to come here right now. We got word from the doctors at the hospital where the bodies were taken. Joe, we both need to get over there right now."

"Why?"

"We don't have all the details, but the doctor over there—Alur, I think his name is—has implemented a class A biohazard lockdown and wants to evacuate the entire facility."

"Christ. Any clue what the disease is?"

"No, but Doctor Alur said they should have that answer by the time we arrive."

"We? You're supposed to be in bed, or was that a different one-eyed Mexican psychiatrist friend of mine who got kicked in the damn face?"

"Joe, I don't want to argue with you," said Rudy. "I convinced Mr. Church to have me discharged and to let me get back to work. I'm not seriously injured. The burn is minor; the head injury is not worth discussing. You've had worse. Many times."

"But—"

"And quite frankly, if I don't get involved in this, if I don't have the opportunity to participate in this case, to use what skills I have, I'm going to go out of my mind."

He did not sound like he was making a joke.

That scared me, because Rudy isn't the type to throw himself into the active side of one of the DMS cases. He was a therapist, a doctor. He counseled the operators between jobs, he kept the spiders locked inside my head, and he worked with victims afterward. He was not a field man. Wasn't trained for it and didn't have the right mental attitude for it. Rudy is the kind of decent human being guys like me try to protect so he doesn't have to run head-on into the fire.

Except . . .

Circe was in a coma, and a psychopath pretending to be a priest had brutalized Rudy. And Rudy had been at the ballpark; he'd seen people blown apart by the drones. He's friends with Bug and Aunt Sallie and was feeling their hurt.

He has skin in this game. A lot of it.

"Okay," I said.

"Okay," he said.

"Brian will drop me off at the hospital. I think you should meet me there."

Brian Botley was the newest member of Echo Team. A hazardous-materials expert who also knew how to cook up useful things that went boom. Code name: Hotzone, which really wasn't much of a stretch.

"Okay, pardner," I said, "but if you look wobbly, I'm putting you back on the bench."

It was the same threat Top had used on me. Rudy ignored it, exactly as I had.

Chapter Ninety-nine

It took Aaron Davidovich very little time to bypass the security system of the empty house. Then he was inside. The house was cold, but it was the warmest he'd been since he'd waded into the waters off the Seven Kings' island.

First thing he did was look for a telephone. Found it. Snatched up the receiver.

Heard nothing. Not even a hiss.

The place was as empty as a dead battery. The furniture was covered in plastic. There was no food in the fridge. The gas and water were turned off. Because of the needs of the security system, the electricity was still on, and the oven was electric. He turned it on and warmed himself by the open oven door. Then he went prowling and found several useful things.

Clothes, neatly folded in moth-proof plastic tubs. Most of what he found didn't fit him, and he soon realized that it was a woman and two kids living here. The kids were young. The woman was short but, he discovered, plump. He could stretch a couple of her sweaters around him. He stripped off his own clothes and draped them around the stove to dry. In one of the cabinets, he found canned tuna, and he opened three cans and devoured the cold fish.

In the attic, he found a trunk with clothes that clearly belonged to an older man. Probably the woman's father. The man had been very tall—inches taller than Davidovich. That didn't matter. Nor did it matter that the clothes smelled of cedar chips and old man. There were no shoes, but he found a pair of good slippers. He stuffed the toes with socks and put them on.

Dressed comfortably in useful layers, he searched in vain for a cell phone. There was no chance he'd find one, but he had to look.

No topcoat, either.

Wearing a dead man's clothes and bedroom slippers, carrying pocketsful of tools, Davidovich slipped out of the house and went into the garage.

He wanted his luck to hold long enough for the car to be functional and fast.

It was a classic 1965 Mustang.

It had no engine.

"Fuck," he said.

But he wasted no time mourning the car. Instead, he left the property through the back gate and headed toward the bridge to the mainland. Caution took time, though, and with every minute he used ensuring his anonymity, he felt a minute of his son's life burning away.

Chapter One Hundred

Sharp Chula Vista Medical Center

Medical Center Court, Chula Vista, California

March 31, 8:54 P.M.

We pulled into the hospital ER roundabout. That whole section of the facility had been evacuated, and someone had brought in a set of police barricades. Two soldiers in hazmat suits stood on the other side. I recognized them through the plastic visors. New guys working for me at the Pier. A couple of MPs I borrowed from the army. A third man, Brian Botley, came to meet us, but he stopped a dozen paces away and nodded to a stack of folded hazmat suits.

"You're going to want to suit up," Brian said. "Believe me."

We each put one on. Since they don't make them for dogs, I'd had to leave Ghost in the car. He wasn't happy about it, and I knew it would be on me if he peed on Mike Harnick's new leather seats.

"They redirected ER function to another hospital," said Brian. "Nobody was happy about it until the staff got a look at what we were bringing in. After that, it was assholes and elbows to clear this place out and button it up."

Another figure in a hazmat suit appeared and came limping toward us, leaning on his cane, which was wrapped in plastic and sealed with duct tape. We didn't shake hands, of course. Didn't go for the big bromance hug. Best friends in protective clothing have to be content with a manly and stoic nod.

"I just got here myself," Rudy said. "I was about to go looking for Doctor Alur."

Brian said, "What do you want me to do?"

"Stay here," I said. "Make sure nobody else comes in here unless they know today's secret password."

He frowned. "Um . . . we have a secret password? What is it?"

"Fuck the Seven Kings," I said.

Brian grinned. "That works."

He went to take up his station. I gave Rudy an up-and-down appraisal. "You look like shit."

"Thank you very much. You're so kind," he said. "I reciprocate the sentiment."

"How's your head?"

"It hurts. How is yours?"

"It hurts."

"Aren't we a pair?"

I nodded to his hands. There were puffy bandages beneath the plastic gauntlets. "I heard something about burns?"

"Yes." Shadows seemed to drift across his face.

"Rude?"

"Yes, Cowboy?"

"We're going to get them."

He said nothing.

"All of them," I said. "Including that sinister little psychopath."

He said nothing.

"This may be damage done, brother," I told him, "but there's life on the other side."

"Joe," he said in a soft but strained voice, "please stop. I don't need the trash talk. I don't respond to it the way you do. All it does is make me realize that I am not strong, that I'm not a fighter. Even if you do manage to take down the Kings and Nicodemus, I will carry the memory of that encounter for the rest of my life. And, before you embarrass us both by trying to explain the effects of trauma, please remember that I do know this. The effects I'm feeling are the very things I treat people for. The parasitic part of my mind is shining light on the irony and looking for the hubris that would be the dramatic root cause of my downfall. I understand that

I am going through the victim process in textbook fashion. Nothing you can say will help. Truly. No threats against them. Not even a successful victory over them will help. This is mine to resolve with myself and for myself."

I nodded. "You're my best friend, Rudy. What can I do?"

He smiled. It was faint but genuine. "Just be my friend. That does more than you might think."

He offered me his hand, and I took it—very gently, mindful of his burns.

Above us, the San Diego sky was a flawless blue. We took a moment and looked up at it.

Rudy cursed very quietly under his breath. When he wants to, he can conjure the vilest expletives known to the Spanish language.

We went inside.

Chapter One Hundred and One

Sharp Chula Vista Medical Center
Medical Center Court, Chula Vista, California
March 31, 9:06 P.M.

It was and cool inside the hospital. The place seemed deserted, and we were dressed like spacemen.

Rudy shook his head.

"What?" I asked.

"I suppose I'm having déjà vu. Have we been in this exact hospital in this same kind of situation?"

We paused, each of us looking around and looking backward into memory.

"Damn," I said softly. "I know what you mean. Feels like half a dozen times I can name. Maybe more."

"More," Rudy agreed, then added. "Too many."

A door opened down the hall and a doctor came out, spotted us, and came to meet us.

"I'm Doctor Alur," he said. "Infectious Diseases. They called me in."

We introduced ourselves.

"Good to meet you, Doctor," I said.

"Yes," said Alur, "though I'm sorry it's under such unfortunate circumstances."

"Exactly how unfortunate are we talking? What is this? Ebola or—?"

"No," said Alur, "but I'm not sure we should be relieved. The two victims both exhibit symptoms consistent with a disease that cannot do what it apparently has."

"You lost me."

"Please explain," urged Rudy.

"Disease symptoms follow patterns," Alur explained. "Even in the cases of mutation, the symptoms are part of a logic chain. We can understand the pathology because we know what diseases of various kinds are likely to do. There isn't much room for them to do things entirely outside of their symptomatological profiles. Do you follow?"

The question was directed at me, the thug without a medical degree.

"Right," I said. "If you catch a flu, your ass won't fall off. Got it."

He almost smiled. Managed not to. "In cases of extreme mutation, where an unforeseen acceleration of the disease has occurred, we can still look for—and generally find—a chain of cause and effect."

"But not in this case?" I asked.

"Not so far."

Rudy frowned. "What disease are we talking about?"

He took a breath. "We believe that this is some kind of extreme or mutated form of necrotizing fasciitis."

I stared at him. "Necrotizing—? Wait, are you talking about the flesh-eating disease?"

"That's a misnomer," said Alur, "but yes. Are you familiar with it?"

"Not really. I know about it, but from a distance."

"Doctor," said Rudy, "Captain Ledger has been around weaponized pathogens for some time. Please give him what you have. If he has questions later, I'll be able to fill in the blanks."

Alur nodded. "We call it NF, though the press likes to call it the flesh-eating disease or the flesh-eating bacteria syndrome. It's a very rare infection of the deeper layers of skin and subcutaneous tissues. Even in ordinary cases, it progresses rapidly, having greater risk of developing in patients who are immunocompromised. In patients, say, with cancer or diabetes. Understand: even in ordinary cases, it is known as a severe disease of sudden onset. Treatment usually involves high doses of intravenous anti-biotics and debriding of the necrotic flesh. It's typically fatal when un-treated."

"This is a bacteria, not a virus?" I asked.

"Yes, but it's more complicated than that."

"It's always more complicated than that," I muttered.

"This disease agent is a Type One polymicrobial, so, actually, quite a few different types of bacteria can cause NF. Group A streptococcus— *Streptococcus pyogenes—Staphylococcus aureus, Clostridium perfringens, Bacteroides fragilis, Aeromonas hydrophila,* and others. And there are other kinds of NF: Type Two, which are triggered by a single kind of bacteria. And since 2001, we've cataloged another serious form of monomicrobial nec-rotizing fasciitis that has been observed with increasing frequency, caused by methicillin-resistant *Staphylococcus aureus—*"

I held up a hand. "Not studying for a test, doc. Hit me with what I need to know."

He looked momentarily flustered, then nodded. My guess was that this was all so big and scary to him that he was letting his clinical knowledge prop up the rest of him. I've seen it a hundred times.

"When we encounter patients presenting with signs of cellulitis, we have several tests we can perform to determine the likelihood of NF. C-reactive protein, total white-blood-cell count, hemoglobin, sodium, creatinine, and glucose. We ran all of those on the deceased, and we hit the right bells each time. This is, without a doubt, necrotizing fasciitis."

"The police and your own people have determined that the disease was spread through contaminated food. Specifically, some Mexican food that was delivered via one of those drones."

"NachoCopter," I said. "It's one of those five-prop commercial drones. A quintocopter made by Sullivan Airdrop in Pasadena. We've got people on there way now, and we had local law shut the place down and quaran-tine the staff."

Alur shook his head. "I read about those kinds of companies, about the drone deliveries, but I can't believe the FAA granted approval."

"Supreme Court overruled the FAA," I said. "The corporations that want to use commercial delivery drones swing a lot of political weight."

"I suppose I shouldn't be shocked or appalled by that."

"Shocked, no? Appalled—yeah, I think you can run with that. Their ads say that the drone will deliver hot food in under twenty minutes. Domino's is doing the same thing. So are Papa John's, McDonald's, and others. Fact of life that this shit's happening. However, it doesn't explain what happened today. How did that happen? Was the NF introduced to the food at the restaurant?"

Rudy consulted a notebook. "From phone records we were able to determine that Mr. Quiñones ordered his food by phone and the drone made the delivery nineteen minutes later."

"Has anyone talked to the drone operator?" asked Alur. "I read that there's someone in a room using remote control—?"

"That's the thing, doc," I said, "NachoCopter doesn't use remote pilots. They're using autonomous piloting software."

Rudy knew about Regis, but there was no need to explain it to Alur. Not yet, anyway.

"Oh." Alur looked deeply troubled. "Was that same drone used for other deliveries today?"

"Yeah, it was," I said. "Seventeen more. And before you ask, our team rolled cars to each location. So far, all of the other customers are okay. No one else is sick. So far, at least. What's the timetable if someone else was exposed?"

"With this version of NF? I don't know. I'd be guessing . . . "

"Guess," I suggested.

"Under two hours. Mr. Quiñones and Ms. Santa Domingo apparently collapsed after eating the food. Possibly no more than sixty to ninety minutes later. They succumbed to deterioration of their tissues and died shortly after that."

I whistled. Rudy shook his head, not in refusal of the doctor's words but because it was like taking another arrow in the chest. Idealism and optimism glow pretty brightly, and that gives the bastards of this world something to aim at.

"Last delivery before we shut it down was four hours ago," I said. "Give it forty-five minutes' max time before someone eats something they've ordered delivered. That gives us three hours for there to be more dead bodies. Why aren't we seeing that?"

Rudy nodded to Doctor Alur. "Are we positive the bacteria was in the Mexican food?"

"Yes," he said. "We were able to analyze the stomach contents."

"How long should it have taken them to die from exposure under ordinary circumstances?" I asked.

"If left untreated, NF could kill in only a few months. Some cases take years."

"Big scary question," I said. "How contagious is this?"

Rudy fielded that. "Generally, not very. However, it's possible for uninfected people to come into contact with patients with the disease and become infected with an organism that may eventually cause necrotizing fasciitis. Transmission from one person to another usually requires direct contact with a patient or some item that can transfer it to another person's skin. Infection usually requires a cut or abrasion for the organisms to establish an infection. However, once contracted, mortality rates can be as high as twenty-five percent."

Alur nodded. "We see about six hundred to a thousand cases each year."

"Here in Chula Vista?" I asked.

"No, here in the United States."

"So, how do two people like this die of a disease like that in a couple of hours?" I asked.

He shook his head. "I don't know."

"Can you take a guess?"

Alur paused, then said, "Come and look at the bodies."

We followed him down the hall and through one of those big leather and plastic doors that flap open and shut. Like they have in meat lockers, which is a visual I wish I hadn't made for myself. We went through several layers of hanging sheets of thick plastic into a biohazard isolation suite. We didn't pass through the last layer of plastic but instead stared in horror at what lay on two identical steel tables. At two bodies. If you could call them bodies. You certainly couldn't call them people.

Not anymore.

There were red lumps on two side-by-side stainless-steel tables. They had arms and legs. There were bony nobs that were about the size of heads. The rest?

God.

They really did look like the kind of melted corpses you see in those old horror movies. But no movie, despite great scripts and acting, despite computer-generated special effects and brilliant cinematography, can capture that one element that will always separate fantasy from reality.

Those were actual people there. Not actors, not stunt doubles. Not animatronic monsters.

These were people, and this disease had stolen their lives, stolen their faces, consumed their futures. Robbed them not just of heartbeat and breath, but of all those moments that make up a life. Small joys, intimate conversations, unexpected excitements, casual insights. Happiness and love. Family. All gone.

Devoured.

"Jesus Christ," I breathed. "How could this happen?"

The doctor's eyes looked strange. Haunted. Deeply frightened.

"If I had to guess," he said softly, "I'd say that this was a deliberate mutation."

Chapter One Hundred and Two

Sharp Chula Vista Medical Center
Medical Center Court, Chula Vista, California
March 31, 9:17 P.M.

The big flap door behind us opened and a man peered in. Hard to say what he looked like beneath the hazmat suit except that he was black, medium height, and wore wire-frame glasses. His head jerked a bit in surprise.

"Oh! Pardon me," he said quickly. "I was looking for the physician in charge."

"Who are you?" I asked.

"Are you the doctor?"

"I'm the man asking who you are," I said, my tone on the sharp side of friendly.

"Sorry, the ER staff sent me down here to ask the doctor to come look at someone they just brought in. They think it might be the same thing."

"Brought in?" cried Alur. "Brought in where? Is the patient alive? Is he conscious?"

The man, who was still only head and shoulders into the room, turned to face Alur. "You're the doctor?"

"Yes," said Alur.

"Okay, great."

The man stepped into the room, and as he did so he brought up the combat shotgun that he'd been hiding.

There was no time to do anything.

Not soon enough.

The blast caught Doctor Alur full in the chest. One magnum twelve-gauge shell tore the man to rags. It shredded his chest, vaporized his heart, and blew out his spine. At that distance—less than fifteen feet—there was no way for Alur to run. Just as there was no way for the killer to miss.

I was in motion before Alur's body could even fall.

I shoved Rudy behind a table and dove for the gunman. My sidearm was in my shoulder holster under the hazmat suit. These weren't combat overgarments, not like the Saratoga hammer suits we usually wore for combat in hot zones. I was unarmed against a shotgun.

But I was so close. Too close for him to swing the barrel toward me. Not in time. Beyond him, I could hear other men shouting. There was another shot. Down the hall.

This was a full-out assault.

That flashed through my brain as I leaped inside the space of a moment, caught the barrel as he tried to bring it to bear, grabbed the barrel with my right, and jerked it high, catching him across the face with a left-hand cutting palm. It spun him as surely as if I'd hit him with a baseball bat. Feels about the same, too. His chin spun around, and his body wanted to follow, but he still had a solid grip on the gun. That grip created resistance. Maybe it sprained his neck. I don't know—I didn't ask. I chop-kicked him in the knee, feeling the cartilage and bones crumble; and as he sagged back, I tore the shotgun from him, reversed it in my grip, jammed the barrel against his cheekbone, and blew his head all over the door.

He toppled outward, spraying the floor outside with blood and brain matter.

Two men stood a dozen yards away, staring in shock and horror at the nearly headless corpse. Maybe they knew who it was. They were all carrying similar weapons. I didn't know who they were, didn't know where Brian and the rest of my team was.

I didn't wait to find out. The Benelli M3 combat shotgun in my hands held twelve shells. Two were gone. I hosed the guys in the hall with the rest. They tried so hard to bring their guns up. To make a fight of this. To have a chance.

I took that chance from them.

The shells tore them into scarlet inhumanity.

The front door opened, and Brian Botley staggered in. He was splashed with blood, and his hazmat suit was torn. He had an M5 is his hands.

"They ambushed us," he gasped. "Riker and Smalls are down."

"How bad are you hurt?"

"Body armor took the hit. I think. Cracked some ribs."

He was wheezing and could barely stand. I pointed the way I'd come.

At the far end of the hall, I heard another shotgun blast. There were more of these pricks.

"Call it, sir," said Brian.

"Alur's dead. Rudy's not. Make sure he stays safe. Go."

He didn't like it, but he was half gone, so he staggered past me through the leather flap doors.

As I ran, I yelled, "Get us some damn backup."

"Hooah."

He vanished inside.

I began running along the hall, bent low, weapon ready. No idea what I would find around the far corner. No idea what horrors would be waiting.

On the other hand, they had no idea what was coming for them.

Chapter One Hundred and Three

Sharp Chula Vista Medical Center

Medical Center Court, Chula Vista, California

March 31, 9:20 P.M.

As I raced toward the end of the hall, my mind tried to assemble this into a shape that made sense.

Why kill the doctor investigating the case? Surely if they were smart enough to concoct a superstrain of NF and cook up the idea of delivering it in takeout food brought by a UAV, then they were smart enough to know that killing the doctor would not end the investigation. Or even stall it. Ambushing the ambulance might have done that. This was too late in the process.

On the other hand, their choice of weapons was significant. Shotguns. Except when using certain solid loads, shotguns typically fired pellets of varying size. Once the round leaves the barrel, the pellets disperse into a wide spray.

I wonder what would have happened had I not attacked? Would the gunman have fired a second shell? If so, would he have tried to kill or wound? Alur had been unlucky enough to be the closest, but a second blast would have wounded the rest of us. The pellets would have punched through the thin hazmat material.

They would have actually killed us.

Not in a room that might have some of the NF bacteria. All they'd have to do was damage the seals.

I skidded to a stop at the end of the hall, then crouched and listened to what was happening around the corner.

There were three separate sounds.

Voices pleading.

Voices weeping.

Voices yelling.

No gunshots at the moment.

I hunkered low and did a quick look around the corner and pulled back, letting what I'd seen in that flash assemble itself into useful details in my head.

Nine people.

All of them in identical white hazmat suits.

Three of them lay on the floor. Bloody and torn. Impossible to tell how badly injured they were.

Three men stood near them, each of them armed with a shotgun.

Three cowering people, who had to be hospital staff.

One of the shooters was yelling orders. "Get a gurney. Bring the bodies outside. Do it now or I will kill you. Do you understand?"

The cadence of the voice and the clarity of the instructions had a military feel. Not surprising. This hit was military in its form, though not the highest grade. Not what I'd call special ops.

Not Kingsmen-level, though that wasn't much of a comfort. Top-of-the-line special operators could sometimes be reasoned with. They were professionals, and, when presented with a no-win situation, they often put a higher premium on their own asses than on their employer's agendas. Second stringers were either zealots of one species or another, or they were amateurs. Both are unpredictable, and each tended to jump at the wrong time and in the wrong direction. And if they worked for the Kings, then they were likely as bug-nuts fanatical as the Kingsmen.

I was stepping into something that was bad and could only get worse.

I didn't know if the air was rife with NF, or if it was even an airborne pathogen. We hadn't gotten that far in our discussions before Alur was killed.

I tried tapping my earbud to get Nikki on the line, but all I got was a whistling buzz.

Jammer?

That was weird as shit, because an active jammer would almost certainly cut off the signal for the intrusion team as well. Unless they had some spooky toys I didn't have.

Rat balls.

I took a second look, noting how the bodies had shifted. I had clear shots at two of the men. I'd have to move in order to safely take the third without spraying the civilians with pellets. I needed to save the innocent and stop the bad guys, but also have someone with a pulse I could interrogate.

So, I decided to take a gamble.

I stood, turned toward the empty hallway behind me, and began firing my shotgun as I backed around the corner.

"They're coming!" I bellowed.

"How many?" demanded one of the shooters, assuming—as I'd intended—that I was one of the other team.

"There's a whole team down there."

One of the shooters ran up to stand beside me, our guns pointed at the bend in the corridor, waiting for the rush that would never come.

I didn't wait for him to realize his mistake.

I pivoted in place and, from a distance of three feet, fired at his mid-section.

At that distance, he caught the whole spray, and it scythed him in half.

"Yuri!" screamed someone behind me, and I whirled as the second shooter darted forward, his gun coming up fast. I shot by reflex, and the buckshot caught him in the thighs and groin. His legs and pelvis were yanked out behind him, and he flopped onto his chest.

The cowering staff shrieked in terror and horror as blood splashed the floor and walls. It was lucky for them that gore was the only thing splashing them.

If even one pellet had hit them and punctured their suits . . .

The third gunman was frozen into a moment of bad decision. He could fire, but I was coming fast, and he didn't have his gun up yet. He could surrender. Or he could take a damn prisoner.

I saw his eyes cut toward a staff member. The smallest of the three. A woman.

"Don't do it!" I bellowed.

He did it anyway. The killer bounded sideways, hooked one arm around a slim waist, and jerked her in front of him as a shield. He jammed the shotgun barrel up under the woman's chin.

"I'll kill her," he declared.

I pointed my gun at his head. "I believe you."

"Put your gun down."

"Or, how about—fuck you?"

"I mean it."

"I know. Me too."

He stammered. The conversation had started badly and already begun to slide down an icy hill.

"Listen to me, Sparky," I said. "Your friends are dead. The two bozos here and the Three Stooges out there. All of them. Dead. You, on the other hand, have the Willy Wonka golden ticket. That means you get the chance to walk out of here alive and in one piece. Now—look at me. I just killed five people. Do you think I'm going to let you walk just because you're hiding behind a hostage? Ever heard the phrase 'collateral damage'?"

The woman's eyes opened wider and filled with even more terror at my words.

"Bullshit," he fired back. "Cops don't risk civilians."

"Not a cop, sorry. Try again."

He jammed the gun harder into the woman's soft chin.

"Please—!" she begged. "Oh God, please."

"Shut up," he growled, jabbing her again.

I moved closer to him. He backed away, but I kept pace with him. We both knew that there were very few options left to anyone. He'd kill her, and we'd fight. He'd let her go, and we'd fight.

He went for option number 3.

With a sudden grunt, he shoved her at me and then leveled the shotgun to try and catch us both.

That was the move I was expecting. The one I wanted him to try. I'd been watching his body language, waiting for the shift of weight he'd need to make in order to push her. As soon as I saw it, I was moving. The girl had time for one staggering step before I snaked out a hand and caught her arm, whipped my hips around for torque, and flung her roughly into the other two civilians. They all went down. That left the gunman free and clear. I swung the stock of my shotgun to try and knock the weapon out of his hands. I liked my chances in a hand-to-hand fight and really did want to have that meaningful chat with him.

But, damn it, he was too fast for his own good.

He evaded my swing, brought his shotgun up, and fired.

I spun out of the way and felt pellets tug at the loose fabric around my middle.

Shit, shit, shit!

Terrified as well as desperate, I used my turn to corkscrew myself down into a kneeling position, shotgun snugged against my chest as I fired.

The blast caught him in the side, and the pellets opened his hazmat suit like an envelope. He toppled backward, geysering blood for torn arteries. I immediately dropped my weapon and scrambled over to him, trying to staunch the arterial bleeding. Needing him alive.

Needing him not to be dead.

Not yet.

"Goddamn it, Sparky," I muttered as I worked, using gloves to staunch wounds that were truly dreadful, "now see what you've gone and made me do."

He tried to tell me to go fuck myself, but he couldn't manage it. His voice was already faint, receding like a train whispering its way down a tunnel. Blood bubbled between his lips and misted the inside of his hood.

"You got one chance to change things for you," I said. "Don't end the game on the wrong team. Tell me something I can use. Who sent you here? Do you work for the Seven Kings?"

"Say good-bye to your world," he gurgled. "Because your world is going to burn."

Then he spat a mouthful of blood at me. While still wearing the hazmat hood. Dumb fuck. It struck the plastic and obscured his face. I couldn't risk taking my hands away from the torn arteries to remove his mask.

Soon, however, I realized that I didn't need to.

The blood stopped pumping.

A last breath exited from him in a bubbling, directionless sigh, and he settled back. Gone.

I sagged back from him.

"Goddamn it," I breathed

Your world is going to burn.

What the hell did that mean?

The three civilians had climbed to their feet and stood in a tight, deeply frightened cluster. I heaved a sigh and stood. However, when I took a step toward them, they all but leaped back, squealing in fear.

"Hey!" I said. "I'm a federal agent. I'm one of the good guys."

But it turned out that wasn't what they were afraid of.

Then I remembered about the spray of buckshot I'd dodged.

I plucked out the loose fabric and stared blankly at a dozen small holes that had been punched through my hazmat suit.

Chapter One Hundred and Four

Warren County, Washington

March 31, 6:22 P.M.

Aaron Davidovich knew that he was a dead man.

Apart from wishing he were dead, and wishing even more that he possessed the courage to kill himself, he assumed that he was being hunted. They had to know he was gone. He'd left enough of a mess.

They would be hunting him. Maybe Boy would be hunting him. Not an agent of the Kings, but her. In the flesh.

Not to bring him back. That ship had sailed. The Kings' project was rolling forward, grinding its way into the history books. All they needed to do now was to cut his throat. They wouldn't even bother to torture him. What would be the point? They didn't need anything from him except his silence.

That would be the thing.

Kill him and silence any possible threat he could pose.

Davidovich stood in the shadows behind a billboard advertising premium real estate. He had no idea how long or how far he'd walked since leaving the house he'd broken into. There was no foot traffic, which meant that on foot a pedestrian would be noticed, so he stayed in the shadows and hid when cars passed. The sun had just tumbled over the nearest clumps of pines, and it felt much later than it was.

He needed something, though. He needed a car. More urgently, though, he needed a phone or a computer with Internet access. He tried to find a pay phone, but if such a thing existed on Fox Island, he couldn't find one. And, looking as he did in ill-fitting clothes and bedroom slippers, no one was going to let him borrow a phone or laptop. No one was likely to float him the money to use a pay phone, providing he could even *find* a relic like that.

Across the two-lane was a small roadside restaurant. Dilley's Classic Roadside Café. A retro-trendy place with expensive cars in the lot. The exceptions were two medium-sized movers' vans. Davidovich figured they had just moved someone into one of the fancy homes and were refueling before driving back to their home base. Dilley's exterior looked like a carhop diner from the fifties, with bright red Coke signs and tin cutouts of burgers piled high with tomatoes and pickles.

His stomach clenched, and he realized that he was hungry. The three cans of tuna he'd eaten earlier seemed to have done nothing for him. He wanted one of those burgers . . .

"Focus, you moron," he told himself, and flinched at the sound of his own voice. He hadn't meant to say it aloud.

Headlights flared as a late-model Ford pickup rattled around the curve and angled toward Dilley's. The truck bed was piled high with bagged grass cuttings and lawn equipment. It rolled to a stop at the far end of a line of parked vehicles and tucked into a slot between the moving vans. Two men got out. A small man with skinny legs and a bulky Seahawks hoodie and a fat man in a thermal vest.

"You going to get something to go?" asked the skinny man.

"I don't know. Need to take a wicked whiz first. If I get something, you want anything?"

"Coffee and a couple of those almond rolls. I'll wait for you. Got to call Gary to tell him we need to go back tomorrow to finish. And we still need to put the mulch down on the Carsons' flowerbeds. Probably need all morning."

"'K," said the fat man as he hurried inside, prancing the way men do who have an urgent need. It made him look like he was walking on fragile glass.

Davidovich was moving out of the shadows and across the street before the door banged shut behind the fat man. The skinny guy had removed a cell phone and leaned his right shoulder against the closed driver's door while he dialed.

Most of the way across the street and over the cracked macadam of the parking lot, Davidovich told himself that he was just going to ask. That was all. Just ask to use the phone. He'd say that he had an accident and needed to call the police. Something like that.

That was all he was going to do.

When he bent and scooped up a piece of rock that had popped loose from a pothole, he did not admit to himself that he was going to use it. Even when he was raising the rock over his head, he kept telling himself that he was not that kind of person. He didn't attack strangers. He didn't hit them in the head with rocks.

The moment of commission came and went, and no amount of denials could change the fact of what he had just done The rock and all of the fingers curled around it were dark with blood. The back of the man's head glistened.

The man fell strangely. His upper body seemed to stiffen, but from the elbows down, the man's arms and fingers twitched wildly. From the knees down, the muscles and tendons seemed to turn to rubber. The man made a small, meaningless gagging sound, and then he fell.

Onto kneecaps and then onto his face, making no effort at all to stop himself from colliding lips and nose first onto the cold, cold ground.

Aaron Davidovich stared at him. He was absolutely shocked to silent immobility.

The man lay sprawled on the ground like an empty suit of clothes. The shape of the bones between collar and baseball cap were . . .

Wrong.

The skull shape was flattened. No. Dented.

Not as grossly misshapen as Steve's head had been, but bad enough. Wrong enough.

His cell phone had fallen from his hand and lay in a pool of light. Davidovich stared at it. The phone was so perfectly placed it was as if a cinematographer had arranged it there for maximum visual impact.

There was a soft thud, and Davidovich looked down to see that he'd dropped the bloody rock.

He heard another sound. Faint and high-pitched, like the whine of a small dog. Pleading and desperate.

The sound came from his own throat.

"I'm damned," he said aloud.

No one and nothing raised a voice to refute him.

Davidovich quickly bent down and snatched the phone with greedy fingers. He clutched it to his chest, turned, and began to run.

Then stopped.

The truck still had the keys in it.

He licked his lips, flicking nervous glances at the diner.

It took less than a minute to roll the dead man's body beneath the bulk of the semi parked next to the Ford. Fifteen seconds later, he was driving off in the Ford. He watched in the rearview mirror for the fat man to come out. The man still hadn't appeared by the time Davidovich turned onto the main road.

He never stopped whining like a frightened little dog.

Chapter One Hundred and Five

Rudy said four words that were not as much of a comfort as we all hoped.

"It's probably not airborne."

"*'Probably'* not?" I said. My voice may have been a tad shrill.

"We're, um, working to determine that, Cowboy," said Rudy.

We were in a room that had been prepped as a replacement for the bio-hazardous exam suite in which Doctor Alur had been murdered. The walls, floor, and ceiling had been thoroughly covered in plastic and sealed with a medical-grade duct tape. It looked like the kind of serial-killer murder room you see on reruns of *Dexter*.

I wore a hospital johnny and had all sorts of tubes running in and out of my veins. Rudy looked even more frightened than me. Behind the thick plastic of his hazmat suit, his face was beaded with sweat and his eye was glassy with shock.

We were alone for the moment, though there were two armed guards outside. Two of my own guys from the Pier.

"Let's circle back to the word 'probably,' " I suggested.

Rudy licked his lips. "That means, Cowboy, that we think its serum-transfer-only but don't have the lab work back yet."

I took great pains to keep my tone very reasonable and not at all like a hysterical Chihuahua. "Can you request, please, that they not dawdle?"

He almost smiled. "I guarantee you, Joe, no one is wasting time on this. I made some demands, and Mr. Church has been on the phone with the hospital administrators."

"You spoke to Church?"

"Yes. He expressed his concern for you."

"Did he really?" I asked.

"Well, no, but it was implied."

"Uh-huh."

Rudy said, "You'll be happy to know that Top and Bunny are on their way back here."

"To do what? Watch my skin rot off?"

"Joe, so far you have no symptoms at all."

"Falling apart here, Rude. I can feel it. I think my spleen is melting."

"Let's face it, Cowboy, falling apart is something of a work in progress for you."

"Oh, hilarious. Psychiatry humor. I get it."

"I don't think you're infected."

I nodded.

"Though, knowing you as I do, you probably think you deserve some kind of injury as penalty for being unable to take one or more of those gunmen alive. You think you failed, don't you?"

I said nothing.

"Joe—you were in a desperate fight with six men armed with combat shotguns. You began that fight unarmed and yet managed to shoot all six of the attackers, and in doing so saved my life, Brian's, and the rest of the staff."

"I didn't save Doctor Alur."

"You couldn't have. That was a surprise attack. Even if you hadn't been wearing a hazmat suit and had been able to draw your sidearm, Alur would still be dead." He shook his head. "You are seldom an unfair person, Cowboy. When you are, it's almost always directed at yourself."

Chapter One Hundred and Six

Boyer Hall Faculty Lounge
University of California, Los Angeles
March 31, 7:33 P.M.

Linden Brierly sat next to the president on the battered old couch in the faculty lounge. Secret Service agents blocked the door and guarded the hall. Alice Houston stood next to the couch, her hand pressed to her mouth. The TV was on, and the cameras showed bodies being removed from a townhouse in Park Slope. Three laptops stood open on a table and set for video chats. The director of Homeland Security was on one; the national security advisor was on another. And Mr. Church was on the third, clearly speaking via cell-phone video.

They were all listening to Church, who was explaining the DMS theory that the Regis system had been compromised by the Seven Kings. The room was as silent as a tomb except for Church's voice.

The silence endured for several moments after Church had finished, though every pair of eyes in the room turned to the president.

Finally, the president blew out his cheeks and said, "I should have stayed in Congress."

No one laughed.

To Church, the president said, "This is still conjecture? Do we have anything concrete?"

"Not at the moment."

"But you believe this to be the case?"

"I do, Mr. President."

"You understand what it would mean to try and shut down everything with Regis installed?"

"Yes, sir."

"You're aware of how vulnerable it would make our country? Not just in terms of attacks from foreign powers, but in defense of what's happening right here."

Church said nothing. Instead, he ate a cookie.

The president fidgeted. Everyone in the room knew that Church had advised against Regis in the first place. Years ago. Just as he'd advised against a delay in responding to the Resort video.

"I'll take it under advisement," said the president.

"Mr. President, there is a time for deliberation and there is a time for action," said Church. "We need to—"

The president leaned forward and slapped the laptop closed. He heard the gasps but did not acknowledge them. Instead, he sank back into his chair and glowered at the closed computer.

After a shocked moment, Alice Houston said, "Mr. President, how would you like us to respond to this?"

"Respond?" The president laughed. "I'm not going to dignify that with an answer. Church is an alarmist. This is his damn fault."

"How so, Mr. President?" asked Brierly.

"Because it was his job to dismantle the Seven Kings organization, and he failed."

Brierly clamped his mouth shut so tightly his jaw creaked. He tried to catch Houston's eyes, but she looked away.

However, the chief of staff said, "Church is coming here to fly back east with you on Air Force One. Shall . . . I tell him not to?"

"Oh no, don't do that," said the president. "I want him with me so I can have a nice little private chat with him. I want to tell him how I will be pulling the DMS charter as soon as this crisis is past. I was warned about him before I took office, and now I can see that those warnings were accurate. Church is a megalomaniac who bullies people into getting what he wants."

"Sir," said Brierly in a tight voice, "what possible motive would Mr. Church have for spinning a story like this if Regis was not a genuine threat?"

The president cut him a savage look. "I don't know, and I damn well don't care. He's done. That's what I care about. And now let's us focus on the realities of what's happening. The ballpark and the video. That's our focus."

Chapter One Hundred and Seven

South 21st Street

Tacoma, Washington

March 31, 8:01 P.M.

Davidovich pulled the truck off the road and drove halfway up the winding private lane to someone's darkened house. He idled there for a few minutes, studying the landscape by moonlight. The place was shuttered up, probably closed since last fall and not yet opened.

Perfect.

He took a breath and drove the rest of the way, then pulled behind the house and parked in the utter blackness of the porte cochere that connected the main house to a large gazebo. He killed the engine and sat for nearly five minutes, gripping the wheel, unable to make himself move.

Although his right hand gripped the knobbed vinyl of the steering wheel, his skin could still feel the exact size, shape, and texture of the rock.

His ears could still hear the meaty crunch as the rock smashed through hair and flesh and bone.

338 | Jonathan Maberry

And brain.

"God," he whispered, but the word came out wrong because his teeth were chattering. Or maybe because that word didn't fit into his mouth anymore.

Tears traced hot lines down the cold flesh of his cheeks.

He wished he felt more pity for the dead man than he did remorse for his own damaged life. He ached to feel that much humanity.

But it wasn't the truth.

He sat there and mourned for himself. For the death of all that he had been and all that he could have been.

The death of a great man.

The death of Aaron Davidovich.

It took a lot of willpower and physical strength to unclamp his hands from the steering wheel. When his fingers finally came free, his hand flopped onto his thigh and then crawled like a white spider over to the passenger seat, searching in the shadows for the cell phone.

He froze.

What if the number wasn't good anymore? What if it had been changed after he'd been taken?

What if there was no one to take his call?

What if?

What if?

Davidovich punched the steering wheel with the heel of his left hand. Over and over again. It hurt. It jarred the bones in his delicate hands. It sent little stinging shocks up his wrist.

It steadied him.

He drew in a breath so ragged that it hurt his lungs.

And picked up the cell.

Even after all these years, he knew the number by heart. It had been drilled into him when he went to work for DARPA and reinforced by the CIA when he was asked to go to Israel for the conference.

The number of his handler.

He punched in the ten digits. Expecting failure. Expecting nothing.

There was a vast, empty nothing for a long moment.

And then it rang.

Once.

Twice.

Before the third ring could start, there was a click and a voice said, "Receiving office."

Davidovich sagged back, fresh tears boiling under his lashes.

"I need to arrange a delivery."

A pause at the other end.

"Foreign or domestic shipping."

"Domestic," he said hurriedly. "I'm here. I'm back in the States."

Another long pause. The voice was not one he recognized. Young but formal. Detached.

"Do you have a billing code?"

Davidovich had not spoken the number for three years, but he never forgot a piece of data.

"Four-six-one-one, M as in Mary, nine-nine."

The young man read it back, but as he did so he transposed the six and the first one.

"Is that correct, sir?"

Davidovich repeated it exactly as the young man had said, with the same numbers transposed.

Another of those long, long pauses.

Then . . .

"Good evening, doctor."

Chapter One Hundred and Eight

Sharp Chula Vista Medical Center
Medical Center Court, Chula Vista
April 1, 4:51 A.M.

We had to wait through the incubation period to see if anything nasty happened to Brian or me. It didn't. They tested every type of fluid and skin sample possible to take from a human being, and they found nothing.

Nothing. We were clean.

Rudy came to disconnect all the tubes.

All he said was, "Thank God."

By the time we were dressed and officially discharged, Top and Bunny were on their way back from the crime scene. The bodies of our two fallen comrades were in the morgue, but there were blood splashes outside to show where they'd been cut down. I hadn't known them very well, but you don't need to be best friends with a fellow soldier to grieve for him. The same went for Alur. He seemed like a decent guy. All of them should have more chapters in the books of their lives.

Another debt to put on the Seven Kings.

The killer had put it in flat terms. *Say good-bye to your world.*

Yeah, motherfucker, I thought, say good-bye to yours.

Because your world is going to burn.

That was a scary threat. Very, very scary.

I wish I knew what to do about it. Where to go with it. While I waited for Top and Bunny, I settled into a doctor's lounge. There was a whiteboard on the wall, so I busied myself listing the timeline we'd come up with on the plane so I could show it to Rudy when he came for me. He was somewhere else doing doctor stuff. I was spinning my wheels.

You know the expression "hurry up and wait"?

I hate that expression.

Especially when it defines my workday. Doubly so when bad things were happening to good people and the best I could manage was killing time.

Oh yeah, "killing time." Another expression that, in context, blows.

Even more so when it becomes the most accurate assessment of the progress of a critical case.

A voice behind me said, "Here—"

I jumped about a foot, spun around, and almost pulled my gun.

It was Rudy holding a cup of Starbucks coffee out to me, his hawthorn and silver cane hooked over the crook of one arm. His expression was halfway between shocked and amused.

"Nerves a little taut, Cowboy?" he said dryly.

"Yeah, well, fuck you, too," I snarled.

"And cranky, too. It's unbecoming."

"And the horse you rode in on."

I took the coffee and sipped it. Hot and delicious, but I was too caught up in the dramatics of the moment to do anything but scowl.

Rudy nodded to Ghost, who had barely managed the energy to swivel one ear when I jumped. "At least somebody around here is managing to keep his blood pressure below the boiling point."

"Don't be fooled," I said, "Ghost is poised for action."

Ghost yawned and rolled over onto his back, legs curled and splayed like a dead chicken.

"So I see," observed Rudy. "As always, I am in awe."

For lack of anything cool or witty to say, I shot him the finger.

"When are we leaving?" he asked.

"Top and Bunny should be here any second. Then we'll go see Circe, Junie, and the others."

Rudy nodded, but there was some reserve in his face, which I immediately—and unfairly—misread.

"My guys swept the hospital," I said, "Nicodemus isn't there. But if you don't want to go back, I—"

That made Rudy stiffen, and he looked at me with one dark brown eye that burned like a laser all the way through me. "Cowboy, my wife is in that hospital. I left with great reluctance in order to come here. If you are suggesting that I am afraid to go back, then I—"

I set my coffee cup down and held up my hands. "Stop. That was me being stupid. I apologize. As you, better than anyone, know, I have more than my share of jackass moments. No excuses. I wasn't thinking, and I'm sorry."

Rudy burned me for another few seconds, then turned off the heat. He nodded, exhaled, sipped his coffee.

"You're right about one thing," he said.

"What?"

"You have an inordinate amount of jackass moments."

I grinned. "Guilty as charged."

We toasted each other with Starbucks—I, with Pike, and he, with his iced half-caf ristretto quad grande, two-pump raspberry, two-percent, no-whip, light-ice, caramel-drizzle, three-and-a-half-pump white mocha. Normally, I would abuse him for the girly-man nature of that drink. Now was not the moment.

"How's Brian?" I asked.

"Bad bruise but nothing broken, thank God. The new spider-silk Kevlar is quite amazing. It'll save a lot of lives. It certainly saved his."

We toasted to that as well.

Church called and told me that he'd struck out selling the Regis shutdown to the president.

"Well . . . shit on toast," I said.

He grunted and said, "Politics."

"What's our play now?"

"I'm still scheduled to fly east with him. First to New York and then Philadelphia. That will give me some time to work on him."

"Working him over would be more useful."

"And probably more fun," agreed Church. "I'll keep you posted. In the meantime, you're heading here?"

"Yes. Maybe I can whip up some kind of game plan."

"I wish you luck."

The line went dead.

Chapter One Hundred and Nine

Sharp Chula Vista Medical Center
Medical Center Court, Chula Vista, California
April 1, 5:07 A.M.

I told Rudy about the call. He made a face of disappointment. Maybe it was a frown of contempt. Hard to say. Either seemed appropriate. We walked outside to wait for Top and Bunny.

"Joe," said Rudy, "I've been thinking about the Seven Kings information we've collected so far. I'm trying to work up a psychological profile on whoever is directing this particular campaign. When the Kings orchestrated the attacks on the Twin Towers and the Pentagon, they used the faux religious zealotry of Osama bin Laden as their mask. With the Ten Plagues Initiative, it was easier to understand because Vox's mother, the self-styled 'Goddess,' was a classic megalomaniacal subtype. The same went for her consort, Sebastian Gault. That plan had their fingerprints all over it. Had they survived and begun another plan together, we may have been able to counter it sooner because of how much we were able to learn about them.

You know, profiling isn't always the shot in the dark it's made out to be in movies."

"Okay, and—?"

"Well . . . have you noticed that there is no face on these attacks?"

"Face?" I asked.

"Think about it, Joe. With the Ten Plagues, the Goddess used social networking to infuse the attacks with a biblical feel. She drew on the heat of racial and religious intolerance and fanned that into a fire so that people were committing hate crimes that were not actually directed by the Kings themselves. Like an avalanche picking up debris. And Mother Night more or less did the same thing. Yes, I know she wasn't part of the Kings, but she'd learned from them. She was with us when we took down the Kings, and she knew Vox. She'd been point person on the science team that dismantled the Kings' operation after the gunplay was over. Surely it's occurred to you that the way she rolled out her pseudo-anarchical Burn to Shine program was modeled after the Kings, just as it was modeled after aspects of her own personality. And she constructed the Mother Night persona to sell it. These things are always more effective when there is a devil among the details. Hitler, Manson, Jim Jones. There are plenty of examples, and it almost doesn't matter whether the face is the directing force or a figurehead."

I nodded.

"Take the *seif al din* matter," continued Rudy, "the thing that brought us both into the DMS. Most of that case was built around the terror-for-profit mind-set of Sebastian Gault. His methodology, his personal intensity. And, let's face it, it's no surprise that he was later recruited by the Kings. He already used a similar style of grand theatrics and showy misdirection to roll out his plan. Only the last part of that, the attack at the Liberty Bell Center, was different, because that bore the more aggressive personality of El Mujahid. Do you see where I'm going with this?"

"I think so."

"So, with this campaign," Rudy said, "where's the element of personality? Why does this seem so"—he fished for a word and chose one that shouldn't fit but somehow did—"clinical? Or, maybe, mechanical."

I repeated the words, tasting them.

"I mean, look at us," said Rudy, "we typically find ourselves giving a case a nickname, and so far no one has done so beyond 'the drone thing.'"

"Regis?" I suggested, but he shook his head.

"No, that's a by-product, and we're still waffling on whether it is, in fact, the core of their plan."

"I'm already sold. Regis is another word for 'king,' for Christ's sake. They put their brand on it, wouldn't you say?"

"Sure, everyone in the DMS seems to agree with that, Joe, but Mr. Church has not had much luck selling that to the president or the Department of Defense. That's complicated by the fact that the earliest proposals for Regis predate our first encounters with the Seven Kings."

"C'mon, that proves nothing. We know for a fact that the Kings have been around, moving behind the scenes for a couple of decades now."

"So Mr. Church has attempted to explain." He made a sour face and repeated, "Politics."

"Politics," I agreed, loading it with the same bile Church had used earlier.

"And the Kings themselves predate the current administration by several years. It's my opinion, Joe, that the president is unwilling to accept that the Kings organization could rebuild itself to this level of threat on his watch."

"Fucking politics," I amended, and he nodded.

I sat on a stone ledge and sipped my coffee. Ghost put his head on my lap. It was clearly time for me to pet him. I did.

"There may be no overall face on this," I conceded, "but their foot soldiers are acting the way we've seen with Kingsmen in the past. They're true believers. The last shooter used his dying breath to drop a tagline on me: 'Your world is going to burn.'"

Rudy nodded. "It shows that internally, at least, the Kings are acting like the Kings. Or, the organization is on an administrative level. But, tell me, Joe, what do you infer from the man's comment?"

I shrugged. "That we've only seen the coming attractions. The main feature hasn't started yet."

Another nod. "And—?"

"Whatever's coming is big."

Rudy looked annoyed. "That's an imprecise analysis, Cowboy. You're smarter than that. What do you, Joe Ledger, senior DMS field agent, head of the Special Projects Division, infer from what that man said?"

I brooded on it, scratching Ghost's fur.

"The line is too dramatic to be an actual dying declaration," I said. "It comes off as scripted."

Rudy nodded. "It certainly does."

"My favorite working theory—one that accounts for the sophistication of their current weapon—meaning drones, the software hijacking, like that—is that Doctor Davidovich is working with the Kings."

"Mr. Church told me you thought so. Why 'with' rather than 'for but under duress'?"

"The QC drive in the pigeon drones," I said.

Rudy frowned. "I'm not sure I follow."

"Developing a workable quantum computer is apparently a very big thing. From what Bug and his geek squad have told me, it should have taken a decade or two. But Davidovich did it in a few years."

"Which means what, exactly, Joe? That under duress Davidovich would only do good work but not outstanding work?"

"Something like that. I know some pretty creative people, Rude. They can do a lot of great stuff under a deadline. But the QC is the kind of thing that will make Davidovich a household name for the next century. How many people create masterpieces at gunpoint?"

Rudy nodded thoughtfully. "An interesting point. I'll consider it. Mr. Church has asked for a profile of Davidovich as a possible player for the Kings."

"At this point I don't think we can discount it."

A police car pulled into the turnaround, lights flashing but no siren. A cop hopped out and opened the rear doors for Top and Bunny. They shook hands with him and then came to meet us. They both looked angry and upset.

"I can't leave you alone for five goddamn minutes," complained Top.

They shook hands with Rudy and asked about Circe, getting the same answers I got. It was still a heartbreaking holding pattern.

Brian Botley came out wearing bloodstained clothes and was no longer in a hazmat suit.

"Glad to see you fellows," he said.

"Glad to see you still sucking air."

Brian looked sad. "Not everyone was so lucky."

Top seemed really furious. "We should have been here, not at the damn crime scene. Nothing new's happening there," he said to me.

"Don't go there, Top," I countered. "There was no way we could have anticipated this hit. And even so, we had three armed agents here."

"'Had' is the damn point, Cap'n," he snapped. "Farm Boy and me would have cut those assholes off at the knees before they ever drew down on our guys. No offense, Botley."

"None taken," said Brian. "I wish you'd been here, too. All the math would be different."

"Top," said Rudy, "please understand something. The only fault lies with the Seven Kings. They are clearly and effectively stretching our resources. Giving us a crime scene and a medical investigation would certainly split our forces. They counted on that, and they used it against us. Instead of looking to blame ourselves, we have to keep in mind the subtlety of their planning. And then we have to develop a response that is appropriate and effective. Do you agree?"

Top looked at him for a three count, then nodded.

"Going to make someone burn for this," he said.

Say good-bye to your world.

My earbud buzzed and I tapped it. "Go."

"Hey, Cowboy," said Nikki. "We ran the prints from the six shooters and got pings on all of them. All six members of the team are ex-military," she said. "Four army, one navy, one marine. All six worked in some aspect of the security industry. All have ties to Blue Diamond Security."

"Figured that." Blue Diamond was a massive private security company that provided shooters to everyone from Monsanto to Uncle Sam. We've had messy run-ins with them in the past, but even though some of their men went to the hospital, prison, or morgue, upper management never took a fall. Contractually, they were not responsible for actions taken by contract employees. Or some legal bullshit like that. When the attorney general tried to sue them, they outlawyered us. They had an apparently unlimited amount of cash to throw at the legal process; the AG had a way smaller budget.

"What about the serial numbers on their weapons? Any leads from those?"

"All of it was stolen from a shipment that went missing back in 2009."

"Ah. And their vehicle? They arrived in an ambulance."

"Stolen the day before from a private EMT service in Rancho Santa Fe. It was actually reported missing, too. The GPS tracker and security lock-out systems were hacked and disabled. Plates were swap-outs stolen from another ambulance company in Solana Beach. Very professional."

"What about the NachoCopter. Anything there?"

"Kind of. We figured out what happened, but that doesn't get us very far," said Nikki sadly. "The UAV left with the food order, and everything was normal for the first four minutes of the flight. Then it landed on a roof-top of a one-story gas station that's been closed for three years. We think that someone hacked into the GPS controls and forced the machine to land so they could plant the disease pathogen in the food. It was done fast, though, and the drone was on its way in under three minutes."

"Anyone see who was on that roof?"

"We have one vague description of a quote 'guy with a San Diego Padres cap and a dark colored T-shirt. Maybe jeans. Maybe the guy was white. Maybe he was black. Maybe he was Latino.' Unquote. The witness wasn't looking and didn't much care. Old retired guy on his porch."

"I used to like you, Nikki. But you're about to fall off my Christmas-card list."

"Doing the best I can with what you give me, Cowboy."

"We anywhere with the drone itself?"

"No. Doctor Hu's team pulled it apart. Everything. It's standard. No QC drive. But it does have the commercial version of SafeZone, so there's that. Yoda's looking for a Trojan horse with a virus, but none of the Mind-Reader scans are pinging anything. Bottom line is the drone was hacked with software that, right now, anyone and their grandmother seems to have access to. SafeZone's everywhere. There are ten versions of it at BestBuy. Any kid in eighth-grade computer-science class could install it."

"Balls."

"The hard part wasn't the UAV," she continued. "The hard part was that NF disease. I spoke with Hu half an hour ago, and he's been working with John Cmar down at Johns Hopkins and a few other top infectious-disease docs. So far, they're all impressed, but none of them know who cooked it up."

"No clue at all?"

"Well . . ." Nikki said diffidently. "Doctor Cmar said it reminds him of something he heard about from a World Health Organization conference ten years ago. A lab in Angola was trying to do something with necrotizing fasciitis, but Barrier shut them down. Supposedly all materials, records, and samples were destroyed. MindReader verified this, and there's nothing else we can find about anyone else trying to develop something along the same lines."

"Another dead end."

Rudy cut in, "Nikki, can you get us a list of everyone who attended that conference? Maybe someone there might have ties to the Kings."

"Um . . . sure. No problem."

She signed off.

We left the hospital and piled into Ugly Betty. A sore, heartsick, and angry Brian Botley was with us. However, Bunny hadn't even started the engine when Nikki called back.

"Joe, oh my God, Joe! I think we caught a break. I think we have something big."

"Talk to me."

"Do you remember the code name Doctor Detroit?"

I stiffened. "Yes, I do."

"I . . . I think he just called the CIA."

Everyone in the car froze.

Doctor Detroit.

Yeah, we all knew that code name. It was the name assigned by DARPA.

It was the name of a man every law enforcement agency in the world looked for.

Doctor Detroit.

Otherwise known as Doctor Aaron Davidovich.

Chapter One Hundred and Ten

We burned a long patch of rubber heading back to the Coast Guard air station. Instead of taking *Shirley*, we hopped aboard a muscular C-130 Hercules that had been arranged for us by Church. That allowed us to take Ugly Betty with us as we flew north to Washington State. The five of us—Top, Bunny, Brian, Ghost, and I—loaded Ugly Betty aboard, and we were wheels up in minutes. I had Montana drive to the airfield to bring Rudy back to San Diego. She wanted to come with us, but I told her I needed the rest of Echo to secure the hospital. The Kings were coming after us from all angles, and Nicodemus had already proved that they could get past the hospital security. She didn't like it, but from the look in her eye I knew she'd take her frustrations out on any Kingsmen who had the bad luck to show up.

Our flight plan was straight as an arrow, and we were riding an executive order. It's about eleven hundred miles, runway to runway, and I told the pilot to push it all the way to the red line. He didn't like it, but he did it.

Once we were airborne, I played the message from Doctor Aaron Davidovich the CIA had passed along to us.

"*. . . not sure if this is the right number. Been a long time since I had to use it. First chance I've had to get near an untapped phone. Please, I need you to pass this along to the Department of Military Sciences. They've dealt with this before. No one else. Please, no one else. Don't try to figure out a better way. Trust me, nothing you do other than to contact Mr. Church's people will work. Tell them this is Doctor Detroit. That's not a joke. It's a code name. This is not a hoax. Tell them Doctor Detroit is alive and he needs help.*"

The CIA handler had tried to stem the flow of words and hold an actual conversation with Davidovich, but the scientist was in full-blown panic mode. His words tumbled over each other in a nearly unbroken flow that floated near the high-water mark of hysteria.

"Is that his voice?" asked Brian. "This was all before my time."

"It's him," said Top. "No doubt about it. That whiny rich-boy voice?

The contempt for lesser beings? Yeah, even scared, it's still there in his voice."

"Don't sugarcoat it, Top," said Bunny.

"Guy's an asshole. Always was."

"Yeah, okay, fair enough. Play the rest, Boss."

I played the rest.

"*I am in Washington State. I'm using a stolen phone. I had to kill someone to get it. I stole some money, too, and a pickup truck. I'm going to find a store where I can buy some burners. Track this phone if you know how to do that. I'm not taking it with me, but it will get the DMS into this area. I'll call again once I find a burner, and then they can come find me. I'll call this same number.*"

"*Doctor, tell me where you are,*" said the CIA handler. "*We can—*"

"*You can't do shit. You guys were supposed to be protecting me in Israel, and look what happened. The Seven Kings came in and took me anyway. Fuck you. I want the DMS. I want Colonel Riggs or Captain Ledger.*"

"Doesn't know Riggs is dead," said Bunny. "He's been out of touch."

The CIA handler kept trying to work his way into the scientist's confidence. "*Doctor, believe me, we can keep you safe. Let us know where to find you and—*"

"*Hey, moron, are you listening to me?*" snapped Davidovich. "*I'm not telling you squat. I'll tell the DMS where I am. For now, all I want you clowns to do is track this phone. I'm not going to give any specific locations. You have to track me, and you have to get in touch with the DMS. Use the GPX-11 cellular satellite system and triangulate my call between that and ground cell towers. Even you should be able to find where I'm leaving this phone.*"

The handler tried, but there was no more from Davidovich. After a few minutes, it was clear the scientist had simply abandoned the phone without hanging it up.

I called the CIA handler and grilled him pretty thoroughly. Even with an executive order, he was reluctant to turn over the case. I insisted. I'm good at insisting. I also had Nikki take control of the number Davidovich had used, and now it was routed directly to us, closing the Agency out completely. There would probably be a sternly written memo. Fine. I can always use fresh toilet paper.

The GPX-11 satellite Davidovich mentioned was another DARPA Tinkertoy. Specifically for ultrafast tracking of cell phones. Davidovich was using burners, though, and that complicated things. Burners were cheap, disposable cell phones that came preloaded with minutes. No plan or contract needed. They are the go-to phone for everyone from drug dealers to global terrorists. Very efficient, but a bitch to trace. I told Nikki to do her best.

I called Church and went over it with him, but he had nothing new to add to my game plan because the plan was simple. Get to Washington and wait for Davidovich to call again. Church took my call while aboard his own plane, which was about to touch down in LA, where he would transfer to Air Force One.

"How's the political shitstorm?" I asked.

"Raging," said Church, and he disconnected.

Our plane was nearly to the airfield in Seattle when Nikki called me.

"Cowboy, we have Doctor Detroit on the line again. New number. A burner. Routing it to you now."

"I'm in a stolen pickup, heading north toward Seattle," said a familiar voice. "Did you idiots get in touch with the DMS yet?"

"Doctor," I said, "this *is* the DMS. We are attempting to locate you now."

"Who is this?" Davidovich demanded.

"We don't use names on an open line," I reminded him.

"Christ, is this Joe Ledger? Holy fuck, it is you."

"Nice use of protocol, doc," I said. "Proves you're smart. Now be smarter and tell me where you are."

"Oh, bite me, Ledger. Like I give a shit about protocol? Where was the protocol when I was taken and——?"

"Really, doc? Now's the time for that conversation? How about you tell me where you are so me and a whole bunch of very scary guys with guns can come and rescue you? Sound like a plan?"

"All right, all right. Let me see. There's a road sign up ahead. I'm on Route Five, heading north. Just saw a sign for Edgewood."

Bunny had a map out and said, "West of Tacoma. Route Five turns north and runs all the way up. We're less than an hour from him."

"Doc," I said, "we can get to you in less than an hour."

"Oh . . . wait," said Davidovich.

"What's wrong?"

"That SUV behind me. I've seen it before. A couple of times now. God. I think they found me."

"Keep driving," I ordered. "Don't stop for anyone. Run red lights if you have to, but don't take any unnecessary risks. We're going to find you, and we will keep you safe."

"Listen, Ledger," he said, "you don't know what's happening. You may think you do, but you don't, and you need to. Those maniacs on the island are totally batshit crazy. I'm not joking. I can help you stop what's coming. But you have to help me first. You need to get me out of this, you understand? And you need to get people to my son. You need to protect Matthew."

"We can do that, but—"

"No. You do that right now. You make sure he's safe. My mother, too. I'm not going to tell you a thing until you can prove to me they're safe. What's the expression? Proof of life? Get them into protective custody, and then I will tell you everything. Screw it up, and this whole world is going to catch fire and burn. Think I'm joking?"

Top signaled to me that he was on it, and I heard him speaking to someone at the tactical operations center in Brooklyn.

"No, doc," I said, "I really don't think you're joking. Neither am I. We're sending teams right now to take your family into protective custody. My people, not the FBI or anyone else. I know you trust us. We'll protect them, but we don't have time to play games here. People are dying. Tell me what's going on and—"

That's where the call ended. There was no sound, no gunshot or anything. Just a drop-off.

The call was gone.

Chapter One Hundred and Eleven

In Flight

April 1, 9:58 A.M. Pacific Standard Time

"Jesus jumped-up Christ in a motor-driven sidecar," I snarled as I jabbed my earbud for a line to the Hangar. "Nikki, please tell me you tracked that call."

"No, there wasn't time. We're working on it."

Then she was gone.

"What happened to Davidovich?" asked Brian. "He playing games with us?"

"There's a game," I said, "but he's not running it."

Bunny nodded. "The Kingsmen could have tracked his call, too. If he just escaped from them, they're closer. They might even have a tracker on him. Don't know. But maybe they worked a car stop or ran him off the road."

"You mean killed him?" asked Brian.

"Maybe," I said. "Maybe not. We lost the call, but it doesn't mean he's dead."

"Hope your angels are listening to you, Boss," said Brian, "because we could use a damn break right about now."

While we waited for more, I made calls to scramble Odin and Java Teams out of Seattle and told them to get onto the road heading south in unmarked cars.

The Hercules pilot bing-bonged to tell us we were on final approach.

"If Davidovich is still on Route Five," I said, tapping the route on the map, "then we might be able to catch him between us and the Seattle teams."

"We don't know how many Kingsmen are out there," said Bunny.

"I don't fucking care," I said. "There won't be enough."

"Hooah," he said, and bumped fists with Brian. They seemed happy about the likelihood of an impending firefight.

Top ended his call. "Okay, Cap'n, we've got three four-man teams on pickup duty. Wife, mother, and son. Local law's running backup. Cars and helos. Anyone looks funny at the doc's family, they're going to get their dicks handed to them in Ziploc bags. All three will be taken to a secure location for assessment and then flown to the Pier."

"Outstanding," I said.

Suddenly Nikki was shouting in my ear. "Cowboy, he's back. He's on the line."

"Christ, kid, put him through."

Just as the wheels thumped down, there was a click, and suddenly I heard the nasal voice of Aaron Davidovich in my ear.

"—another burner . . . they . . . oh, God . . . "

The call was nearly drowned by static, and Davidovich's voice was thick and nearly unintelligible.

"Doc, what's happening?" I yelled. "Are you injured—?"

" . . . oh, Jesus . . . I can't stop it . . . can't find the bleeder . . . "

After that, nothing but static.

But it was the static of an open line.

"Nikki," I said, "tell me something I want to hear."

"The call's still going," she said. "I think he dropped the phone."

I heard Bunny whisper. "Did he fucking die on us?"

The plane stopped rolling.

"What's happening with the trace?" I asked.

Nikki said, "We're closing in. Looks like it's north of you. I'll send you the location as soon as we complete the trace."

Top spun around, and in a leather-throated voice bellowed at the flight crew. "Offload this vehicle. Do it *right goddamn now*."

They did it right goddamn then.

We scrambled into Ugly Betty, and Bunny hit the gas. Despite the car's size and weight, Mike Harnick hadn't lied about its power. The machine leaped forward and continued to accelerate. The needle was tapping ninety-five when Nikki came back on the line.

"Got it, Cowboy. Twenty-nine point four miles north. Signal is moving. It's on Highway Eighteen heading northwest."

"On Eighteen? Confirm?"

Brian found it on the map. "Eighteen spurs off from Route Five and cuts inland past Tiger Mountain State Forest toward North Bend and Snoqualmie."

"The signal's stopped moving," said Nikki.

"What's happening?" I asked.

"Signal's steady but—no, wait. Yes, confirmed the signal is heading southeast again. Looks like he's heading back to the Five."

"Get me a satellite, damn it."

"No satellites in range, Cowboy."

"Find me one."

"Proceed south on the Five," she said. "If you hurry, you might reach where it intersects with Eighteen before he does."

"You heard the woman, Farm Boy," said Top. "Stop driving like my Aunt Gertie."

"Your Aunt Gertie's dead," said Bunny.

"Exactly my point."

The Escalade roared down the road.

"Cowboy," said Nikki, "Java Team has a drone in the air, and we're waiting on a picture."

"Gosh," said Bunny. "A drone. How lovely."

"At least it's one of ours," said Brian. "Got to be some irony in that."

"Fuck irony."

Nikki said, "Okay, Cowboy, we have the feed. Sending live feed to your computer now."

Top, Brian, and I bent over my screen. The gray-tone image from the drone painted a bull's-eye on what looked like a landscaper's pickup truck hauling ass along Route 18. There were two black SUVs with it, one behind and one in front, maintaining the exact same distance from the pickup truck.

"What are you seeing?" asked Bunny as he weaved in and out of traffic.

"Classic pickup," said Top. "I think our boy's in the center vehicle, lead and follow cars have his truck boxed. Looks like they grabbed him and are taking him and the truck he stole."

"Nikki, does our drone have thermals?"

"Switching to thermal scan," she confirmed.

The lead SUV had four glowing dots; the follow car had five. The pickup had three.

"Count fourteen signatures," said Nikki. "Maybe thirteen hostiles and Doctor Detroit."

"Copy that," I said. "How many assets do we have from Java?"

"Four agents in two cars. Sending a detail map."

My screen changed to show a map of the area. The three cars in the convoy were assigned green lights. Java and Echo Teams were yellow. We were all heading toward each other at high speeds.

"Thirteen to eight," said Brian. "Pretty good odds."

"Not for them," said Bunny.

"Thirteen to nine," said Top, scratching Ghost between the shoulder blades. Ghost showed his titanium teeth.

Brian grinned. "Almost doesn't seem fair."

"Don't get cocky, kid," I said in a fair approximation of Han Solo. At least I thought so.

"Call the rules, Cap'n," said Top as he began a final weapons check.

"Priority one is to retrieve Davidovich alive," I told them. "I need to ask that son of a bitch a few thousand very important questions. After that, try to bag some bad guys while they still have a pulse so we can get some idea of what the hell these ass-clowns are up to. But don't take risks. We all go in, we all come out. Capisce?"

"Hooah," they said.

Bunny crunched down on the gas pedal.

"Any ideas what the 'big thing' is that these Kings guys are about to throw at us?" asked Bunny. "So far, this shit is already pretty frigging big. Not sure I want to know how much bigger they want to take it. But . . . not knowing makes my nuts want to crawl up inside my chest cavity and hide."

Top grunted. "And all this time I didn't think they'd dropped yet."

"Blow me."

"Point taken."

I said, "We don't know, but it more or less corroborates what the shooter at the hospital said. '*Say good-bye to your world.*'"

Brian shook his head. "Seriously, where do they get this stuff? I mean, is there a class these goons take to learn how to drop cryptic messages while they're bleeding out? Are they trying to die as clichés?"

"Apparently they are," I said, "but that doesn't change the fact that we should probably be scared out of our bloomers. The pattern Top, Bunny, and I came up with on the flight from Philly suggests that the Kings have been testing their systems and their efficiency. The nature of those tests did not, as far as we could see, jibe with the kind of attack they launched at the ballpark. That actually might have been either a last test or an opening salvo."

"Yeah, but what's the main attraction?"

"Let's hope we can grab Davidovich before we have to find out."

Brian nodded. While we talked it out, he reached over to pet Ghost. Brian had only been out on two jobs with us, and Ghost hadn't been part of either.

"Wouldn't do that, son," warned Top.

"It's okay," said Brian, "I'm a dog person."

Ghost wrinkled his muzzle in what was clearly not a smile.

"He's not a people person," explained Top.

"And he had a bad day yesterday," I said. "But, hey, if you can shoot a gun with no fingers . . . by all means."

"Taking it back," Brian said, withdrawing his hand and smiling at my dog. Ghost continued to show his teeth. "Nice doggie."

"No," said Bunny, "not really."

Chapter One Hundred and Twelve

Los Angeles International Airport
April 1, 11:32 A.M.

Air Force One taxied to the runway. Although the plane did not usually fly with fighter jets in escort, the current situation required a military presence. A pair of F-18s were already in the air, circling the airport to fly close support. Like Air Force One, the F-18s had been retrofitted to replace Regis with the safer Solomon program.

Church found this significant but did not comment on it to the president. A better moment for that kind of observation would likely present itself.

Church and Linden Brierly sat with the president in the onboard conference room as the plane lifted off. The commander in chief looked worn and much older than his years. He had his jacket off, tie loosened, and there was a sallow cast to his skin and red rime around his eyes.

"God, this is a nightmare," said the president.

"We'll get it sorted out, sir," said Alice Houston, and Brierly gave a tight-lipped nod. The look in his eyes told a different story.

POTUS nodded but cut a look at Church. "You're unusually silent, Deacon. Hope there are no hard feelings about how I ended the conference call earlier."

Mr. Church offered a faint, bland smile. "You are the president. I work for you."

That put a slight frown on the president's mouth. As intended.

Brierly cleared his throat, but he said nothing.

"Tell me, Deacon," said the president, "how confident are you that we'll get in front of this? Brierly seems to think you do magic. Is he right, or is he just stroking my political fur?"

Church shrugged. "Do you want a straight answer or a political one?"

Brierly turned away to hide a wince. Houston's face became a slab of wood. Even the generals in the jet's conference room seemed to wilt into the background.

The president leaned back and considered Church. "You really don't give a damn about me or my office, do you?"

"My first concern is doing my job, Mr. President. All other concerns are of less importance to me."

"Damn, you aren't afraid of shooting from the hip, are you?"

Church said nothing.

The room was silent for several heavy seconds.

"You really think this is the Seven Kings manipulating Regis?" asked the president.

"It is the leading theory," said Church. "No other scenario holds as much water."

"What if you're wrong?"

"Then I'm wrong. Fire me if it suits your needs."

The president's face flushed red, and he clearly had to bite down on something he wanted to say. Another few moments dragged by. The others in the conference room wore expressions like they were holding their breaths.

"You're not going to let me off the hook on this," said the president. "Are you?"

"I was not aware, sir, that you asked me aboard to massage your feelings. Perhaps I should be sitting back with the press corps."

"Christ, Deacon," growled the president, "you're more thin-skinned than I am."

Church chose not to reply to that.

Brierly interjected and tried to change the subject. "Is there any word on Aunt Sallie?"

"Nothing new," said Church. "And nothing new with any of my people who have been hurt by this."

The president sighed. "Right. I'm sorry. I guess I'm being an insensitive ass."

No one commented. Church opened his briefcase and removed a package of Nilla Wafers. Tore it open, ate one.

After a moment, the president tried a different conversational path. "Will your boy Ledger get Davidovich? Alive, I mean?"

"As my psychic powers aren't working at the moment, I won't hazard a prediction. I trust, however, that Captain Ledger will do his very best. His best is considerable."

The president looked away for a moment. He was angry but also clearly frustrated. "I don't know how to have a damn conversation with you today," he muttered. "I'm sorry."

Church looked at the cookie he held, sighed, and set it down. "And I'm not making matters any better by my attitude. I apologize, Mr. President."

The president grunted. "Wow. I was warned that you never apologized."

"I try to avoid having to do so, but I'm wrong here. I think it's fair to say that we are all under considerable strain."

"That's generous of you." The president looked at the tabletop for a moment. "I'll give some genuine thought to Regis. It would be useful to have something more concrete to work with. My stock with Congress is at an all-time low right now."

Church finished his cookie. At no point did he offer one to the president.

After a moment, Brierly said, "I was reading over the report from the attack on the hospital in Chula Vista. One thing stands out for me."

"Oh?" said Church.

"That pathogen. The fast-acting necrotizing fasciitis. My people tell me there's nothing like it. Nothing that made it beyond the initial experimental stage. So I called your friend, John Cmar, the infectious-disease doctor at Johns Hopkins. He said that the possibility of it was discussed once at some World Health Organization conference years ago and that an Angolan lab was raided that had been trying to develop it. Barrier shut them down, correct?"

"Correct. All notes and samples were destroyed. Nothing was kept."

"Then how is it in California?"

Church said, "I think we've figured that out. The conference was held some years before DMS first encountered the Seven Kings. Before, in fact, Captain Ledger joined the DMS. One of the speakers at the conference was an internationally known and respected pharmaceuticals manufacturer, a man who was also a brilliant pharmacologist. He gave a rousing talk about how all bioweapons research should be shut down, and those seeking to develop new weaponized pathogens needed to be tracked, shut down, and arrested. The bulk of his speech was quoted verbatim in *Time* magazine, and it's available on YouTube."

"I vaguely remember that," said the president. "That guy's dead, though, isn't he?"

"He is," said Mr. Church. "He was killed by Hugo Vox."

"Oh? Did the Seven Kings target him because of his stance against bio-weapons?"

"Hardly," said Church. "The scientist in question was a member of that organization but apparently had a fatal falling out with Vox."

Brierly narrowed his eyes. "Wait a minute . . . are you talking about the King of Plagues? Christ, are you talking about Sebastian Gault?"

"I am. Gault gave that speech back when his cover was that of a global power for good. This was before his true nature was revealed during the *seif al din* matter, which preceded the Ten Plagues Initiative by nearly a year."

"What of it, though?" asked the president. "Gault's dead, Vox is dead, and as far as we know, all of the original Seven Kings are dead. Bin Laden was the last of them, and we damn well know he's dead. For real, I mean."

"Gault may be dead," said Church, "but that doesn't mean his research is."

"Are you saying that Gault developed this new strain of NF?"

"It seems likely. After the raid on that lab in Angola, there was such a fear of NF that several foundations and at least nine governments including Great Britain channeled millions into research for a treatment or some prophylactic measure. Gault's company was one of several that led the way in research for those treatments."

"Why would he do that if he was behind it?" asked the president.

"Because it's a very controlled way to do supply and demand. Create a demand for what you can supply. We've since learned that Gault created several pathogens—and in some cases introduced new viral and bacterio-logical strains—and then rushed to market with treatments so quickly that he was universally viewed as a great man. He was compared to Salk. And he produced treatments for unfashionable diseases that afflicted isolated third-world populations. Treatments we now believe were invented for diseases he had developed or modified. In the case of NF, his company made tens of millions from research and development. In the case of, say, African river blindness, it was to elevate himself as something approaching a living saint. A great man."

Brierly nodded. "I remember that very well. We all thought the man walked on water. Even the release of *seif al din* was done to scare us into putting billions into new R and D to combat it. He never really planned to release it. But the threat of it had to be real or the plan wouldn't have worked. It almost worked, too."

"Still leaves Gault dead and the NF in Chula Vista," said the president. "What are we supposed to think about that?"

"It seems pretty clear to me," said Brierly.

Church nodded. "Whoever the Seven Kings are now . . . they apparently have Sebastian Gault's research. And that is a very, very troubling thing."

Chapter One Hundred and Thirteen

Tiger Mountain State Forest
Washington
April 1, 11:39 A.M.

"Heads up, guys," said Brian as he studied the electronic map. Nikki had switched the drone's video-surveillance controls to him. "They're making a turn."

The truck turned left onto a fire-access road in the state park.

"Where's he going?" I asked Brian, who was integrating the drone feed with Google Maps. He hit some buttons to overlay the image with data collected by MindReader.

"Nothing out there except a two-man ranger station," he answered. "And after that there's a whole lot of nothing."

"Side roads?"

"Hiking paths, some utility roads. Scattered Forest Service buildings. Mostly empty this time of year."

"What about a clear space for a helicopter?" I asked.

"Plenty of places if the pilot has some stones. Oh, wait—on the far side of the park, there's a concrete slab used by fire department helos. No birds on it now, but that could be where they're going. You could put a Chinook down on it."

I tapped my earbud for the team channel. "Cowboy to Java and Odin. Be advised, target has gone into the forest. Sending possible coordinates. Find an alternate route in to take them from the far side." I growled at Brian. "Where's that drone feed? All I'm seeing is trees."

He put the thermal scan back online, and the heat signatures from the three vehicles flared from under the dense canopy of leaves.

"Got 'em."

"Jumper to Cowboy," said a voice in my ear. Jumper was the top kick of Odin Team. "We're fifteen minutes out. Can you hold the party for us?"

"Doesn't look like it.

"Traffic's a bear, and there's construction on the shoulder. Can't get around it in time, so this in on you. Don't stop for coffee."

"Copy that."

"I have a gravel road that cuts around to the far side of the landing pad," said Brian. "Sending coordinates to the GPS now."

"Got it," said Bunny, and he swung the wheel to send the Escalade crashing through some weeds. He thumped and bumped over underbrush and then skittered onto the gravel.

"Boss," said Brian, "we're going to hit the road they're on directly in front of them. Shit, this is going to be close."

"Perfect," I said.

We left the gravel road, and Bunny spun the wheel as we thumped back onto the service road. In the side-view mirror, I saw the convoy right behind us. The lead SUV braked for a moment, then began accelerating toward us. The passenger-side window opened, and an arm leaned out with an AK-47. Even over the drone of engines, the buzz-saw roar of the machine gun filled the air, and rounds pinged and whanged off the armored skin of Ugly Betty.

"Okay, kids, party time," I said. "We're going with a Baltimore slam. Hit it!"

Bunny punched a button on his steering column that popped the rear hatch and launched a spike net. It shot backward as a rolled bundle but immediately sprang open and dropped flat sideways across the road. The spike net was fifteen feet long and shaped like a carpet runner, except that it was covered with heavy-grade steel spikes. The front wheels of the lead SUV hit the spikes and exploded.

The driver tried to control the vehicle, but he was going too fast, and there was no room for ballet. The pickup truck slammed into the back of the SUV and sent it into a wild fishtail. We could all feel the thump as the SUV crunched sideways into a ponderous maple tree.

The pickup driver was in trouble from the impact, too. It began a long, bad turn that chunked the sides of two tires against the uneven side of the road. The truck canted over and went crunching down into a slide, the metal skin hissing as it rasped over stones and tree roots.

That left the follow car.

"Can I, Boss?" asked Bunny.

"Have some fun," I told him.

"Fun with what?" asked Brian.

Bunny just grinned and hit another button. We heard the rumble as the rear taillights swung down and two M242 Bushmaster 25 mm chain-fed autocannons rolled out.

"When you only care to send the very best," said Bunny. He pressed the button again, and the air was filled with thunder. The heavy rounds punched into the SUV and tore it apart.

No joke.

The armor-piercing Sabot rounds killed the engine, blew apart the windshield, and turned everything inside that car to junk. Red, screaming junk.

The vehicle slowed to a smoking stop and died.

Bunny stamped on the brakes, spun the wheel, and turned us around so fast that a tower of smoke rose all around us. We were out and running before the echoes of that screeching turn had reached the far wall of trees. I had my Sig Sauer P226 in a two-handed grip and began firing as I stepped through the smoke. Top and Brian had CQBR carbines, and Bunny had his drum-fed combat shotgun.

Men were crawling out of the crashed SUV and up through the windows of the fallen pickup. They were all dressed in unmarked black BDUs. None of them looked like Aaron Davidovich.

I have to give them credit for trying to make a fight of it.

We weren't here for a fight. Not a fair one, anyway.

We cut them down, and we didn't feel a flicker of mercy, compassion, or regret.

One of the men staggered away from the SUV and was clearly dazed by the crash. His face was covered with blood, and his eyes were wild. His pistol was in his hand, but it was pointed at the ground. He looked at the bodies that littered the grass and the road and then at us. We stood in a line, our smoking barrels pointed at him.

I aimed my Sig at his face. "Drop the weapon."

Blood ran from a broken nose into his mouth, and he spat it at me. Too far to reach me, but he made his point. I took a step closer.

"Drop the weapon or I will kill you."

He suddenly smiled at me. His teeth were bright red. "Say good-bye to—"

"Yeah, yeah, I know. My world's going to burn. Blah, blah, blah. Put the gun down right now."

The man kept smiling.

He was still smiling when he jammed the barrel of his pistol up under his chin and blew off the top of his head.

Chapter One Hundred and Fourteen

Tiger Mountain State Forest

Washington

April 1, 12:22 A.M.

Brian Botley said, "Well . . . holy shit. Why did he *do* that?"

"Fanatic much?" murmured Bunny, annoyed but unimpressed. "Frigging Kingsmen."

"Welcome to the DMS," grumbled Top. "Okay, stop gawking. Hotzone, check the lead car. Green Giant, check the follow. Go."

Brian and Bunny ran forward, weapons up, eyes wary. Top and I approached the pickup from two sides.

"Clear!" called Brian, and a second later Bunny echoed it.

I squatted down in front of the shattered windshield of the pickup. The interior of the truck was a shambles. There was a lot of blood but only one body.

And thank God it still had a pulse.

Strapped into the passenger seat, his wrists bound by zip ties, a trickle of blood on his forehead from a small cut, was Doctor Aaron Davidovich. He looked absolutely terrified.

"Please," he begged. "Please don't hurt me."

I lowered my gun. "Doctor Davidovich," I said, smiling at him, "we're the good guys. No one's going to hurt you again."

He stared at me in doubt, in disbelief. Then his eyes widened. "J-Joe . . . ?"

"Good to see you alive, doc."

"My . . . my son?"

"We have him. Your wife and mom, too. All safe."

A fragile smile blossomed on his face. Then he put his face in his bound hands and began to weep.

"Doc," I said, "we need to get you out of there." I took out my knife and cut the zip tie. "How badly are you hurt?"

"It's my thigh. I was shot!" He said it as if that was the most extraordinary thing that had ever happened to anyone. He raised his head, and I could see that he was a few ticks away from falling off the edge of the world. I had no idea what he'd been through since he'd been taken from the CIA safe house, but there wasn't a lot of what you'd call sanity burning in his eyes.

"Let me take a look," I said, and I climbed into the truck. He had a rough field dressing taped to his thigh, and I peeled it back to reveal a nasty-looking exit wound. The wound was bleeding sluggishly, though no arteries were ruptured. From what Davidovich had said on the radio, I expected something far worse than this. Of course, to the average person, any kind of violent wound was huge. I replaced the dressing. "It's not too bad. You're not in any immediate threat, and once we get you out of here, we can give you something for the pain. First, though, we need to get you out. Looks like you're in here pretty good, though. I'll need to get some tools from my truck."

He tried to protest, but I assured him that I wasn't going to abandon him. I began worming my way out when he caught my wrist.

"Joe," he said, gripping me with desperate force, "you swear that my son is safe? You swear that Matthew is going to stay safe?"

"You have my word of honor, Doc. No fucking around."

He studied me for a long moment, his eyes jumpy and wild. "You're telling the truth? You're not lying to me so I tell what I know."

"No, Doc," I said, "we're helping your family, and we're here to help you, but you have to help us. If you know what the Kings are doing, then tell me. Help us stop them."

"God, you have to stop them. They're insane. Pharos and the Gentleman. They took me and tortured me and did things to me . . . "

His voice trailed off and he started to cry, but there was something about it that seemed like performance.

"Who's Pharos?" I asked. "Who's the Gentleman?"

He shook his head. "It doesn't matter. They're crazy, and you have to stop them before they can hurt Matthew."

"Focus, Doc. Did they make you work for them?"

He nodded, not meeting my eyes.

"Doc, did they make you tell them about Regis? We think they're hacking it."

"Of *course* they are. Those maniacs . . . They're going to use the system to launch missiles, make ships crash, open valves on submarines, take over firing controls on jets. And not just military. It'll cause autonomous cars to crash. I think they even want to override active controls on planes in flight and initiate a suicide firewall."

"How can we stop them?"

"The reset codes will shut the whole thing down."

I almost sobbed with relief. Reset codes. Jesus, Mary, and Joseph.

"*What are the codes?*" I begged. "And how do I—?"

He shook his head. "There's a whole set of them. You have to input them manually. No cut and paste or it triggers a deadfall subroutine."

I knew about those from other jobs. If you try too many times to input a password, or in this case use the wrong password, the deadfall kicks you out and won't allow your computer to connect again. Ever. Bug has stuff like that in MindReader.

As if he could read my thoughts, he said, "And don't let Church use the MindReader system. I built countermeasures for that. My QC can spot MindReader a mile off, and it will retaliate by giving all the go codes at once. You have to log on with a regular computer and Wi-Fi."

"Okay, but where are the reset codes?"

"They're still on the island in my notebooks, hidden in a piece of old game code that I stopped working on. It looks like junk unless you know the key to using it."

"Which fucking island?" I said, losing patience with him.

He didn't answer but instead kept rambling. "Get my notebooks. The key to finding the codes Pi from nine, backwards," he said, as if that should mean something. "Page two. I'd have put them in myself, but I had to get out and took the first opportunity I could. Had to go right then."

"Doc, you're not making sense. Tell me what—"

"Fuck it!" he snarled. "You're too stupid to understand. You *all* are. Get me out of here. If I can get to a computer, I can—"

Suddenly a voice yelled in my ear. "Jumper to Cowboy, Jumper to Cowboy, do you copy?"

I touched my earbud. "Go for Cowboy."

It was Nikki, and she sounded hysterical. "Be advised, we have lost control of the drone."

"Say again?"

"We have lost operational control of the drone. We're getting signals that the bird has gone weapons hot. Jesus Christ, Cowboy, it's coming right at you. Get out of there!"

Outside, I heard Top and Bunny and Brian yelling.

I heard gunfire.

Hands reached through the smashed hole where the windshield had been. I fought them, fought to hold on to Davidovich as he tried to cling to me.

There was a hissing sound outside, above me.

Then the world seemed to come apart. There was so much heat, and yet my brain seemed to go dark. I felt my body moving through the air, pushed by a burning fist of superheated gas. Then leaves and branches were whipping at me. I was falling, crashing, tumbling as I plummeted through the brush. I still had hold of Davidovich's hand. Somehow, impossibly, I still clutched his hand in mine.

It was only after I landed that I realized that his hand was all I held.

Chapter One Hundred and Fifteen

On the big screen, they watched the lawn-service truck erupt into a fireball. The plume of fire rose, carrying pieces of the truck and its occupants with it. Smoke billowed up and was torn by the forest winds.

Doctor Pharos was surprised that he felt some sadness at the death of Aaron Davidovich. Not much, but some.

The burned man's reaction was different.

"Good," he said, nearly spitting the word at the TV monitor. The screen was dark now, though a moment ago it displayed the video feed of the hijacked DMS drone. "There's an end to it."

"He was more useful to us alive than smeared over half of Washington State."

"How so? We have Regis. We have the other programs. We milked that cow for all there was."

Pharos shook his head. "He can control all of the programs."

"*We* control them."

"We *use* them. It's not the same thing."

The Gentleman chuckled. "Of course it is. A soldier doesn't need to know how a bullet is made. He needs to be good at killing his enemies with it. Davidovich loaded our guns very, very well."

Pharos got out of his chair and walked around to the foot of the hospital bed so that he could be face-to-face with the burned man. He leaned on the steel foot rail.

"Most of his programs are running now. The rest will kick in automatically according to the timetable, but—"

"Which is exactly what we wanted."

"Please, let me finish. Your bullet-and-gun analogy is flawed. What Davidovich did for us is much closer to building a nuclear reactor than casting a bullet. We are going to use the power of that reactor to accomplish every item on our checklist, and that's fine. But once all of that has been accomplished, we have to be able to shut the reactor down; otherwise it becomes a danger to us every bit as much as to our enemies."

"It will shut down by itself, Michael. That's part of the timetable, too."

"Theoretically, yes. Optimistically, yes. But tell me, my friend," said Pharos, "what if it doesn't? What if runs on and on until it goes critical and melts down? Which, as Davidovich so often warned us, is a real possibility unless carefully managed. What then?"

The Gentleman turned aside and did not answer.

What disturbed Pharos most was that the burned man kept smiling.

Chapter One Hundred and Sixteen

Tiger Mountain State Forest
Washington
April 1, 12:41 P.M.

Short version, Top shot the drone down with a rocket-propelled grenade.

Saved everyone else's lives, because the thing was turning for another pass.

Long version? Well, time would tell. Doctor Aaron Davidovich was dead. Blown to bits, burned to ash. Taking all of his secrets with him.

The reset code.

The notebooks.

The identities of Doctor Pharos and the Gentleman.

The name of the goddamn island where the Kings had held him.

Gone.

All of it, just . . . gone.

Me?

I was flash-burned and bruised. My hearing might never be right. And I had about a hundred small cuts to add to the damaged suit of skin I was already wearing. None of which I cared about.

Davidovich was dead, and so was our only lead.

I sat on a log and drank water while Brian applied some kind of burn salve to my skin. Odin and Java Teams showed up and milled around and made the kind of too-little, too-late grumbling comments you'd expect them to make.

I called Church and told him.

He didn't say much. Didn't tell me he was happy I was alive. I guess he had about as much enthusiasm and optimism as I had.

Chapter One Hundred and Seventeen

Naval Base Kitsap

Kitsap Peninsula

Puget Sound, Washington

April 1, 12:46 P.M.

The boat was named for a former president of the United States, but the class of submarines was named after a fast and aggressive Atlantic fish. The USS *Jimmy Carter* was a Seawolf-class nuclear-powered fast-attack submarine. Lethal, powerful, and reliable. And rare. Twenty-nine of the boats had been planned, but only three built once the Cold War ended and took a big chunk of the defense budget with it. Instead of building more Seawolf hulls, the navy switched to the less expensive Virginia-class subs.

The *Jimmy Carter* kept sailing, though. Above and below the waves. Doing her job, making a difference in both direct enforcement and covert operations. Built to go toe-to-toe with the Russian Typhoon missile boats and still be agile enough to duke it out with the Akula-class attack subs, these subs were a perfect balance of muscle and speed: they were armed with eight torpedo tubes and laden with fifty UGM-109 Tomahawk cruise missiles.

The *Jimmy Carter* was easing out of its home port at Naval Base Kitsap and edging toward the deep blue Pacific water. The stay in port had been at the end of thirteen months of continuous duty. The boat had been part of a new series of exercises in the troubled waters between Japan and China and had twice been sent to openly lurk in plain view of the North Korean navy. No shots were ever fired, however its presence was a statement made with cold eloquence. Since returning to Washington State, the *Carter* had received a thirteen-million-dollar computer upgrade. Hardware, software, and firmware. A team of DARPA engineers had crawled like ticks all over the boat, removing old systems, installing new ones, uploading software that was supposed to give the boat a new level of operational efficiency that would ensure a lightning-fast reaction-time counterpunch.

The crew and officers were used to this sort of upgrade. The Department of Defense loved its toys, and refits were a fact of naval life.

Now the refit was done, the systems double and triple checked, and the boat was on its way to a run to Pearl Harbor and back to test the systems.

Doctor Sarah Ghose tried not to be a total obstructive pain in the ass, but she knew that everyone thought she was. She wasn't a sailor, and despite her degrees and a lifetime of advanced schooling, she couldn't reliably tell starboard from port or fore from aft. Every time she thought she had that down, she discovered she was wrong. She also found herself transgressing against the countless rules and policies aboard a naval fighting vessel, and a submarine in particular. She often called the chief of the boat "Chief," which was apparently wrong; and she called him "sir," which was clearly a sin against God.

The only reason she hadn't been loaded into a torpedo tube and fired into the depths of the ocean was that she understood the BattleZone and Enact software packages and could debug any glitches as they happened.

Which is why the captain allowed her to remain on the bridge.

Or, as she'd been told at least fifty times, the control room. The bridge was that tall conical thing that sometimes stuck out of the water.

Ghose was sure he loathed her as much as everyone else.

She watched as the crew went through the process of preparing to dive the boat.

"Stop engines," ordered the diving officer. "Switch to battery power."

Ghose watched as this was done. Everyone seemed to move without concern and with a fluid and practiced ease.

"Close main induction."

Ghose remembered some of what they'd told her the first four times the boat had gone through this process, and if she couldn't remember policy, she could grasp the mechanics. The main induction was a large air-intake pipe, located at the rear of the conning tower. It has to be closed before diving or the engine rooms would fill with water. The executive officer told her that this happened once way back in 1939 to a submarine called the USS *Squalus*. The boat sank and half the crew died. She licked her lips nervously, hoping this crew was doing everything right.

The diving officer went through the rest of it with the crew. Making sure the main induction opening was sealed and checking this against a row of green indicator lights. Testing it by releasing air pressure into the hull.

"Open main vents," said the officer, contriving to sound bored. Ghose wasn't fooled. No one in their right minds could be anything but terrified by willingly sinking a big iron casket into the depths of the ocean.

"Rig out bow planes," said the officer. "Close vents."

As this was done, Ghose felt her heart hammering in her chest.

"Blow negative."

There were sounds and creaks, and the big metal coffin dropped down into the water. Ghose could not see this, but she was sure she could feel it.

"Level off. Slow to one third."

After a moment, the diving officer turned to the captain and informed him that everything had been done right and that the boat was at the proper depth and speed—and, Ghose hoped, that they were not about to implode like a crushed Dr Pepper can.

The captain, who had spent this entire procedure leaning over a light map table, straightened and said, "Very well."

He turned to Doctor Ghose, a big, bland smile on his face. Everyone in the control room looked at her.

Today, after all, was the big day.

It was her day.

"Doctor . . . are we ready to play our game?" asked the captain. He gestured toward the computer console that had been installed at Kitsap. It looked simple enough. A deck-mounted swivel chair and a computer workstation that had a thirty-inch screen and an extended keyboard. There were two key ports on the upper right side, similar in design to the key slots used on the missile control system. Most of the new systems could be activated and managed by a trained specialist even for one feature, ADAD— the autonomous drive and defense package. ADAD was for submarines what the ComSpinner was for planes. In the event of catastrophic injury to the crew—such as a fire, loss of breathable air, or flooding—the self-contained system would continue managing all systems on the boat, from lights to defensive countermeasures, following a very specific set of the rules of war. In an extreme emergency, such as a nuclear attack on the United States, the president could transmit a control code that would authorize a deeper level of software that would direct ADAD to launch its Tomahawks in retaliatory strikes.

Today's exercise would not take things that far. What Doctor Ghose and the captain would do was similar to what happened during a missile-testing exercise. They would agree to proceed, break and read authorization codes, insert their keys, turn the keys, and step back to let ADAD do the rest. Except that ADAD was loaded in safe mode only.

If the emergency was real, the captain and any surviving officer who had a key could activate the system.

If everyone was dead or incapacitated, ADAD would self-load after a certain span of time. At any time, a human operator could input a reset code and stop the launch of weapons.

In theory.

"Doctor—?" prompted the captain.

Ghose licked her lips. "Yes, of course."

She unfastened the top button of her blouse and fished for the metal chain, hooked it with a finger, pulled it out, and held the red key up for the captain's inspection.

He smiled at her. A tolerant smile.

"Say the words, doctor."

"Oh," she said flustered, "right." She cleared her throat. "Captain, I have the red key."

"And . . . ?"

"And I am ready to continue."

"Very well," he replied. "I acknowledge the red key."

He dug under his collar and found his own chain and brought a second key out. He showed it to her.

"I have the blue key. I am ready to continue. Do you agree?"

"I agree."

He nodded approval and crossed to the computer station, gesturing for her to join him. She did, but remained standing as he punched in his personal code on the keypad of a small safe built into the wall. The door popped open to reveal a pair of plastic envelopes slightly longer than playing cards. They were identical and marked ADAD / TESTGROUP C / AUTH.

He took them out and handed one to her.

"Chief of the Boat," said the captain, and a stocky man with a Cherokee face stepped up, "will you witness and verify that I have removed the code sleeves from my safe?"

"Yes, sir. I verify that you have removed two code sleeves from your safe." He then described the code sleeves in a very loud voice.

"Chief of the Boat," continued the captain, "will you witness and verify that I am handing one code sleeve to Doctor Sarah Ghose? And verify that Doctor Ghose has received a code sleeve."

The chief of the boat did, and Ghose had to fight to keep from rolling her eyes. She understood the need for procedure, but some of it seemed awfully silly to her. Still, she waited it all out.

When she held the plastic envelope, the captain addressed her. "Doctor Ghose, I am breaking the seal of my code sleeve."

He did so by bending it in half. It broke with a sharp sound. The captain pulled it apart and removed a white plastic card on which a short string of numbers and letters was printed in bold typeface. She broke hers, and they compared the codes, agreed that they were identical, showed them to the chief of the boat, who verified all of this, and then turned to the control console. Doctor Ghose slid into the seat and tapped a few keys to bring up a pair of empty fields. She deliberately typed in her code, had it witnessed and verified, and then watched as the captain did the same.

Immediately, the previously quiet computer came to life. Lights flared and a series of small overlapping windows appeared. One gave detailed information about the state of the boat and its readiness for action. Another screen fed telemetric intel from the RFID chips each of the crew had in the fatty tissue under their arms. A third screen showed the status of the weapons systems, and a fourth was a direct link to a roomful of sailors, scientists, and engineers who were clustered around ranks of computers to oversee this test. Because of the attack in Philadelphia and the pervasive belief that a greater threat was poised to strike the United States, everyone wanted this shakedown cruise to succeed. If it worked on this boat, then the Regis systems already being installed on the navy's ten active carriers and more than two hundred and eighty fighting vessels would be brought to the highest possible level of combat readiness.

The air force was doing the same with its jets, as were the army and marines with everything from helicopters to tanks. A lot was riding on the success of ADAD.

"System is green and fluid," said Ghose. "All meters are at midpoint, and the redundancies are showing online."

"Very well," said the captain. He removed his keychain and waited for her to do the same. He inserted his key and nodded to her to do the same. They made eye contact, and she saw it then, hidden behind his blasé expression, that spark of excitement. He was enjoying this. He wanted it to work, too. There was a twinkle there.

She smiled at him. He managed to keep a poker face.

"On zero," he said. "Two, one, zero, turn."

They turned the keys.

The ADAD system came online smoothly and without pause. All throughout the control room, the lights changed as the autonomous systems activated and took operational control of the submarine. The chief of the boat ordered everyone to stand down, and they obeyed, standing or sitting at their posts, watching as software did what it had been trained to do. The ADAD ran through a series of diagnostics that included making subtle changes to airflow, trim, position, speed, course, and every other system. The telemetry was sent back to Kitsap, where it was analyzed.

Ghose could not see the smiles on all those faces, but she knew they had to be there. She wore one of her own. And now, so did the captain.

"Running a weapons check," said Ghose, and the captain turned to see the lights on the torpedo and missile systems flick on and off. The mine-deployment systems flashed. The countermeasure-deployment systems did likewise.

Everything was running perfectly.

"Well, Doctor Ghose," said the captain, "I must admit that this is mighty damn impressive. You and your team have done something remarkable here. On behalf of my officers and crew, I want to congratulate you."

He held out his hand.

Ghose took it.

And then the lights went out.

Everything except the screen on the ADAD console. In the one second she had left to live, Doctor Sarah Ghose saw something that was impossible. According to every safeguard, every design feature, every failsafe bit of computer code, it was absolutely impossible.

All fifty of the Tomahawk cruise missiles went live.

Every single warhead on the harpoon torpedoes went from inactive into the green.

All of the firing systems instantly went from disabled/inactive to active launch.

In a microsecond. Faster than any human involvement could manage.

Far too fast for any human intervention to stop.

The torpedo tube doors and missile launch doors, however, did not open.

Ghose saw all of this in a second.

And then there were no more seconds of her life.

Chapter One Hundred and Eighteen

Air Force One
In Flight
April 1, 12:59 P.M. Pacific Standard Time

The president asked Church to go over the Regis thing again for the benefit of the gathered generals and senior advisors. Church took them through it step by step, adding to it the fact that the Kings clearly had abducted Doctor Davidovich and had hacked a DMS drone to kill the scientist.

As Church spoke, though, the president shook his head and kept shaking it. So did most of the military officers. Alice Houston sat next to Linden Brierly, and they kept exchanging worried looks. This was not going well. No matter how it would ultimately play out, it was not going well.

Finally, he slapped his hand flat on the tabletop with a sound as loud as a gunshot.

"Damn it, Deacon," he growled, "you do realize that what you're asking is impossible."

"It's not impossible, Mr. President," said Church. "It's merely difficult. You need to shut down every piece of military hardware that has had Regis installed, and then you need to remove that program. There is no other reasonable alternative."

"I can't and won't do something like that on the say-so of a captain in the DMS."

"You don't need to take Captain Ledger's word for this, Mr. President.

Would you like me to replay the tape of him interviewing Doctor Davidovich inside the crashed truck? You heard him say, in no uncertain terms, that the Seven Kings have control of Regis."

"But nearly everything has Regis. Most of the fleet, most of—"

"We don't need an inventory, Mr. President. We need leadership."

The president bristled and pointed a finger at him. "You watch yourself, Deacon. My predecessor and half of Congress may have been afraid of you, but I'm not."

"I won't budge from this request, Mr. President."

"And I won't damn well do it. You're wrong about this. Davidovich was a traitor and a liar and—"

There was a sharp knock on the door, and Bain, the national security advisor, burst in. He looked shocked, even horrified.

"Mr. President," said Bain, "we have a situation."

"God. Now what . . . ?" said the president.

"It's the *Jimmy Carter* . . . "

Chapter One Hundred and Nineteen

Tiger Mountain State Forest
Washington
April 1, 1:01 P.M.

Brian sat in Ugly Betty's passenger seat, and the rest of the team stood around the open door and watched the news Nikki forwarded to us. The *Jimmy Carter* was lost with all hands.

While test-driving the new Regis system.

Top closed his eyes and rested his forehead against the frame of Ugly Betty's open door. He murmured a prayer for sailors lost at sea.

"We commit your bodies to the deep," he said, "to be turned into corruption, looking for the resurrection of the body, when the sea shall give up her dead . . . "

Instead of saying "amen," Bunny punched the side of the car with a sound like an iron gong.

I felt like the ground beneath my feet was turning to quicksand.

If there had been any doubt left about whether the Kings controlled that software, it had blown itself into atoms along with a lot of good people aboard that boat.

Gone. All gone.

At that moment, I got a phone call from the unlikeliest of sources. I stepped away from the others and punched the button.

"Junie?" I said. "This really isn't a good time."

"I know," she said, "we're all watching the news. It's so horrible."

"It is. Look, baby, let me call you—"

"No, Joe, I need you to talk to someone. He might be able to help."

"Who?"

She paused. "Toys."

"Toys?"

"He's here at the hospital. He wants to help."

"I'd like to help him by putting my foot up his ass. I told you he shouldn't be there, Junie, and you know it."

"Mr. Church said it was all right."

"Oh, please."

"Joseph," she snapped, and damn if I didn't snap to attention. If the guys had seen this, I'd be Mr. Whipped for the rest of my life. Damn it. "You need to speak with him. I wouldn't ask if I didn't think this was important."

"Yeah," I said, "okay. Put him on."

The next voice I heard was someone I hated with every fiber of my being. I am not usually an inflexible and unforgiving prick, but I have my moments. Toys was a pet project of Mr. Church, I get that. I know that Junie and Violin worked with him at FreeTech. I know that he is supposed to be trying to redeem himself. But . . .

"Ledger?" said a familiar voice.

"Toys. Tell me why I'm talking with you."

"It's not to swap recipes or gossip about celebrities," he said dryly.

"Glad to hear it. You have thirty seconds. You've already wasted ten of them. Tell me something that I need to know, or we're done."

"They're saying that Aaron Davidovich escaped from the Seven Kings."

"People shouldn't be telling you anything. Fifteen seconds."

"I heard something about him escaping from an island."

"So what? Ten seconds."

"An island in Washington State," said Toys. "Near Seattle. Or maybe near Tacoma?"

I said nothing.

"You stopped your countdown," he said.

"No, I haven't. You're telling me what you heard. Now tell me what I need to hear or fuck off."

"I think I might know the name of the island," he said. "Would that be what you need to hear, or should I go and fuck off now?"

In a voice I didn't even recognize as my own, I said, "Tell me what you know and how you know it."

Toys said, "I'll admit I'm guessing, but I think it's a good guess. A few years ago, after Sebastian and I joined the Kings but before your lot tore them down, there was one night when Hugo, Sebastian, and I were having drinks and talking about the future. About what we might do after. You understand? After the Kings had stopped playing their games. After we'd had our fill and wanted out. Hugo often talked about that. He liked the idea of retirement, though I don't think he would ever have retired. Anyway, we talked about where we'd like to live. Sebastian wanted to live in the Caribbean or the Bahamas, but Hugo said it would be too risky. Even with good plastic surgery and enough money. Hugo said that it would be better to pick a place that was inside the protection and financial stability of the United States but outside the mainstream flow. He favored the Pacific Northwest because there are so many private islands up for sale. If you remember, his estate during the Ten Plagues thing was on an island he owned in the Saint Lawrence River."

"Get to a fucking point, Toys," I warned.

"I am. Keep your balls on. I'm telling you what Hugo said. He told Sebastian that there were some good prospects that would allow a boat to slip out to sea or a seaplane to make a quick getaway to somewhere in Canada."

"Toys . . . "

"Hold on. Remember, this was just conversation. This was Hugo being Hugo, telling everyone what the best way to do anything was. He always wanted to be seen as the one who knew things. I don't think any of the Kings actually owned property in Washington, but Hugo talked about his 'great escape' so often that everyone knew it was a solid bet as a safe haven."

"A name. Give me a name."

"The one Hugo liked the most was a small island in Puget Sound called Tanglewood. After what Davidovich said, it makes sense, doesn't it? Maybe that's where the Kings are."

Chapter One Hundred and Twenty

Air Force One

In Flight

April 1, 1:25 P.M. Pacific Standard Time

The president sagged back against the leather cushions of his chair. The conference room was utterly silent. On the screen, video footage from a helicopter showed the massive whirlpool that was all there was of the USS *Jimmy Carter*.

The president dragged a trembling hand across his mouth.

"How many men?"

"Fifteen officers, one hundred and twenty-six enlisted. Four members of a DARPA team."

"Merciful God," said the president.

Linden Brierly looked past him to where Mr. Church sat, his fingers laced tightly together on the tabletop.

Those two words seemed to hang in the air, a mockery of their own meaning.

Into the silence, Church said, "This is the Seven Kings."

"But . . . why target the *Carter*?" asked the president blankly. "Is it something tied to his presidency? Something about the class of submarine?"

"No," said Church. "This is Regis. This is exactly what I've been telling you about."

"Why *that* sub, though?"

Church leaned forward. "I still don't think you understand, Mr. President. This isn't about the *Jimmy Carter*. I'm not sure how else to make my point. The Seven Kings are hacking Regis. Do you understand what that means? They have just proved that they have the technological reach to take control of any U.S. military craft which has been fitted out with the Regis autonomous command software."

"But . . ."

"Right now, to a very real degree, they can turn our own weapons of war against us. The *Carter* was a statement. There may be demands to follow, or they may choose to make other statements before issuing those demands."

"What can we do?" snapped one of the generals. "Every damn thing has Regis in it. We can't very well shut down our entire military."

Mr. Church's eyes were ice-cold. "We may have to."

"That would leave us vulnerable to attack," said the national security advisor.

"Vulnerable?" said Brierly. "What do you think we are right now? This isn't just about shutting down our military. It's about preventing those automated systems from turning every plane and warship we have against us."

Chapter One Hundred and Twenty-one

Tiger Mountain State Forest
Washington
April 1, 1:38 P.M.

We were already in motion when Church texted me to say that the president was issuing an executive order for all land, sea, and air craft to have their autonomous systems shut down. Since Regis controlled so many ordinary functions on ships and aircraft, it meant that for now the bulk of our military power would be inert. Even the Seventh Fleet in China.

I told the others, and Bunny's only response was to step harder on the gas.

"The whole fleet?" gasped Brian. "The air force? All of it?"

"Most of it," I corrected.

"Goddamn big set of paperweights," mused Top. "And right now that's all they're good for."

Brian looked worried. "What's going to happen? What if someone attacks us?"

"We'll throw rocks," said Bunny. Then he shook his head. "It won't happen. Nobody's going to start a war with us. They know we'll recover."

I wish his voice carried more conviction. He didn't get any "hooahs" for that.

"If we can find that reset code," Brian said, "we can get it all back online. Right?"

"Kid," I said, "I am completely open to suggestions."

Chapter One Hundred and Twenty-two

Beale Air Force Base

Marysville, California

April 1, 1:58 P.M.

The demonstration of the new generation of QF-16X Pterosaur superdrones was delayed by the news about the *Jimmy Carter*. However, after the initial shock, that same news galvanized everyone into action.

Unlike the other jets in the new tactical-combat-drone program, the Pterosaurs did not run on the Regis software. The team at DARPA had wanted to try something newer and better. The Pterosaurs were pure Solomon.

The advisor from the congressional oversight committee, Senator John Langan, had been a champion of the Solomon package. It had no commercial version, and it had never been in the hands of Aaron Davidovich. It was clean. And it was, in many ways, his. He had spearheaded the approval for the new project, and he'd made sure it was funded and watchdogged. No leaks of any kind.

He was here in Marysville to see the drones in action. Until a few minutes ago, this test had been on the verge of being canceled because of the national emergencies. Now it was more important than ever. Solomon was easier to install than Regis, and it could be used to replace that other corrupted package in almost twenty percent of the infected ships and twenty-eight percent of aircraft. Langan felt like a hero. Anything with Solomon was going to be part of saving the whole damn country.

He was absolutely sure he would be able to ride that wave out of the Senate and into the Oval Office. Oh hell yes.

If the North Koreans, Russians, or, more likely in his view, the Chinese, tried anything during the scramble to pull Regis and upload

Solomon, then Langan was going to help the military kick ass and take names.

The other men and women in the stands here in Marysville were probably thinking similar thoughts. They were all, to one degree or another, part of Solomon. They would all stand between America and those Seven Kings parasites and whoever wanted to exploit the Regis vulnerabilities.

Langan genuinely thought it would be the Chinese who would jump.

Bloody Chinese were waiting for something like this.

Langan did not consider himself a racist by any stretch, so it was nothing against the Chinese people. But the government? They were the most ruthless political force he had ever encountered, and he thought they were the most dangerous force on earth. Look at how they treated their own people, not to mention the things they did to the rest of the damn world. And they were hypocrites while they were at it. The core of the People's Republic didn't care a single speck of dog shit for anything Marx had to say. That wasn't communism. They hid behind the "dictatorship of the masses" bullshit and used it as a platform for establishing a tyrannical empire larger than any the world had ever seen. Financially canny, merciless, built on misinformation and disinformation, and hungry for conquest.

No, Langan was not a fan of the Chinese government. If there was a government behind the Seven Kings, he would bet it was China. If he ever made it to the White House, then maybe China's communist government would be to him what the Soviet Union had been to Ronald Reagan.

On the dais in front of the stands, General Dearborn stepped up to the microphones. His face was grave for about a millisecond.

"Ladies and gentlemen, distinguished members of Congress, our friends in the press," he began in a stentorian voice that, when amplified by the speakers, sounded like the voice of God. Langan knew that Dearborn was aware of the effect. The general had white hair and bright blue eyes and looked like central casting had sent him to play the Lord of All Creation. "Tragedies like what has happened in Philadelphia and in Puget Sound are proof that our nation is not as safe as it should be, not as safe as it needs to be. We live in an age where our enemies are dangerous, and they are devious. They hide in the shadows, they strike without warning, they fight without honor. And they are many."

He paused; the sea of faces on the bleachers were all turned toward him. Langan knew they were all eating out of his hand.

"Here in the twenty-first century, we have fought two terrible wars," continued Dearborn. "One of which was the longest in the history of this great country. It was one where we suffered great losses and constant threats. Our brave men and women in Afghanistan not only had to deal with the Taliban, they were frequently betrayed by members of the Afghani military—by spies hidden within that military. Lives were lost that should never have been at risk. That is the nature of the twenty-first-century terrorist. They hide in plain sight. They do not and cannot put an army in the field. They know that in a stand-up fight they can't hope to defeat American power, and so, like the cowards and bullies they are, they set bombs and take cheap shots." He paused for effect. "This, my friends, is the war we are forced to fight."

Another, longer pause.

Senator Langan covertly glanced around, noting—as he had at other times—how completely Dearborn owned this audience. Langan knew that the invitation list to this event was a careful job of crowd seeding. Many of these people were already supporters of Dearborn, and the others were those who had known interests in the drone programs. Manufacturers and designers, researchers and developers. Even the members of the press in attendance were science writers of the kind who typically broke stories in support of advanced weaponry systems.

For his part, Langan was ambivalent. He was all in favor of what UAVs, properly managed, could do. They reduced risks to American lives, and that was always at the top of Langan's personal agenda. But he did not believe they were the surgically precise instruments they were touted to be. The disaster at Eglin Air Force Base showed that. Langan wanted this technology to go through many more months of field-testing. General Dearborn, on the other hand, was lobbying to become the "Drone General," as some of his pet reporters had already begun labeling him. Dearborn wanted the history books to remember him as the man who reduced the military human element—and its associated human danger—to less than forty percent. To take the soldier out of the field and out of the cockpit. Even, if he had his way, out of the driver's seat in most of the submarine and surface fleets.

That was what Langan expected Dearborn to say today, and the general went in exactly that direction. Langan listened to him rattle off impressive statistics, cite case studies, quote remarks—often taken out of context—by eyewitnesses to drones in combat.

The general's remarks went on and on, very nearly to the point of tedium. But the general stopped short of actually boring his own packed crowd. He gave another of his dramatic and, Langan had to admit, effective pauses, and then he turned to the field that stretched out, broad and green beyond the stands. Thousands of acres of grass bisected by asphalt runways. A control tower stood like a lighthouse on the far side. Above the field, a few puffy white clouds sailed through the endless blue, all of it providing a picturesque backdrop to what was about to happen.

General Dearborn nodded to a lieutenant, who in turn spoke into a small mike.

Within seconds, there was a screaming roar as a flight of six jets swept into view.

Each sleek smoke-gray aircraft had crimson wingtips and tail fins—a different color scheme than the charcoal and orange used on the QF-16 aerial-target drones. These were not targets. That's what the general told the crowd.

"Welcome to the new age of aerial combat," announced Dearborn with obvious pride. "The QF-16X Pterosaur is a true variable-use combat aircraft that can be remote-piloted by two qualified ground-based pilots, or, at the flick of a switch, they can become fully autonomous fighters. That means that in the event of an interruption of power or a disruption in communication with ground support, these aircraft will continue to carry out their missions against preselected targets. Now, ladies and gentlemen, we are switching to autonomous flight. Let's see how these babies can perform with no one but a computer at the joystick. Prepare to be amazed."

The Pterosaurs flew at one thousand feet above the grass, soaring straight and true above the ground, then they split apart, with two peeling off high and left, two going high and right, and the remaining two curving directly upward. Then each pair of fighters began a difficult maneuver, rolling as they climbed so that they moved around each other like two moons in an orbital dance. The jets rose and rose until they were black dots. Then they turned and split apart once again so that all six arched downward toward the field, like the petals of some vast flower. Their vapor trails chased them down, down, down. When it seemed like they were far too low to possibly avoid crashing, the jets turned with incredible precision and perfect synchronicity, leveling off less than five hundred feet above the deck.

As Dearborn had promised, the crowd was, indeed, amazed. The jets circled and turned, flew at each other and passed so close it looked like they must have scraped paint off each other's wings. They swept apart, came together, made shapes in the air, and even buzzed the grandstands. It was all great theater. The crowd oohed and ahhed at all the right moments.

"And now," said the general, "let me show you why American air superiority will remain unchallenged despite adversity, despite treachery, despite attacks by terrorists and world powers. This will be a live-fire exercise—but don't worry, it's all going to happen up there in the wild blue yonder."

There was another growl of heavy engines as four more jets flew over the stands. Langan recognized them as F-18s. Very fast, very reliable jets on the cutting edge of air combat.

"We have teams of pilots operating the four F-18s. These pilots are all experienced, and they are the best of the best. Let's see how they stack up against our Pterosaurs and the latest generation of the BattleZone tactical combat system."

The F-18s flew over the field and then, just as the QF-16Xs had, they split apart and rose into individual climbing turns, racing toward the four corners of the field. The Pterosaurs were circling high up now, and suddenly four of them broke off and blew off into wide circles that would bring them into direct opposition of the F-18s. Like four mirrored images of the same encounter, the superdrones zoomed toward their enemies at incredible speeds.

Air-to-air missiles burst from beneath the wings of all eight aircraft. Instantly, the Pterosaurs banked and dropped. The F-18s were a second later in breaking away from their flight paths, but they did, each of them accelerating to shake the computer locks in their heat signatures.

Missiles flashed across the sky.

Boom!

One of the F-18s transformed into a glowing orange fireball as an AIM-7 Sparrow punched into it and detonated. The blast was six miles up and out, but the sound of it came rolling and tumbling across the field to buffet the crowd in the stands.

"Shit," muttered Langan, though not loud enough for anyone to hear above the roar of engines, the echo of explosions, and the sound of delighted gasps.

A moment later, two more of the F-18s blew up.

"Shit, shit."

The fourth F-18 slipped the missile that had been fired at it and began a series of very deft, very clever maneuvers. Langan could imagine the ground-based pilots trying every trick they'd learned from their own combat missions to slip the punch of these new superdrones. He was impressed. This was superb flying, even if it was remotely done.

But it couldn't last. The drone that had targeted it was now joined by the three that had destroyed their targets, and, like a flock of flying monsters, they pursued the F-18. The four Pterosaurs belched out a collective sonic boom as they throttled high and broke the sound barrier. Langan had to squint into the distance to see the smoke as two of the craft fired simultaneous Sidewinders.

It took a long time for the explosion to roll all the way to the stands.

The crowd sighed with an almost orgasmic release as the last of the four F-18s fell like fiery rain to the ground far below. Langan sagged back, blowing out his cheeks, knowing full well that this demonstration was far too perfect for him to be able to offer any objections. All four F-18s had been taken down in seconds.

Seconds.

From start to finish, the whole dogfight—if such an antiseptic slaughter could be called that—took nineteen seconds.

"Holy mother of shit," he mumbled.

Then he heard someone say something that snapped him instantly out of his own political musings and fully back to the moment.

"Where are the other drones?"

He turned to the man who'd spoken, the junior senator from Ohio.

"What—?"

The Ohioan pointed to the empty sky beyond where the four Pterosaurs were regrouping. "The other two drones. Where are they?"

"Maybe they landed," said another congressman.

"No," said a fourth, pointing. He had a good pair of binoculars and held them to his eyes. "There they are. Way over there."

Langan borrowed the glasses to take a look. Indeed, the two remaining Pterosaurs were up there, but they were no more than dots, fading quickly into the distance. Heading northwest at high speed.

"That's weird," he said, then turned toward Dearborn. The general was also looking off to the northwest. He was no longer smiling. His face was cut by a deep frown of confusion.

The general suddenly bent and said something to the lieutenant, who apparently repeated it into his mike. The lieutenant didn't look confused. He looked frightened.

No . . . "frightened" was wrong. It was too weak a word, and Langan knew it.

The man looked absolutely *terrified*.

Chapter One Hundred and Twenty-three

Tanglewood Island
Pierce County, Washington
April 1, 2:04 P.M.

Doctor Pharos turned to the burned man.

"See? See?"

"Yes," said the Gentleman. "I see."

He was pale beneath his burns. His hands shook with palsy and spit glistened on his lips.

"This is what you wanted, isn't it?"

The burned man was impotent and crippled, disfigured and incontinent, but in that moment there was such heat in his eye that even Pharos recoiled. Never once in his entire life had he ever seen such malevolence, such fundamental hatred in the eyes of another man. In the eyes of another person. The looked that flared in the Gentleman's eye rivaled the inhuman hatred and contempt of the freak Nicodemus.

Or . . . maybe in some impossible, unnatural way it was the evil priest himself staring out of that one baleful eye. That single orb was like a hole burned through the floors of this world from the ceiling of hell.

That was the thought, the startled reaction that filled Pharos's mind.

And in that moment the color of the Gentleman's eye seemed to change. To metamorphose from a human blue to a swirling mélange of colors. Feces-brown. The mottled green of toad skin. Jaundiced yellow.

Pharos felt himself leaning too far back, sliding from the chair, falling onto the floor. That eye followed, tracking his collapse. The mouth below it curled into a snarl that was unlike anything that had ever troubled the mouth of the Gentleman—before or after he was maimed. And yet it was such a familiar smile.

So familiar.

"I see," said a voice that was not at all the voice of the burned man. "I see very well."

Pharos scuttled backward, a small cry bursting from his throat.

"Dear God!"

"I see," said the voice. Then, in a voice that was filled with the promise of pain and horror, he said, "Now show me more."

Chapter One Hundred and Twenty-four

Air Force One

In Flight

April 1, 2:09 P.M. Pacific Standard Time

Bain, the national security advisor, took a call on his reserved line. When he stiffened and went white with shock, everyone else in the conference room fell suddenly silent. Bain instantly began snapping his fingers for his aide.

"Channel nine, channel nine!"

The aide snatched up a remote and began punching buttons to reach the channel, which was one of four secure feeds from the Department of Defense. The big screen on the wall burst with sudden color and movement.

"What is it?" demanded the president. "What's happening?"

"There's been another incident," barked Bain.

"No," said the president very softly. "No more. No more."

"It's the base commander at Beale Air Force Base in Marysville,

390 | Jonathan Maberry

California," said Bain. "They've been testing the QF-16Xs out there, and two of them have gone rogue."

The president bristled. "What do you mean 'gone rogue'? I ordered that all drones with Regis be grounded."

On the screen, a satellite was tracking the flight patterns of two jet fighters traveling at thirteen hundred miles per hour. Fifty nautical miles behind them was a pack of other fighters.

"Mr. President, these drones aren't using Regis. They have a different software package. Something new. Nothing that connects them to anything Davidovich worked on."

"Christ," said Brierly, "they're heading toward San Francisco."

The jets were blurs as they tore across the screen.

"What's our response?" demanded the president.

"We scrambled four F-18s from Vanguard Group. They're in close pursuit. Permission to—"

"Granted," barked the president. "Shoot them down before anyone else gets hurt. Don't let them reach the city."

One of the generals spoke into a phone. "This is Air Force One to Vanguard Group, do you copy?"

"Copy, Air Force One. We are forty miles back and closing."

"Permission has been given to go weapons hot. Vanguard, you are cleared to engage. Repeat, you are cleared to engage. Put them down."

"Roger that," said a voice that, typical of fighter pilots, was calm despite the circumstances. Brierly thought that level of calm was admirable but unnerving.

"This is Vanguard Two, fox one," said a second pilot, and everyone tensed as they waited for the AIM-20 AMRAAM missiles to burst from beneath the wing and drill their way through the air toward the rogue drone at Mach 4.

The moment stretched.

Nothing happened.

"Vanguard One, I detect zero missiles fired. Confirm."

The radio was silent.

"Vanguard Two, do you copy?" yelled the general.

Silence.

Then . . .

"Air Force One, we are experiencing——"

The voice vanished.

A moment later, another voice cut in, clearly from the tower at the airbase. "Vanguard One, I am reading a system malfunction. Confirm status."

As if struck by a harsh sideways wind, all four of the pursuit craft shuddered, their tight formation wobbling. The operator of the satellite video feed tightened the focus to show thin streamers of smoke or steam whipping backward from the cowls of each jet.

Then the tower voice was back. Yelling for each of the pilots to respond.

The jets flew on, still gaining on the two drones.

But no one was answering.

The president turned to Church. "I don't understand. What's happening? Why aren't they responding?"

Church set down the water glass he had lifted to his lips. "Dear God," he said.

"What? Will someone please tell me what just happened?"

Mr. Church said, "The eject controls of all four pursuit craft have been activated."

"What? Where? I didn't see anyone eject."

"In order to safely eject the cockpit, cowling has to be removed. It's done by firing explosive bolts."

"But——"

"Those bolts never fired. The cowling is still in place."

"But the pilots . . . ?"

"The pilots are dead, Mr. President," said Linden Brierly.

"Jesus Christ! Is this Regis . . . ?"

No one answered.

"Is this fucking Regis," screamed the president.

"No, sir," said the air force general. "We scrambled jets that did not have the Regis upgrade."

"Then how——?"

"Solomon," said Church. When the president turned to him, the DMS director looked as stricken as everyone else in the room.

"Yes," said the general. "They were part of the first test group for Solomon."

"Oh my God," said the general, but it was not in sympathy with the president's words or in mourning for the dead pilots. Everyone turned back to the screen and watched in absolute horror as all six jets—the two drones and the four pursuit craft—fired their missiles.

Each of them.

Missile after missile.

The weapons flew from under the wings at four times the speed of sound. They streaked across the sky above the California landscape. Flying straight.

And true.

Toward a giant of steel that stretched its arms from Marin County to San Francisco. Steel that glinted gold in the light.

No one spoke.

No one could.

As the missiles slammed into the vast span of the Golden Gate Bridge and blew it into fiery dust.

Chapter One Hundred and Twenty-five

Tanglewood Island
Pierce County, Washington
April 1, 3:29 P.M.

We went in like silent birds.

Like the ghosts of some great old predators of the air.

Echo Team riding the breeze, coming through slanting rain out of a leaden-gray sky, carrying within us an even deeper darkness in our hearts.

The TradeWinds MotorKites were something Church had commissioned from a company that made ultralight aircraft. The frame was made from a new aluminum-magnesium alloy that was lighter than a lawn chair but far stronger. Big silk bat wings filled the frame and extended beyond it, ribbed with flexible polymers. The motors were tiny two-strokes built for stealth rather than speed. Virtually silent.

No one heard us coming.

And unless they could make out shadows against shadows, they couldn't see us.

We wore a new generation of combat sealskin that had a network of cooling wires to keep the surface temperature of the suits in harmony with the air around us. Our own thermal signatures was masked. The rain helped with that, too. It was a dreary April morning. No one would be outside looking up.

I led the way, with Bunny riding shotgun on my left. Top was on my right, and his kite pulled a second machine from which Ghost was suspended. He was in a close-fitting dog-shaped outfit that hid him as effectively as ours did. The motor of his kite was synched with Top's, and the fur monster had been well trained for this kind of landing. Ghost loved the kites. Unlike his pack leader, who hated heights.

Brian Botley brought up the rear.

We were all still reeling from what was going on in San Francisco.

The Golden Gate Bridge? Gone? And all those people.

More innocent lives.

More proof that we were losing this fight to the Seven Kings.

Who even knew if Tanglewood Island was the right target? If it was, did that mean we had our first real chance? If it wasn't . . . then what?

Really. Then what?

I would have liked to have had a bigger team in case this was the big play, but this is what we got. Odin and Java Teams were on their way down to San Francisco to help with the disaster and offer support to Homeland. We had a SEAL team inbound, but they wouldn't be here for nearly an hour. I didn't think we had that much time. No, check that, I couldn't risk *wasting* that much time.

Ten miles over the horizon, our launch ship rocked on the waves. Not a military ship. No one trusted any of them right now. No, we commandeered a fishing trawler. Not much of a ship. It had engines and not much else. We didn't need much else.

In my ear, I heard Nikki's voice. "We have an Osprey in the air with an E-bomb."

"A trustworthy Osprey or—?"

"They pulled all of its computers."

"Welcome to the world of the Luddites," I said.

We sailed closer and closer to Tanglewood Island, our kites and gear invisible against the storm clouds. The winds were steady but not heavy.

No gusts—and the rain was a relentless drizzle rather than a crushing downpour. We had our Google Scout goggles on, and telemetric feeds projected onto the lenses gave wind speed, altitude, angle, pitch and yaw, distance to the island, and other data.

"Okay, listen up," I whispered. "We go in exactly as we rehearsed."

I thought I heard a soft grunt from Bunny. Our rehearsal had been all of twenty minutes. That had been all the time we could spare. It wasn't much, and I prayed that it was enough. The smallest mistakes could cost lives. Not just among Echo Team, but across the nation. We needed those reset codes. If we bungled the landing, if we failed to take the island, if we couldn't gain access to the chamber of the Kings, if, if, if . . .

If we made any mistakes, America was going to grind its way into a new dark age. Although the president was grounding all military aircraft, there were still a lot of ships with missiles. Crews aboard each one were cutting cables to the computer systems in a desperate rush to keep Regis from launching a self-inflicted war.

In some cases, though, the efforts were too little and too late. A destroyer, the USS *Momsen*, leaving Pearl Harbor tried to self-launch Tomahawk missiles. The crew managed to secure the launch tubes, but the warheads went live. The *Momsen* blew itself in half. Rescue crews were searching for survivors. At last count they had only found three.

In the waters off Yokosuka, Japan, the USS *Ronald Reagan*'s engines and navigation system went active and autonomous. Before the crew was able to physically disable the motors, the massive aircraft carrier had smashed its way through twenty-six commercial vessels in a fishing fleet and rammed the helicopter carrier JDS *Izumo*. Both ships were taking water and listing badly.

The butcher's bill kept growing, tightening the knot of tension around our throats. Thousands of lives. Billions of dollars.

And no end in sight.

All banking in the United States had been shut down. Schools were closed and most other activities were canceled. All trading was suspended. However, around the world, the stock markets were going wild, much of the panic fed by our own news media.

The Seven Kings were winning.

Winning.

It was like playing chess when the other guy had all the pieces.

It was impossible to know if the Regis agenda was working as planned. If this was exceeding their expectations, then fuck them. If this was falling short of their hopes, it was still bad enough.

The DMS computer team was working to track whoever was raking in profits from the swings in the global market. The problem was that there were so many people getting rich that it was hard to point at anyone who stood out as clear agents of the Kings.

Already, Yoda's computer models were suggesting that the system couldn't take much more of this. Some kind of collapse was coming. All it needed was one more push. One more punch.

Echo Team rode the dark winds trying to beat that punch.

We had no idea if we were already too late.

Chapter One Hundred and Twenty-six

Air Force One

In Flight

April 1, 3:33 P.M. Pacific Standard Time

On the conference-room screen, the towers of the Golden Gate Bridge were bowing toward the water. Fire was woven inside great cables of smoke, and they coiled upward toward the clouds. Small dark objects continued to fall.

Cars.

People.

Lives.

"Goddamn you all to hell, you miserable pricks!" screamed the president as he whipped his arm across the table, sending laptops and papers and coffee cups flying, showering the generals and Marcus Bain and Alice Houston. "You let this happen. You fucking let this happen."

The conference-room door burst open, and two Secret Service agents stepped in, hands reaching for their sidearms. Brierly waved them back.

"Mr. President," said Bain, pawing hot coffee from his eyes, "we couldn't stop this."

"You should have seen this coming!"

"Mr. President," barked one of the generals, "no one could have foreseen this."

For a moment it looked like the president was going to go over the table at him.

The moment held, stretching as taut as a fiddle string. The tension hummed in the air of the small conference room. Then the president shoved himself back from the brink of violence and turned toward the big man who sat at the far end of the table.

"Mr. President," said Church, "which control system was installed on Air Force One?"

The president gaped at him. He tried to say the name, but he simply could not. For a moment, none of them could.

So Church said it. "It's Solomon, isn't it?"

The president whispered, "God save us all."

Mr. Church launched himself from his seat, pushed past the dazed advisors, and made for the door.

He almost made it before all the lights on Air Force One winked out and plunged the interior of the aircraft into total darkness.

Chapter One Hundred and Twenty-seven

Tanglewood Island

Pierce County, Washington

April 1, 3:35 P.M.

Below us, the rain-swept island swelled from a dot to a lump to a piece of rocky terrain with features I could now pick out. There was a long, slender pier thrusting out into the choppy waters of the sound, and a smaller boat dock on the far side that allowed medium-sized pleasure crafts to offload under a canopy. From what we'd been able to determine via the satellite images, the best angle of approach was the northeast, between the long pier and the maintenance wing of the hotel.

"Cowboy to Echo, Cowboy to Echo," I said. "Let's go in and end these evil sons of bitches."

"Hooah," they all said.

On the way here, Top and Bunny and Brian called this for different people. For Bug and Auntie. For Dilbert Howell. For Circe. For Philadelphia and San Francisco.

In truth, though, it was for everyone from sea to shining sea. No joke, no trash talk. This one was for everyone.

I dipped my kite to spill the air from the black wings, and then I was falling, falling, dropping toward the black water fifty yards from the jagged rocks. The altimeter told me I was fifty feet up, forty, thirty. I usually sweat heights, but today wasn't the day to give in to little fears. Not when people were dying right now. Not when people were in pain right now.

At twenty feet, I angled the wings to stall my rate of drop; and at ten, I hit the big release button on my chest. The wings collapsed backward, the tubing and frame slithered around my chest and thighs and waist, and I was in free fall. I pressed a hand to my goggles to keep them from bouncing and bashing my face to Ledger paste. Then my heels hit the surface, and I went down into the cold waters of Puget Sound.

Behind me, the others dropped down.

As the waters closed over me, I kicked hard and shot back to the surface, angled forward, and struck out hard for shore. My gear weighed a ton, but we'd prepared for that. I popped a cord on my chest harness, and two small tanks shotgunned compressed air into a buoyancy bladder. My body rose toward the surface, and I broke through and gulped in the clean air. Fifty feet away, I saw Top and Ghost break the surface, too. Then Brian. Bunny was somewhere off to my left, too far away to see.

Even with the bladders, the gear was heavy, but if you wanted to survive, you pulled your weight. Otherwise, you either went unarmed onto the beach or you drowned. Not a fan of either.

We'd picked an angle where the visibility and the movement of the tide were in our favor, but soon the danger shifted from drowning to being smashed on jagged black rocks. I lowered my feet until I found the bumpy surface and then reached for handholds among the boulders. I let the waves help me move forward one awkward step at a time. The surf splashed up to slap me in the face, but that was okay. The noise masked our sounds. The water shoaled quickly, and suddenly my knee was on a muddy slope.

The water thrashed and flew in wild directions, and a misshapen form shot past me, bounding through the cold water and rushing up to solid ground.

398 | Jonathan Maberry

Ghost.

He ran low and fast, as silent as his name, head whipping to either side. There are times he looks a lot less like a dog and a lot more like some kind of primitive wolf. I am very glad he's my friend. I've seen what happens to his enemies.

Then two more shapes rose up like gods of the deep. One vast and tall, with a monstrous sweep of shoulders, the other shorter but no less broad.

Bunny and Top.

Behind them, Brian Botley stood up as if he were coming out of a pool after a leisurely dip. He even grinned at me as he stalked up the beach. Weird kid.

We clustered together in the dense shadows beneath a corner of the building that jutted out into the sea. There was a narrow wooden walkway with a slat rail and, beneath it, stout pilings driven deep into the rock. Rain pinged and popped on the pressure-treated lumber.

Without Sam Imura we had no sniper, but Top was a pretty good shot. Better than Bunny or me. He took a sniper rifle and crawled up onto the island to find a shooter's perch that provided good angles.

Bunny and I went in opposite directions as we circled the island on the rocky slope, keeping to the shadows under the walkway. We met again at the same spot.

"I got four guards on the east and north sides," he reported. "Plus one guarding the finger pier. There's a speedboat out there, too."

"Three on this side," I told him. "And another pair inside a boathouse."

"Lot of guys. Everyone I saw was in black battle dress uniforms. My guess is either Kingsmen or Blue Diamond."

"None of them are friends of ours," I said quietly.

"Call the play."

"I want it quiet until I'm inside. I'm going to see about taking out the two in the boathouse. There's a door with a keycard scanner, and sentries working that spot will probably have cards. You watch my back. If anyone comes close or gets nosy, take them out as quietly as possible."

He nodded and began screwing a Trinity sound suppressor onto his sidearm.

I did the same. Ghost saw it and actually seemed to perk up. Dog loves a fight.

"Hotzone, I want this whole place set to blow. Every load-bearing timber. And put up a few party favors we can use as a distraction. Something to call them out so Top can have some fun."

Brian grinned like it was Christmas. He drummed his fingers on the canvas cover of the big bag that was slung across his chest. It was crammed with small but very powerful waterproof explosive charges. Like C4's angrier cousin. Something Doctor Hu's team cooked up for us. Each bomb had a radio detonator keyed to our mission channel. Any of us could detonate the bombs one at a time or all at once. Without a word, Brian moved off around the underside of the building to begin planting his charges on the support struts. He was smiling as he worked. Brian likes blowing things up. Everyone needs a hobby.

I checked the mission clock. It read: 00:09:33.

I nodded to Bunny, and we moved off to get this party started.

Chapter One Hundred and Twenty-eight

UC San Diego Medical Center

200 West Arbor Drive

San Diego, California

April 1, 3:39 P.M.

Nicodemus came out of a closet that had been checked three times. Everyplace in the hospital had been checked. That did not matter to Nicodemus. He went where he wanted to go. It amused him when the soldiers with their hard eyes and their guns looked at him and did not see him. They saw shadows. They saw clothes on pegs. They saw corpses on slabs or patients in beds. They did not see him because he did not allow it.

Once he looked out from between the curtains around a dying woman's bed and saw, far down the hall, a man that he had entertained in the chapel. Dense and slow, one-eyed and lame, *tok-tokking* his way down the hall on his cane with a soldier walking behind him like a Chinese bride.

Nicodemus could have taken him then. He almost did—it was that tempting.

But the moment wasn't right.

He had agreed to do it a certain way, and he was bound to that bargain. Annoying, but there it was. A deal was a deal was a deal.

Now, though . . .

Well, now the time was as ripe as a peach.

Smiling to himself, Nicodemus walked out into the hall.

Where everyone could see him.

He loved the look of shock on their faces. He loved the way they turned. He loved the sound of their shouts. So bold, full of military jargon. He simply adored the sight of guns coming up, of barrels pointing his way.

He even raised his hands.

"It's okay," he called to them. "I'm not armed."

Chapter One Hundred and Twenty-nine

Air Force One

In Flight

April 1, 3:39 P.M. Pacific Standard Time

The door locks clicked into the locked position. When Church tried the manual control, he found it frozen.

A Secret Service agent pushed him aside. "Let me try."

"Protect the president," called Linden Brierly.

"What's happening?" asked another voice. Then everyone was yelling. Fists hammered on the door from the other side, and there were more muffled yells from agents trying to get in.

"Where are the lights?"

"Turn on the security lights."

"I have a penlight."

A small light flared on and swept around the room, sweeping across faces filled with panic and fear.

Then the president's voice rose above everyone's. "Will someone tell me what the hell is happening?"

Everyone tried to, all at once; but it was Mr. Church who made himself heard.

"Enough!" he roared, and in the brief silence that followed, he spoke in his usual controlled tone. "Mr. President, it is clear that Solomon has been compromised. We need to assess our situation and regain control of the plane."

"How?"

Church said, "Everyone with a laptop, open it and turn up the brightness. Cell phones, too. We need light to operate. If you have a flashlight feature, turn it on. Do it now. Then I want everyone back in your seats."

Although Church's voice was filled with calm command, the senior staff looked to the president for confirmation.

"Do what he says."

They did.

"Linden," said Church, "is your radio controlled through the plane's Wi-Fi?"

"We have battery backup and our own hot spots. But our cell phones are—"

"One thing at a time. Tell your men to use a breaching tool to open this door. President's orders."

Again the president nodded. Brierly gave very specific orders to breach the door but leave weapons holstered.

"Everyone else get back from the door," said Church. "Cover your faces with your arms. There will be splinters."

Everyone complied, and within seconds there was a heavy thump on the door that shook the cabin. The door shuddered but did not open. Three seconds later, the agents on the other side tried again. This time the lock tore itself from the frame. Bits of metal and a storm of wood splinters filled the air, grazing arms, lodging in hair. Secret Service agents began to pile into the cramped conference room, but Brierly ordered them to stand down.

"Mr. President?" said Church.

"Go," said the president. "Do whatever you have to do."

As he spoke, though, there was a ghostly movement in front of his face. They all saw it. And for the first time they all felt it.

"What—?" murmured Bain.

"The heat," said Brierly. "They cut the heat."

The jet flew through the air at 506 miles an hour, flying at thirty-six thousand feet. The temperature outside was fifty-seven degrees below freezing.

Church left the conference room and moved quickly through the darkened plane. He pulled his cell phone and switched on the beam.

"On your six, Deacon," said Brierly.

"You should stay with the president."

"He's secure. You'll need help with this."

They reached the cockpit door. Two Secret Service agents were fiddling with a keypad, trying to bypass the security.

"What have you got?" asked Brierly.

"We got a dead lock," said one agent. "All electronics are frozen, and the onboard countermeasures have kicked in. Door is sealed against hijackers. Can't get in without force. It's hardened against breaching tools."

"Can you contact the flight crew?"

"No, sir. They are totally unresponsive."

Brierly glanced at Church. "Solomon controls everything, including oxygen. It can also release a sedative vapor. Nonlethal but effective. And . . . yes, it's part of the countermeasure package your team advised against."

"What other surprises are there?"

Brierly shivered. "The same system is shipwide. They can freeze us, dope us, or kill us. And the system controls explosive bolts on the doors in case of emergency evacuation after a crash that's killed the crew."

"You knew about this and didn't tell me," said Church. It wasn't a question or an accusation. It was, however, an eloquent statement of disappointment.

"This was approved by the president and—"

"Don't embarrass yourself, Linden. All we need to do is focus on solving this."

"How?"

"Not sure yet." Church reached into an inner pocket of his jacket and removed a small device about the size of a paperback book. From another pocket he removed a leather case that opened to reveal an array of very delicate tools. He knelt and shined his phone light on the keypad of the security-bypass terminal fixed to the bulkhead outside the cockpit. The terminal was there for emergencies and could only be accessed under very specific circumstances.

"Is Solomon keyed to defend against this system?" he asked.

Brierly was too long in answering.

"Solomon was built as a can't-fail system in the event of a hijacking by technologically savvy intruders."

"How clever. You must be proud."

Church removed a set of wires and plugged the leads into ports on the terminal. Several lights flicked on along the face of the device he held. The lights were all red.

"Is that good?" asked Brierly. "Can you access the system?"

Church ignored the question. He pressed a button that caused two thin panels to open like wings from the lower part of his device. As they locked into place, tiny lights switched on to illuminate a holographic touch-screen keyboard. Church peeled away a strip of plastic film and pressed the top end of the device to the bulkhead below the terminal, held it in place for ten seconds, and then released it. The device stuck fast.

"What is that?" asked Brierly, his breath pluming with frost. "Portable MindReader?"

"Something like that."

"Will it allow us to bypass Solomon? Or should we wait for——?"

"For what, exactly, Linden?"

"The Kings to make their demands. We can negotiate something with them."

Church turned and looked at him for a moment. "Linden, do you grasp what's happening here?"

"Yes, the Kings have taken over the plane. They probably want to kill POTUS, or hold him hostage for some kind of payoff."

Church shook his head. "I don't think it's that simple."

"Then what?"

"The Seven Kings have spent a lot of time and money to infect the Regis and Solomon systems. They've outsmarted us at every single turn. If this was a grab for money, they'd have made their first hit on a Monday after opening bell at the market. They didn't. They hit the park and killed a great hero of the war in Afghanistan while also inflicting an injury on the American people at the launch of our national pastime. Seen together, that looks more like a symbol than an attempt to influence the market. In fact, it's become harder and harder to connect the chain of events with any kind of big-ticket swindle."

"Then what?"

"I think the Kings may have other motivations."

"Like?"

"Revenge comes to mind," said Church. "We did considerable damage to their organization. It is entirely possible they built a fail-safe into their infrastructure. Something to throw the last punch. It would be very much like Hugo Vox to do that kind of thing. Even if he loses, he wins."

"Wins how? Wanton destruction?"

"Or a historical statement. Perhaps a political one. After all, the last King to be killed was Osama bin Laden." He nodded to indicate the plane around them. "This would be a very apt statement."

"How?"

"Because the very first major attack by the Seven Kings was to hijack planes and fly them into the World Trade Center. Into the symbol of American financial power. And into the Pentagon, the symbol of our military superiority. If the fourth plane had hit its target instead of being forced to crash, it would have hit the White House, the symbol of leadership. Using Solomon is so appropriate."

"I don't see how. By killing the president?"

Church sighed. "Where are we headed, Linden?"

"New York."

"Correct. The Seven Kings have taken control of Air Force One, turned it into a drone, and aimed it at New York. Would you like to guess what their target is going to be? Now that it's been rebuilt? Now that it's a gleaming spike symbolizing how America rises from any defeat? You tell me, Linden. What could the Kings do to strike a more devastating blow than that?"

Brierly said nothing. His mouth hung open.

Church pointed toward the window. "They blew up the Golden Gate Bridge. Now they're going to destroy the World Trade Center with Air Force One. From sea to shining sea. And we are all fools for not seeing it soon enough."

Chapter One Hundred and Thirty

Ghost and I moved along the dock as silently as we knew how. Any noise that rose louder than the rain, and we were dead. Maybe my whole team was dead. There were rows of wooden barrels on shelves and stacks of supplies in metal or plastic tubs. Through the plastic I could see canned fruits in one tub, boxes of medical gauze in another.

The two sentries were not winning points for alertness or vigilance, which meant I liked them a lot. But they were on an island, inside a boat-house, carrying automatic weapons and wearing microphones. They probably felt safe.

Suddenly I heard a voice and nearly had a fucking heart attack.

"Deacon for Cowboy. Deacon for Cowboy."

The earbud transmitted directly into my ear. No one else could hear it, but I froze and became part of the stacked supplies. I think I even adopted a wood-grain pattern on my skin. I was that determined not to be seen.

The guards didn't turn my way, and after about five seconds my sphincter unclenched, and my heart started beating again. I shifted slowly to my right and ducked down behind a stack of wooden boxes. There is a track-ball stitched into the lining of my pocket, and I used it to activate my Scout glasses. The screen display flicked on and confirmed that the incoming call was indeed from Church. I used the cursor to indicate that I couldn't make a verbal reply but was able to receive intel. Church began speaking quickly and quietly.

He told me very bad things.

He told me about Air Force One.

He told me about a bunch of people freezing to death in a drone that was heading for New York.

"Bug thinks he can help me bypass the security and gain access to the cockpit. If that happens, I'll be able to key in an override. Have you secured the reset codes from the target?"

I tapped the cursor once to indicate that I had not.

Church's voice was calm. Too controlled, too dry. "We're running out of time, Cowboy. You know they can't let this plane cross into New York airspace. Not near the city. They'll shoot us down before they let that happen."

He disconnected the call.

I sat there, stunned. Horrified.

And really goddamn pissed off.

I raised my Sig Sauer and took it in a comfortable grip, left hand cupping the right and supporting the gun, finger laid along the trigger guard. I made a small clicking sound to tell Ghost to stay back and stay silent. He sat and seemed to turn to stone.

Then I moved forward. Not running, but taking many small steps that allowed me to limit sound, move quickly, and keep the gun rock steady. The guards were looking in the wrong direction, laughing at something one of them said, unaware that I was there.

I opened fire from twenty feet away.

Shot after shot.

Taking them both in the body and then the head. Watching them go down. One of them fell over the edge into the water. The other collapsed like a scarecrow onto the deck. Four shots, two seconds.

Dead.

"Ghost," I said quietly, and he bounded forward. "Clear."

He veered off and moved as silent as his name around the dock, looking with keen dog eyes and sniffing with his incredible dog nose. Then he cut and returned to me. If there had been another man standing somewhere out of sight, Ghost would have taken him.

I slipped my gun into my shoulder rig and squatted down over the dead man, praying that it wasn't the other one who had the keycard.

I sighed with relief when I found the keycard in his trouser pocket.

Unfortunately, that's where my hand was when the door behind me opened.

Chapter One Hundred and Thirty-one

UC San Diego Medical Center
200 West Arbor Drive
San Diego, California
April 1, 3:44 P.M.

Lydia Ruiz saw the man first.

Him.

The priest.

For reasons she could never explain to herself, she touched her chest, where, beneath her clothes and body armor, a silver cross hung over her heart. Her mother had given it to her for her first confirmation a million years ago. Another life ago. She wasn't even sure she believed in God anymore. Not after the things she'd seen. The things she'd done.

But now the cross and all that it meant to her mother, her aunts, her grandmother, her family seemed to pull at her hand. She touched the shape of it beneath her clothes.

Lydia had never met this man before. Not in the flesh. She'd been on the fringes of DMS actions involving him, including the thing in Iran with the Red Knights.

The priest smiled at her.

"I'm not armed," he said.

Lydia's hand left the cross and drew her gun faster than she had ever done anything in her life. The Glock was in its holster and then it was in her hand and her finger was inside the trigger guard and she was firing.

The priest was forty feet away. At twenty-five feet, she could put nine rounds into a hole the size of a dime. At fifty, she could kill anything she aimed at. Even at fifty yards, she could put eighty percent of her shots through a six-inch dirty-bird target. She was a superb shot, and she'd killed hostiles with handguns and long guns on five continents.

The priest did not fall.

Did not stagger.

And he did not stop smiling.

When the slide of her Glock locked back, Lydia dropped the magazine and reached for a fresh one with the smooth fluidity of years of practice, even though her mind was reeling. As she slapped it into place, she heard her own voice reciting a prayer the nuns had drilled into her.

"Holy Mary, Mother of God, pray for us sinners, now and at the hour of our death."

Nicodemus said, "Amen."

Behind him, the doors to the stairwell banged open and a horde of Kingsmen came rushing out.

Chapter One Hundred and Thirty-two

Tanglewood Island
Pierce County, Washington
April 1, 3:46 P.M.

There was no time to draw my gun. I wheeled and saw another pair of guards in the doorway. Shift change? Who knows. Two men. Big, startled, armed.

"Ghost," I said. "Hit!"

He was a blur as he shot past me and leaped high at the first man. Ghost is one hundred and five pounds of muscle and teeth. All that weight hit the guy in the solar plexus and drove both guys back inside. As I leaped after Ghost, I whipped my rapid-release folding knife from its pocket sheath. It flicked open and snugged into my palm.

Ghost sank his teeth into the first man's throat, and blood sprayed up and hit the ceiling. I jumped over him, slapped aside the barrel of a machine gun the second guard didn't quite have time to raise, and slashed him across the throat. The short, wicked blade took him just below the Adam's apple and cut a two-inch red trench.

He staggered backward and sank down to his knees, eyes bugging out as he used both hands to try and staunch a flow that could not be stopped. I bashed his hands aside and shin-kicked him in the throat. He flopped backward and down and stopped moving. I pivoted to see the man beneath Ghost give a final frenzied kick of his legs and then settle back into that terminal stillness that can never be mistaken for sleep. Blood pooled out beneath him, and Ghost raised his head and turned toward me.

When he does a kill there is a little bit of a disconnect from the dog I know and love and the predator that lives inside his heart. I'm sure there is a similar look in my eyes when I let the killer out to play. So for a moment we stood there, two monsters, linked by the blood we had just spilled.

Then I pulled myself back from the edge and listened to the building around me. For shouts, for alarms. Heard nothing except the slap of water against the pilings outside.

When I was certain that no one was coming, I tapped my earbud for the team channel.

"Cowboy to Echo. The boathouse is clear. Four hostiles are down. I'm inside the building."

"Copy that," replied Top. "Did you get the message from Deacon?"

"Affirmative. Clock is ticking. I'm going for it."

"Call the play," said Top.

"Give me five minutes and then kick the doors."

"Hooah," he said.

I glanced at Ghost. He was himself again, but I knew the wolf was not far away.

"Let's go," I told him, but he was already moving. He'd tasted blood, and he wanted more.

Chapter One Hundred and Thirty-three

Air Force One
In Flight
April 1, 3:46 P.M. Pacific Standard Time

"How's it coming?" asked Brierly. He was shivering and stamping his feet.

Church knelt with a blanket draped around his shoulders. His fingers were nearly blue, and the tools kept slipping as he gradually lost muscular control to the biting cold.

"Questions aren't particularly useful right now," said Church.

"I need to do something."

"Then go find me a satellite phone. I don't care if you have to take it away from the president. I've hit a wall here and I need to call in an expert."

Brierly nodded and backed away, then turned and ran. In the main cabin, the press and the White House staff had clustered together into huddled masses under layers of coats and blankets. The air inside the jet was sub-zero and falling. He could hear people weeping. A few were praying.

When he reached the conference room, he saw the president hunched in his chair with the others sitting close. Not quite a communal huddle, but it was getting there. The president wore his blue parka and gloves. A few others had coats, but there weren't enough on board for everyone.

The president had the satellite phone to his mouth and was speaking softly, tenderly, soothing someone at the other end. The first lady, no doubt. POTUS looked up as Brierly came over.

"Any luck?"

"Some," lied Brierly, "but the Deacon needs the sat phone."

The president looked reluctant, but he nodded. "Honey," he said into the mouthpiece, "I need to call you back. No . . . no, listen to me. I will call you back. Just trust me. We have the best people in the world working on this. It's all going to be fine."

He ended the call and handed the phone to Brierly.

"Did I just lie to my wife? Is this going to work out?"

"I'm sure it will," said Brierly, because lying was the only thing they could all do right now.

He hurried back to Church and gave him the phone.

"Thanks," said Church and immediately punched a number and waited through five rings before it was answered. Brierly was close enough to hear the voice on the other end. Small, lost, filled with pain.

"Y-yes?"

"Bug," said Mr. Church, "I need your help."

Chapter One Hundred and Thirty-four

UC San Diego Medical Center
200 West Arbor Drive
San Diego, California
April 1, 3:47 P.M.

Lydia dove behind the nurses' station as the Kingsmen opened fire. Heavy-caliber bullets chased her and tore the counter to matchwood. Lydia hit, rolled, kicked herself around, and reached around the end of the counter with her gun hand. Blind firing was usually a waste of bullets, but the hallway was packed with killers. Even behind the wave of gunfire, she heard screams.

And then she heard more guns open up, and for a wild moment she thought she was caught in a hopeless crossfire. But the sound signature was wrong. The Kingsmen all had AK-47s, and the new shots were Heckler & Koch CQBR carbines firing NATO rounds. She turned to see Montana Parker crouched in a doorway, her rifle snugged into her shoulder. Two other DMS agents were running up the hall, firing as they came.

The three Kingsmen at the forefront of the charge staggered and collapsed, blood flying front and back from through-and-through wounds. But more of the killers kept pouring from the stairwell.

Chapter One Hundred and Thirty-five

Tanglewood Island
Pierce County, Washington
April 1, 3:51 P.M.

Ghost and I moved through a silent building. I knew there were people here, but it didn't feel like it. The place had a dead vibe to it that was hard to describe. There was a wrongness to it that went beyond even the evil of the Seven Kings, and yet I didn't feel the kind of malevolent vitality I expected.

The halls were lined with dark wood that was polished to such a high shine it looked like a museum display. The carpets underfoot appeared to have never felt a footfall. We knew there were people in this hotel but somehow the place had a disused quality. Or, maybe it was soulless. That's how it felt.

The hall was lined with doors. None of them had a fancy lock or anything requiring a security keycard. Most were unlocked, and when I checked I found evidence of occupancy. Men's clothing, mostly. Many pairs of black BDUs and rubber-soled shoes. Weapons and extra ammunition. Porn magazines. Books of all kinds. Laptops. Nothing that looked like a room where a short computer genius might have been held. I plugged uplinks into the

USB ports of each laptop I found, hoping that none of them were of the quantum variety. I doubt I could tell the difference.

I exited the next-to-last room along that hall. My knife was back in its pocket, and I had a fresh magazine in the silenced Sig Sauer. The door to the very next room down the hall opened, and I instantly ducked back inside as a woman dressed as a maid emerged pushing a small cart laden with towels. She began moving off, then stopped and looked my way. She couldn't see Ghost or me, but she frowned as she looked at the runner carpet. I didn't have to look to know what she was seeing. Footprints. Wet and new.

What she did next was going to determine her future. If she was an ordinary maid and decided to turn and run for help, I'd catch her and juice her with horsey. If she wasn't an ordinary maid, then she wasn't going to have a future.

Still frowning, she crept down the hall, and as she did so she reached under the sweater she wore over her maid's costume and pulled a Glock 26.

I stepped out of hiding and shot her through the heart and the forehead.

Bad guys come in all shapes and sizes, and sexes.

I hooked an arm under her and caught her as she fell. There was no time to hide her body, so I laid her down on the carpet. I tucked her gun into the back of my belt, clicked my tongue for Ghost, and ran up the hall. I paused to peer into the room she'd just left. It was empty, but I knew as soon as I stepped inside that I'd struck gold.

There was a pile of clothes on the floor that looked way too small to belong to one of the Blue Diamond thugs and a pair of shoes that couldn't have been larger than a seven.

"Ghost," I said, "watch."

He went back into the hallway.

I tore through the room. I wanted to find a computer, but there was nothing. No electronics. Not even a Gameboy.

Fair enough. Once Davidovich had bugged out, they would have taken his computers to see if he'd left anything useful on them. Would they do the same for his notebooks?

I cut over to the desk and saw that it was piled high with papers of all kinds. Reams of computer printouts, scores of file folders, three-ring binders, and loose pages torn from yellow legal pads. Nothing that I could see screamed "Hey, this is what you're looking for!"

Until it did.

Sitting on one corner of the desk was a stack of spiral-bound notebooks with cheap cardboard covers. The kind they sell for a buck at Staples. There were maybe forty of them bundled together in sets that were bound with oversize rubber bands. Either Davidovich had stacked them haphazardly or someone had already gone through them. I tended to believe the latter. Davidovich had many flaws, but sloppiness was not one of them.

I set my gun down and picked up one of the books, flipped it open. On the inside cover I saw a handwritten name. Not Aaron Davidovich's own name. It was Matthew. His son's name. Written over and over again. In pencil, in felt-tip marker, in three different colors of ballpoint. Hundreds of times. The pages were filled with computer code. Meticulously written in pencil in a small, crabbed hand. Flipping through, I saw that the book was completely filled. Almost. There were a few blank pages, maybe to separate one program from another, or one set of functions. Something like that. I'm talented with spoken languages, but computer speak isn't even Greek to me. I can speak and even write Greek. This was an alien language. What had Davidovich said?

They're still on the island in my notebooks, hidden in a piece of old game code that I stopped working on. It looks like junk unless you know the key to using it.

Then he'd rambled on and on, losing his shit in the midst of panic. I picked through my memory everything he said. Every detail, fishing for something useful. He'd said something . . . something . . . I closed my eyes and willed my brain to replay the conversation.

Pi from nine, he'd said. There was more and I had to claw for it. I mouthed the words I remembered, and as I spoke them aloud they congealed into something that maybe sense. A kind of sense.

"Pi from nine, backwards," I murmured. "Page two."

That's what Davidovich said.

I opened the notebook to page two, but it was merely the middle of a code string that began on the previous page. I tossed it down and began going through the others and very quickly discovered that I was totally out of my depth. None of it looked right to me. The only thing that I could understand was the name Matthew. Davidovich had spent a lot of time writing his son's name on the inside covers of his notebooks. Why? Obsession? Regret? Who knows.

So I took a risk to break radio silence and tapped my earbud to get Yoda on the line. In the absence of Bug, Yoda was the software genius of the DMS. His real name, by the way, is Yoda. He has a sister named Leia. His parents could use some therapy.

"Mmmm, what have you got, Cowboy?"

"I think I found Doctor Detroit's notebooks, but there are a lot of them and I don't have time to exfil with them." I tapped the camera on my Scout glasses so Yoda could see what I saw. "He said it was game code on page two."

I could hear Yoda take a breath. "Okay," he said, "start with the, ummm, first one."

The clock kept ticking.

Ticking.

Ticking.

Chapter One Hundred and Thirty-six

UC San Diego Medical Center
200 West Arbor Drive
San Diego, California
April 1, 3:51 P.M.

"Is that thunder?"

Rudy Sanchez and the infectious-disease specialist looked up from the NF reports they had been discussing. Above them, the building seemed to tremble.

The doctor had asked the question, but he was frowning.

"No," said Rudy.

"It sounds more like fireworks," said a nurse who was on the other side of the room taking updates from the printer.

Rudy murmured, *"Ay Dios mío.* That's not fireworks. Doctor, call the police. Do it right now."

He reached for the silver handle of his cane and pushed himself up. Rudy tapped the earbud Lydia required him to wear. He tapped it to bring her online, but there was no answer. He tried Sam. Montana.

No one answered his call.

He tried Church. Nothing.

Finally, he contacted the DMS headquarters at the Hangar on Floyd Bennett Field. The duty officer answered at once.

"This is Doctor Rudy Sanchez—"

"Combat call signs only on this line—"

"To hell with that. I am at UC San Diego Medical Center. Send immediate help. We are under attack."

Chapter One Hundred and Thirty-seven

Tanglewood Island

Pierce County, Washington

April 1, 3:52 P.M.

Doctor Pharos felt his phone vibrate, and when he looked at the display, he smiled.

"Boy," he said into the phone, "I was waiting for your call."

"Father," she said, "it's started."

"Ah. Excellent."

"And . . . Father?"

"Yes, my dear?"

"After this, I get to come home?"

"Yes, my dear."

"Thank you, Father."

"No, honey, thank *you*."

The line went dead. Pharos slipped the phone back into his pocket and glanced at the burned man, who in turn was watching the news coverage coming out of San Francisco.

"So beautiful," said the Gentleman. "So beautiful."

Pharos said nothing. Instead, he stood and walked without haste to the door. This was all accelerating now. He had to make sure that the twelve separate escape routes he'd arranged were all prepped and ready. Once he had the codes from the burned man, he was going to be out of there like a bullet leaving a gun.

And if those codes were never to be his . . . ?

So sad.

But his feelings were soothed by all of that gold.

He was smiling as he left the dying man's room.

Chapter One Hundred and Thirty-eight

Fort Myers, Florida

April 1, 12:53 P.M. Eastern Standard Time

Bug sat in his hotel room. His clothes were draped over the edges of his suitcase, empty sleeves reaching like dead arms, head collars collapsed in defeat. A pizza box stood open, one slice missing, the cheese cold and congealed. More than a dozen cans of Coke stood on the night table or lay on the floor. The TV was on, and news footage of the horrors in San Francisco was like something from a summer disaster movie. A box of tissues was within reach on the small dining table. Dozens of crumpled tissues overflowed the metal trash can.

Bug listened to what Mr. Church was telling him, and as he did so he could feel the malaise in his mind and the grief in his heart fusing into a wall of indifference. He didn't care about the president, the ballpark, the bridge, the submarine, or any of it. He wasn't even sure he cared about Mr. Church. He certainly didn't give a shit about the president or anyone on Air Force One. None of it was quite real.

Only one thing was real to him, and it was going to be buried in a closed coffin. He wasn't even sure all of her would be in there. The blast had torn her to pieces.

Pieces.

The thought was too horrible to fit into his head.

His mother had been torn to pieces. Bloody chunks. Broken bits of bone. Burned blood.

That face, the one that was always filled with smiles. The first thing he had ever seen in this world. Those eyes, brimming with laughter and love. That heart. That noble and loving heart. The hands that had bathed him.

The laugh that could burn away the darkest shadows. The mind that held a fierce intellect and a generous nature. The personality.

Gone.

All of it blown to pieces by a bomb.

All of it gone.

All of her gone.

Gathered up in bits and put into a bag so it could be buried in a box.

So sorry, the police and the doctors and all his friends had said. So sorry.

Now the world itself was being blown to bits, and that seemed only right. It should all blow up, all fall down, all go into the cold, cold ground.

Like Mom.

Like her.

Like his own heart, which was so badly broken that Bug knew it could never be fixed. Some things can't be fixed. Some things had no reset button.

"Bug," said the voice on the phone.

"I can't," Bug told him.

"Please."

"Get someone else. Get Yoda."

"Yoda isn't up to this," said Mr. Church.

"*I'm* not up to this."

"Bug . . ."

"It's not fair!" Bug suddenly screamed into the phone.

After a long moment, Mr. Church said, "No, it's not. They took your mother away from you, Bug. They're trying to take my daughter away from me. They may have killed Aunt Sallie, and they will kill me."

"I'm sorry . . . but you shouldn't have called me."

"Who else could I call?"

The silence washed back and forth on the line.

"It doesn't matter anyway," said Bug. "If they have a quantum computer, even MindReader can't beat it."

"They may have a QC, Bug. They probably do. But if so, it's not on this aircraft. The Solomon program is."

Bug said nothing.

"I need to bypass a computer lockout system with a set of pocket tools and a Warlock handheld. I've tried everything that I know how to do. I can get about a third of the way in, and then it locks me out again."

Bug said nothing.

"We have about forty-three minutes of flight time left before we cross a certain line."

"What line?"

"The president cannot let Air Force One cross into the New York metropolitan area. If we cannot take control of the plane in under twenty-five minutes, the president will have to order ground-based missiles to blow us out of the sky."

Bug said nothing.

For a long time.

Then he sobbed once and pressed a tissue to his eyes and clenched his jaws to stifle the scream that he wanted to give as the only reasonable answer.

He struck himself in the forehead with his cell phone. Once. Again. And again.

Then he dragged a forearm across his eyes, sniffed to clear his nose, and mumbled a single word.

"Okay."

Chapter One Hundred and Thirty-nine

UC San Diego Medical Center
200 West Arbor Drive
San Diego, California
April 1, 3:53 P.M.

A figure emerged from the crowd of Kingsmen. Small, slim, female, with a Cambodian face and eyes like a shark. She wore a full set of high-tech body armor and carried a .22 automatic in her hand. Nicodemus hissed something at her and vanished into a doctor's office. The Cambodian took charge and immediately yelled to the Kingsmen, who began overturning gurneys to create shooting blinds. Lydia rolled out and fired four quick shots, catching one of the men in the throat and sending the others for cover. The Cambodian woman spun and fired and bullets chipped the desk an inch from Lydia's face.

She squirmed back under the desk, peering through a splintered hole as she reloaded.

The Cambodian knelt quickly, aimed, fired. There was a sharp cry, and one of the DMS team simply sat down, coughed red, and fell over onto his side.

"The cow is in the room at the end of the hall," yelled the woman. "Take her. Kill the others. Do it now!"

The Kingsmen began pouring it on even heavier, turning the hospital floor into a whirlwind of flying lead and jagged splinters.

Lydia slapped the magazine in and then leaned out to fire at the newcomer, but there were two shooters in the way. She shot one through the side of the head, and he fell sideways into his companion, dragging them both down. That gave Lydia a clear shot at the Cambodian, but the slim Asian wheeled and snapped off a shot that punched into the center of Lydia Ruiz's chest.

Lydia collapsed backward, the air rushing from her lungs. Fires ignited in her eyes, and for a moment she could neither move nor breathe. She turned to see the Kingsmen rushing forward, howling as they fired.

Circe O'Tree-Sanchez's room was across the wide hallway from where Lydia lay. Bullets hammered into the glass and exploded it inward, filling the room with a million glittering splinters. There was sudden movement as two figures came up off the floor and threw themselves down across Circe. Junie used her body to cover Circe's chest and face; Toys bent his body like an arch over her distended belly. Not touching her, but shielding her as the glass tore through their clothes and painted their bodies red.

Chapter One Hundred and Forty

Tanglewood Island
Pierce County, Washington
April 1, 3:56 P.M.

"Tell me something good, Yoda."

"Ummmm, Jesus, Cowboy, this is very advanced stuff. Some of this must be for the, ummm, QC and—"

"We're not looking for the frigging QC," I snapped as I threw down one notebook and opened another. "We're looking for old game code. Does any of this fit?"

He started to answer, faltered. Started again, faltered again.

"Goddamn, focus. The clock is ticking."

"I know, I know. Mmmmmmmm, God . . . I wish Bug was here."

I flipped through the pages of the notebook. "He's not. Pay attention. Is this game code?"

"I don't know. I think it might be, but . . . "

I wanted to scream. Somewhere in the skies over Ohio or some Midwestern state, Air Force One was racing to punch into the New York airspace. Minutes were breaking off the clock. My heart was racing so hard it hurt.

"No," said Yoda. "Not that one. Ummm, let me see the next one . . . "

Chapter One Hundred and Forty-one

UC San Diego Medical Center

200 West Arbor Drive

San Diego, California

April 1, 3:56 P.M.

Lydia pressed her fingers to her chest and looked at them, expecting to see blood.

All she saw was her own copper-brown skin.

Kevlar. She wanted to laugh, but it hurt too much. The vests stopped the bullets, but they could only do so much to diffuse the pounds of force.

"Get the cow!" screamed the Cambodian woman.

Then another voice, older, male, snarled, "Bring her to me."

Nicodemus.

Lydia growled, took a big bite of her pain, and rolled back to her knees. The Kingsmen were racing toward Circe's room. Montana took three of them down, but it didn't even slow their rush. Then a heavier weapon spoke from the far end of the side hall. A big, throaty cough, and in the same instant one of the Kingsmen seemed to fly apart. There was a second shot, a third, a fourth, and with each one a Kingsman died. Heads exploded. Chests ruptured.

Lydia could not see where Sam Imura was positioned, but he kept firing, killing everything he aimed at. He'd brought his "indoor" gun with him, an M21 semiautomatic with a twenty-round box magazine.

Except that the gun needed to be reloaded and the hall was choked with Kingsmen. How many magazines did Sam have? One spare, tops?

As Lydia shifted back into a shooting position, she saw another DMS agent go down, his upper chest torn apart by a dozen rounds. The fusillade drove Montana back from the doorway. Police officers and the support team from Homeland poured out of the fire tower, down near Sam. They opened fire at once, and the Cambodian woman sent half her team down the hall to intercept them. There were a lot of DMS, SWAT, and Homeland shooters in the hospital.

There were five times as many Kingsmen.

Nicodemus and the Cambodian woman had brought an army.

An army.

Why? Lydia couldn't understand why they would send such overwhelming force to abduct one pregnant woman. Who was Circe to them? Why did she matter?

These thoughts and questions ran through her head as she fired and fired, killing and wounding, emptying her gun, dropping the spent magazine, reloading, aware of how many rounds she had left.

Not enough.

Even if she put one bullet in every Kingsman here, she did not have enough ammunition to win this. Nowhere near enough to survive it. And far too little to protect Circe and her baby.

Nicodemus came stalking along the hall, his wizened body canted forward like some predatory dinosaur. His smile was an awful thing to see. Totally inhuman, filled with obvious delight at the chaos and blood that swirled around him. Again, Lydia tried to shoot him, but a pair of Kingsmen rushed at her, and she had to waste bullets on them instead of taking out that perverse parody of a priest.

"The cow is mine," said Nicodemus, his thin voice rising above the din. "Mine!"

Suddenly something came bounding out of Circe's room. With a howl that momentarily stilled the fighting in the hallway, it leaped through the shattered window frame and struck a Kingsman with such force that the man bent backward, folded nearly in two. The man's spine snapped with gunshot clarity.

"Banshee . . ." breathed Lydia.

The enormous wolfhound drove the dead man to the floor and sprang forward, tearing the throat out of a second man.

"Kill it!" shrieked a voice. "Kill it!"

The voice belonged to Nicodemus. He pointed at the dog as he backed quickly away.

"Kill it!"

He sounded different.

Not boastful. Not confidant.

Nicodemus sounded terrified.

And Lydia Ruiz was certain of it.

Immediately, a half dozen of the Kingsmen hurled themselves at the hound and dragged it down out of sight.

Chapter One Hundred and Forty-two

Air Force One

In Flight

April 1, 3:58 P.M. Pacific Standard Time

"The green wire's next," said Bug. "I think."

"Bug," said Church as he lifted the green wire in the jaws of a pair of needle-nose pliers, "I need something better than 'I think.'"

Church's teeth were chattering, and his fingers had turned a dusty purple.

"I know, I know, but I can't see the circuits. Move the light."

Church picked up the light, dropped it, picked it up again, dropped it. He took a breath and tried once more and managed to position the light. He could not actually feel the cell phone he was using as a flashlight. Almost all nerve conduction was gone from his fingertips. Where his fingers weren't completely numb, they screamed with pain. Strange how the pain of frostbite could feel like fire.

"Can you see it now?" he asked, forcing his voice to be calm.

"Yeah. It's not the green wire. It's the blue one. Strip it and hotwire it to the white one. That should connect you to the battery and give you power to run the locking computer."

"You're sure, Bug? I won't be able to do this twice."

"Blue and white. Absolutely."

Church began stripping the wire. His dying hands were clumsy, and the tools kept falling. Each time he picked them up and continued. He didn't waste time with cursing or any of the dramatics of frustration. He worked as efficiently as the biting cold and thinning oxygen would allow. He could feel the beginnings of confusion at the edges of his focus. Carbon dioxide was building up in the cabin.

Bug said, "I . . . I wish I was there to do this for you."

"You are here with me, Bug," said Church.

Chapter One Hundred and Forty-three

Tanglewood Island
Pierce County, Washington
April 1, 3:59 P.M.

"Ummmm, Cowboy—?" said Yoda, "I, ummm, think that's it."

"Wait . . . *what's* it?"

"That page. No, no, the book you just put down. Let me see that one again. Second page. Hold it steady so I can take a screen shot. Got it. Okay, give me a minute."

"We don't have a minute."

"Half a minute." Yoda said, and then just hummed at me for what seemed like an hour. Probably only fifteen or twenty seconds, but it felt longer. Too long.

"Yoda . . . "

"Umm, holy shit, Cowboy," he blurted. "*That's definitely it*. Flip the page. No go to page nine. Davidovich said it was Pi and to work backward from nine. The value of Pi is 3.141592653. Keeps going from there to infinity. The ninth value is three. Hold it so I can see line three."

I did, and I noticed that in his excitement he'd stopped humming.

"Let me input the code from the third line. Got it. Now page eight, line five . . . "

Chapter One Hundred and Forty-four

Rudy Sanchez took the elevator up to the floor where his wife lay pregnant and helpless. He gripped his walking stick with hands that were slick with sweat. He had to clutch his hands into fists to keep them from trembling. Never in his life—not even when the burning helicopter plunged into the brown waters of the Baltimore Harbor—had he been this terrified.

Circe.

Dear God, he prayed in Spanish, *please . . . not Circe. Not her.*

He could hear gunfire and screams. And through it all the bone-chilling howl of a monstrous hound.

Banshee.

Rudy had no gun. Joe had tried many times to teach him, but, even before he lost an eye, Rudy had been an indifferent marksman. Now, with the loss of depth perception that came with being one-eyed, he was worthless with any gun except a shotgun. He didn't have a shotgun.

All he had was the hand-carved walking stick made of hawthorn and topped with an ornate silver handle. He had used that stick to try and fight back against Nicodemus and failed. He clutched it now and wondered if he was rushing to help his wife or to simply be murdered.

Dear God and all Your saints . . . not my wife. Not our child. Take me instead. If you need a life, take mine. Show them Your mercy.

The elevator stopped, and the doors opened to reveal a scene from hell itself. Hieronymus Bosch could not have painted a more horrific tableau.

Bodies lay sprawled on the floor; the walls were pocked with black bullet holes and splashed with red blood. Shell casings glittered like discarded jewels. The combatants fought at close quarters. With guns. With clubs and stun guns. With knives. With bare hands. Rudy saw four DMS agents, including Agent Cowpers, lying dead. SWAT officers and agents of Homeland's tactical response teams lay entangled with Kingsmen.

Lydia Ruiz knelt beside the nurses' station, firing into the crowd. Across the hall, Rudy could see Circe's room. The big window was gone except for a few jagged glass teeth. On the bed, Rudy could see one sprawled form. A man's body. Bloody and inert.

He could not see his wife at all.

Oh God . . . where was Circe?

Please, God of all. Not my love. Not Circe.

A man stood directly outside the elevator car, and as the doors opened he turned toward Rudy. A Kingsman. He grinned as he turned. He had a marine bayonet in his hand, and with a cry of murderous glee he threw himself at Rudy.

Chapter One Hundred and Forty-five

Tanglewood Island

Pierce County, Washington

April 1, 4:01 P.M.

"That's the last one," I said. "Do you have it all?"

"I do."

"Then upload the rest of the fucking code. Do it right damn now."

I could hear his fingers hammering on keys.

Then, "Oh Jesus . . . "

"Don't 'oh, Jesus' me, man. Tell me it went through. Tell me you're shutting this down."

"No," he said. "It's, ummmmm, not working. There was a URL built into the code. It brought up an, ummmmm, Web site. Password-protected."

"What's the password?"

"How would I know?" Yoda protested. "I, ummm, don't know it . . . "

Ever been punched in the face? Really hard? The kind of punch that knocks the air out of your lungs and all of the thoughts from your brain?

Yeah.

That's what I felt.

Chapter One Hundred and Forty-six

Rudy Sanchez fell back as the Kingsman rushed him. With a desperate cry, he brought his cane up in both hands to try and parry the fall of the knife. The Kingsman's wrist slammed into the hawthorn shaft and rebounded, and the jolt—against all hope—hit the right nerves. The man's hand sprang open, and the knife flew over Rudy's shoulder and fell behind him.

The Kingsman looked as surprised as Rudy felt, but the killer recovered at once and swung a punch that caught Rudy across the jaw, spun him, and dropped him to his knees. Then the man grabbed Rudy's chin in one hand and knotted the fingers of his other hand in Rudy's hair. He began to twist, forcing Rudy's head to turn on his neck. First to the edge of comfort and then past it.

Too far past it.

Rudy could feel the bones in his neck begin to grind.

Chapter One Hundred and Forty-seven

I staggered as if I'd really been punched and had to catch the wall to steady myself. I stared down at the stack of notebooks.

Then I stiffened.

"Yoda!" I cried. "I think I know the password. Christ—it's Matthew. His son's name. Matthew, type that in."

"Cowboy, if you're wrong, then the system could lock me out."

"It's Matthew. I'm sure of it. He wrote it on every single book, over and over again."

"Okay. Putting that in now."

I heard him type.

Then I heard a sharp, scolding ding of a computer-generated bell.

"Ummmm, Cowboy . . . that wasn't it. I have a pop-up screen telling me that I have two tries left before it goes into permanent lockout."

"How about his birthday. Matthew's. We have it in our files."

"Mmmmmm, okay. I have it."

"Put it in."

He did.

We heard that same goddamn bell.

"Mmmm, one try left and then we're dead, Cowboy."

Chapter One Hundred and Forty-eight

Air Force One

In Flight

April 1, 4:04 P.M. Pacific Standard Time

It took Mr. Church five times longer than it should have to twist the wires together. He could smell how the electricity burned the skin of his fingers, but he couldn't feel it. He couldn't feel his fingers at all. Even applying pressure was done through observation rather than feel.

"It's done," he told Bug.

"Good, now see that little gray switch? Hit that."

Church took a breath and flipped the tiny switch.

Immediately, the control panel flashed with lights. At first they were all red, and then one by one they popped with a bright and promising green.

Church closed his eyes for one moment.

Then he punched in a five-digit code on the keypad.

There was a sharp metallic click as the locks disengaged and the cockpit door swung open.

"Thank you, Bug," he said quietly.

"Boss, I can see your hands. You're getting frostbite."

Church didn't comment as he rose shakily to his feet. His knees hurt, and his body was still with intense cold. He pushed open the cockpit door and stepped inside. The air from inside smelled of chemicals, and the members of the flight crew were toppled sideways in their chairs, unconscious. Solomon's hijack-defense system had released the tranquilizers. Church opened and closed the door like a fan to dissipate the drugs, wafting it out into the main cabin. He removed a handkerchief from his pocket and pressed it to his nose and mouth and then entered the cockpit.

As he expected, all of the flight controls were still locked by Solomon.

However, there were manual systems for cabin airflow, lights, and heat.

Church staggered forward and collapsed against the wall by the controls. His fingers were turning black now, and he had to fight with the dying nerves to make them work. In the end, he had to paw with the side of his hand, slapping sloppily at the switches.

Around him the cabin lights came on.

Air hissed from the vents.

Church looked out of the windows to see if the fighter escort was still there. And, if so, would they shoot Air Force One down to keep it from hitting its target?

The skies around the plane were clear. The jets were gone.

Where? Forced to crash by Solomon?

Or sent out to do more harm?

Church could feel the first tentative touch of heat rising from the floor, and he sank slowly to his knees and pressed his hands against the vent.

Air Force One, however, still hurtled through the skies toward New York City. The irony was not lost on Church that now he and the others would be alive, awake, and able to feel everything when the plane hit the World Trade Center.

Chapter One Hundred and Forty-nine

UC San Diego Medical Center
200 West Arbor Drive
San Diego, California
April 1, 4:06 P.M.

Boy sent wave after wave of Kingsmen down the hall toward the room where Nicodemus's prize waited. The pregnant woman. "The cow," the priest called her.

However, Boy knew what she really was to the old monster.

Not a victim. Not exactly. Victims were a dime a dozen. Everyone associated with the Seven Kings was ankle-deep in the blood of victims.

No, Circe O'Tree-Sanchez, daughter of Mr. Church, key to the destruction of the DMS, was a sacrifice.

Nicodemus had plans for Circe. And for all of the psychosis that Boy knew she kept penned in her own soul, the things Nicodemus had planned sickened Boy.

Still . . .

It would help the Gentleman. It would help her father.

When this was over, when the fires of this world had burned down, then she and Pharos would walk away from it all. They would find a quiet, beautiful place to live. A place where they could be family together forever.

Off to her right, she heard the great wolfhound howl, though if it was a cry of triumph or of pain, Boy did not know.

She held the thought of her father and her in the front of her mind. As a shield against the fundamental disgust of what Nicodemus was going to do. As armor to keep her moving through this fight.

Boy set her jaw, raised her gun, and fired at the Latina who had foolishly leaned out from behind cover.

Chapter One Hundred and Fifty

Tanglewood Island
Pierce County, Washington
April 1, 4:07 P.M.

They say that the most dangerous person is the one who has nothing to lose.

I believe that's true for some.

Not for me.

When Yoda told me that the second password attempt failed, I didn't lose hope. No. That's not how I operate.

When they try to steal away the last shreds of my hope, then I go cold. So cold.

The kind of hate that lives inside me isn't a flame. It's an emptiness. It's the deep arctic nothingness that once upon a time had been filled with my innocence. When Helen and I had been attacked, when they raped and brutalized her, when they stomped me and nearly killed me, they tore a hole in me. Innocence leaked out, and into that vacuum flowed an icy wind.

We couldn't access Davidovich's program. We couldn't upload the reset code.

There was now only one way to stop this thing.

At the source.

I stuffed the notebook into my shirt and turned toward the door. Somewhere in this building were the Seven Kings. Some or all of them.

And some or all of them would know how to stop their own program. Solomon and Regis, the kings of destructive programs, had their own masters.

Here in this building.

I drew my pistol, checked my magazine, and looked down into Ghost's dark brown eyes. I've trained him to obey hundreds of verbal and hand signals. He's a smart dog. He understands his job, and he understands me.

However, I didn't say anything to him. The killer in me looked at the killer in him, and the coldness flowed between us, more eloquent than any language.

I smiled at him. He snarled at me. It all meant the same thing.

Without a word I turned, and together we went hunting.

Killers with nothing left to lose.

Chapter One Hundred and Fifty-one

UC San Diego Medical Center
200 West Arbor Drive
San Diego, California
April 1, 4:07 P.M.

As he exerted his strength to crack Rudy's neck, the Kingsman bent and whispered in his ear.

"I know who you are," he sneered. "Your that doctor. The cripple. The husband of the sacrifice. You should be thankful you won't live to see what the Trickster will do to her. And to that worm inside of her."

Rudy Sanchez screamed.

It was a huge sound that tore itself from his chest as he raised his good leg and stamped down as hard as he could atop the killer's foot. Smashed with the heel, grinding. Just as Joe had taught him. He felt the metatarsals collapse, felt the hardness of the foot become like a crushed shell. The Kingsman screamed, and in the same instant Rudy's bad leg buckled. They fell together.

Rudy could feel his consciousness becoming separate from his body, and at first he did not know if this was death. Was this the separation of the spirit that is sometimes reported by those who are at the edge of the abyss? Do victims of murder get to watch their own slaughter?

However, his body was not collapsing, and it was not dying.

His body was fighting back.

He was still inside that body and yet standing apart from it, watching himself fight for his life.

Rudy twisted around and drove an elbow backward into the Kingsman's face, hitting a blocking arm, hitting a collarbone, hitting a cheekbone, then a nose, then a mouth. He felt punches hammering into his back. He felt his own ribs crack.

His arm kept hammering.

The Kingsman suddenly shoved him and turned to reach for Rudy's walking stick. He laughed as he snatched it up.

Rudy felt something hard beneath his thigh. He snatched at it, swung it blindly. Saw the flash of silver.

Saw the look of triumph in the Kingsman's eyes disintegrate as the point of his own bayonet punched through his chest. Rudy screamed as he drove the knife deep. The Kingsman screamed, too.

But the killer's scream did not last as long, and it was filled with a gurgling wetness.

Chapter One Hundred and Fifty-two

Tanglewood Island
Pierce County, Washington
April 1, 4:08 P.M.

I tapped my earbud and got Top on the line.

"Go for Sergeant Rock," he said.

"The plan's for shit," I said. "Kick the doors."

There was a brief pause, and I could imagine him wincing with the pain of it. Then he growled a single word. "Hooah."

"Nobody here's our friend," I told him. "The Kings are mine. Kill everyone else."

He said "Hooah" again. This time it held a different, darker meaning.

I ran on with Ghost ranging ahead. The corridor fed into a lobby, and as I entered I saw three people. A thin man behind a reception desk, a tall bearded man in an expensive suit, and a Blue Diamond guard standing just behind him.

Ghost shot forward and was in the air before I could say a word. The security guard shoved the bearded man and tried to pull his sidearm. Ghost hit the guard like a missile and drove him down into an overstuffed chair that tilted backward and fell. Screams and snarls filled the air.

I saw the guy behind the counter reaching down for something. Probably a gun or an alarm bell. I put two center mass, and he went down hard. That left the bearded guy in the suit. I figured him for midforties, fit, tanned, with Greek features and an air of importance.

Was he important enough to have some answers for me? It was his bad luck that I had to find out.

"Who are you?" he demanded, edging backward, reaching into a pocket of his expensive suit.

"I'm Joe fucking Ledger," I said, and blew off his left kneecap. His scream was enormous, and he fell into a twitching, thrashing heap.

I don't know why I announced my name. There was no way for me to think he'd know it. Maybe it was because this fight had become so personal. I didn't want these pricks to think this was all cops and robbers. This was people.

He stared up at me in abject horror.

And he mouthed my name.

"L-Ledger . . . oh my God."

Despite the pain, he managed to pull a little .25 Raven Arms pistol out of his pocket. Tried to point it at me.

I shot him through the elbow, and the gun thumped to the floor.

The man screamed.

And screamed.

I knelt in front of him and put the hot barrel of my gun into his crotch.

"Stop screaming," I said. I only had to say it once. His screams ended on a strangled note of new fear. He stared bug-eyed at me, his olive complexion turning a greasy gray-green.

"Who are you?" I asked. I did not ask nicely.

"F-f-fuck you."

"Wrong answer," I said, and shifted the pistol. I blew his other kneecap off. "Try again."

He screamed and screamed until I used my free hand to slap the screams from his mouth. Then he started crying. This time I placed the barrel against his temple while I picked his pocket, flipped open his wallet, and read the name on his driver's license.

"Michael Stefan Pharos, M.D.," I said.

Ah . . . now that was a name I'd heard before.

I leaned close. "Listen to me, shitheels, we both know this is over for you. Question is how you want it to end. Alive, with good doctors fixing your parts and lawyers trying to keep you alive for a long time. Or do I fuck you up right now so badly that your last hours are going to be a screaming hell? You think you're in pain now? Look into my eyes, Doctor Pharos. Look at me and tell me if you think there are any limits to what I am willing to do to you. If you know who I am, then you know you are in the wrong place with the wrong damn person."

His eyes were huge and filled with absolute understanding.

"You need to tell me right now," I said.

"T-tell you what?" he gasped.

"Reset codes. Tell me how to stop Regis and Solomon."

He wanted to lie. We both knew it. Even now, with three gunshot wounds, with shock setting in, with his blood pooling around him, he wanted to lie. But you can only lie when you think you have a chance to get away with it. The mistake he made was doing what I told him to do. He looked into my eyes.

He saw what I wanted him to see. The killer, crouched there, hungering to take him into that world of endless cold. He knew that death wouldn't be his ticket out any more than lies would.

"The . . . King . . ." he said. "The last . . . King."

I leaned so close that our faces touched. A kind of intimacy that only exists there at the edge of sanity.

"Where is he?" I asked.

Very softly.

Chapter One Hundred and Fifty-three

Tanglewood Island

Pierce County, Washington

April 1, 4:09 P.M.

Top Sims rose from behind a boulder and aimed his pistol at the Blue Diamond guard. He said nothing. He was not the kind of man who needed to mark an event of this kind with a comment. A joke. A smart-ass witticism. They did that in movies. Real soldiers just pulled the trigger.

He shot the guard in the back. One, two. The bullet punched in between the shoulder blades, shattering the spine, severing the spinal cord, bursting the heart. The man was dead before he knew he was in threat. Before the body could even react to the loss of central nerve conduction, Top turned and put another two rounds into the second guard, who was smoking a cigarette and looking out at the slanting rain.

Brian Botley saw Top's face as he fired those shots. And he saw no flicker of emotion.

Jesus, he thought.

Then he tightened up his own resolve and followed Top over the rails and onto the porch.

Bunny was somewhere on the far side of the inn.

He heard the big man's voice in his earbud.

"Green Giant to Sergeant Rock. Three down, no problems."

"Copy that. Two on the deck here."

"Ready to kick some doors and make some noise?"

Top smiled then. "Yes, I am, Farm Boy. Yes, I damn well am."

He turned to Brian. "You're up, Hotzone."

Brian nodded and held up his sequential detonator. "Fire in the hole."

He pressed the trigger, and the finger pier exploded in a fireball. The force lifted the speedboat out of the water, turned it over, and smashed it down on the rocks.

Three seconds later, the doors of the inn banged open, and Blue Diamond security operatives came pouring out, weapons ready.

Brian clicked the button again.

And again.

And again.

With each click, one of the charges planted beneath the decking exploded. Huge fingers of flame and smoke reached for the men of Blue Diamond and crushed them in fiery fists.

While the blasts were still rolling outward toward the mainland, Top, Bunny, and Brian began firing into the smoke.

Chapter One Hundred and Fifty-four

UC San Diego Medical Center

200 West Arbor Drive

San Diego, California

April 1, 4:09 P.M.

Lydia and Boy fired and dodged, fired and dodged as the fight raged around them. And in a freak moment of combat synchronicity, both guns locked empty at the same moment.

Instantly, Lydia was up and running straight at the Cambodian woman, even as they both fished for fresh magazines. Out of the corner of her eyes, Lydia saw something, though, that nearly stopped her midstride. Someone stood in the doorway to Circe's bedroom. Bloody, gasping, holding a chair as he swung and smashed at Kingsmen. The killers were not shooting. They clearly wanted to take Circe alive, and they had the numbers to overwhelm the sole defender.

Lydia slapped the magazine home and threw it even as she bellowed out a name.

"Toys!"

He looked up to see the pistol pinwheeling through the air toward him. One of the Kingsmen made a grab for it, but Toys kicked him in the groin and then snatched the weapon out of the air. That was all Lydia saw before Boy tackled her and drove her down onto the floor.

The fight was immediately intense.

The Cambodian woman was lethally quick and much stronger than she looked. The wiry kind of strength that is always surprising. Always dangerous.

Boy hit her in the face with a palm heel, kneed her in the crotch with a bony knee, head-butted her, and tried to spoon her eyes out with hard thumbnails. All of it in a tumbled tangle of two frenzied seconds.

Lydia knew she was in trouble.

This woman was so god-awful fast.

The kind of person who had the power of confidence because she'd probably won every important fight she'd been in.

The blows kept coming from every direction.

If she tried to defend herself, Lydia knew that the Cambodian woman would simply dismantle her. There are times when a defense is no defense at all.

So Lydia said, "Fuck it."

And attacked.

She slapped her palms together like a diver and thrust them up between the pummeling arms. Then she whipped her arms apart and grabbed Boy's biceps. At the same time she bucked her hips up to shove Boy forward and flopped sideways to roll along the inside of the woman's thigh. The leverage swatted Boy onto the floor, and Lydia immediately hip-checked into the woman's crotch. Lydia wore a full equipment belt, and even though Boy did not have testicles, everyone is vulnerable to a sudden, harsh assault in the groin.

"Like head-butts bitch?" snarled Lydia, and thrust her head between both sets of struggling arms, aiming to explode the woman's nose.

But Boy was too good a fighter to become helpless because of pain and surprise. She twisted her face and took the blow on the point of her cheekbone. It hurt, but it hurt Lydia more. She reeled back, and the world began whirling around her.

Boy tore her arms free and hit Lydia in the face and chest and throat.

And then Lydia was falling backward toward a great darkness that reached up to take her.

Chapter One Hundred and Fifty-five

Doctor Pharos told me where to find the King.

The last King.

The *only* King.

He told me that the King had the codes. And the password.

Toward the end, he begged to tell me everything he knew. Everything.

Here's the thing, though. I don't think he was so completely forthcoming because I'd shot him or because of the threats I made. Sure, that was a part of it. A big part.

No, there was something else.

When he spoke about the King, his face was twisted into a mask of horror and disgust. And hatred.

Something else, too. Hurt, maybe? Hard to tell, but my gut told me that was it. All of those emotions wrapped up into a tangle of contempt that allowed Pharos to betray this man.

Who Pharos was and what his part in all this was, I had no idea. That was for later, if there was a later.

For now, all that mattered is that he told me where I could find the last of the Seven Kings.

I stood up and stepped back from him. He was a broken doll on the floor. Blood still flowed from the bullet wounds in knees and elbow. I was tempted to end it for him there, to pop one last cap and say adios.

Didn't, though.

Instead, I left him there to bleed.

If he was still alive when I was done, maybe we'd explore a first-aid option.

Maybe.

"Come on," I said to Ghost, and we went running. The building shuddered with explosions, and outside I heard men shouting and guns firing. The soundtrack of war. Maybe the last movement in the symphony of the American apocalypse.

Too soon to tell.

Chapter One Hundred and Fifty-six

UC San Diego Medical Center

200 West Arbor Drive

San Diego, California

April 1, 4:11 P.M.

Alexander Chismer—Toys to everyone who knew him—was a monster, and he knew it. A murderer and enabler of murderers. A killer with so many deaths on his conscience that he could not name all of his victims.

Had the Kingsmen's bullets killed him, he would have accepted it as justice. Ironic, but just.

Had the shattered glass of the window cut him to pieces and left him bloodless on the floor, he would have thought it equally just.

Instead, he was alive.

Behind him, Circe O'Tree-Sanchez lay in her bed. Junie Flynn knelt next to her. Unarmed, lacerated, bleeding, terrified.

In front of him, a knot of Kingsmen rushed forward to take Circe. Behind them stood the impossible figure of Father Nicodemus. Toys had heard enough stories to know what kinds of things the priest would want to do with the woman and her child.

Death was the kindest gift Nicodemus ever bestowed on his victims. Being alive and in his custody was far, far worse.

Toys knew all of this.

Just as he knew that he was the worst kind of person to stand between Nicodemus and his prey. Hugo said that a valiant soul could do it, but he was probably joking.

Toys's soul was as sullied and black as it was possible for a human soul to be.

When Lydia threw the gun, he considered letting it pass over his head. He considered grabbing it and giving it to Junie.

He even considered grabbing it and turning it on the two women. Killing them rather than letting them discover how much worse being alive could be.

He watched his hand rise toward the gun, not sure if he would slap it away or catch it. The world seemed to have slowed, to become unreal.

The plastic grips of the pistol handle smacked into his palm. Real and immediate. The weight of it pushed his hand down.

The Kingsmen came at him.

Nicodemus laughed aloud with a sound like screaming cats.

And then there was the thunder of gunfire. The glitter of a spent cartridge flying up and away out of sight. The thud of the handle punching back into his palm. The shiver of shock running up his arm.

He saw the face of a Kingsman break apart three feet in front of him.

Another bang. A chest burst open and red flowers filled the air.

Toys did not know how many bullets were in that gun. He did not consciously aim and fire. But his finger tightened and his arm shifted, and with every shot a Kingsman died.

Every.

Single.

Shot.

Chapter One Hundred and Fifty-seven

Tanglewood Island

Pierce County, Washington

April 1, 4:13 P.M.

I was expecting a long elevator ride to a hidden dungeon far below the inn. I was expecting an airlock or some kind of high-tech security wizardry to bar my way.

Instead, when I followed Pharos's directions I found a big set of wooden doors.

The sons of bitches weren't even locked.

I turned the handle, took a breath, kicked the door, and leaped into the room.

Big room. Wall covered with TV monitors. Hospital bed in the center of the room. Couple of chairs. Five people.

Two of the Blue Diamond thugs right inside the door.

A pair of guys who looked like grad students.

And a wreck of a man in a hospital bed.

On the TV screens I could see bridges burning. I could see ships sinking.

440 | Jonathan Maberry

Columns of smoke rising from the hearts of cities. Massive multicar pile-ups on highways. Planes falling from the skies.

I saw what the King saw.

Regis and Solomon at work.

When I entered the room, the man in the bed was watching the screens and smiling.

I knew immediately that he was the last of the Seven Kings.

A withered, broken scrap of a man.

This was what the Seven Kings had become? A dying man and his stooges.

I raised my gun and pointed it at the King.

"Nobody fucking move!"

Everyone fucking moved.

Chapter One Hundred and Fifty-eight

UC San Diego Medical Center

200 West Arbor Drive

San Diego, California

April 1, 4:13 P.M.

Lydia hit the floor hard. She could barely see through the bursting white lights in her eyes. She saw Boy raise a foot to stamp and forced herself to turn. The kick clipped her hip but struck only the floor. Lydia rolled into the leg as hard as she could and sent the Cambodian flying face-forward.

The woman caught herself with a skillful front fall and then stabbed out with a counterkick to Lydia, catching her midthigh. Lydia rolled away and got to toes and fingertips and started to rise, but it was a fake; the Cambodian jumped high to intercept, and Lydia flattened and dove low, catching her around the thighs and bearing her down. It made the woman sit down hard on her tailbone. The shock snapped the woman's teeth together and dimmed the lights in her eyes.

It was Lydia's doorway back into the world. She fell on her side and chop-kicked the woman in the face, knocking her onto her back. This time the woman fell badly, rapping her head on the ground. Lydia reached over and clawed her way atop the Cambodian. She shimmied forward and dropped her knees onto the woman's biceps, trapping both arms.

Lydia could have wasted time pummeling her. She could have broken her own hands by hammering at the woman's face with her fists. But Lydia wasn't stupid. That kind of fighting is for ring competition, where there are rules. Instead, Lydia grabbed the woman's ears, used them to pick her head up and them slam it back down. Then she slapped her left palm flat over Boy's face, drew back her right hand, folded it into a half fist, and punched down with her secondary knuckles. Once, twice. A third time.

With each blow, the shape of Boy's throat changed.

After the last punch, there was no useful shape left to it.

"Besa mi culo, puto," she snarled and then spat into Boy's face.

Gasping, nearly spent, Lydia toppled off of the thrashing, dying woman.

Immediately, something brushed her face, and she swung a punch, but her knuckles brushed something soft, and a dark blur passed above her. She gaped at it.

Banshee. Covered in blood, foam flecking her muzzle, racing for a fresh kill.

Lydia turned to see that behind the hound lay a dozen bodies that had been torn to red ruin.

Chapter One Hundred and Fifty-nine

Tanglewood Island

Pierce County, Washington

April 1, 4:15 P.M.

The two Blue Diamond guys were the closest. They tried rushing me while going for their guns at the same time. I shot one, but the other one body-blocked the guy I shot, so they collided into me. We all hit the edge of the doorway. Ghost went after the second security thug, got his titanium teeth locked into the guy's wrist, and pulled him down for some fun and games on the floor.

That left the grad students. I wasn't sure what or who they were. I was hoping they were computer nerds or part of the tech team. But from the enthusiastic way they rushed me, I knew that wasn't it.

The guard I'd shot had a death grip on my gun arm, and as he fell his two-hundred-plus pounds tore the Sig Sauer from my hand. I had to let it go or fall with him. I let it go and danced sideways as the first of the grad students slashed at me with a double-edge British commando dagger that he produced from God knows where. The thing was razor-sharp and cut through the top shoulder strap of my Kevlar.

I backpedaled and then jumped back as he darted in, quick as a cat, with a second and third slash. The little bastard was good. In and out.

The other kid began circling to my right, and as he did so he snapped his arms toward the floor, releasing a pair of weapons that fell right into his hand. Not knives. Scalpels.

I don't like knives at the best of times, but there is something appallingly frightening about scalpels. They glide through whatever they cut, and in the hands of an expert they are dreadful. From the way he moved, I could tell he was an expert with them. His weight was on the balls of his feet, knees bent and springy, elbows bent and tucked close to protect his body, blades up to protect his face and throat. He moved like a dancer, gliding across the floor.

I began moving with him, retreating in a broad circle so that I moved to Surgeon's left and away from Boy Commando. They followed and immediately began adjusting to my retreat.

In combat, the worst thing you can do when fighting multiple opponents is to retreat in a straight line because it allows them to get closer to each other while creating an aggressive wall in front of you. Circling helps, but if they know that trick and are used to working together, they can make a lot of small, quick shifts to cut you off.

"That's Ledger," yelled the man in the bed. He had an English accent, clipped and cold. "Be careful."

The grad students only smiled. Their confidence was disheartening.

Ghost was having his own time of it. The Blue Diamond guy was tough, and he had clearly been trained in how to fight a dog. Maybe the King had all of his best guys here.

I would much rather have had to deal with the Marx Brothers or a couple of the Stooges.

Suddenly another explosion shook the room. Dust puffed down from the ceiling. Now it was my turn to smile.

"Hear that, your highness?" I said, continuing to circle. "That's my team breaking this place apart."

"Who cares?" he said. "Let them come."

Surgeon darted into me with a one-two lunge that was so goddamn fast that, even though I spun out of the way, I trailed blood from a pair of burning cuts on my arm. No idea how deep they were. Blood welled through the slits in my sleeve.

He lunged again, but as I shifted to avoid him, Boy Commando made his move. He whipped his hand high, turned it into a fake, checked and slashed a vertical line down that would have severed the femoral artery in my leg if he'd connected. He missed by maybe a quarter inch.

Then Surgeon was in again, using my evasion as his opening in exactly the way an expert would. He used a right-left-right jab combination and then went for the long reach to try and take me across the eyes. I couldn't counterslash him, but I used my left to punch upward into his arm. I caught him wrong—hitting elbow instead of triceps, but it knocked his arm high. It was a tiny window, but I took it and threw myself at him, hitting the exposed rib cage with my shoulder and barrel-slamming him ten feet across the room. He hit the edge of the bed and cried out in pain as the steel rail punched him in the hip.

I could hear Boy Commando rushing up behind me, so I grabbed Surgeon and spun him. I felt something bite me in the side and knew it was one of the scalpels. Pain exploded beneath the right side of my rib cage.

But Surgeon screamed.

We were face-to-face at the end of my spin, and when I saw the horror in his eyes, I knew that my timing had been good.

Good for me.

Totally sucked for him.

He was pressed all the way back against Boy Commando, and over his shoulder I could see his partner's eyes bug wide as he realized what had just happened.

The double-edged British fighting knife is excellent for slashing, but it also makes one hell of a hole on a straight thrust. Boy Commando had tried to drill me in the kidney, but instead his blade was buried to the hilt in the Surgeon's back.

My knife was free.

I let go of Surgeon, reached over his shoulder, grabbed the back of Boy Commando's head with my left, and used my right to bury my knife into his left eye socket. I corkscrewed half a turn and tore it out, then buried it again, this time in the center of his throat.

They collapsed together, locked in a terminal embrace that seemed somehow intimate. As they dropped away from me, I felt something jerk at my side and looked down to see blood trailing from the scalpel that was still clutched in Surgeon's dying hand.

That's when the pain hit me.

Enormous pain.

He'd gotten me good. Beneath the ribs. Maybe in the liver.

I was bleeding inside and out, and I knew it.

The clock was ticking.

Ticking.

I wheeled around to see what was happening with Ghost.

Ghost stood panting by the wall. There were parts of things around him that probably added up to one Blue Diamond guard.

Ghost looked past me to the man on the bed. He snarled with all the primitive ferocity of a wolf. With all the hatred of a member of my tribe.

I leaned on the bed frame and looked into the face of the man who had orchestrated so much harm. The face I looked into showed no fear. Only disappointment at the failure of his men to kill me. If there was compassion for their deaths or their suffering, none of it showed on this man's face.

He was hideous.

His face had been melted away by some terrible blaze. He had no legs and only one arm. One eye was a boiled egg white in his skull; the other was filled with a kind of calm hatred that I'd never seen before. As if he had no fear of whatever I might say or do. Or threaten.

His mangled lips wore a contemptuous smile.

"Somehow," he said, "I knew it would be you. Joe Ledger. Thuggish captain of Echo Team."

"I like it," I said, hissing a little with the pain. "I can put that on my business card."

"Please do. Truth in advertising."

"You know why I'm here," I said. "Mind if we skip the banter section of this and go right to the point where you take it as read that I own your ass and you give me what I want?"

"Let's not."

"Dude," I said, "not sure if you've taken inventory yet, but the Kings are dead; your men are dead or dying."

As if to emphasize my point, there was a rattle of gunfire from down the hall. A man screamed. Pretty sure it wasn't one of Echo Team.

"I don't give a fuck about them," said the burned man. "And I don't give much of a fuck about you, Ledger. You've invaded the island fortress of the mad scientist. Bravo. You've killed the villains and all the supporting characters. Now you are going to threaten to kill me. Or torture me."

"I'm open to it. 'Specially the last part."

"To what end?"

"Reset codes."

"Ah. And would you like the password to access Davidovich's Web site? That way, you can save the world just like that." He snapped the fingers of his good hand.

"That would be nice. It would save you a lot of discomfort."

He smiled at me. "No," he said. "Of course . . . no. There's nothing you can do to me that you haven't already done. You've ruined my life over and over again. Well, here's the kicker, Ledger—I'm already dying. I have enough diseases and conditions firing all at once that I'll be dead inside a week. And if you torture me, all you'll do is hasten the inevitable. You see, you have no leverage. I get to watch you fail, and I get to go to my grave knowing that I destroyed you and that I destroyed this country."

"Why?" I asked. "You've got a real hard-on for me. Who am I to you? What the fuck have I ever done to make you this pissed off? I mean . . . if you want me to suffer, shouldn't I know that much?"

He cocked his head to one side.

"Seriously?" he said. "Even now, you don't recognize me?"

"Nope. You look like a can of fried SPAM. Somebody cooked you over a nice slow flame. Makes it hard to figure out who the hell you are."

He flinched. Ever so slightly at that.

"Hugo said that you were tough but stupid."

And I think that's when it all went *click*. A lot of little clues, a lot of floating pieces. It all fell into place right there. He watched my face, and from the delighted smile that he wore, I could tell that he knew that I had it. That I finally recognized him.

You see . . . we'd never actually met. He was a photo in a case file, a body in a piece of video. And he was supposed to be dead.

I had to take a breath, because there was no air in my lungs to speak his name.

But I said it.

"Jesus Christ," I said. "You're . . . *Sebastian Gault*."

Chapter One Hundred and Sixty

UC San Diego Medical Center

200 West Arbor Drive

San Diego, California

April 1, 4:15 P.M.

The elevator doors opened again, and Rudy staggered out.

There were more bodies scattered around, but the fighting still raged. Montana Parker had a collapsible metal rod in her hand and was smashing at a Kingsman with a knife. Sam Imura sat on the floor with his hands pressed to his stomach and blood trickling from his mouth and nose. Lydia Ruiz stood above him, firing an AK-47 that had bloodstains on it.

But across the hall was the worst of it.

Toys stood in the doorway to Circe's room battering at Kingsmen with an empty gun. Five feet away, the massive wolfhound, Banshee, was tearing at their throats and groins.

Twenty feet way, closer to Rudy than to Circe's room, stood Nicodemus. He was looking the other way, yelling at his men, directing the relentless attack. In fact, for the moment, no one was looking at Rudy. Everywhere he looked, people—Kingsmen, police, Homeland agents, the last few members of Echo Team, even Toys—were trapped inside their own fragments of this drama. A sea of violence separated Rudy from his wife and their unborn child.

Rudy bent and picked up a gun. It was another AK-47, dropped by a dead Kingsman. Rudy had no idea if it was loaded, or how to check that.

He simply hooked his cane in the crook of his arm, raised the gun, pointed it at Nicodemus, and opened fire.

The gun bucked heavily in his hands, and fire burst from the barrel, sending a dozen rounds into the crowd around the priest. Kingsmen spun like dancers, collapsed like dolls.

And then the bolt locked back, the magazine spent.

Nicodemus turned toward him. He extended his hand and pointed a withered finger at him.

"You," he said. "I'm so glad to see you."

Rudy let the gun clatter to the bloodstained floor as the priest walked slowly toward him.

The battle raged around them, but the priest and the doctor stood facing each other across five feet of space. The wild glee of battle faded from Nicodemus's face, and for a moment he looked like an ordinary man.

"Why are you doing this?" asked Rudy.

"Even a man as smart as you pretend to be," said the priest, "would never understand."

"Try me."

"No, sir, I do not think I will. I would much rather have you wonder about it. There are few things more entertaining than letting the worm of doubt have its way with someone."

"No," said Rudy, taking a step forward. His limp was very bad and he swayed. That seemed to amuse Nicodemus. "Why us? Why my wife? What could she have possibly done to offend you?"

"Her?" Nicodemus laughed. "I couldn't care less about that slut. Or you. Or the wriggling grub in her belly. Not you as people. I care less about you than dog shit on my shoe. Lordy-lord, how arrogant you must be to think such thoughts."

Rudy gripped his stick like a club. "They why, damn it? She is helpless. Our baby is innocent . . . "

"And nothing hurts him more than to see the innocent suffer."

" 'Him'? Who . . . ?" Rudy's voice trailed away.

Nicodemus watched him like a cat. "Ah, I can see that you're getting it now. At least the tiniest part of it."

"This is about Church?"

Nicodemus snorted at that name. "Church. Oh, he does love his little jokes, doesn't he? The names he picks for himself. Church. The Deacon. Sexton and Pope, Eldritch and Saint Germaine. Magus and Prospero. How many others?" He took a step toward Rudy, and now they were close enough to touch. "Ask him your question, doctor. Ask him why I will burn worlds to have my revenge on him. Ask, but don't expect an answer. He'll never hear you over the screams of all those who have died for him. All those who have died because of him."

"You're insane. And you're not making sense."

"Do you think not, doctor? Your Mr. Church is the cause of more hurt and misery than you can possibly imagine. Why, I suspect it would burn you to know who and what he is. Yes, sir, it would pure burn the heart right out of you. And to know that you sleep with his daughter. That your child carries *his* seed. Good lordy-lordy-lord. And you think *I'm* a monster."

Between clenched teeth, Rudy said, "No, I think you're a liar."

He slashed at Nicodemus with the hawthorn cane.

Not with the shaft.

This time, he used all of his strength, all of his hurt and rage and terror, to swing the carved silver handle at the priest's face.

Chapter One Hundred and Sixty-one

Tanglewood Island
Pierce County, Washington
April 1, 4:17 P.M.

"Yes," said the burned man. "Sebastian Gault. Would you like to gloat now?"

I stared at him.

This man was the reason that I joined the DMS. He paid to have the *seif al din* pathogen created. He very nearly caused an outbreak that, according to every statistical model, would have ended the world.

Ended.

We all thought he died when the laboratory of his lover, Amirah, the scientist who actually created the plague for him, was destroyed during a geothermal explosion. We later learned that Toys saved him, dragged his burned body through a tunnel and out onto the sands in Afghanistan.

Months later, after extensive plastic surgery and recuperation, Gault and Toys were brought into the Seven Kings by Hugo Vox. There, Gault became their King of Plagues, and he created several terrible bioweapons for them, including a version of airborne quick-onset Ebola. That was the cornerstone of the Kings' Ten Plagues Initiative.

Once more the world trembled on the very edge of a global pandemic.

Vox told Toys that he had blown Gault and the Goddess—Vox's treacherous mother—to bits with a bomb he'd planted aboard her yacht. The Coast Guard only ever found small fragments of the yacht in the Saint Lawrence River. Gault was once more presumed—hoped, wished—dead.

And now here he was again. The sole surviving King. No longer just the King of Plagues, but the only reigning member left.

Crippled and burned, but still vastly powerful.

Still cruel. Still vindictive.

And, with the protection of certain death a short step behind him, he held all the cards.

He knew it, too.

He watched my face, watched me work it out, and he laughed.

I shook my head. "So all of this—the Regis and Solomon programs, the hijacked drones, the attacks on the ballpark and the bridge—"

"And Air Force One," he said. "Let's not forget about that."

"No, let's not. All of this is what? Revenge?"

He held his hand wide to indicate what was left of him. "What else do I have?" he asked. "What else have you left me?"

"Whoa, dickhead, *we* didn't actually do this to you." I paused, wheezing. My side was bleeding heavily, and I tore open a package of gauze and pressed it against the wound. It hurt like a son of a bitch. There was surgical tape on a side table, and I wound it around my waist to hold the bandage in place. I was going to need more than that. Maybe surgery. Maybe a lot of surgery. The room was spinning. "As I recall," I continued, "it was *you* who blew up Amirah's lab."

"Of course. To stop her destroying the world."

"With your fucking doomsday weapon."

He shook his head. "That was designed as a threat and you know it. Don't pretend to be even stupider than you are. I wanted to be rich and to live rich, and I couldn't very well do that in a dead world. I saved the world."

"Yeah, good try. If you build a doomsday weapon, you don't get points for not using it."

He shrugged. "Oh, fair enough."

"And as for the boat thing. Hugo Vox blew up the damn boat. We didn't."

"He was on the run from you and cleaning up loose ends."

"Still doesn't put it on our tab."

Another shrug.

"Then who's the revenge against?" I asked.

His eye glittered with hatred. "For everyone who is going to be alive tomorrow and next week and next year."

"Wow. You're doing this because you got yourself all fucked up so everyone else has to pay?"

"Small minds can make anything sound petty."

"If there's a better explanation, then tell me. Historians will want to know, and that is actually not a smart-ass comment. We both know you've made your mark. No one is ever going to forget this week. No one. And Sebastian Gault will be remembered forever. Bravo for you. You'll be universally hated, but you'll be remembered."

"One takes the immortality that's afforded them."

"I suppose."

I began walking around the bed. I was careful to make it look casual, but my feet were getting wobbly. "Let me see if I get this straight, though. You have the codes to reset Regis and Solomon, yes?"

"Of course. I'd be an idiot not to have that information."

"And you know that Davidovich built a Web site that allowed him to control those programs."

"Yes." He watched me as I paced. It was difficult for him to turn enough to see me. "We knew everything that he was doing."

"Then you have the password for that Web site, right?"

"I do."

I passed above the headboard and came down the far side of the bed. His head swiveled around to watch me again.

"Is there anything I can say or do that would encourage you to give that password to me?"

He smiled. "Nothing comes to mind."

"If you've read my file, you know I can play rough."

He held up a withered hand so I could see his burned flesh. "Really? Rougher than this? They pulled me from the sea while I was covered in burning oil. I felt my own skin melt. There's nothing worse than that, Ledger. Go get your thumb screws if you think it'll help, but I've already been through hell."

I kept circling. As I completed one circuit, I saw that I was leaving a trail of bloody drops.

"I could just kill you," I said. "Deny you the chance of seeing the end. Air Force One hasn't crossed into New York airspace. Not the metropolitan area, at least."

"That would be disappointing," conceded Gault. "But I would die knowing that it was inevitable. Stop fucking circling like that. It's childish."

I stopped at the foot of the bed. "And there is absolutely nothing I can say or do? Nothing? Not one thing?"

"No," he said with finality.

I nodded thoughtfully. The sound of gunfire was dying away. None of the recent shots came from AK-47s. Top and the others were cleaning things up. Ghost started to come over, but I waved him off. "Family," I told him. "Find family."

He paused, then turned and ran out of the room. Looking for any of my guys who were still alive. Once he was gone, I tore open a Velcro flap and dug something out of my pocket, holding it out for him to see. It was a small cylinder about two inches long, set with a tight screw top.

"What's that?" he asked.

"Let's find out." I unscrewed the top and shook the contents out into my palm. There were six of them. I leaned over the steel foot rail and showed them to him so he would understand.

Gault said nothing, but there was doubt in his eye.

I picked up one of the objects. It was wooden and had a red bulb at one end with a dot of white at the tip.

"Wooden kitchen match. My grandpa used to call this kind a Lucifer match. Know why? 'Cause it'll light anywhere. Has its own sulfur."

I scraped the match along the steel rail.

Nothing happened, of course—the metal was too smooth. But for a moment Sebastian Gault flinched. Fear bloomed in his eye, and he recoiled as far as the mattress would allow.

I held up the unlit tip and gave it a comical frown. "Oops. No friction. My bad. Almost anywhere."

"What the hell are you doing?"

I removed my pistol from its shoulder holster and scraped the match along the crosshatched grip. It ignited at once. Gault flinched again.

"Stop mucking about," he cried. "You're wasting your time. I won't tell you."

"I know," I said. "But I guess I'm like you. Since I can't have what I want, I might as well sit and watch my enemies burn."

I bent and held the match to the sheet.

He screamed and tried to kick hard enough to prevent the cloth from catching. Might have worked if he had legs.

"Stop it, you fucking maniac."

I straightened and blew out the match, leaving only a black scorch on the sheet.

"Five more matches," I said. "I have those five, and I have a gun."

He stared at me.

"Maybe you don't know," I said, "but Amirah didn't die in that blast. She escaped, too. Or, at least the thing she'd become had escaped. I went hunting for her in the Afghan mountains. I found her. She was a mess. Rotting away. Being tortured by soldiers. It was horrible. I offered her a choice. The existence she had or a quick trip to paradise and peace."

He said nothing, but his lips parted.

I showed him the matches in one hand, the gun in the other. "I'm going to offer you the same choice. You can give me that password, and I put a nice, quick bullet into what's left of your head. I'm a very good shot. You'd never feel it." I leaned forward again. "Or I'll *burn* you. I have matches, and I have time. Tell me, Sebastian, do you want to burn? Again? Is that how you want this all to end? Do you want to bet that you have enough healthy nerve endings left to feel every inch of flames as they crawl over you? And don't think I'll let that happen fast. Fuck no. You're a monster, and you're going to kill people I care about. I'd want it to last."

A small whimpering sound came out of his mouth. A tear, bloody and viscous, broke from the corner of his eye.

"Now you tell me," I said in a voice that came from that cold, dark place, "this or paradise?"

I lit another match.

"Give me the password."

Sebastian Gault screamed.

"Matthew!" he shrieked. "It's Matthew."

I held the match closer to the sheet. "It's not Matthew. We tried Matthew."

"No . . . no! It's Matthew. In binary code. Type it in. The ones and zeros that make up the boy's name. Type it in just like that."

I straightened and tapped my earbud. "Cowboy to Yoda, do you copy?"

"Right, mmmm, here, Cowboy. We can't figure out—"

"It's the boy's name. Matthew. Type in the binary code for his name. That's the password."

"Are you sure? If this doesn't work—"

"Do it!"

I shook the match to extinguish it. Gault lay there, weeping, panting, hating himself and me with equal intensity. I heard Yoda's fingers hitting the keys.

Then nothing.

Nothing.

No bell.

"It worked," he cried. "We're in."

"Start uploading the reset codes. Do it now!" I bellowed. But I don't think Yoda was even listening to me.

I sagged back and collapsed into the leather guest chair. The room was filled with the dead and dying. I figured I was one of the latter.

"You're a bastard," said Sebastian Gault.

I holstered my pistol. He frowned.

"Aren't you going to kill me? Isn't that what you said? This or paradise?"

"That's what I said."

"Then do it, you sick fuck. Take your shot. End this."

I looked at the four remaining matches.

After a moment, I got slowly, wearily to my feet. The pain in my side was a white-hot howling thing. I went to the foot of the bed again and leaned on it. Sweat was running down my face. Even with the bandage, I was losing way too much blood. I still held the matches.

"Well, damn you," he said, "go on! *Do* it. If you want to send me to bloody paradise or bloody hell, then fucking do it."

"Yeah," I said. "I think I will."

I took a match. Popped it alight with my thumbnail. Held it to the others. They all flared.

"What the hell are you—?"

I dropped the matches onto his sheet.

One at a time.

In different spots.

He began screaming, thrashing, wailing.

I staggered over to the guest chair, pushed it ten feet back, and lowered myself into it.

Gault screamed so loud, I thought it would crack open the world.

I sat and watched.

The fire caught fast, spread too quickly for him to escape. The air shimmered, plumed outward, touching me, touching my skin. I know that it was hot.

So hot.

Hot as hell.

But to me, all I felt was a deep and endless cold.

Chapter One Hundred and Sixty-two

Air Force One

In Flight

April 1, 4:19 P.M. Pacific Standard Time

"Church," said Linden Brierly. "Good Christ, *Church!*"

Church heard the voice, but it seemed so far away.

So far.

He knew that he must have collapsed.

The cold.

The lingering chemicals in the cockpit.

He knew. He understood.

But there was nothing he could do about it. The darkness was so big. Too big.

All of his life, he had stood against that darkness, and now it had come for him. Vast, shapeless. And so powerful.

So powerful.

As the darkness took him, Church spoke a single word. A name.

"Circe . . . "

And then he was gone.

Chapter One Hundred and Sixty-three

UC San Diego Medical Center

200 West Arbor Drive

San Diego, California

April 1, 4:20 P.M.

Rudy Sanchez stood there, holding the walking stick in his hands. The silver handle was gone, snapped off midway down the shaft.

It lay on the floor. Half melted. The wood that was still attached to it was charred.

Behind him, men were running.

Kingsmen fleeing. Screaming. Mad with terror.

Soldiers with guns. Police with guns.

Lydia and Montana, the only two members of Echo Team left on their feet, fired at them. Everywhere, from all of the fire towers, poured uniformed men in riot gear.

So many guns.

So many screams.

Rudy looked down at the twisted figure on the floor. Broken, bleeding. Dressed in black rags. Smoke curled upward from hollow eye sockets in a face that was nothing but white bone.

It made no sense.

Because nothing made sense.

The massive hound, Banshee, stood amid the carnage, sides heaving, eyes filled with magic. Mouth dripping red, steam rising from her coat. The dog looked at him for a long, long time. Then threw back her head and howled.

The cry echoed through the halls and slowly, slowly faded into silence.

"Rudy!"

A voice cut through the fog and damage in his head. It was as crisp, as clear, as a vesper bell. It hit him with the force of cold water on burning skin. He turned, stared.

"Rudy," she said. She spoke his name. Rudy.

He took a single staggering step toward her, and his bad leg buckled. He fell. Onto the bloody linoleum.

"Rudy. Oh god . . . Rudy!"

Because he could not run to her, Circe O'Tree-Sanchez ran to him.

Junie Flynn held one arm to steady her. Toys held the other. Both of them were painted in blood. Splinters of glass glittered like diamonds in their skin.

They crossed the battlefield, where only the dead lay. He got to his knees as she came to him, and he wrapped his arms around her and pressed his face to the side of her swollen belly. He kissed her, and then he used her hands and Junie's to pull himself up. He kissed her belly. He kissed her over her heart. Then he took her face in his hands and kissed her lips.

"Oh God," he said, kissing her lips, her cheeks, her eyes, her hair. "Oh dear God . . . it's over."

Circe gasped.

And Toys said, "It's not quite over, mate. I think her water just broke."

Chapter One Hundred and Sixty-four

Tanglewood Island
Pierce County, Washington
April 1, 4:25 P.M.

It was Brian who found me. He followed a barking, blood-spattered dog and found me on the floor beside the chair. Between the seat I'd slid out of and a bed on which a twisted thing was wreathed in fire and slowly turning to blackened ash.

"He's in here!" he yelled. "Christ! We need a medevac."

I opened my eyes and saw shapes over me, around me. The hulking, improbable shape of Bunny. The face of Top, lined with concern. Ghost's big nose.

Brian looked past me to the dead thing on the bed. "What the hell is that?"

I told them. I mumbled a name.

But they all thought I was delirious.

That was fine. Maybe I was.

Maybe none of this happened.

I closed my eyes and let it all go away.

Epilogue

1.

The world didn't burn down.

Not completely.

But the country will never be the same.

The Golden Gate Bridge has become a symbol of how impervious we're not. It's the new Twin Towers, equally potent, terribly painful.

Maybe there's a philosophical or political discussion to be had about whether we dropped our guard in the years following 9/11, that we became complacent. That we forgot the lesson the planes taught us on that September morning.

I don't know.

My part of the world never forgot. The people I work with never forgot. We never lost a step getting to first base. We were ready; we were fighting that fight alongside soldiers, cops, and spies. And ordinary citizens.

Maybe it was just that the Seven Kings—or whatever the hell you want to call what that organization had become—had wanted us to doubt ourselves. Probably. Their whole agenda, built on misdirection, misinformation, and screwing with minds, was the kind of thing they did so damn well.

Eleven warships had been destroyed. Sixty-three aircraft. Ninety-one tanks.

The death toll kept rising.

Rising.

Rising.

But we all knew that it was going to slow, to stop.

The password was real. It was "Matthew" in binary.

01001101 01100001 01110100 01110100 01101000 01100101 01110111.

Crazy, right?

It stopped Regis. It stopped Solomon. It ended the terror.

The world didn't burn.

But damn if we didn't nearly choke on the smoke.

2.

Over the next few days, I spent way too much time in hospitals.

My knife wound was tricky, but it was blood loss more than damage that nearly took me. They pumped me full of high-test, and the trauma surgeon more or less told me to stop whining about what amounted to a sissy injury. Nice guy.

Everyone else I know seemed to be in worse trouble.

Aunt Sallie lost one kidney, but she would live. The doctors were trying to tell her that she should retire. I hoped the doctors had good health coverage of their own.

Sam Imura took a bullet in the stomach and lost four inches of his large intestine. He was expected to recover. His parents flew out from California and brought Sam's infant brother, Tommy. They stayed with him until he was released.

Toys had 119 stitches.

I sat vigil with Ghost while surgeons picked thirty-one glass splinters out of the woman I loved. Junie's back looks like it's covered in red lace. I tried to explain to her that I thought the scars would be sexy. She doesn't believe me. She should. Scars to me were proof of life. Or a life lived. She was not a killer, not like me; but Junie was born in the storm lands. She is a warrior, too.

I love that woman with all my heart. More every day. More than I thought was possible.

"You ever planning to put a ring on that?" Top asked while Junie was in surgery. He expected me to make a snappy comeback. I didn't. He stared at me for a while, and then he went off to find us some coffee.

He was smiling.

3.

I walked—very carefully, out of respect for my stitches—with Church down the long hallway of the hospital. Not the same floor, of course. That was an ongoing crime scene, and it was a charnel house. No, we were two floors up and in another wing, one untouched by the violence of that day. Church still wore cotton gloves over the damaged skin of his hands. The frostbite had been bad. One of the doctors had wanted to amputate most of his fingers. Another doctor, a top specialist from Switzerland, thought they could be saved. They were using radical treatments. It was a work in progress.

Church had to be in great pain, but he wouldn't show it to me. I've wondered many times before if his stoicism is a sign of great power and therefore something to be admired or a sign of a tragic disconnect from a normal life. I felt sorry for him, but that's something I would never show to him.

I also respected him. Maybe even loved him like a second father.

Yeah, that's another conversation we'd never have.

Church had me go over what happened on Tanglewood Island. I told him as much as I cared to share. Maybe he guessed the rest. Our people managed to save the life of Doctor Michael Pharos, and he was medevac'd to a hospital in Seattle. And then he vanished into the big, dark system of the DMS. It is unlikely he will ever see the light of day again.

"Doctor Pharos is doing his best to be useful," said Church. "He has been remarkably forthcoming."

"Lucky for him."

"No," said Church, "not really."

Down the hall, a figure sat on a chair outside a patient's room. She stood as we approached. Tall, slender as a knife blade, beautiful. Alien.

"Hello, Joseph," she said.

"Hello, Violin."

She craned her head forward to kiss Mr. Church's cheek. Then she took his gloved hands and kissed them. He spoke to her very briefly in the ancient language used by Arklight. They don't know that I've picked up some words and phrases. Languages have always been easy for me. I caught two words that I probably misheard, and certainly misinterpreted. I thought Mr. Church said, " . . . my daughter."

But I'm sure I'm wrong.

Maybe Church was referring to Circe. Thanking Violin for helping protect her. Sure, that was probably it.

Even so, there was a strange look in her eye. And in his.

"Thanks for bringing that dog," I said. "I heard stories about what she did."

Violin nodded. "Still, I wish I'd been there when they attacked. I'm sorry."

"No need to be. Soldiers can't be on every battlefield."

She nodded and stepped back. Church and I entered the patient's room.

The bed was empty, and the patient was getting dressed with great care and slowness. Much of his body was wrapped in bandages and surgical dressings. When he heard us enter, he turned, and I could see that his face was bruised and lacerated. He had stitches in his lip, through his eyebrow, and across the bridge of his nose. Only his eyes were untouched, and they were filled with a bleak acceptance, as if such physical injury was right and proper and in no way unjust.

"I did not hear that you'd been discharged," said Church.

Toys tried not to wince as he pulled on a lemon-colored dress shirt. "They've already done a patch job. There's nothing else they can do for me here that I can't do for myself at home."

I expected Church to object, but he merely nodded. "Brick will drive you."

"No need. I called a cab."

"Brick will drive you," repeated Church, and Toys shrugged. That did make him wince.

As he began buttoning his shirt, Toys looked up at the ceiling, and maybe through it into the center of his own thoughts. "Sebastian," he murmured.

"You had no idea?" I asked.

"God, no."

"He never tried to get in touch?"

Toys shook his head. "Why would he? We hardly parted on the best of terms. The last time we saw each other, we tried to commit mutual murder."

"Shame you didn't try harder," I said.

Toys didn't meet my eyes. "Something else I need to work out."

He sounded really sad, genuinely remorseful, and I felt like an ass for having said anything.

"Toys," I said, "look . . . I wanted to—".

The young Brit shook his head. "Don't."

"You don't even know what I'm going say."

"I don't care what it is. Whatever you have to say, whatever you think you have to say, say it to someone else. Not to me."

"Why not?" I asked.

He raised his eyes and looked into mine. "Because I don't want to hear it. Not from you or anyone else. Not ever."

He made to leave, but I shifted into his path.

"No," I said, "I think you will hear me out, because I need to say it. Church, can you give us the room?"

"Captain—" began Church, but I shook my head.

"Close the door, too."

He left and shut the door.

Toys stopped and stood there, bracing against it, jaw set, eyes glassy with dread at whatever I was going to say.

"Listen to me," I said. "We both know what you've done. We both know that it's going to take a lot more than good works to make you feel better about who you are. If you're expecting me to forgive you, that's not what I wanted to say. If you expect me to thank you, I'm pretty sure that's not what you want me to say."

"No," he said hoarsely. "Please don't."

"Don't worry . . . I won't. But I will say this. Call it a confessional moment, one sinner to another."

His gaze sharpened on mine.

"I've wanted you dead for a lot of years now. If it wasn't for Mr. Church and Junie, I'd have killed you already. Probably wouldn't have used a gun or knife. Might have used my hands, because it would have felt good. What you did while you were with Gault and Vox is unforgivable. I don't give a pint of cold piss if it was because you had a rough childhood. Believe me, so did I. There's nature, there's nurture, and then there's choice, you dig what I'm saying?"

He nodded.

"If you're on some kind of road to redemption, that's between you and

Church or maybe between you and God. I wouldn't even hazard a guess as to how many good works it takes to undo the death of one innocent person. And you know what? I don't care. I'm not in the forgiveness business. I'm a hunter and I'm a killer, and none of that trains me to be compassionate to my enemies."

Toys said nothing.

"What I want to say to you is this. I don't forgive you. I don't like you. I don't ever want to be friends with you. But . . . After what happened? After the other day? You and I are no longer enemies. We're not even, but we aren't at war. Not anymore."

Toys said nothing.

I stepped back, took a breath, let it out, and turned toward the door.

"What," he said quietly, "no kiss?"

I cracked up. When I turned, he was smiling, too. A sad smile, but a real one.

"Fuck you," I said.

And I left.

4.

The ashes of the political fires are still falling.

No one thinks the president will do well in the next election. The bin Laden video, however unfairly, stained his presidency. So did the rise of the Seven Kings organization. It didn't matter that ultimately it was one diseased mind, one money-hungry bureaucrat, and a self-sustaining infrastructure that nearly ended things. Someone has to take the bullet, and the president was captain of the ship. Mixed metaphor. Fuck it.

Either way, I don't much care. The more I become aware of the way politics works, the less invested I become in politicians. I don't fight for them anyway. I have my own agenda.

In the wake of Regis and Solomon, the drone thing became the center of the national conversation. Everyone can see the benefits; everyone is aware of the dangers. Like most things, it's all about the gray areas. We'll have to wait to see what fills our sky tomorrow. For today, the skies are clear and quiet.

5.

On a bright and sunny Sunday morning, Junie and I dressed in our very best clothes. I wore a suit that made me look like a million bucks, and a tie that brought out the blue of my eyes. Junie wore a gorgeous dress that fit every delicious curve while still hiding the scars that were now healing nicely. She had a pair of shoes that it took her two weeks to find. I thought they looked great, but they also looked like six other pairs of shoes she already owned. I am not brave enough to say that to her.

We drove in a limousine provided for the occasion. All of the guests were being chauffeured. As we stepped out of the car, I saw Bunny standing on the steps, he on a lower one and Lydia on a higher one. She was adjusting his tie. They kept smiling at each other.

Everyone was smiling. Top, Montana, and Brian. Violin—who appeared in one of those outrageous European hats that straddle the line between high fashion and comedy. Even Lilith was there, though she was not smiling. I don't know if she understands how that process works. I have never before seen her in civilian clothes. She sat next to Mr. Church. And, weird thing, she looked kind of hot. Most of the guys in the place couldn't take their eyes off of her. But then they'd see Church looking back at them, and they'd turn away so fast you could hear their necks creak.

Bug was there, and it was the first time I'd seen him since his mother's funeral. I hugged him. So did Junie. I think he liked Junie's hug better, which is fair enough.

Bug even managed to smile. Maybe his first in a long time. Was there less innocence in that smile? Less optimism? Less of that rare and precious quality that defined him, that made him—far more than his computer savvy—the heart of our dysfunctional little DMS community?

God, I hope not.

He was coming back to work soon and seemed eager to begin playing with Davidovich's science. We'd recovered all of his design notes. Everything. It was a good bet that MindReader was about to take a quantum leap forward. Pun intended. We'd need it. We needed an edge. With enemies like we have, we needed any edge we could get.

But that was tomorrow's concern.

Today wasn't about the war. It wasn't about weapons or damage or loss.

For once, it wasn't about any of that.

We all walked up the steps and into the big Catholic church. Doctor Hu and Jerry Spencer were seated together. They stopped smiling when they saw me. But Aunt Sallie, still in a wheelchair, was parked up front and she actually gave me a smile. Or maybe it was a wince. Hard to say.

The organist was playing something pretty. There were flowers everywhere.

Mr. Church sat near the front. His official presence was as a friend of the family. A few of us knew different. He now wore black gloves in place of the white cotton ones. I would never see him without those gloves again.

The organist changed his tune to something more formal and official. We all took our seats. Then they came in.

The three of them.

So beautiful.

So happy.

They walked down the aisle together. Past all of us. Past friends and coworkers. Past people who, even then, wore guns in concealed holsters. Even in that place. Even on a day like this.

Rudy leaned on his new cane. Another hawthorn stick, another silver handle. I was with him when he bought it. The silver is as pure as it gets. He didn't tell me why that mattered to him.

Rudy's suit was gorgeous. It had been impeccably cut and tailored for him by someone Mr. Church knew. A friend in the industry.

Circe looked radiant. I use that word in a literal sense. She seemed to glow. She walked straight and proud. There were cornflowers in her hair that matched her dress. Every woman there wanted her shoes. Every man there probably fell a little bit in love with her.

But the brightest light in that place, the glow that drew us all there, was the tiny form that Circe held in her arms. Dressed in white, with intensely black hair and eyes that were as blue as the cornflowers. Circe and Rudy brought their child to the front of the church. And then the priest called for the godparents to join them.

Junie and I held hands all the way up the aisle.

I'm not Catholic, nor were more than half the people there. Some of them were from different religions; some belonged to none. Some of the people didn't believe that there was anything beyond this world. No spirits, no angels. No devils or demons.

That was okay. People should be allowed to believe what they want to believe. If some of us have seen things that make us question the limits of the world and the possibilities of a larger world, then that's on us. It's ours to consider. To fear or not to fear as we each choose.

Rudy has less fear in him than he's had for years, even though he knows there is more to be afraid of. It happens that way sometimes. He's more like his old self, and I'm glad to have him back. He is the best person I know, and—let's face it—he keeps me sane.

Ish.

So, on that morning, we all stood there and watched a priest dribble water on the head of Albert Joseph Rudolfo O'Tree-Sanchez.

The water was cold.

The baby cried.

We all smiled. We all wept.

And the world did not burn down.

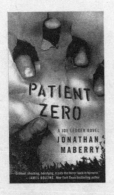
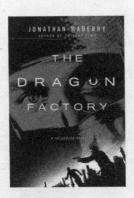

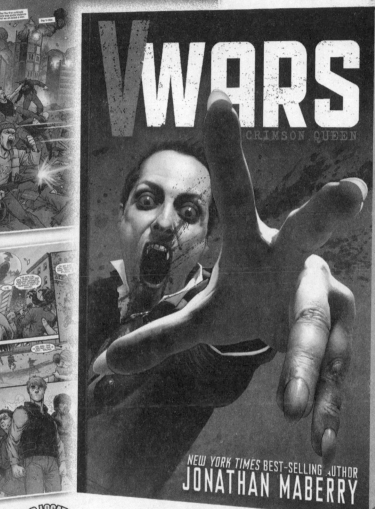